# *Breakfast at Timothy's*

Richard Tyler Jordan

Breakfast at Timothy's
© 2023 Richard Tyler Jordan
All Rights Reserved

This book is a work of fiction. People, places, events, and situations are the product of the author's imagination. Any resemblance to actual persons, living or dead, or historical events is purely coincidental. No part of this book may be reproduced, stored in a retrieval system, or transmitted by any means without the written permission of the author and publisher.

Cover design by Dar Albert,
Wicked Smart Designs, Bellingham Wa

*For David Edmund Kernaghan*

*(My heart is filled full of you.)*

## Books by Richard Tyler Jordan

Nonfiction
*BUT DARLING, I'M YOUR AUNTIE MAME!*

Novels
*REMAINS TO BE SCENE*
*FINAL CURTAIN*
*A TALENT FOR MURDER*
*SET SAIL FOR MURDER*
*OVERNIGHT SENSATION*

Novellas
*ALL I WANT FOR CHRISTMAS*
*SUMMER SHARE*
*MAN OF MY DREAMS*
*GIRL'S KNIGHT OUT*

Writing as Mike Melbourne

*TRICKS OF THE TRADE*
*HUNK HOUSE*
*GAY BLADES*
*ONE NIGHT STAND*

For preview and purchase details,
and much, much more, visit
richardtylerjordan.com

# Chapter One

First days on new jobs are generally fraught with anxiety and diarrhea. It was no different for aspiring novelist Timothy Trousdale, who had just landed a job as an assistant to his all-time favorite movie star, Mercedes Ford. He was excited and nervous and panicked and jittery because not only was he going to his new office but his new home as well. Curiously, the position required that he live in Mercedes' super-swanky Tribeca penthouse, The Colton. That was totally cool with Timothy, who was thrilled that he could finally escape the hell of sharing an eight-hundred-square-foot studio apartment with two present—and future—losers.

However, August mornings in Manhattan have no respect for auspicious beginnings, and this one was punishingly hot and humid. Timothy had taken an MTA bus from 45$^{th}$ Street, and by the time he arrived for work—wearing his only pair of dressy jeans, a classic Oxford powder-blue button-down shirt, and used-to-be-white tennis shoes—he was more wilted and stinky than poised.

Dressed in a pseudo-military livery, the grouchy doorman casually surveyed the splotches of perspiration leeching through Timothy's shirt. After a phone call to somewhere within, he unlocked the building's front entrance and allowed Timothy inside.

Ahh! Heaven! Timothy had walked out of the sweltering

steam of the city jungle and into an oasis of refrigeration that was the building's two-story, glass-atrium lobby. He instantly and affectionately dubbed the space Arendelle in honor of his favorite animated movie, *Frozen*. "Let it go, let it go," he whispered, lyrics from the film's hit song, trying to stave off a full-on panic attack. Other than that, and the squeaking sounds made by the gooey melting rubber soles of his shoes meeting the cold, polished marble floor, the place was as quiet as a mausoleum.

Timothy had been instructed to meet with the concierge, Mr. Fulton, who would provide him with the key to the penthouse. *Key?* He quickly found that with all the super-rich and famous people living here, access to their condo units was only possible if you had a bunch of technological ways to be individually and specifically identified and authorized.

After Timothy provided his Alabama driver's license, a debit card desperate for an infusion of paycheck funds, and a Piggly Wiggly supermarket rewards card that he'd retrieved from the bottom of his rucksack as proof that he was indeed Timothy Truman Trousdale, Mr. Fulton tapped some numbers into his cell phone. Timothy heard him whisper the cryptic words "Du jour" and "two weeks, tops." In a short moment, a burly man with a high forehead and no discernable neck, wearing a blue police-like uniform, appeared through a doorway marked Authorized Personnel Only.

Without so much as a goodbye from Mr. Fulton, Timothy was turned over to this imposing, no-nonsense guard whose badge read Griffin. Timothy couldn't tell if it was a first or last name, but he was nonetheless intimidated by the guy. Griffin ushered Timothy into a suite of rooms that looked the way he imagined the Pentagon's War Room must look. There were half a dozen computers and television monitors and an equal number of uniformed people watching screens and typing notes, presumably reporting the contents of their video displays: mainly empty corridors, the front entrance, and side exits of the building.

"Palm there," Griffin said, pointing first to Timothy's hand, then to a device that looked like an ATM. But where a keypad on an ATM might be, there was a flat, white surface with a red-lighted outline of a hand. He touched the pattern, then splayed his fingers between the lines. A moment later, the outline turned green.

Griffin then cocked his head to another device that resembled what Timothy's eye doctor used during exams. "Retinal scan," he said (although Timothy initially thought he said something a bit more personal and anatomical) and indicated for Timothy to place his chin on a rubber pad just below two lenses. He peered in, and a mesmerizing kaleidoscopic lightshow of colors swarmed before him. It was so hypnotic that he would have loved to watch it for hours. But, after a muffled ping sound, the machine automatically went dark.

"Voice encoding," Griffin said, holding a digital audio recorder. "Speak clearly into the mic. State your full name, address, and the home telephone number you had as a kid."

"What's next? A microchip in my neck?" Timothy said. "Arff-arff!" The joke bombed. "How now, brown cow?" he added, enunciating each word distinctly. That, too, failed to elicit anything more than a look of irritation on Griffin's face, so Timothy got totally serious and followed the instructions. Shortly afterward, with all the warmth of the monotone voice in a GPS app, Griffin said, "Your personal body characteristics have been extracted. You can go."

Body characteristics? Extracted? Timothy looked at his palms. Then, at his arms. No signs of skin puncture. Griffin said that the information was entered into what he called "The Colton's impenetrable security database." No key cards or passwords or PINs in this highfalutin place!

Timothy shrugged, stood up, and walked to the door. There wasn't a knob or handle. He turned and gave Griffin a quizzical look. Griffin stared him down, testing him to see if Timothy could figure out how to get out of the place.

Well, Timothy Trousdale may have been a nervous wreck, but he wasn't a complete idiot. He quickly caught on and placed his right hand on the ATM-like pad next to the door. After a mere second, the light around his fingers turned from red to green. Then he looked into the kaleidoscope machine and heard that ping of approval. As the lenses went dark, he heard the almost inaudible click of the lock being released inside the door. The portal slowly opened outward, and he turned to Griffin with a look of arrogant satisfaction. Then he walked out into the lobby.

Although alone—with Mr. Fulton nowhere in sight—he knew that the security automatons behind the computers kept their eyes on him. He was sometimes paranoid, and now felt sort of like a felon under house arrest. But he knew the security measures were for his and the residents' protection.

As Timothy approached the bank of elevators, the doors of the middle car parted without him even pushing a call button. Stepping inside, he was super impressed by the high-tech look of the interior: lots of colors, LED lights, and mirrors. He scanned the tiny room for the panel of buttons to select the penthouse floor but found only the hand outline and a smaller version of the retina-scanning machine. Patting himself on the back for catching on so quickly, Timothy followed the security procedure, and the doors closed. Then a sweet voice that sounded like an angel with a British accent said, "Please state your desired destination."

Timothy wanted to say, "Buckingham Palace." Instead, he said, "Penthouse-A, please."

"With pleasure."

In only a moment, the doors parted again, and Timothy gasped in awe at the scene before him. He was suddenly Dorothy Gale from black and white Kansas, entering Technicolor Oz. Dumbstruck, he stepped out of the elevator and into the foyer. For a moment, he just stood there and stared. It could be a movie set, or where he imagined someone super-rich, like that Tesla car inventor/X owner, lives. A round, Lalique crystal glass pedestal table holding a massive arrangement of Casablanca lilies occupied the center of the entranceway.

Timothy gingerly moved farther into the condo, and his eyes were drawn across the sweeping expanse of high-tech open-plan living space to an entire wall of windows two floors high. To his immediate left a curved acrylic glass staircase ascended to another level. Presumably, it led to the bedrooms. Further to the left of the staircase was a dining room with a long marble-top table set with two ornate gold candelabras. Looking ahead again, Timothy could see a wide terrace beyond glass doors.

As he slowly walked into the main room, the view beckoned him, and he could see that one of the doors leading to the terrace hung open. Timothy had a curious nature—useful for writing stories but sometimes detrimental to his health and safety. Still, he wanted to step outside to view the cityscape. It was utterly breathtaking, with a long terrace appointed with wrought iron furniture and a fire pit bordered by a colorful collection of blooming stacked potted plants and flowers against a barrier of more acrylic glass. The muted sounds of car horns and emergency response vehicles wafted up the 45 stories, but rather than the irritation he usually felt from all the noise in the city, he had a sense of calmness and serenity. He became almost hypnotized as he looked out at the other ritzy buildings in the neighborhood. In the distance way beyond, he could see the Empire State Building and Central Park. His heart pounded joyfully from the thrill of it all. *This is where I get to live*, he thought.

Timothy forced himself to step back inside the penthouse. He wandered around the living room as if he were visiting a museum. It was nearly as quiet as an exhibit hall, too. Rooms make a definite sound, even when they appear silent, and this place had an almost audible vibration. Although Timothy had seen fancy brownstones and apartments on *Million Dollar Listing*, this was off the charts in terms of elegance and size. Absolutely massive! With contemporary furniture—but not the cold steel and leather some designers use to insinuate modern sterility. *Neo Art Deco*, Timothy said to himself, wondering if that was even a real decorating style.

Spotlighted on the wall to his right, over a Lalique console table, hung an immense painting of a Black woman with a white gardenia over her left ear. Remembering an interview with Mercedes Ford in which she said she was a fan of Diana Ross; he realized it was a painting of Miss Ross as Billie Holiday in the old movie *Lady Sings the Blues*.

As he tried to keep his jaw from dropping from all the wonder around him, he recalled his dead father's voice saying, "So this is how the other half lives." His dad always made that comment when he saw a big house or fancy car or boat. "No, Dad, this is how the 1% of the 1% live," Timothy whispered.

A photo in a silver frame on another console table caught Timothy's eye, and he reached out and picked it up. Of course, he knew he shouldn't touch anything, but he'd instantly recognized the picture of a young and beaming

Mercedes Ford, the biggest movie star since Bette Davis. In the photo, Mercedes, with shoulder-length blonde hair, wore a blue turtleneck sweater and embraced a little girl on her lap with yellow ribbons in her auburn hair. Timothy remembered seeing this very picture in a television retrospective of the star's life and career. It had originally appeared on the cover of *Vanity Fair* magazine long before Timothy was even born. Mercedes looked to be about the age when she made her feature film debut forty years ago in the British period drama *The Rose of Shaftesbury*. Her tour de force performance brought audiences and critics to tears, and she was instantly crowned an international star.

Mercedes won that year's Best Actress Academy Award, and several more of those gold statuettes followed. Timothy wondered if it was true what Mercedes had once said on a TV talk show when asked where she kept her Oscars. "I think they're in a shoebox under the stairs in the basement," she'd laughed.

If Timothy had one of those status symbols, he'd be showing them off to everyone—especially his mother, who couldn't understand why her son considered himself smart enough to be a writer. But then, Mercedes was known for being an actor who graciously accepts the accolades but values her family and her art above all else.

Timothy continued wandering around the room and gravitated toward a grand piano on a slightly elevated platform beside the wall of windows. The elegant black Steinway had a lustrous mirror-like finish. Timothy had always wanted to play the piano. Unfortunately, after years of lessons, none of his practicing sank in. He consoled himself by saying that he had other talents. But it was really a case of wanting to be an artist but having zero ability or confidence. He stared into the high-gloss shine of the raised piano lid and became lost in a long reverie about playing at Carnegie Hall.

Then, something in the shiny surface of the piano lid caught Timothy's eye. A slight, almost imperceptible, movement. A reflection of someone standing behind him! Timothy whirled around.

"Who the hell are you?" shouted a woman in her mid-70s with a loud, gravelly smoker's voice. "I'm calling security!"

In that nanosecond, a startled and confused Timothy dropped the picture frame. Its glass shattered on the marble floor, and a gazillion shards scattered everywhere.

"Idiot!" the woman screamed. She couldn't have been more maniacal if Timothy had just tossed a pet puppy over the terrace balcony. "Don't touch what isn't yours!" Again, she demanded Timothy's identity.

"Timothy. Timothy Trousdale," he stuttered, horrified by his clumsiness, and this barking beast scared the wits out of him. So many things in New York frightened or intimidated Timothy. The sheer size of the city, the fast pace, and the cost of living were constant worries. He was even afraid to pull the stop-I-want-to-get-off signal cord on the cross-town bus, fearing another passenger would be irritated with him. "I work here," Timothy added. "Starting today."

The woman scrutinized Timothy and came to a conclusion. "Oh, I get it. They're spyin' on me again. They wanna get dirt so they can get rid of me. It's not going to be easy. No siree. I know my rights. Too old, they think. But I'm not goin' without a fight. Ageism, I tell you! Well, you can say anything you want about me, but it'll all be lies. Lies, I tell you! And I know a lawyer!"

Of course, Timothy had no clue what the woman was yelling about. "No, no, no!" he wailed. "I'm just working here. To answer emails and do online social media stuff for the fabulous Mercedes Ford. I'm not a spy. I'm just a writer with a debut novel coming out." Timothy blushed a little at the lie as he hadn't yet even found an agent, let alone a publisher. But then, he hadn't said when his book was coming out, had he?

The woman looked at Timothy with even deeper suspicion. "Writers are all liars," she hissed. "Fake news!" Then she sat down on one of two identical extra-long sofas facing each other perpendicular to the magnificent city view. Slowly, the old battle-axe melted. She looked defeated and tired. "I've been puttin' up with this sorta bull for the past 50 years," she said in a softer but still defiant voice. "At my age, I've had it with takin' orders from upstarts like you."

"Orders?" Timothy scoffed. "I'm not your boss. I'm no one's boss. I'll do my work, and you do yours. We'll be best friends and have a fabulous relationship. I'm just here to make a buck until my novel comes out. Um, let's start over, shall we?"

"Shall we?" the woman mocked Timothy's grammar in a grandly affected voice, which he didn't think sounded anything like his own. "Shall we dance?" the woman added. "Shall we have a spot o' tea?"

Timothy rolled his eyes. *Oh, so this is how it's going to be*, he said to himself. "Might we pretend that I just arrived?" He rephrased his question. "I'll introduce myself—Timothy Trousdale. And with whom do I have the fabulous pleasure of meeting?" Of course, his language sounded even more stilted and elitist the second time. He saw it in the woman's face, too.

"Okay. I'm just Timothy. And you are?"

The woman sat mute for a long moment. Then, without looking at Timothy, she confidently said, "Fabiola."

Timothy reached out his hand to shake Fabiola's, but the old woman simply glowered and offered a loud harrumph.

"You do a fabulous job keeping this place so neat and clean," Timothy tried, to win the woman over.

Fabiola didn't respond, and they sat silently for another long moment, both trying to figure out where their fragile détente would lead.

"Must be a lot of work…" Timothy again attempted to open a civil dialogue as he looked around the room with admiration. Then, he became aware of the muted sounds of wind chimes filtering through the air.

Fabiola heard them, too, and looked up. "Someone's at the door," she said.

"That would be Moi," a man's voice said as Timothy looked up and rose to his feet.

It was Jared Evans, the creepy guy from Muriel Maynard's office whom he'd met during his interview a few days earlier. There was something unpleasant about him—Timothy had felt it when they were briefly introduced—but he couldn't exactly put his finger on what it was. Jared seemed to seethe as if he were always looking for an opportunity to make a biting comment or judgment. Timothy could almost always find something attractive about another man: a smile, eye color, beard, talent, or intellect. But Jared was too peculiar and unnerving for Timothy to find him even remotely sexy.

Jared had a slight body frame, narrow shoulders, dough-colored skin, and although he appeared to be in his mid-30s, most of the hair on his head had already disappeared, leaving a short-cropped semicircle that made Timothy think of a toilet seat in a public restroom. With his pointed nose, thin lips, overbite, and beady eyes, he looked like someone Timothy didn't want to cross.

"You two have met," Jared stated redundantly. "I wanted to be here to introduce you, but things got insane at the office. Muriel's in one of her assault modes. It's always this way when she's negotiating with one of our clients. I'm not allowed to say which one, of course, but she's going to be really big, and Muriel's giving ulcers to the Disney execs desperate to cast her as a character voice in their new animated musical film." He paused for air. "That's Muriel's favorite thing in the world to do, you know, make Hollywood people throw up."

"She even begins negotiations by handing out personal-size bottles of Imodium to the tough-guy execs," Fabiola agreed.

Distracted momentarily by Fabiola's apparent awareness of business negotiating tactics and the visual image of a boardroom full of Suits being sick around a conference table, Timothy said, "We were just getting to know each other." He smiled at Fabiola and added, "I know we'll become fabulous friends." He offered a big smile, but Fabiola looked away.

"Right," Jared said, "time to put you to work. I brought the laptop. Follow me to the office. I'll set things up and provide you with passwords and such. All very hush-hush, you know. Let's get it over with."

Timothy eagerly followed Jared down the main corridor, and when they reached the office near the far end, Jared unlocked the door and relocked it behind them. "Always keep it secure," he commanded.

Timothy's smile grew wide when he looked around the small but smartly decorated office space. The forward-facing wall was another floor-to-ceiling smoked-glass window with an eye-popping cityscape view. A yellow mid-century style leather sofa sat centered against the window. To the left, running the entire length of the wall, was a sleek, shiny, gray-enamel, built-in desk with an executive chair that matched the color of the sofa. A professional-grade computer printer sat like a lump of heavy clay on the desk next to an I ♥ NY coffee mug containing an assortment of pens. Fitted above, taking advantage of the entire remainder of the wall, were built-in storage cupboards and shelves for binders and decorative ceramic art pieces. Turning to the right, Timothy was thrilled to see another entire wall of books. Recognizing fancy gold-embossed spines with titles by Jane Austen, Charlotte Brontë, and Ian McEwan, he instantly felt a swell of pride confirming that his movie star idol was a connoisseur of classic literature.

Withdrawing a MacBook Air from his canvas shoulder bag, Jared said, "And this not only never leaves the penthouse, but you must also lock it up in the safe if you ever have to leave it unattended. That's extremely important. Even if you only go to the bathroom, it goes in the safe."

Jared moved to the other side of the room, removed his cell phone from his pocket, and swiped through a series of apps until he came to an icon that resembled a key. Tapping it, he entered a password code. Suddenly, after the clicking sound of a lock, the floor-to-ceiling bookcase pivoted to reveal… a hidden room.

For the second time that morning, Timothy's jaw dropped. Of course, he'd seen hidden rooms and secret passages behind bookcases on TV shows and in the movies, but he'd never been inside one.

"Follow me," Jared said.

It was a relatively small space, more like a walk-in closet. But instead of a wardrobe, the carpeted room contained an old leather desk chair on casters, a step stool, and a few tall shelves with several shoeboxes on the top. Dominating the space was a five-foot-tall beige-colored steel safe, the variety of which one might find in an old bank. Impossibly sturdy and strong.

"This is where the laptop goes," Jared said. "And no one

is to know this room exists. Not even you, if you get my drift. Give me your phone, and I'll download the security app."

Timothy was mortified when he reluctantly showed Jared his old flip phone. He was too broke to even dream about owning an iPhone. Jared took one look, and horror registered on his face. "We'll have to do something about that!" he snapped, then sniggered at the pathetic, old device. "What a loser," he said under his breath, but loud enough for Timothy to hear and make him feel more inadequate than usual. Timothy was used to this feeling of inferiority but it still wounded his sensitive soul. "You'll have a new one later today," Jared said, pushing another combination of numbers and letters on his phone. The safe made a sound that suggested it was now unlocked. Jared pulled the handle on the obviously heavy door and revealed shelves packed with folders and papers. Timothy had expected tiaras, velvet trays of precious gems, rings, and necklaces. He thought the stuff in the safe belonged in a simple filing cabinet.

"No need to examine any of this," Jared said. "Just contracts and files. All very ordinary but none of your business."

Timothy shrugged and nodded. "Trust me; discretion is my middle name."

"Actually, I don't trust you," Jared snapped, giving Timothy a look of disdain and revulsion. "While you're working for me—"

"I thought I was working for Mercedes Ford," Timothy interrupted.

"Same thing," Jared barked. "And just so you know, you're the most recent in a very long line of assistants who also pledged their discretion but were nosey and couldn't keep their paws to themselves." He dragged his index finger across his throat to indicate what had happened to the previous assistants. "I'm just sayin'," he offered before closing the door to the safe and reversing the procedure to relock it. He ushered Timothy out of the secret room. "Now, let's discuss your duties," he said.

"Muriel told me on Friday what my job entails, and I'm excited to start. Email and Facebook posts and some Instagram for Mercedes."

"I knew this would happen," Jared said, throwing his hands up in a *Why me, Lord* pique. "Look, dummy, nothing about this job is ordinary. Things change as needed. What did you think?"

Timothy blanched at being called a dummy. He'd never dealt with workplace abuse before and didn't know how to respond. "Only that you needed a writer—someone to answer fan mail and stuff," he said, remembering the job description from SwellHire Top Temps.

Jared shook his head and grimaced. "Social media is just the tip of the iceberg. You're here to make everyone's life easier, Muriel's—and my own. Although from the look of you, I can't imagine you'll succeed at that. You're on call 24/7. Why else do you think we need someone to live here? Any one paw monkey can do email from a cage at the zoo, for crying out loud."

Timothy was still determining if his previous job as a host at The Chili Exchange was so terrible after all. "I thought you just needed a writer," he said cautiously. While Timothy wanted to take advantage of this amazing opportunity, nothing about being on call 24/7 had been mentioned in the interview with Muriel. "If I'm always on call, will I get overtime pay?" he asked. "I was hoping to work on my new novel in my free time."

Jared sighed and sat down on the arm of the loveseat. With his hands in *open the church and see all the people* position, he stared at Timothy for a long moment before asking, "Timothy, how many hours are in a day?"

Oh darn. Timothy felt as though he were back in grade school being tested about how long it takes for two trains traveling at 30 miles per hour to reach Philadelphia after they leave the stations in New York and Boston with 36 passengers aboard and stopping a couple of times along the way to let 17 people off. "Twenty-four hours in a day, the last time I checked," Timothy said, feeling further diminished.

"Time is one of our common denominators," Jared said. "It's how each of us uses those twenty-four hours that matters. If you're really a writer—and to me, you don't look bright enough to write a coloring book—you'll carve out time for your little creative endeavors. On your own time. Do you follow me?"

Timothy nodded slowly. Jared was probably right. Timothy had a friend in junior college who worked two jobs, went to the gym daily, took figure skating lessons, cared for his ailing mother, and still made time to write and publish short stories. The guy was amazing, and Timothy had wanted to be more like him.

"I thought this might happen, so I brought along a printed job description. Study this," Jared griped as he slapped a half-dozen stapled pages against Timothy's chest. "I'll also migrate all the phone numbers you'll need into your new phone, which, by the way, is only to be used for business purposes. Capisce?"

"Oui. I mean sì," Timothy said, unsettled by his new boss's rude behavior, and gave a cursory glance at the pages.

"Alrighty," Jared said as he essentially ended the meeting. He punched a password into his phone, and the bookcase pivoted back into place, leaving no indication that it was a portal to a secret room. "As for the old bird," he cocked his

15

head toward the door and Fabiola beyond, "don't get too chummy. She's not long for this world."

"She's sick?"

Jared shrugged. "Let's just say she won't be here much longer."

"I think she already knows," Timothy said. "She thought I was sent here to spy on her."

"She's also paranoid. That's one of the reasons she's on her way out. Again, lips sealed," Jared said as he unlocked the office door. Timothy followed him back into the corridor, and Jared locked the door again. As they walked toward the elevator in the foyer, Jared suddenly turned around. Timothy followed as he retraced his steps and went beyond the office to a room at the far end of the condo. "She's supposed to stay in here," he said, knocking tentatively on the door.

After getting no response he turned the knob and let himself into the bedroom. Timothy was aghast at the sheer messiness of the room, with clothing strewn everywhere, an unmade bed, and laundry left unfolded.

Jared sighed. "Keep me posted if she starts treating the rest of the place like this."

At the elevator, Jared asked if Timothy had any last questions. Of course, he did.

"How do I get my assignments? Which bedroom is mine? When is payday?"

"Log onto the website listed on the pages I gave you. Check the dashboard several times an hour. Muriel or I will forward whatever requires your attention. As for your room, take your pick. They're upstairs. Mercedes has only been here half a dozen times since she bought the place. Right now, she's on a film shoot. Then, with awards season coming soon after that, she'll be in LA. She'll unlikely be visiting here until early next year unless she drops in after her current movie wraps. You'll be paid every other Friday."

"What about having friends over?"

"Nope."

"So, I'll be a cloistered monk?"

"You're not in quarantine, for crying out loud," Jared spat. "You have an hour off for lunch, and the office gets plenty of invitations to opening nights on Broadway, art galleries, and parties. I occasionally need a Plus-One."

Jared's Plus-One? Eww, Timothy thought as he momentarily imagined being Jared's date for anything where they'd be seen in public. More and more, this job sounded a bit crazy. What had he gotten himself into? And was he to be a prisoner in this gilded cage? That was definitely not for him. And Timothy told Jared so.

"See your little friends," Jared said sarcastically, "just not here. You shouldn't have to work past 7:00 or 8:00 each night if you're efficient. But, of course, you always have to be available for emergencies. Which reminds me, I've got to run over and get you a phone." He sighed heavily with annoyance and shot Timothy a filthy look.

Jared stepped into the elevator. He performed the whole biometric reading thing and curtly said, "Ciao," as the doors closed.

"Ciao to you, too," Timothy repeated disinterestedly as the doors closed. He stood in the quiet foyer looking at the Casablanca lilies and telling himself that he had to stop being so negative. "This is the best thing to ever happen to you," he said. "You have a beautiful place to live—rent-free. A paycheck that you can save because you'll have very few expenses. And it's a quiet place to write—when you aren't at the beck and call of Muriel and Jared, that is. Think of this as an adventure! Just grow a spine, and you'll be fine."

Timothy tried to convince himself that he'd landed in

17

Clover. And then, from down the hall, he heard the loud and violent sound of glass shattering. He raced to find out what was going on.

# Chapter Two

Timothy knew where the sound was coming from and who was making all that noise. It had to be Fabiola. Sure enough, when he arrived at her room, he could hear something else shattering against a wall. He knocked and called out Fabiola's name. Silence. He knocked again and asked if there was anything he could do to help.

Eventually, a softer version of the harsh New York accent Timothy had first been introduced to cheerfully said, "Everything's fabulous."

"Not from the sound of things," Timothy said. Then, after a long silence, he slowly turned the door handle and eased the door open. He was met with a strong perfume scent and saw the carnage of broken atomizer bottles scattered on the floor.

Fabiola looked at him with red-rimmed eyes and shrugged. "Just expressing myself," she said in a matter-of-fact tone. She looked at the stained wall and added, "What? You've never heard of postmodern abstractionism painting? I call this masterpiece Madonna and Child."

Timothy stood looking at the wall and the sad woman before him. He pressed Fabiola to say why she was so angry. "Must be hard to get old, eh?" he stupidly said. The words just slipped out of his mouth.

Fabiola looked at Timothy as if he were nuts. "Yeah, and I really miss my daddy, Methuselah."

"Anything I can do?" Timothy asked. "We're living

together now, at least for a while, and..."

"And I'm scaring you. I know. I get it," Fabiola spat. "Don't worry; this doesn't happen very often. I haven't killed anyone in days."

"Hey, sometimes I get mad too." Timothy tried to make Fabiola's distress more of a universal thing. "We all have our ups and downs. I sometimes think I'm way too sensitive for this planet. A guidance counselor at school said that I have 'generalized anxiety disorder.' Heck, whenever an agent sends me a rejection for my book, I'm miserable for the whole rest of the day."

"I thought you said your book was about to be published," Fabiola said.

Oh, phooey! Timothy regretted the little lie he had told; it just made him feel more like a failure. "I mean, I got lots of rejections before I finally *sold* the book," he said, continuing the sham. "I have a file full of emails from agents and editors telling me that my project wasn't right for them."

"You're telling me I'm a rejection, like one of your stupid letters?" Fabiola shot back. "You don't know a thing about me, Mister. And that's an understatement!"

Timothy could tell where this conversation was going. If he tried to make Fabiola look on the bright side of things, she would say that he was too young to know what he was talking about and couldn't possibly understand. It would go back and forth, so Timothy simply said, "You're right. Let me know if you want to talk... or anything." Then he closed the door and decided to select a bedroom for himself. Two boxes with his meager possessions were being sent to The Colton in the afternoon, and he wanted to figure out where to put his stuff.

After living with two other guys in a studio apartment not much bigger than a cargo shipping container, Timothy knew that he was pretty much now at Downton Abbey. "Please, dear God," he begged, "don't let this be like those dreams about winning the lottery that always ends with the alarm clock going off!"

After examining all the rooms, Timothy went for one with a queen-size bed and an en suite with travertine tile in the shower and double sinks in the vanity. A recessed alcove boasted a combination toilet and bidet. Again, he thought of his dad. This is how the other half lives.

As Jared had placed the laptop in the safe and Timothy didn't yet have a phone with the app to access it, there wasn't any work Timothy could do, so he decided to familiarize himself with the rest of the penthouse. He returned to the living room and discovered that the shattered glass from the picture frame was still all over the floor. He was about to summon Fabiola to clean it up, then thought better. The poor old woman was having a rough day. Instead, he wandered into the huge kitchen and began rooting through drawers and cabinets for a broom and dustpan. He found the utility closet and all the items anyone might need to keep a condo this size in shape. He swept up the shards and returned the silver frame where he'd found it. And then the wind chimes/elevator doorbell wafted through the air.

"That was fast," Timothy said as Jared entered the condo.

"They don't mess with me at the Apple Store," he said, withdrawing a white, rectangular box from a plastic drawstring bag. "I need you to get to work right away."

My gosh, the phone was absolutely beautiful! Timothy couldn't believe he'd finally possess modern telecommunications. He felt he was possibly the last person in New York to lay his hands on one of these beauties.

Jared walked him through the security app. "Memorize the code," he snapped. "You can't write it down anywhere."

Thankfully, Timothy had a decent memory. In an instant,

he was able to access the phone and its contact list. "What about getting into the secret room and safe?" he asked.

Jared cocked his head toward the office, and Timothy followed him down the hallway. Once again, Jared opened the door and locked it behind them. "Go to it," he said and gave Timothy a four-digit code for the phone.

"Voila!" Timothy said when he successfully opened the bookcase portal.

"You only have three tries to get the codes right. Otherwise, you'll be locked out," Jared warned. "It'll take Muriel's master code to override your error. You think that fat guy with the weird hair in North Korea is scary? By comparison, Muriel makes him look like the Buddha."

Timothy made a face Jared obviously interpreted as concern because he said, "Yeah, you'd better be afraid. And I can't wait to watch what happens when you screw up. Open the safe and take the laptop out."

Timothy reached among all the papers and file folders and lifted the computer from the safe. He closed the heavy steel door and repeated the security process. He breathed a sigh of relief, but Jared seemed disappointed by his successes.

"Okay, then," Jared said as he left the secret room.

When they were both on the other side, Timothy tapped the security app again and entered the passcode. He was almost drunk with success as the bookshelves pivoted back into place. "Easy-breezy," he said triumphantly.

"Check the emails," Jared demanded in a tone that suggested Timothy had already neglected a duty. "Should I stay to make sure you've got the right username and password?"

"How many tries do I get before I'm locked out of the computer?" Timothy asked.

"Oh, dear God! Pretend you only have one shot," Jared

cried. "You should get all the codes right the first time. And don't tell me there are too many. You probably remember your address and your phone number and your mother's birthday. I'll bet you never get those wrong. In your case, you probably do."

*Jeez! Why is this guy being so negative?* Timothy thought but wanted to appear totally confident, so he said, "I'm good. No problem-o. I've got it down. We're cool." He wondered if he was overselling himself.

Jared gave him a dubious look. "You're a cocky little dweeb, aren't you," he said, then they walked back toward the foyer, with Timothy cradling the precious laptop firmly against his chest. "And don't bother me unless it's an emergency," Jared added. "I call you—no need for you to call me." He stepped into the elevator and placed his palm on the biometric pad. The doors closed, and Timothy was alone. He returned to the office, closed, and locked the door, sat at the desk, and opened the computer.

He marveled at the beauty of the machine. The casing was brushed silver with a backlit keyboard. His own PC was a cracked and often not working piece of rubbish. He hit the On button and heard the pleasant startup chime from this beautiful piece of equipment. He typed in the password, opened the browser, and then clicked on the mailbox icon. A short list of only five incoming messages appeared. He decided to start with the earliest one, from Muriel, who had attached another file containing fan mail. That one was loaded with messages! In the body of her short message, Muriel said: "From today, the emails arriving at the Mercedes Ford fan site will be forwarded automatically to the Inbox on your computer. We don't make fans wait more than twenty-four hours for responses."

Timothy recalled that Muriel had mentioned during the

interview that the replies were going to appear to come from Mercedes Ford but that there would also be a line stating 'This message was sent on behalf of Mercedes Ford' to offer Mercedes legal protection in case of any errors made by the actual sender. Not that Timothy would ever dream of making a mistake while writing on behalf of his idol.

So, Timothy immediately downloaded the correspondence and began to read the messages, eager to answer each one. The weight of responsibility of representing the iconic Miss Ford pressed heavily on his mind.

The messages all had a similar theme. They loved Mercedes' work and wanted autographed photos. A few of them had sob stories about being down on their luck and asked if Mercedes could find it in her heart to make a mortgage or car payment for them. Those were really sad, and Timothy didn't have a clue how to answer them. He'd have to talk to Jared about it. And what about pictures and autographs? Jared had yet to tell him how to reply. For a moment, he thought about calling him, but he'd been warned, and this certainly wasn't an emergency. He didn't want to appear as if he couldn't figure these things out for himself. He remembered the sheaf of pages with his job description. There was indeed a paragraph about fan mail and instructions for finding templates for responding to all sorts of inquiries. "Simply fill in the blanks," it said. Timothy selected the weirdest letter first:

Dear Mercedes, (Such inappropriate familiarity, Timothy thought.)

Me and my boyfriend Thomas, I LOVE, LOVE, LOVE you and your movies. We go all the time to the discount theater here in Siminac. You have certainly given us hours and hours and hours of many happy hours. Well, except for that one movie that was supposed to be a comedy, but you weren't very funny in it. We think that you are so talented and hear that you are a very generous star.

I am writing to you because I think you are a nice person. All the magazines at the Walmart checkout line say so. Like Julie Andrews and Sandra Bullock. Not like Amy Schumer, who may be nice, but we're Christians and don't like her potty mouth.

Here's the main reason why I'm writing. We've had a bit of a spell of being unlucky lately. Thomas had to quit his job at the warehouse because he didn't get along so well with the foreman and broke his arm, but it wasn't entirely Thomas' fault. And I can't work because I have a social anxiety situation caused by being on the heavy side.

Since we pay to see your movies, we want you to pay us back. Just this one time, for sure. We need to buy a new truck so that Thomas can start his own business. He's tired of working for mean bosses. He wants to haul people's junk away. We figure that since everybody has junk, we can make a good living from taking it to the dump. We'll be selling the good stuff. We only need $35,582.62 from you.

Please let me know immediately when the money will be coming so we can get the truck. We thank you very much and know that Jesus will pay you back for us, with lots of interest for sure, because you are a good person.

Very sincerely,
Rebecca Ritter

Timothy knew he shouldn't have laughed when he read that letter, but it was so pathetic that he couldn't help himself. He couldn't imagine the nerve of someone asking a stranger for a lot of money. But then he realized that to some people, Mercedes Ford wasn't a stranger at all. She was a real person whom they saw in movies and on TV talk shows. Some misguided people apparently thought it was quite acceptable to believe they could mooch off of her—like a rich cousin.

Timothy opened the folder titled Correspondence Templates and scrolled down the list of possible responses. When he saw one titled Never a Lender Be, he clicked on the document. Bingo! It read:

Dear [Insert Name],

Thank you very much for taking the time to write to me. I sincerely appreciate the wonderful people like you who let me know they enjoy my work. Honestly, I love my job so much that I don't consider it work at all. I know how lucky I am.

I read your kind letter with great interest, and although I have enormous sympathy for your [inset specific situation], I am not legally allowed to provide the money you requested. It's a long story, but it all has to do with the

IRS and laws in [insert state name] that my attorney and accountant tell me are quite explicit about celebrities sending money to people they don't personally know. I blame everything on Washington. Don't you?

Although I am unable to help you at this time, please know that you remain in my thoughts and prayers. I am enclosing an autographed color photo of myself.

I hope you will see my new movie [Title], which opens nationwide on [date].

Good luck to you!

Yours sincerely,
Mercedes Ford

It seemed a perfect response to poor Rebecca and Thomas' delusion that they could squeeze Mercedes for all that loot. Then Timothy proceeded to the next letter. And the next. This went on for hours. Eventually, he realized that dusk had begun to settle over the city, and he was feeling hungry. He turned off the computer, successfully opened the secret room and safe, and locked away the laptop. Such a great first day, and I'm sure I'll get used to Jared, he said to himself as the bookcase again closed to conceal the room. He opened the office door, relocked it, and wandered to the kitchen.

There was little food available, at least nothing in the refrigerator or freezer that appealed to Timothy. Just then, Fabiola walked in. Perfect timing, Timothy thought; she'll be starting dinner soon. "What are we having tonight?" Timothy asked. Fabiola gave him a look that made Timothy feel she thought he was an idiot. "For dinner, I mean."

"You tell me," Fabiola said.

"Lasagna sounds good," Timothy said. "Or maybe something Mexican?"

"Sounds good to me, too," Fabiola smirked and wandered out of the kitchen toward the terrace. "In the meantime, pour me a glass of white wine," she called back. "And I'll have some crackers and the rest of that Brie in the fridge. Oh, and use the correct stemware. I hate drinking white wine out of a red wine glass."

Timothy quickly got the picture. Fabiola obviously was not going to cook for him. He wished he had the nerve to complain to Jared but knew he wouldn't. He did the next best thing and tried sarcasm. He looked back at Fabiola, who was smiling evilly at him. "And would madam care for caviar on toast points to go with her wine?" Timothy teased.

"Fabulous," the old woman whinnied like a horse.

Timothy actually did find a jar of caviar in the fridge. And he served Fabiola a glass of wine, too (he just guessed at the right stemware). They both finished the bottle together in silence, and by then, Timothy wasn't hungry anymore. And he also asked himself, What's wrong with this picture? I'm a writer employed by Mercedes Ford in her New York penthouse condo, and I'm acting like I still work at The Chili Exchange. Again, it occurred to him that this job, which seemed like a godsend at first, might not be so great after all. Then his brand-new cell phone rang.

The screen said, Jared Evans. "Hi, Jared," Timothy said in a chirpy greeting. Then Jared told him that he'd monitored the responses to the fan letters and thought he'd done a totally crappy job. "Incompetent? Substandard? Pathetic? You can see what I'm doing when I'm on the computer?" Timothy asked incredulously. He looked over at Fabiola, who was smirking and nodding her head. "Isn't that illegal? It's certainly intrusive."

Jared reminded him that the computer belonged to Muriel Maynard Management, that Timothy worked for Muriel Maynard, and that it was right to keep an eye on the owner's property. Timothy supposed that was true, but he was still unnerved by Jared playing Nosey Neighbor. But considering all the surveillance he'd already been subjected to at the condo, he realized that he shouldn't expect privacy on a business-owned laptop either.

But that was not the entire reason that Jared was calling. He told Timothy to go back to the computer, read his latest email, and respond immediately. Timothy looked at his wristwatch. It was 8:30, for crying out loud. Jared had previously told him he would not be expected to check emails after 8:00 p.m. Plus, he'd already had a few glasses of wine and wasn't altogether sober. However, he ended the call and told Fabiola he'd catch her later. Then he went back into the office.

When Timothy retrieved and logged on to the computer again, he found a dozen more emails had arrived. However, the one from Jared was flagged with a small icon of a jagged lightning bolt. He clicked and opened it.

Timothy read the message twice, trying to decipher why it was so urgent. It was merely a text from Muriel saying there was to be a party at the penthouse the following Saturday night. The guest of honor was Virginia La Paloma, the Italian soprano. Timothy thought, Woo-hoo! My first swanky showbiz party! Suddenly, the good day that had turned into a not-so-good day was a good day again. Very cool, he thought, and immediately emailed Jared. "Of course, I accept! I accept! I accept!" his words practically skipped across the screen. "Sounds like fun! However, I have nothing appropriate to wear to a fancy party."

Jared immediately responded. "How nice of you to accept. And yes, it should be fun. As for what to wear, check the utility closet in the kitchen."

Timothy thought it was an odd response. However, when he opened an accompanying attachment, he realized he had misunderstood Jared. He wasn't reading an invitation. He was to be the freakin' catering assistant! With that, Timothy closed the computer, returned it to the safe, and went to bed. For the next hour, he watched a Netflix Original Series, a comedy about a dysfunctional clan of New York City sewer dwellers who find a winning lottery ticket and move into the Park Avenue mansion next to the Kardashians. A modern-day *Beverly Hillbillies*, he decided. Then he fluffed up his pillow and closed his eyes.

## Chapter Three

When the grey light of morning seeped through the window drapes in his room, Timothy didn't want to give up the comfy sheets and pillows. Then he looked around at his elegant surroundings and started humming the song *If They Could See Me Now*.

Then the blasted phone rang!

Of course, it was Jared Evans. "An ice sculpture? Of two human lungs?" Timothy repeated as Jared started rattling off a list of what Muriel had told him to acquire for the party. "Oh, it's a charity event. A respiratory disease? The guest of honor wants who invited?" Timothy was astonished when Jared repeated the name Dr. Reuben Wrightwood, the famous Amazon rainforest bug scientist. "Arrange for his travel? I wouldn't even know where to begin to find him. I know he's always in the news, but that's because he lives among snakes and panthers and finds new exotic species of insects and rescues disgusting creepy-crawly things from extinction," he said.

Jared taunted, "Is the widdle moron too stupid to do a simple job?" He sounded exactly like a schoolyard bully. "Are you going to disappoint yourself, Timothy?"

"I don't want to disappoint *you*," Timothy countered, stung by the unfair derision.

There was a discernable condescending edge to Jared's voice. "You're the one who needs a job, not me," he said with a steely tone. "Frankly, I'd be delighted to see your skinny little butt kicked out the door. There were a thousand better applicants for this position than you." His tone bore a striking resemblance to Timothy's mother, especially the time she made him feel like a failure for coming in third place—out of three entrants—in his hometown's city-wide essay competition (*My Responsibility as a Citizen*). "I have no problem if you want to quit," Jared added. "But how will you feel knowing that you're such a loser that you can't make a few simple travel arrangements?"

"Wow. I'm new at this, Jared. I'm just trying to suggest that you've given me a rather tall order. And on short notice. But of course, I'll try to get it all done."

"Try?" Jared said, his tone patronizing. "Try?"

Although there was silence on the other end of the line, Timothy could sense that Jared was fighting a losing battle to remain calm. After a few long moments during which the only sound Timothy could hear was heavy breathing, Jared said something surprising: "'Do or do not. There is no try.' A quote from Yoda." And then he hung up.

Wearing only his sleeping shorts and sitting stone-still on his bed, Timothy held his phone in one hand and wiped away tears of frustration with the other. A knock on his door startled him out of a Jared-induced trance. Without an invitation, Fabiola peeked in. "The Tuesday guys are here," she said, giving a raised eyebrow and approving nod to Timothy's shitless, slender torso. Timothy must have looked mystified because Fabiola repeated, "The men who come on Tuesdays. For the folders."

"What do they want?" Timothy asked, genuinely interested.

"The folders," Fabiola repeated. "They come like clockwork every week."

Timothy gave up and said he'd be out in a few minutes. Fabiola shrugged and gave him an appreciative once-over again. Her eyes seemed to linger for a moment longer than necessary on the silky wisps of dark hair blanketing his narrow chest, and then she closed the door.

Timothy needed to splash some cold water on his face, brush his teeth, comb his hair, jump into his jeans, and put on a clean T-shirt. It would only take a moment—or ten.

When he eventually arrived in the living room, two model-handsome men in their mid-twenties wearing striped, cotton, seersucker suits were milling around, taking sips from plastic bottles of spring water. Each was of average height, clean-shaven, and quickly losing the hair on their heads. Neither of them smiled. Timothy was always conscious of men's fashions; even though he couldn't afford so much as a Ralph Lauren T-shirt in the bargain bin at TJ Max, he knew their suits were expensive. Maybe Armani?

"You must be the new one," said the man with a plaid pocket square.

Timothy offered a frown. "I am a bit new here, yes," he said. "I'm Timothy. And you are?"

"We're here for the folders," said the one with a red and black striped pocket square. He could tell Timothy was in a cloud of confusion. "The papers that Jared gives us each week. I'm returning these…" he held out a file folder, "…we exchange them for a new one. Isn't it just like ol' Jared to do his best to make the new guy screw up…"

Timothy held up his hands. "Hold on, hold on. I don't have any instructions about folders or files. I don't know what you mean. Let me make a phone call."

Both men simultaneously exhaled long breaths. They apparently weren't too happy having to cool their heels while Timothy searched for answers. Timothy went into the office and closed the door. He called Jared and explained the situation.

"Why did Muriel hire such a disaster?" Jared spat with irritation. "I told her you'd be worthless! She never listens to the truth! You read the job description I gave you! Go get it."

Timothy walked to the desk and found the pages. He started reading and discovered a bulleted list of responsibilities.

**TUESDAYS: 9:30. Exchange materials. Only one file per week. Yellow tabs. Place the returned file on the bottom shelf. These files are top-secret and are not to be opened under any circumstances.**

"Got it," he said. "Sorry to bother you."

"Sorry?" Jared countered, "You're going to be really sorry." Then he abruptly ended the call.

Timothy was not one who liked to ask for too much help with anything. He figured it was probably an Aries trait. So, he didn't confirm with Jared that the files were in the safe. He just came to that conclusion and hoped he was right. He opened the secret room, and when he accessed the safe, he quickly saw that there were many files with different colored tabs. A few were yellow and placed on the bottom and top shelves. He deduced that since the returned ones were to be put on the bottom shelf, it made sense that the ones on the top were for distribution. He took one and closed everything up again.

With the file in hand, Timothy returned to the living room. The guys were on the terrace, enjoying the view. "I'll show you mine if you show me yours," he said to get their attention. However, just like his lame attempt at banter with Griffin in security, neither of these guys smiled. So, I'm no

Joan Rivers, he thought. And yes, it had occurred to him that perhaps he should find an evening adult education class—Wisecracking 101.

"Next week," one of the guys said, in place of "goodbye."

"If he's still here," the other smirked as they strode to the elevator. The guys entered the car and waited... For? Timothy realized that security had let them up to the penthouse, and he had to do the biotech thing for the elevator door to close and send them back down. *Gosh, what people have to go through to come and go from this place*, he thought.

Timothy was totally bewildered. Why did it take two men to pick up one lousy file folder? And who were they, all dressed up like they were men's store mannequins? He wondered what could possibly be so important about the folders that they had to be in a safe and doled out just one at a time. He rolled his eyes. It was none of his business, he decided. He had a job to do, and it wasn't for him to question the duties and procedures. But he figured he'd better read that job description all the way through.

After showering and making a buttered bagel for breakfast—thankfully, there were some food supplies in the pantry—Timothy returned to the office. He took out the laptop and started his workday. The emails had piled up during the night. The last time he looked, there were twenty-seven. Now, the count was up to seventy-five. Again, he started by opening the ones that came in earliest. There were more requests for money. An acting class teacher requested that Mercedes lecture to his students. Another was hopeful that Mercedes would perform at a charity event for helping to save bees.

But the one that totally caught his attention came from a woman named Fiona Carter. It seemed bizarre. Fiona was from England and claimed to be Mercedes' long-lost daughter! To prove her case, she was offering results from a DNA test she'd taken through one of those ancestry companies that use spit to document one's heritage and which claimed that Fiona and Mercedes shared the same genetic markers. Of course, it proved absolutely nothing since millions of other people shared similar traits. Also, this Fiona character wanted to come to America to meet her "Mum." Of course, she wanted Mercedes to pay her way. Timothy shook his head and thought, It takes all kinds.

Timothy read the message more closely. The woman offered the usual accolades to Mercedes. She had attached a photo of herself and said that all her friends told her she looked a bit like Mercedes Ford. Timothy looked at the picture of a woman with a mop of curly hair on her head and a large gin nose. "The most deluded people are those who choose to ignore what they already know," he said, quoting something he'd read somewhere long ago in a college philosophy class.

Timothy shook his head and began to type up a draft response. He cut and pasted from other templates. The first paragraphs were always identical: Mercedes appreciated receiving the message and how thankful she was for the time and effort it took for them to write. Then, for the next paragraph, Timothy started to use his creative writing skills and really got into it. Of course, he would never send what he was composing, although he totally wanted to. This was just for fun. Stuff one wishes they could really say but would never dare to.

Dear Crazy Fan Lady.

[Insert text from the template.]

Thank you for clarifying that the attached image was your photo. I thought it was a manatee. Oh, and I lost count of how many chins you have. There is no chance you'll ever be anorexic, is there? And what can I say about your unibrow? Don't they have tweezers in England?

So, your friends think you look like Mercedes Ford, eh? They probably mean that you are the size of a Mercedes SUV and built like a Ford F-150 truck. And you obviously have nothing more to do in your little unfulfilled life than have fantasies about being a movie star's daughter. How are the cats? I bet you have a lot of them in a small flat (as you call apartments in England). Probably stinks from the pee of a dozen or so of the flea-bitten critters. And I'll bet that your windows are covered with newspapers because you're afraid that aliens are trying to get pictures of you when you undress. Am I right?

But Mercedes thanks you anyway for your letter.

Again, Timothy could never send that message. He would never alienate Mercedes Ford from her adoring public. Then he pasted in the paragraph about seeing the new film when it was released at Christmastime and pushed Send…

He pushed… SEND…!

"Oh, no, no, no! No freakin' way! No!" Timothy began to yell and violently pressed Delete, Delete, Delete! Nothing! "Oh, please, dear God, no! I couldn't have sent that! It was a terrible and mean message. It could go viral if that lady Fiona posted it on social media. Please, dear Lord, how do I retract it?" He was in an all-out panic. He knew there were ways to sometimes get sent messages back, but how? He'd never had to do that before!

Timothy kept ranting and hyperventilating and practically crying. He frantically went to Google and typed, "How to unsend an email message." Instantly, a list of ways to withdraw sent messages popped up. He clicked on the first link and followed the instructions, but nothing happened. Nothing!

Timothy stopped for a moment and took a deep breath. He looked at his watch. There was a five-hour time difference between New York and England. He hoped that maybe Fiona Carter was at work and wouldn't see the message until she got home. Or that she was preparing afternoon tea and was too busy to check messages. Or… anything that would save his worthless butt! Timothy went back to Google and found a link to a video that showed precisely how to retrieve sent mail. At the end of the four-minute demonstration, the narrator said, "And if that doesn't work, you're toast since the message has been opened, and there is nothing you can do to save your miserable, worthless skin. And you're a little good-for-nothing screw-up who shouldn't be anywhere near a computer or your favorite movie star, and you should just quit right now and hang yourself!" The narrator didn't say that last sentence, but Timothy was thinking those words.

Yep, Timothy was toast, all right. Blackened. Burned to a crisp. So much for having a cool new job, a swell place to live, and a larger paycheck than he could ever get at The Chili Exchange. He had to face the fact that he was a pathetic excuse for an assistant and was utterly and completely screwed. As he sat before the computer screen, paralyzed from the shock of what he'd done, his survival instincts began to kick in. Maybe no one other than Fiona Carter would see the message. He was the one in charge of correspondence. The messages arrived at the Mercedes Ford fan website and were forwarded to him. He felt a cautious sense of optimism when he realized that he alone was in contact with Fiona. He was exhausted from dispensing all the adrenalin that comes with blood-curdling horror. And then he remembered that Jared monitored his work. He was going to be fired after only a few hours on the job, which must be some sort of a record for a personal assistant. On the other hand, surely Jared couldn't possibly read every email Timothy sent; that would be a full-time job, wouldn't it? Timothy desperately needed to take a break.

Timothy left the office, and when he came into the kitchen, Fabiola was there making herself a turkey breast sandwich. Timothy was starving and said so. However, Fabiola was, if not deaf, then clearly not interested in anyone else's empty stomach. "I'm going out for a bite," Timothy said. "Back in an hour."

Timothy had forgotten how hideous the weather was outside. He could feel sweat dripping down the nape of his neck in no more than a minute of walking. He only went one block before he found a deli-style restaurant. He couldn't believe a few nuts were sitting at tables on the sidewalk. He entered the place, but it wasn't any cooler inside. Two filthy-looking fans were mounted on the walls behind the counter and food-display case, but they didn't do much more than stir the stultifying air around. He ordered a hot dog with mustard and relish and a Coke. He also grabbed the one available seat, ignoring an old woman who was clearly navigating toward the same spot.

Timothy eagerly consumed the hot dog and quickly drank the Coke until only melting ice was in the plastic glass. Then he took out his phone to check for messages. He rolled his eyes when he saw the list. "How on earth could there be seventeen more messages just in the short time I've been away?" he moaned. "I know that Mercedes is internationally famous, but why do people actually take the time to write to celebrities?" It was a mystery to him.

Then he saw an email from Jared. It was flagged as urgent. The subject line read, ASAP! "Oh God," Timothy said. "He knows about the terrible message. I totally deserve to be fired!" He really didn't want to open his email, but Timothy had a thing about facing challenges that he wanted to get over quickly. He opened it and immediately felt relief. It was just a confirmation that he'd be home to receive the piano tuner at 2:00. He took a deep breath, then read the rest of the message. Naturally, there was a PS. "Let me know exactly what time Virginia La Paloma's flight is expected to arrive on Saturday. And by all means, make sure that Dr. Wrightwood is deloused before setting foot in the penthouse. Don't want parasitic larvae from the Amazon depositing their pupa under the skin of New York's 1%."

Despite the oppressive heat in the deli, Timothy shivered at the thought of Jared's last line. He'd once seen a movie about documentary filmmakers working in the jungles of some tropical rainforest and how their bodies became hosts for maggot-like insects that peeled back a couple of layers of human epidermis and gave birth to their even creepier offspring under the person's skin. That thought was enough for Timothy. He got up, tossed his trash in a bin on his way out, and walked back to The Colton.

When he stepped off the elevator, Fabiola was waiting for him. She had her arms crossed and a smirk across her face. Then she sang, "*Somebodysintrouble.*"

Timothy panicked. "The email. I accidentally sent a stupid email. Jared must have found out. I'm dead."

Fabiola just shrugged and walked away. But before being out of voice range, she added, "You have a visitor in the office. I'm sure he's *dying* to see you."

"Darn it all!" Timothy said as he gingerly walked down the hallway and into the office. Of course, Jared was standing there with the computer in his hands. He could have been a spokesmodel on *The Price is Right*, the way he held out the machine as if it were some sort of coveted prize.

Timothy instantly realized he hadn't secured the computer in the safe before leaving. He was such a mental mess from accidentally sending that email; he had just wanted to escape. "Oh, my gosh!" he burst into apology mode. "I'm so sorry, Jared! I'd been working all morning and got so hungry that I forgot about the computer. I'm hypoglycemic, you know," he lied. "If I didn't have something to eat right away, I would have died on the spot. Really and truly!"

"Saboteur!" Jared exploded. "The email! How could you? I knew you were a miserable little moron, but…"

Timothy knew it had been too good to be true that Jared was only angry because the computer had been left out. And, of course, Jared had every right to be furious with him. No matter how many times he tried to express his apologies, Jared wasn't buying it. To hear Jared's version of the situation, Timothy had singlehandedly destroyed Mercedes Ford's reputation and career.

"Timothy! Timothy!" he screamed. "We hired you on Friday; it's now Tuesday. You can't use the excuse that you're new at the job! Honestly, I've never had more trouble with an assistant. Ever! Whoever gave you a college degree must have been a knobhead, too! Oh, that's right, you only went to a junior college!"

Again, Timothy flooded the room with apologies. He knew that he deserved to lose his job. And his new home. But where would he go? By now, someone else had surely taken his place in the studio apartment he'd been sharing in Bed-Sty. The only person he knew well enough in the city to even consider asking for help was his ex-boyfriend Ted, the nerdy poet he'd met at the Strand bookstore. But Timothy certainly could not go back to Ted—although Ted would probably take him back in a nanosecond.

"Didn't we basically pluck you from some filthy, rat-infested hellhole?2 Jared said, shaking his head. "You get to work for a major, internationally famous movie star. We give you a fantastic place to live. And this is how you repay our kindness?"

"Please, Jared," Timothy implored, "I'm so, so sorry! I'm usually a very quick study. I'll get the hang of this job in no time. I won't make any more excuses for my mistakes."

"Hey, Timothy, 'Love means never having to say you're sorry.'"

*Huh?* Timothy gave Jared a look that told him he had no idea what he'd just said.

"It's a line from an old movie. In other words, don't make mistakes, and you won't have to apologize."

Oh, brother, what a stupid saying! Timothy wanted to roll his eyes and tell Jared to jump in front of a speeding subway train. But that's the type of thing you save until the last day on a job when you have nothing to lose by calling out the boss for being a gigantic dick. And this could certainly be that final day for Timothy. But instead, he agreed, "Absolutely. I get it. I'll never try to be funny again. And I'll never leave the computer out of the safe unattended."

Jared took a deep breath and shoved the laptop into Timothy's arms. He exhaled loudly and said, "How many

RSVPs have you received?"

*RSVPs?* Timothy said to himself in a panic. This must be a trick question. He's trying to trip me up. But it wasn't worth the time and effort of trying to pretend that he knew what Jared was talking about. Timothy had to admit defeat. "Sorry, Jared, I'm not sure what you mean."

Jared looked at him coldly. "Timothy," he said in a steely tone, "what did we just discuss about uttering the word 'sorry'?"

"Right. Sorry. I mean, I'm not sorry. I mean..." Timothy fumbled for words. "Just tell me what I did wrong, Jared. I'll fix it."

"Fix what?" he asked coyly, clearly toying with Timothy.

"You tell me," Timothy said, trying to show a bit of backbone. "Something about RSVPs." Suddenly, the answer dawned on him. "Oh," he said.

"Oh," Jared parroted with a sneer.

"I'm supposed to email reminders to Saturday night's party guest list. Shoot. I'm sorry! I mean, I'm not sorry. I mean, that was my very next project. In fact, I've already started. No one's confirmed yet, but I'll get back to it right now. It would have been finished, but then the whole hypoglycemia thing happened, and then I came home, and you were mad at me. And all that."

Jared took another deep breath. He was always taking deep breaths around Timothy. Timothy thought maybe he had that *Infectious chronicosis* lung disease that they were organizing the benefit for or an asthma issue, and the scent of Timothy's constant anxiety triggered a physical response.

"Timothy, I wasn't mad at you. I don't get mad at people. I only get upset with the stupid, half-witted, imbecilic things that certain stupid, half-witted imbeciles do. I suspect that most people would say that I'm a sweetie. I've heard things like, 'Bless his little heart.' And 'Isn't he an interesting piece of work.'"

Coming from the Deep South, as Timothy had, he knew those were hardly terms of endearment, but Jared didn't seem to realize it. Timothy didn't really know what to say. A part of him felt more at ease, while another part knew that Jared was a cobra in the grass. He was totally aware that he had to watch his every step. He tried to force a bit of calmness into the atmosphere and said, "Well, it's back to work for this busy boy. Thanks for dropping by. And again, I'm…" He caught himself from using the word sorry. "…happy that I'm working with you."

"Working *for* me," Jared smiled evilly. "And not for long if you don't step up to the plate and start pulling your weight around here. Oh, and recharge that unit," he said of the computer. "You've let the battery level go below fifty percent. Don't let that happen again. What if there was a blackout and we lost electricity?"

Timothy followed Jared to the door and locked it as loudly as possible. He wanted Jared to hear that he was following security protocol. Then he stuck out his tongue and whispered, "That's for you, you arrogant, condescending, self-centered little prick-maniac!" Then he sat down at the desk… and cried. Timothy cried easily. Almost anything could set him off. TV news stories about war refugees. Good Samaritans visiting elderly people in rest homes. Even that old television commercial where the husband asks for a second cup of coffee at a dinner party when he never wanted his wife's coffee at home. He was almost always just on the verge of tears. And now, well, Timothy was exhausted from Jared torturing him. He'd had mean bosses when he did office temp work, but nothing like this power-hungry monster. Although he agreed that he'd made a horrible mistake by writing and sending that email, the overwrought tongue-lashing he received was definitely not commensurate with the offense.

Timothy sat silently for a few minutes, trying to figure out how to escape from this punishing job. But he knew he was cornered. He had no money and nowhere else to live. All he could do was make the best of a rotten situation that had been camouflaged as a fun and exciting opportunity. He told himself that life would surely improve. It had to. After all, he wasn't living in some squalid, third-world country. But he did have an evil, tyrant dictator who seemed determined to control and ruin his life.

And then Timothy heard Fabiola knocking on the door. "The piano guy's here," she called through the door.

Timothy's first response was a roll of his eyes and a silent, Why do I care? Let him do his job, then leave. But he decided he'd better at least tell the man how important the upcoming party was, and that Broadway people would be attending, so the piano had to be in perfect tune."

Timothy wiped his eyes and nose with the bottom of his shirt, checked his face in the smoky reflection of the window, and pulled himself together.

In the next instant, his prayer that life would improve was answered. The guy who'd come to adjust the tension of the piano strings made up for all Timothy's misery. Timothy thought only geeky dorks did this type of work. And this guy may have been a geeky dork, too, but if so, he was the sexiest geeky dork on the planet. He looked like a super-fit soccer player, and his jeans and his faded *Rolling Stones* concert souvenir T-shirt emphasized his packed physique. His left inside forearm was etched with a tattoo of a treble clef, and he introduced himself as Brad.

Timothy's first thought was: After you finish with the piano, I need tuning, too!

Brad was adorable, and Timothy practically swooned as he watched him work. When Brad lifted the piano lid and leaned into where the tuning pegs and strings were, his T-shirt hiked up several inches, revealing the top of his underwear (it was rainbow-colored with a designer's name stitched on the waist) and a hint of mossy hair on his tummy. And Timothy was literally dizzy with infatuation.

When Brad finished, he sat at the keyboard to test the instrument. He played beautifully. Wow, good-looking and talented, too! Timothy thought to himself. It's true that Timothy fell in love very quickly, especially with piano players. At junior college, he used to go to a piano bar off Interstate 210. The guy at the eighty-eights there could play anything that anyone requested. All of Timothy's favorites from the old days—the late 1990s—that his parents had listened to. He had fixated on the guy's long, milky-white fingers and the tufts of prematurely gray hair in a well-maintained field of curly black. And he had a really good singing voice, too. They actually dated for a short while. At the time, he was everything that Timothy thought he wanted in a boyfriend, but the fact that he worked at the bar until two in the morning was a bummer. He was hardly ever available for dinners or movie dates. Plus, although Timothy thought they'd have made a smart and attractive couple, he was determined to set out for New York City and find literary fame and fortune. He couldn't give up that dream for anyone.

And now, here was Brad, and he wasn't wearing a ring, which was the first thing Timothy always looked for when he saw a cute guy.

"Do you have a favorite?" Brad asked as he resolved one melody and went into simply noodling the keys.

For a moment, Timothy was stupefied. He wanted to say, "You're my favorite!" But he realized that Brad meant a favorite song. His all-time, best-loved song was obscure, and he was pretty sure Brad wouldn't know it. "*Long Ago and Far Away*. From an old Rita Hayworth and Gene Kelly movie musical that my dad liked," he said.

"*Cover Girl.* Nineteen Forty-four," Brad correctly identified the film's title and year of release. And to Timothy's total amazement and astonishment—as well as instant images of the two of them walking hand-in-hand on a tropical beach—Brad played a few chords and then went into the melody. Timothy was transported back to a time in early childhood when his dad had held him in his arms and danced around the family rec room to this very song. *So sad that he's dead*, he thought of his dad. *Life can be so unfair. And also, very fair indeed, considering this guy who is now making me totally nuts with his gorgeous looks and musical talent.*

Timothy smiled throughout Brad's performance and applauded wildly when he stopped. And for once, he saw a bit of positive emotion in Fabiola, who had been drawn from her room to hear the music. She and Timothy clapped enthusiastically as Brad stood up, took a humble bow, and collected his tuning implements. "You're very kind," he said. "Sorry that I have to leave." He spoke that last sentence as he focused his brown eyes onto Timothy's blue ones.

Timothy was sorry, too. "How about some water to take with you," he said. "You're darn hot out there. I mean the *weather's* hot. Oh, you are too, but… I mean…" He felt like a blathering idiot.

During the brief moment that they stared at each other, Timothy wanted to memorize how Brad looked but tried not to be obviously imprinting Brad's face and body. Then, he went into the kitchen to retrieve a cold bottle of spring water.

He met Brad in the foyer. "Thanks for the beautiful song," he said, not knowing what else to say. "I'm surprised you know it."

"I surprise a lot of people with a lot of stuff," Brad said and looked into Timothy's eyes again. "You surprise me, too. You're a definite improvement over the last several people who worked here. To them, I was no more than a handyman. You're very egalitarian."

*Egalitarian*, Timothy repeated to himself. As a writer, he really appreciated Brad using a word like that. He bet that if he told him he likes polysyllabic words, Brad would know exactly what he meant. (His mother would have said he was showing off.) As Brad stepped into the elevator, they took one, longer, trance-like look at each other, and Timothy said, "You need my hand to make it go down."

"Or up," Brad winked as Timothy blushed again and placed his palm on the biometric pad. When the outline turned green, Brad put his larger hand over Timothy's. "Stay in tune. I mean in *touch*," he said, revealing that he was just as much a nervous idiot as Timothy. "I'd really like that. If you ever feel like going to a concert or seeing a band, let me know." He pulled a business card from the back pocket of his jeans and handed it to Timothy. Timothy loved the feeling of the warmth of Brad's body on the card, and he blushed again. And then the elevator doors closed.

What just happened? Timothy said to himself, unable to recall ever feeling such a sense of lightness and physical excitement. He totally forgot about how dreadful the day had been. He was pretty sure that if he climbed over the terrace railing, he'd float above the city like the Snoopy balloon in the Macy's Thanksgiving Day Parade. Weird, he knew. That never happened with Ted, the poet. Not even with David, the other piano player.

And then reality punctured the Timothy balloon. His phone rang. The caller ID assured him it was trouble.

## Chapter Four

Why do bosses think you can do twenty different things all at once? They need to understand the law of physics that states that no two objects can occupy the same space at the same time. But they insist on piling up more work than can ever be accomplished in a day. It's one of the great cosmic/employment mysteries.

Now Jared was calling to tell Timothy that he had to somehow get the general manager of the Crown Theater to give Muriel Maynard tickets to *Metamorphoses: The Musical*. It's the 21st-century updating of that weird classic Kafka play about a guy who turns into a cockroach. Seriously, a *roach*! The hit song, *Little Buggers!* had made the show such a massive hit that scalpers were getting up to $1,200 per seat, even for matinee performances. "She wants to attend tonight?" Timothy exclaimed. "I hear tickets are impossible to get!"

More silence ensued from Jared. Then, with another sigh of disappointment, he said, "Remember what Audrey Hepburn once said, 'Nothing is impossible.' The word even says, 'I'm Possible.'"

*And it's possible that you're a total cuckoo!* Timothy wanted to say but, of course, didn't.

"Muriel wants two seats in the sixth row on the left center aisle, Jared demanded. "And she needs a table at Joe Allen before the show. And a car to take her home. Not Uber!" And then he hung up.

Timothy went back into the office, frustrated by all the work. In the contact list on his phone, he found the name for the head of house seats at The Crown Theater. He called and said he needed two tickets for that night's performance.

After the guy stopped laughing hysterically and pleading, "Amy, is that you? I know it's you. It's not even April Fool's Day!" Timothy told him who the seats were for, which did nothing to make the man stop sniggering until he told him that Muriel Maynard represented Mercedes Ford and that Muriel had to see the show because Mercedes was considering doing the film version. "Naturally, she'll be changing the role from a disgusting cockroach to a water bug," Timothy insisted.

"Ain't they about the same repulsive thing?" the guy asked.

"Mercedes Ford makes every role she plays unique," Timothy flatly stated, trying to sound as though he were a tough representative for the legendary star. "Muriel Maynard will be at Will Call just before curtain. May I have a confirmation number, please?"

When Timothy called Jared back, he thought he'd get a great big commendation for obtaining the near unobtainable. Something like, "You go, winner!" No such luck. Timothy had a long way to go before he would understand that he'd never do anything right in Jared's dark, beady eyes. "Now she wants to sit on the other side of the row," is how Jared responded. "And tell the stage manager to hold the curtain if she's late. And what about Joe Allen? Her usual table, the one under the poster of *The Prince of Central Park*. And find out the name of the driver for the car."

The restaurant. The car. In all the excitement of obtaining the impossible-to-get theater tickets, Timothy had totally forgotten about booking a table! As for changing the seats to the other side of the house, hell no! If Muriel complained to Jared the next day, Timothy would simply feign innocence and tell him that he had been assured the seats would be switched. After pulling off the coup of arranging for house seats in the first place, Jared would probably believe him. No, of course, he wouldn't. As for holding the curtain? Yeah, right. No way would Timothy make that absurd request! Still, he felt brilliant and accomplished.

After reserving Muriel's table and ordering a car (the driver's name was unpronounceable), it was time to email confirmations to the swanky "do" that was taking place at The Colton on Saturday. Timothy knew the easy part would be writing the invite. But typing all those email addresses from the contact list would take forever. He'd have to peck slowly at the keyboard to ensure he correctly entered all those letters, numbers, and symbols. *Why can't email addresses be simple?* he whined to himself. Then he had a sudden and terrific idea—copy and paste! That would save a ton of time and be accurate, too!

Timothy finished just before 7:00 p.m. and then jumped into the body of the text. But Jared never specifically told him what the party was for except for some charity. With those ice-sculpture lungs, it was probably a dreary disease, but he also didn't know if it was formal or informal. Probably formal. Timothy decided to write a quick, silly draft. He'd just wing it. He figured that once Jared saw a bare-bones, rough sketch, he'd provide the details, and, in seconds, everyone would have their invitation reminders. But to make completely, positively, 100% certain that Jared absolutely knew he was only showing his creativity (he didn't want any email foul-ups like last time), he added a disclaimer right at the very tippy top. In bold! In Red ink!

Then, to amuse himself, he started typing:

*Breakfast at Timothy's*

**DRAFT COPY**
**FOR JARED'S EYES ONLY**

Dear Stinking Rich and Famous Friends,

Muriel Maynard would like to remind your mountains of disposable moolah that her annual *Infectious chronicosis* fundraiser is this Saturday at 8:00 p.m. We'll share an intimate evening of boring opera arias and tedious slides of rare and creepy bugs from the Amazon rainforest. Special guests include internationally acclaimed diva Virginia La Paloma (whomever she is!), warbling her greatest hit(s). As well as the celebrated explorer and entomologist Reuben Wrightwood, fresh from his trek through the jungles of Taratonika. He'll be scratching lice from his scalp and passing out creepy rainforest spiders for fun and games. Antidotes for anything venomous will be provided. Please RSVP right away to Ms. Lolita Loquat at the above-referenced email address.

Ciao, darlings!

He even added a watermark to the page, diagonally and in italics, that announced **DRAFT** just to make sure that this time Jared knew he was only playing around and wasn't being a pinhead. Never again! Great, he thought. And now my busy day is over. He would just send that little puppy over to Jared, and the remainder of the evening was all his. He'd pour a glass of vino, then toss a frozen pizza into the oven. It also looked like an excellent evening for dining on the terrace, muggy though it might be. Heck, he was feeling so good he decided to invite Fabiola to join him for drinks. And by morning, he'd have Jared's changes to the invitation and a commendation for not only showing a better sense of humor than to that British fan but also for arranging the theater tickets, hiring a car, and dining at Joe Allen for Muriel. *Aren't I just the best thing since the Roomba vacuum robot? You bet I am!*

And off the email went.

\* \* \*

After their second glass of Pinot Noir, Fabiola and Timothy found themselves in a kittenish whimsy about Brad, the piano tuner. "God in Heaven is indeed mean and vengeful," Timothy mused. "He makes only a very few ridiculously gorgeous men, sets them down on this planet, then just sits back on his cloud stroking his beard and watching as we ordinary mortals lose our dignity and self-control over them!"

"If only I were about fifty years younger," Fabiola sighed in agreement, and for the first time since they'd met, it seemed they might be breaking the ice. Timothy came to the realization that people in the twilight of their lives could still feel the need for romantic companionship. Fabiola was somewhere between seventy and The Pearly Gates, but she apparently still thought about guys. Timothy should have known that intimate feelings didn't stop when people reached an older age. Although, he couldn't imagine there was any age at which his own mother felt anything remotely like what he was feeling for Brad. His mother had stopped being lovey-dovey somewhere between Timothy's conception and the severing of his umbilical cord.

As Fabiola seemed to be in a mellow mood, and curious Timothy was always eager to find out what makes people tick, he began to weave a few innocuous questions into their conversation. "What astrological sign are you? Do you prefer liquid or bar soap? Thin or thick-crust pizza?" Just ordinary small talk. Totally innocent queries. And indeed, the answers were a snap: "Taurus. Liquid. Thin." However, the fourth question, "Why were you so upset that you went on a rampage with those perfume bottles?" came with an unexpected accusation. They were getting along so well, and then Fabiola's face turned from amused to wary. "Spy!" she said, repeating what she'd said the day before.

Timothy was stunned! What had he said to cause such an outburst? All he could say was that he was sorry for intruding on Fabiola's privacy. But Fabiola wasn't interested in apologies. She got up, took her glass and the almost-empty wine bottle, and returned to the penthouse. After a few minutes, Timothy noticed the scent of something burning. He sniffed the air. In a split second, he raced back into the condo. The kitchen was filling with smoke from the oven. He couldn't turn it off before the alarms blasted everywhere, and the house security phone started ringing. He turned off the oven as quickly as possible and took out a blackened circle that was once a beautiful pepperoni and meatball pizza—with extra cheese. A strident robotic voice issued God-like through the condo's speaker system: "In case of fire, do not use the elevator. I repeat…"

All the while, the house phone continued ringing, and then Timothy's cell phone rang, too. He was frantically dashing around, fanning the smoke with a dishtowel, and trying to coax it through the terrace doors. While still fanning, he picked up the house phone. It was, of course, security. He quickly explained what had occurred, and then the alarm was silenced. He assured Griffin that all was under control.

During all the commotion, Fabiola never bothered to come out of her room to see what was happening. Timothy wouldn't have put it past her to have turned the heat up on the oven. And why wasn't she helping to clean up the kitchen? Timothy felt like leaving the charred disc that used to be food sitting on the counter for her to dispose of. But no, Timothy was a bit of a neatnik. He ripped up the darn thing and shoved it down the garbage disposal, tossed the box into the recycling bin, and washed his wine glass.

When the condo was quiet again, Timothy looked at the ceiling and asked, "What's next?" It was a rhetorical question, but it served as an invitation. Timothy really needed to be more careful with the words he spoke.

* * *

When the sun spread into Timothy's bedroom the next morning and snatched him from a dream about Brad and his talented fingers, he was cranky. He definitely did not want to face another workday.

With a huge sigh, he pushed the covers off and got himself out of bed. Timothy was the kind of person who didn't like to put off doing difficult things; he'd much rather just get them over with. But when he looked at the multiple messages on his phone, he decided they could wait until after his morning routine. He got into the shower, performed his ablutions, and dressed. Fabiola hadn't made his bed the day before, so he figured that was another job in the house he was responsible for. He made only a slight effort to smooth out the sheets and comforter and fluff up the pillows. It was a lazy job, but he thought, who's gonna know? Probably not Brad. Ever.

When Timothy arrived in the kitchen, desperate for a cup of coffee, he could see Fabiola out on the terrace, reading a book. Timothy was always interested in what others read, so he popped his head out to say good morning. He was determined to make a fresh start with the maid. "Taking a break?" he said in a cheerful voice. He didn't mean anything by that harmless comment other than another way of saying hello. But no, Fabiola did not take it that way.

"Spy." She repeated last night's accusation without looking up from her book.

Timothy was positively mystified by why Fabiola not only couldn't warm up to him but also kept thinking that Timothy was somehow her adversary. "And good morning to you, too," he said in jest. No response. Timothy noticed that Fabiola was reading the new mystery by Millie Monroe. Ted, the poet, had loaned him his copy of the bestseller, and Timothy had quite enjoyed it. Lots of suspense, plot twists and turns, and interesting characters. He thought talking about the book might be a good way to show that reading was a common interest between them.

"How far into it are you?" Timothy asked, sitting down at the wrought-iron and glass-top table. "The book, I mean."

As he'd hoped, Fabiola sort of mumbled, "Almost finished. I'm at the part where Shannon is hiding in the hunting lodge about to escape from the insane serial killer and his machete."

"Ooh, that's a great scene," Timothy said. "I was so upset when he found her hiding behind the water boiler in the basement and chopped her head off."

Fabiola looked at him with fire in her eyes, then closed the book as loudly as the crack of an auctioneer's gavel.

Timothy instantly realized what he'd done. "Darn! I'm so sorry! I hate it when people spoil story endings! Want some coffee?"

Timothy was quickly left sitting alone on the terrace in the already oppressive morning heat. Hungry but afraid of having to confront Fabiola in the kitchen, he picked up the dreaded cell phone. He saw that there were 10 voicemails and only then realized that he had put the ringer on silent mode when he and Fabiola had started to get so chummy last night. He hadn't wanted any interruptions as they tried getting to know one another. Of course, all the messages were from the same number: Jared's. And Timothy could be a dummy, so he suspected they were tributes for Muriel's successful evening of dinner and the theater. Timothy was eager to finally receive well-deserved praise. As was his practice, he played the messages in the order received.

"Yes!" he shouted and offered a fist bump to the gods. Jared was happily reporting that Muriel, indeed, had had a fun evening. He said that the star cockroach in the play was out sick with some kind of bug (Timothy thought that was ironically hilarious), and the understudy cockroach went on in his place. Apparently, a star was born in that performance. A critic from *The New York Times* had been in the audience, and the entertainment section of the morning paper had a rapturous review. Timothy was feeling terrific as he selected the second call. And that was the end of his high spirits and the beginning of a sentence that would have made a visit to the biblical Lake of Fire a picnic.

With all the hysterical screaming in Jared's voice, he could only make out a few words. Something about Saturday... opera... insects... email list. He really had no idea what the man was blathering on about until suddenly, a berserk Jared was up close and personal, standing beside him on the penthouse terrace, explaining it all.

"Fool! Cretin! Dipstick!" Jared exploded. "You are nothing but a screw-up!"

"I don't... what are you talking about... what've I..." Timothy stammered, tears already flowing from his eyes.

Jared continued his tirade, jumping around like a

hyperactive brat at Walmart, demanding mommy buy him a new toy. Then he suddenly stopped and took a deep breath. From past experiences with Jared, Timothy knew that he was definitely ready to kill someone but was at least making an attempt to compose himself. "Follow me," Jared demanded.

As they left the terrace and walked through the condo to the office, Timothy blotted his tears with the bottom of his T-shirt. Jared unlocked the door. Timothy stood to the side as the maniac opened the secret room, then the safe, and withdrew the computer. Jared set the laptop down on the desk. "Sign in," he said in a calmer voice that Timothy knew barely concealed rage.

Timothy's hands were shaking as he entered the username and password.

"What do you see?" Jared asked as if he were a prosecuting attorney cross-examining a criminal.

Timothy looked at the screen and shrugged. "RSVPs. You wanted the invitation reminders to go out ASAP, so I stayed late in the office last night—on my own time—and wrote…"

Timothy instantly brought his shaking hands to his mouth and made an audible sound that was a combination of surprise/anguish/fear/distress/agony. He'd sent that absurd draft invitation meant only for Jared to every guest on the party list!

"Why? Why? Why!" Jared erupted like an exploding gas pipeline. Then he took another deep, calming breath. "Open the message from LmoreCrane@seemail.com," he said in an officious tone.

Timothy was nearly paralyzed with fear. He scrolled down the list of messages until he found the one Jared wanted. He double-clicked on the envelope icon next to the name.

"Read it aloud," Jared said, his voice changing to saccharine.

Although Timothy's mouth was dry, he reflexively swallowed and tried to wet his lips with his tongue. His voice had a rasp, and he had to repeat the first few words. He started again.

"Dear Ms. Lolita Loquat,

Thank you for taking the time to remind our *mountains of disposable moolah* about your *intimate evening of boring opera arias* by our dearest friend on the planet, Virginia La Paloma, as well as *a tedious slide show* presented by Dr. Reuben Wrightwood, whose entomological research we sponsor in full. Alas, we shall RSVP—in the negative. And, for the record, may I say that your attempt at levity for an annual charity fundraising event that we have always magnanimously supported for children suffering from *Infectious chron*icosis was beyond inappropriate.

Good luck to you in all future fundraising endeavors.

Sincerely,
Mr. and Mrs. Stinking Rich and Famous, aka Loretta and Raymond Crane."

Timothy stopped and stared at the computer screen. He couldn't look at Jared. He was aware that he was clenching his sphincter. In a soft, repentant voice, he said, "It was a draft. I even wrote that at the top, in bold red letters. For your eyes only. A small joke that only you would see. You'd look at it, think I was clever, and then send me all the pertinent information to include in the real email reminder."

"Blame-shifting is so unattractive," Jared sneered.

Timothy sat still and silent. He had nothing to say. Jared was absolutely right. And why, he wondered at that moment, did he ever think of himself as a writer just because he typed two hundred thousand words and gave the collection a title—especially the stupid title *Suffer Fools*. He was the fool. And he completely owned it. He knew that words could hurt. His words had possibly hurt the *Infectious chronicosis* community. He was beyond mortified.

Tears slid down his face as Timothy sat there, humiliated, and appalled by his stupidity. Jared stepped back and crossed his arms. "I'm not through with you yet, you pathetic little piece of…" he scowled. "Read Fineman27@seemail.com."

Timothy wondered why this horrible man was torturing him. He felt like an injured animal on the side of a road that Jared continued to poke with a stick and laugh at its agony. "I can't," he said and stood up to leave. "I'm incredibly sorry… and yes, I know you don't like that word, but it's the best I can do right now. I don't expect to be paid for my time here. And I'll send a check for the glass in the picture frame I broke."

"Not so fast, Mister," Jared snarled. "Sit your skinny ass down and read Fineman27!"

Timothy was trapped. He wouldn't have been able to reach the office door and unlock it before Jared could stop him. So, he resigned himself to more humiliation. He sat down and located the email. Opening it, he saw it that was, thankfully, very short. He started to read aloud.

"Ha! Sounds like my kinda do. I hate opera, and I'm squirmy around crawly things from rainforest jungles. But I love humor. I'll have a blast if the evening is anything like your draft invite reminder. And by the way, I am

'Stinking Rich and Famous.' Ha! I'll bring a blank check. See you Saturday."

—Eric Fineman

Stunned would be an understatement for how Timothy felt. How about euphoric? At least relieved. Definitely not crying anymore. He looked at Jared, who appeared even more perturbed than earlier. But why, Timothy thought. This was a good response. And from a guy with deep pockets. In fact, he recognized the name. "Is that the same Eric Fineman who invented the air-tight seal used on screw-top wine bottles? The one who owns CreditEase online layaways? The one who…"

"That's not the point!" Jared erupted again.

"What do the other RSVPs say?" Timothy asked, hedging his bet that they weren't all so terrible.

Jared folded his arms in exasperation. He took a deep breath and exhaled loudly. "There are words that I wish my mother, bless her soul, would let me say. This is the perfect opportunity to use every single last one of them." Jared turned away and started toward the door. He stopped and hissed, "Recall every email that hasn't been read. Right this minute!" He looked at his watch. "And, by two o'clock, I want a report with all the info about the caterer, the security detail, the private jet, limo service, and hotel accommodations for Virginia La Paloma and Dr. Wrightwood. Oh, and media coverage. Anderson Cooper and Don Lemon and their boyfriends better be there!" Jared then withdrew a typed page from his shoulder bag, crumpled it into a ball, and threw it at Timothy. Then he practically raced down the hall to escape being anywhere near his loathed assistant.

Thanks to the YouTube videos that Timothy had watched

explaining how to recall emails, he discovered that as long as the message hadn't been opened, he only had to do this and that to retrieve it. And the page that Jared had tossed at him was language to use in the real invitation.

At about 6:00 p.m., Fabiola knocked on the door. "Jared called," she said. "He's been trying to reach you. Is your phone on silent mode?"

With all the drama of the day, Timothy had totally forgotten that he'd never turned the sucker back on. The moment he did, the ringtone Jared had selected, which was way too strident, blared out. Of course, it was the man himself.

"Now, what have I done?" Timothy challenged the ninny.

"It's what you haven't done. I had a call from Fancy Florists. They haven't been paid this month. You know they come every Sunday after their church rounds with cut flowers for the foyer, for cryin' out loud."

"What do you want me to do about it?" Timothy asked. "You never said anything about paying vendors, where the checkbook is, who the accountant is, and who pays the bills around here."

"You still haven't read the job description!" Jared snapped.

As a matter of fact, Timothy had read that sorry excuse for job responsibilities all the way through to the end. He knew exactly what his duties were supposed to be, and there was nothing about flowers or writing checks. And he told him so.

"You obviously didn't read down to the *very* end. I have a copy on my computer screen. It plainly states, '... and various, assorted, mixed, sundry, and disparate activities as they may arise.'"

"You obviously use your Thesaurus a lot," Timothy said, but should have known better.

"You have an attitude problem, Mister," Jared snarled.

"You're lazy and disrespectful! Why can't any of you stupid people anticipate what needs to be done in the private home of a legendary movie star? It should be totally obvious, even to a moron like you, that if someone performs a service, such as delivering flowers, they must be paid. You've been on the job long enough to know what's required."

Timothy had rolled his eyes so often that his sockets were starting to bleed. Was it just him, he wondered, or was this guy absolutely Trumpian in the despot department? It crossed his mind that maybe he wasn't as smart as he'd always believed. Maybe most people do anticipate every little thing that a boss needs. Perhaps to be a successful personal assistant, one had to also be psychic, a mind reader, an astrologer, and a tarot card reader, all rolled into one. He should have been born with a crystal ball in his cranium instead of a brain.

"By the way," Jared said, "Muriel wants a meeting with you at 8:30 tomorrow morning. Don't be late." Then he hung up the phone.

Timothy groaned out loud. Since he was going to be fired anyway, he decided he'd been insulted enough for one day, so he put away the computer and went to join Fabiola, who was having a glass of wine and reading another book in the living room.

Fabiola looked up when Timothy came into the room. "Nice day?" she smirked, knowing full well that it had been a Jeffrey Dahmer dinner invitation of horror. "I'm surprised you've lasted this long," she added.

"I'm hungry," Timothy said in response. "I'll eat anything you make. I'm dying, so I'm not fussy."

Fabiola gave him a quizzical look as if she were almost amused by what Timothy had said. "Who do you think I am? Or better yet, who do you think *you* are? And can't you see that I'm busy?"

Well, whatever Muriel Maynard had on her agenda to speak with Timothy about in the morning—and he suspected it was his termination—Timothy had something to tell her, too. He'd never seen Fabiola do a lick of work, and now she was essentially telling Timothy to get lost because reading her book was more important than doing her job.

"Fine," Timothy said with obvious indignity. Then he grabbed Fabiola's book and read the title. "Just so you know, Doris is found not guilty of the murder of her lover, Miles. But just as she leaves the bank after depositing the check for five million dollars that she got from duping the insurance company, she gets hit by a speeding motorcycle and ends up in a brain-dead vegetative state for the rest of her natural life. Karma sucks," Timothy said, throwing the book back at her as he stormed up to his bedroom.

\* \* \*

Dinner that night was at La Strega, a small Italian restaurant a few blocks from The Colton. Timothy finally consumed an unburned pizza and enjoyed two glasses of wine. No sharing with the irritating and mean-spirited Fabiola. If she wasn't going to be polite to Timothy, Timothy saw no sense in beating his head against a brick wall with the hope that Fabiola might throw him a bone of respect. Forget it. This job was challenging enough, and he didn't need some lazy, old housekeeper to make him feel any lower than he already did!

And just as he was about to hail the waiter for the check, Timothy got the biggest and best surprise: Brad, the piano tuner, walked in. Timothy watched for a moment as Brad was escorted to a table. He was alone. Surely, someone was going to join him. But no, apparently not, because the waiter took away the second wine glass at the place setting, then returned with a carafe of red wine and poured it for Brad.

How could such an amazing-looking and talented guy be dining alone? Timothy thought. There must be something wrong with him. Maybe he has webbed feet. As Timothy sat staring at Brad from across the room and wishing he dared to just go over and sit down at his table, an idea suddenly occurred to him. Yesterday, Jared quoted Audrey Hepburn. He had meant it as an insult, but Timothy remembered the part that said, "I'm possible." With that bit of advice from a legendary movie star, Timothy stood up and walked over to Brad's side. *Hey, you luscious, irresistible, sexy man, you*, he wanted to say. He settled for, "Hi! Aren't you Brad Bradbury, the piano tuner? You came to The Colton?"

Brad smiled, his dimples popping to life, and his perfect Colgate White Strips teeth sparkled. "Hey, Timothy!" he said, standing up like the true gentleman he obviously was.

*He remembered my name!* Timothy instantly decided that all the drama would be worth it if nothing more than a date with Brad came from working at Mercedes' penthouse.

"Are you alone? Join me for dinner?" Brad asked. "Please?"

Of course, Timothy had just consumed an entire pizza—with extra anchovies—but Brad didn't have to know that. "Seriously? Sure, I'd love to. I'm practically starving to death," he fibbed. Naturally, at that very moment, the waiter walked over with his bill. "Just had a glass of wine," he lied, then handed over his debit card to the server.

## Chapter Five

Timothy didn't need to set the alarm on his new phone to wake him up the next morning. His nearly sleepless night had been divided between thoughts about incandescently desirable Brad and worrying about his meeting with Muriel. "Why can't life be simple? Just let me have a few precious drama-free days when I don't have to worry about anything more than how to steal Brad's sweaty gym workout clothes to wear in bed each night," he whined.

Timothy reluctantly got up at 6:30 and followed his usual routine. When he finished and wandered into the kitchen, Fabiola was already there sipping a mug of coffee. Timothy had no idea what time Fabiola generally woke up, but she always made him feel that he was a sloth for staying in the sack as long as he did. Did he dare wish Fabiola a good morning? Well, he wasn't one to hold a grudge, and he really wanted Fabiola to like him, although he suspected that any attempt at rapport would be fruitless. So, he not only greeted Fabiola with a big smile and a warm "Hey!" but he refilled the woman's coffee mug too.

"I'll have a dollop of half and a half and two cubes," was Fabiola's way of saying thank you.

When Fabiola wandered out to the terrace with a copy of the morning paper, Timothy followed her. "Headlines?" he asked. "Have those fools in Washington blown up the planet while we slept?" He was doing whatever he could to get this woman to talk. Fabiola sat down at the table, turned to the daily crossword she'd apparently started earlier, and said, "Nine letters. Blank Arch in London."

Timothy thought for a moment. "How 'bout Admiralty Arch? It's the right number of letters."

Suddenly, as if the sunshine had broken through a cloudy sky, Fabiola smiled. Well, not many people would call the thin stretch of Fabiola's lips a smile, but Timothy knew it was a smile, just the same. *Hallelujah!* Timothy didn't say. Instead, Fabiola gave him another clue to the puzzle. "Four letters. Fitzgerald or Raines."

"Um, Ella? You know, Ella Fitzgerald, the singer? Ella Raines, the old-time movie star?"

Fabiola gave another hint of a smile and, without looking at him, said, "You're not as stupid as Jared says you are."

"Shocking, isn't it?" Timothy replied as he finished his coffee and left the terrace. He called back, "Have to run. Meeting with Muriel Maynard."

Timothy didn't expect a response. His expectations were met.

\* \* \*

It was another sultry morning, and the Uber ride across Midtown was excruciating, with constant stopping and starting for traffic lights and pedestrians. The air/con was apparently not working; the driver reeked of perspiration and Patchouli and was too talkative. Timothy was nervous about the meeting with Muriel and didn't want to discuss sports, which never interested him anyway unless it was the men's Olympic gymnastics athletes or 10-meter platform divers in their tiny Speedos. The ride took much longer than Timothy expected, but finally, they pulled up to the curb outside The Oxford Building on Park Avenue. He thanked Abdisalan (the driver's name was on Timothy's Uber app) and stepped out of the gray Prius.

The moment he looked up at the towering steel and glass monolith, Timothy got a horrible feeling in his stomach. It was the sort of feeling he always got before visiting his dentist. He was on unsteady ground as he moved forward to the entrance doors. It seemed like thousands of people were filing into the building all at the same time for work or appointments. Although Timothy was enveloped in trepidation, he tried to walk with as much confidence as everyone else around him seemed to have. *Am I the only one on the planet without a smidgen of self-assurance?* He joined a line for the elevators and shuffled into a car stuffed with about 20 other people. When the doors reopened on the 15th floor, he had to practically beg to squeeze his way out.

As he'd been there for his interview only a week before, Timothy knew to turn right and walk to the end of the hallway. There it was, a mahogany door with a sign announcing MURIEL MAYNARD MANAGEMENT and a logo of three interlocking M's. From the outside, it could have been an office full of accountants instead of a talent management team representing some of the industry's major stars. Of course, movie icon Mercedes Ford was the firm's biggest asset, and Timothy suspected she knew it. He thought it must be fun to know that you're so important that a whole office full of people would jump off the Chrysler Building if you even slightly suggested they do so.

Timothy opened the door and walked into the noisy office, which desperately needed a *Love It or List It* decorating makeover. The place probably hadn't seen a new coat of paint or modern furnishings since before the turn of the 21st century. But there was plenty of activity. The whole vibe was one of frightened little rats scurrying around a maze, desperate not for food but rather not to get in the way of Muriel Maynard. It reminded Timothy of *The Devil Wears Prada*. The only difference between Muriel Maynard and Meryl Streep was that Ms. Streep (both she and her character in the film, Miranda Priestly) had talent and knew what they were doing. It was an open secret that Muriel Maynard, who ruled by fear, had started out like gangbusters, but 30 years on, she was sort of long in the tooth. She had always hired people who knew what they were doing, and she took all the credit. Her one talent was intimidation, which made her a natural-born barracuda in the contract negotiating rooms of Broadway and Hollywood.

Timothy walked up to the receptionist rat, who was munching on a wedge of cheese (well, maybe it was a cheese Danish), and announced that he had an 8:30 appointment with Muriel.

"So, you're the wanker who stole my job," the receptionist sneered and gazed at Timothy contemptuously.

Timothy blanched at the bizarre greeting, not having the teensiest, weensiest clue what the receptionist was talking about. "Good morning to you, too," he said sarcastically.

"I worked my tail off, and Jared demoted me and hired you," the guy sneered. "You're no better than Eve Harrington. Let's see how long you last. And how will you feel when you're evicted from The Colton as I was!" Without so much as a "May I get you a cup of coffee," the little rat boy whose haircut was military-short, his facial bone features chiseled, and who wore fashionably ripped jeans over reed-thin legs led Timothy to a small conference room. "She's running late," Rat Boy said. "Sit tight." Then he looked at Timothy with disdain again and scampered away.

All sorts of thoughts were skipping through Timothy's head at the same time. With each second that ticked by and every mental image of facing Muriel that flashed through his mind, he definitely needed to go to the bathroom. Just like when he was waiting to face the dentist's monster Novocain needle and drill.

Finally, the door opened, and Muriel walked in, along with Jared. Timothy stood up and thought, why couldn't they have simply fired me over the phone and made it easier on everyone? He figured they probably wanted to do it away from the penthouse to prevent him from taking revenge, like tossing the laptop computer over the terrace balcony or lighting a match to the papers in the safe. But why not have Griffin from security merely send a few security goons on his team to escort him off the premises?

Now that Timothy was certain of their plans, he was suddenly quite calm. It's interesting how we often spend so much time worrying about the inevitable, but when it finally arrives, we've already psyched ourselves up to acceptance. A sort of ethereal calmness takes over. At least it did for Timothy.

Muriel had a stern look on her face (but then she always did). Jared... was Jared. Just another sycophantic rat kissing the boss's ample tail. Timothy imagined this was how Muriel started her clients' contract negotiations, immediately intimidating her foes. They all sat down simultaneously.

Muriel's first words were, "We have a problem."

"So, let's just cut to the chase," Timothy blurted out, eager to get the whole ugly situation over with. "I hate drawing out the inevitable, don't you? Just rip off the bandage. Don't peel it back slowly, tearing away the scab and little hairs."

"Agreed," Muriel said.

"One request?" Timothy interrupted. "I hope you won't report this to the recruiters at SwellHire Top Temps. They're the ones who put me up for the job, and I don't want them to know how it all worked out."

"Naturally," Muriel said, looking totally confused.

That's when Jared handed Muriel a #10-size white business envelope. Something to sign to waive any rights to unemployment benefits, Timothy figured. Or some document saying he won't sue the agency for harassment—which, considering his treatment by Jared, he'd probably win.

Muriel withdrew a couple of tri-folded pages and said, "Sorry, it didn't work out," as she handed them to Timothy. "I can't go," she explained. "And Gopher here," she snapped her head toward Jared, "is on the TSA's No Fly List." She turned to Jared and glared. "You can't threaten to bring a plane down just because you think they've made the peanuts smaller!" she said.

Muriel looked at Timothy. "You'll be back tomorrow night," she said, as Jared handed him a zippered leather bag—like the ones small-business owners used to use to deposit cash in overnight bank drawers. It had a tiny padlock on it. Certainly, nothing that couldn't be easily opened, but it gave the impression of being important. "You'll deliver this to Mercedes' husband, Sage Slater, on the set of *Blind Trust.*"

"That's the name of the movie," Jared added, "not how we feel about you."

Muriel sneered at him, obviously not amused by his comment.

"I'm not fired?" Timothy said.

"Not yet," Jared said fiendishly.

"I'm going on a business trip?" Timothy straightened up in his seat, trying to take it all in. This was nothing like what he expected. He opened the envelope and found a printout of boarding passes and travel itineraries. He looked at the leather satchel and asked, "So what's inside? What am I delivering?" He picked it up, and it didn't feel like anything that airlines forbid: guns, bombs, emotional support pythons.

"It's nothing, dear," Muriel said. "Just papers."

"Nothing you need to know about, at least," Jared added with what Timothy thought was a slight chuckle.

Timothy sat silently for a short moment before twisting his mouth and making a dubious face. He figured that since he had come there to be fired, but for some weird reason, they apparently trusted him with this assignment, he didn't have much to lose by asking a few critical questions. "I don't know," he finally said. "I don't know you guys all that well. I wouldn't want to be one of those unsuspecting drug mules."

Muriel laughed, and Jared looked aghast.

"What if you're spies and trying to turn me into a courier for transporting espionage materials?"

"What, exactly, are espionage materials?" Jared snort-laughed.

"Or Mafia, sending me out to do a hit job."

"A hit? With what?" Muriel asked. "A leather purse? Yes, it looks lethal!"

"Hey, I'm just wondering," Timothy offered. "I don't want to be one of those gullible people who wind up dead just because they followed any random order given to them by their boss. I remember that news story about a secretary who was gunned down by her boss's jealous wife when she blindly followed orders and tried to stop Mrs. Boss from entering the office, where Mr. Boss was having rumpy-pumpy with someone who definitely looked a lot younger and friendlier than Mrs. Boss."

"Pfft," Jared made a nonverbal sound with his lips as if Timothy were being overly dramatic.

"So just tell me what I'm carrying to the set," Timothy said firmly. "I don't do drugs!"

"Fine," Muriel said. "You don't have to go." She tugged the bag out of Timothy's hands. "And you also don't have to work for us any longer."

Oh rats, Timothy thought to himself. Now I really am getting fired! Why couldn't I keep my trap shut, follow orders, and just drink the darned cyanide-laced Kool-Aid like a good Jim Jones Peoples Temple disciple?

But then it seemed that Muriel had a sudden change of heart. "I understand, dear. You're a naïve young man, newish to the city and show business. But trust me, I don't need to supplement my income with drug dealing; I'm an agent to one of the biggest stars in the universe. And Mercedes Ford doesn't do drugs, either. Let's be honest; that stuff about spies and the Mafia is just plain ridiculous. And we'll upgrade your seat to business class," she offered.

Timothy smiled and said, "Are the peanuts really getting smaller?"

\* \* \*

Obviously, Timothy was overwhelmed by what had just happened, and by the time he got back to the penthouse, he wasn't any clearer about why he was chosen to deliver something to a film set in South Carolina. It was nearly 11:00, and Fabiola was again outside on the terrace, reading another book and sipping iced tea. Did this woman ever do any work? Timothy asked himself as he stepped out to join her.

Fabiola looked up and showed Timothy the cover of her book. *Lincoln's Life and Death.* "Spoiler alert," she mocked. Then, with more interest than she'd ever exhibited about anything before, she asked, "What's up with Muriel? Did she and that little worm Jared discuss their plans for me?"

Timothy wanted to pretend they'd given an ultimatum that if Fabiola didn't start doing housework, she'd be out on her keister in no time. But Timothy was still too puzzled by why, instead of being out on his own butt, they'd given him an obviously important job. "Not a word about you," he said. "They want me to fly to South Carolina tonight to deliver something to Mercedes and her husband."

Fabiola took another sip of iced tea. "One of these days, that little case will end up in the wrong hands," she said, nodding at the zippered bag that Timothy still carried as if she knew what it contained. "Remember, things often are not as they seem."

That started Timothy thinking. What had happened to all the other assistants who had worked there before him? Why had they all come and gone with such apparent frequency? What had they done to warrant termination? He looked at Fabiola and said, "Just how many assistants have worked here before me?"

Fabiola closed her book. "Let's see. Just before you, there was Sandy. Then, Clarissa—she was here for a couple of weeks. Marta, the one before that, had a hard time adjusting. I think she lasted only five or six days. Chrissy was cute. A bleach blonde. I actually liked her a little. But she asked too many questions, and Jared couldn't cope with that. Belinda was good too but said she couldn't stand all the intrigue."

"Intrigue, indeed," Timothy said. "It does seem like something fishy is going on around here. I mean, all the security in the building and Jared monitoring my activity on the computer. And now I'm flying off to…"

Fabiola interrupted. "And then there's the secret room behind the bookshelves that Jared doesn't think I know about," she almost cackled. "Let's just say I know where the bodies are buried. Sorta my insurance policy." Then she went back to reading about Abraham Lincoln and the mess he left behind in the Presidential Box at Ford's Theater.

Timothy had no idea what Fabiola meant by "knowing where the bodies are buried," so he removed himself from the stultifying heat on the terrace and returned to the office. He thought he'd better spend what time he had between now and Ubering to the airport working on more emails. Naturally, among the incoming messages was one from ol' Jared, or "Gopher," as Muriel had condescendingly called him. He clicked on the message. "On your way to JFK, stop at the following address. Ask for Max. He's expecting you."

"Oh, great," Timothy said, rolling his eyes again. "Another job that I don't have time to do." He looked at his watch. It was close to 11:30. Then he reread the address Jared had sent. It looked like the same block in Midtown as Muriel's office. So why couldn't Jared do the job or have one of the rat assistants go there? He looked at the 5:45 boarding time on the printout of his airline ticket and started to count backward from then. "Um, okay, give yourself an hour to get through the security line," he said. "Which means arriving by 4:45, which means I should leave here by 2:00 to get to this Max guy by 2:30. It better be quick because it'll take at least another hour to get to JFK." Timothy was feeling stressed and decided he'd better not waste another moment with the stupid emails. So, he closed the computer and returned it to the safe.

Fortunately, it was only an overnight trip, so Timothy could travel light. His rucksack—a knock-off of a Louis Vuitton piece he'd picked up from a sidewalk vendor on 5th Avenue—would hold everything he needed. He only required one change of socks and undies, and his electric toothbrush and other toiletries fit nicely into a large Ziploc bag. He ordered an Uber, and just before he left the penthouse, he peeked out to see Fabiola turning the pages of her book. He thought he'd better remind her that he'd be gone overnight—not that Fabiola gave a hoot. "I'm away until tomorrow," Timothy said.

Fabiola raised a hand in acknowledgment but never looked up from the page. Then she said the oddest thing. "Kisses to Max."

This stopped Timothy in his tracks. He hadn't mentioned where he was going other than to South Carolina. In fact, he'd only been told about this stopover near Muriel's office a few minutes earlier. Timothy stepped out onto the terrace and faced Fabiola. "Anything more I need to know?" he asked with curiosity and concern.

Fabiola tore her eyes away from her book and looked up at him. "You tell me," she said.

"I'm only asking because I'm definitely in the dark. Am I being played for a sucker or something?" he answered.

"What makes you think I know anything?" Fabiola countered weakly.

Timothy didn't have time for games. He was in a hurry. But he was intrigued and suddenly very apprehensive. "You seem to know about things that maybe I need to know about, too," he said. "Like, who is this Max guy? I mean, I didn't tell you that I was going to meet anyone named Max."

Fabiola looked as though she were weighing how much information to share and as if she had a lot on her mind but didn't want to spill the beans or get herself in trouble. Finally, she said, "Look, I'm just guessing about Max. Whenever Muriel and Jared send an assistant on an overnight trip to see Mercedes, they all have to see this Max guy first."

"Why?" Timothy asked.

"Beats me. I've heard that maybe he gets some fountain of

youth herbal supplement from an indigenous tribe in South America for Mercedes' husband," Fabiola said. Then she added, "Look, I don't know anything, really. I'm a nobody. Nothing more than a bird trapped in this gilded cage. But I still have two eyes. And they both tell me that Mercedes' gold digger of a husband, Sage, is a louse. She was warned not to marry the creep but wouldn't listen to me or anyone else."

Timothy swallowed hard as his mind raced with thoughts about all sorts of illegal or immoral problems that he could be getting himself into. "You don't like Sage," Timothy said. "He sure looks handsome in the magazine stories about their happy marriage."

"Sleaze!"

"Why would someone like Mercedes, one of the most famous and talented women in the world, and classy, and probably really rich, stay with someone beneath her?" Timothy asked.

"That's always the first question a spouse gets asked after the one they trusted gets found out," Fabiola said cryptically. Then she added, "Just go. But be wary."

Timothy nodded his head. "Don't miss me too much," he joked as he got a text message saying his Uber was waiting. He returned to the penthouse, grabbed his rucksack, and was off.

*  *  *

When his Uber finally made its way through Midtown, they arrived at a restaurant/bar called La Maison Eleganté. Timothy walked into the nearly empty place, gave his name to the host, and said that Max was expecting him. The host stepped away, and Timothy waited by the door. Then he heard someone call the name Eve Harrington. "Yeah, you," the voice said as Timothy looked around.

But it wasn't the host and probably not Max. It was coming from the bar area. There was only one person seated there. Timothy walked over, and although he couldn't quite place the face, he couldn't mistake the trendy ripped jeans the young man was wearing. It was Muriel's rat-boy receptionist from that morning. "You obviously don't remember my name either," Timothy said. "We weren't really introduced. And you are...?"

"San'y," the young man slurred, then tried to enunciate more clearly. "San'y."

"Nice to see you again, Sandy," Timothy said and didn't tell him that, in fact, he thought Sandy had been rude for calling him "a wanker" that morning. Instead, looking at the martini glasses on the bar, he said, "Liquid lunch, Sandy?"

As Sandy lifted a martini glass to his lips, he said, "Medicinal. Nursing my woun's."

Seeing two empty glasses, Timothy said, "Looks like a pretty good prescription for pain. Major surgery?"

Sandy snort-chuckled. "Am'utation," he said. "Severed from my job. No anesthesia! First, Jared demoted me from your stupid job and made me a stupider receptionist in the office. How mean is that! And now he's gone and fired me for good and ever. To'ally not cool."

"Fired?" Timothy said. "What happened?"

Sandy shrugged his shoulders and shook his head slowly. He was obviously sloshed. His body slouched as if he didn't have the strength to sit up straight on the barstool. "Usual stuff," he slurred, unable or willing to focus on Timothy. "Gopher... an' Muriel... always had it out for me." He offered another small laugh. "He hates when people call him Gopher. That makes it all the more fun. Ha!"

"Yeah, he blushed this morning when Muriel called him

that in front of me. How'd he get that nickname?"

Sandy again shook his head. "Pro'ly 'cause he's s'pposed to go-fer this and go-fer that. It's what assis'ants do," he chuckled again.

Timothy was completely surprised. "Jared's just an assistant?" he said. "I thought he was one of the talent managers on Muriel's team. He acts like he's totally in charge."

"Course!" Sandy said as if Timothy had made an inane observation. "Jus' a li'l gopher, but he's got tons-a-power. Muriel enables him. Nee's him 'cause he's cunning. And vicious. But he sh'nah messed with me and my career. No siree. Boy, will he be sorry."

Timothy looked at his watch, eager to meet Max and be on his way. But there was no sign of anyone else in the place, not even the host. "So why were you fired?" he pushed.

"Maybe 'cause I f'got t' give you coffee. Or maybe 'cause I f'got t' give Jared coffee. Or maybe…"

Sandy seemed to be wracking his brain to recall the exact reason for his termination. Finally, a light dawned. "Pro'ly 'cause I di'n't follow the rules of that stupid office. Made a big boo-boo. Got caught."

"Caught? Doing what?" Timothy was now very intrigued. "What did you do that was so wrong it got you fired?"

"No one's s'posed to use contacts at the agency t' get ahead. But hey, I'm an actor." He stabbed the polished bar countertop with his finger to punctuate his words. "I! B'long! On a Broa'way stage! Not. In. Some. Stinky. Sweatshop agency!"

Again, Timothy looked at his watch. He didn't have time for this conversation, let alone wait for whomever Max turned out to be, but he was also curious about the terrible thing Sandy had done to get himself sacked. "Nothing wrong with trying to get ahead," he said. "Unless you do something really terrible like murder the leading man to get his role," he grinned.

"This was worse," Sandy said emphatically. Then in a conspiratorial whisper, he said, "I did the naughty with someone I shou'n'a. Someone I thought could help my c'reer. He di'n't do bu'kis f'r me. Just 'cause he's married to the rich 'n famous… Shhhh. Not s'posed t'say. Afraid-a bad pu'licity. Well, I got news f'r him…"

This sounded good to Timothy, and he was totally intrigued. Sandy was revealing just the kind of showbiz gossip Timothy lived for. Celebrity love triangles were definitely his thing. Timothy's curiosity was aroused, and although he was afraid of being late for his plane, he hoped that Max wouldn't see him for at least a couple more minutes. "Who do you have news for? Jared? Muriel? Good news? Bad news?"

"Baaah news," Sandy said, drawing the word out like a bleating sheep. "Someone's gonna get it real good. I swear on my mother's grave."

Sandy wasn't making any sense, but Timothy tried to coax him along. "Are you saying you'll get even with Jared and Muriel for firing you?"

"Let's jus' say there's a not nice person doin' some not nice things to a nice person. Got it?" he said. "But my lips'r sealed. Better keep your lips sealed, too. F'rever' n' ever."

Sandy was ready to fall off his seat when the host returned and said Max was prepared to receive Timothy. Timothy turned back to Sandy. "Sorry, I have to go, but I wish you all the best," he said, patting him on the arm. "You'll find another job right away, I'm sure. Then you'll go on to Broadway and forget all about working in a crummy office. I guess it's called paying your dues. I'm sure you're very talented. Can't wait to see your name up in lights on a marquee someday!"

"It'll happen," Sandy slurred. "First, I gotta take care of a creep. I'll keep ya pos'ed."

And then Timothy left to follow the host.

He was escorted to a back office. The host knocked once, then opened the door for Timothy. Max—who else could it be—was seated behind a desk when Timothy entered the room. Max motioned for him to take a seat. "Jared says you're more than a few French fries short of a Happy Meal," Max laughed at his little (and very old) joke. "So, why's he trusting you with this?"

"Probably because I am a few fries short and doing a fool's errand," Timothy said, starting to totally believe it.

Max looked to be in his 50s. He wore rimless glasses, his hair was cropped short, he needed a shave, and the buttons on his Hawaiian shirt strained against the watermelon that sat where his stomach was supposed to be. "Did ya bring the bag?" he said. "The little zipper guy. Gimmie."

Timothy realized that Max wanted the bag that Muriel and Jared had given him. He opened his Louis Vuitton knock-off, withdrew the leather clutch, and handed it to Max, who left the room with it.

In a moment, Max returned with the bag and handed it back to Timothy. Yes, he'd definitely added something. The bag was now bulky and felt like it contained maybe a bottle of vitamins.

"You can go," Max said, dismissing him. Then, with just a hint of sarcasm, he added, "Hugs to the happy Hollywood honeys."

When Timothy returned to the bar, he saw that Sandy was no longer there. He looked at the host. "I hope he'll be okay," he said.

The host shrugged. "I totally pity the dude who done him

wrong. I know the type. They don't just get mad; they get even."

"Yeah, I know the type, too," Timothy said and thanked him for the character analysis.

The lighting in the bar had been dim, and when Timothy stepped outside, the bright sunlight nearly blinded him. And the hot, humid air instantly wilted his shirt. He opened the Uber app on his phone and entered his destination: JFK.

\* \* \*

Timothy was generally really good about being able to fall asleep on airplanes. Even if he were rich, he wouldn't fly first class unless someone else paid for it because, for him, it would be a way too expensive nap. As long as he had a window or aisle seat, he was just fine. Unfortunately, he didn't get the seating upgrade that Muriel had promised for this trip. He was stuck in economy wedged between two people who must have been on the Pillsbury Doughboy diet. He discovered what being a hot dog in a bun was like. A bun that hadn't used its Old Spice maximum protection triple defense underarm-odor stick. Thankfully, the flight was under two hours. Still, if he'd needed to get up to use the toilet, extricating himself from his seat would have been like putting an inflated raft back into its original packaging… without first letting out the air.

When he finally arrived at the Columbia Metropolitan Airport, Timothy headed straight for the curbside to call for a car. An hour later, he checked into the motel reserved for him. When Timothy got to his room, he practically collapsed with exhaustion. Another hideous day! And he didn't care if the nine-ounce bottle of wine in the mini-fridge cost $25.00. He opened it anyway. Along with the teensy-weensy, $5.00

bag of Doritos (they were definitely getting smaller!). It kind of made up for the flight attendant not being able to see him between the two orcas when she passed out the bags of mini pretzels.

Yes, Timothy was tired, but he also felt isolated and alone. Although he knew the iPhone was only for work purposes, he decided to call Brad. He didn't want their new friendship to evaporate just because he was a busy working man. And he didn't care if Jared somehow monitored the call. He tapped in the number printed on Brad's business card. Some of him hoped he'd just reach the voicemailbox so he could leave a quick message. But on the other hand, he really wanted to hear Brad's voice and to profess his true and endless love (which he'd never in a million years have the guts to actually do). As Timothy listened to Brad's phone ringing, he looked at the time and hoped it wasn't too late to be calling.

"Timothy!" Brad said eagerly.

"How'd you know it was me?" he asked, happy that Brad seemed pleased but curious because he didn't remember giving him his number.

"Jared gave me your contact info," Brad said. "I called him and lied that I'd left a tuning fork at the penthouse and used that as my excuse for needing your number. So how are you?"

Aww, what a sweet guy! He actually took the time to commit a sin in order to find out Timothy's phone number. Suddenly, the lousy day just got a whole lot better. "I'm terrific," he said, which was absolutely true because Brad was on the other end of the line. "I'm in Summerville, South Carolina. Business trip. Back tomorrow."

"As a matter of fact, I was just about to call you," Brad said. "I wanted to know if you'd be interested in seeing *Metamorphoses: The Musical* with me on Saturday night. It sounds weird, and the reviews have been mixed, but people seem to like it."

"Like it? Tickets are impossible to get!" Timothy exclaimed. "And they cost a bloody fortune! How'd you manage it?"

"I don't know; clients just give me things. I guess they like my work." Brad was so adorable in his naiveté. They lose their minds over your brown eyes, deep dimples, and what they imagine is stuffed into your jeans! Timothy wanted to say but refrained. Then he remembered the party on Saturday night at The Colton. "Oh, shoot! I have to work at a charity event at my boss's place. That's why you came to tune the piano. There's no way for me to get out of it."

"Of course. I totally forgot. Some other time, for sure," Brad said, genuinely disappointed.

Phooey! Timothy couldn't let a stupid job stand in the way of his future as the adoring husband of the best-looking man on the planet, so he tossed out a brilliant idea: "What if you come to the party after the show? You can bring your date too" (although he hoped there wouldn't be a date to bring). Timothy could almost hear the smile in Brad's voice when he said, "Sounds great! I'll be there."

The fact that he hadn't said, "We'll be there," was not lost on Timothy! Picturing Brad dressed to the nines for the theatre was the first time Timothy had imagined him wearing clothes. Either way, dressed or undressed, he looked stunning in Timothy's mind's eye.

Before they ended the conversation, Brad confessed that he hadn't lied to Jared about why he needed Timothy's number. "Actually, I really did leave a tuning fork in the piano. But on purpose." In that moment, Timothy knew that not only was life perfect, but there was a perfect plan—and an ideal man—for his life!

## Chapter Six

Despite the fantasy engendered by Brad's phone call and cradling his pillow, pretending that he was in Brad's arms, Timothy conked out almost right away. When the combination of morning sunlight and a noisy garbage truck emptying a dumpster outside his motel room window began to permeate his brain, he lethargically looked at the time on his phone and then vaulted out of bed. It was a little after 8:00, and, according to his itinerary, he was supposed to meet Mercedes' husband on the movie set at 10:00. He couldn't be late. Although he was famished, he didn't even think about stopping for breakfast.

After a quick shower and taking time to kiss his phone (because it was as close to Brad as he could get), he tapped his Uber app to summon a car. Nothing. That little whirly thing just kept going around and around, searching for an available vehicle. He realized there was no Internet connection. Timothy decided to go into the motel's office and check their service. He had to pay his bill anyway because, after the set visit, he was going straight to the airport for the flight back to New York.

Timothy gathered his things and stepped outside. He had been so tired the night before that he hadn't realized what a one-horse town Summerville was. Except for a gas station, a coffee shop, and three churches, the motel was the only other building in sight. When he walked into the office, the woman behind the desk cheerfully asked, "You one of them movie peoples?" It was the same question that the night manager had asked.

Timothy smiled and explained that he was merely on the periphery of the film business, that he was really a writer and had come to town to visit the *Blind Trust* location and to meet one of the producers. He was still determining Sage Slater's role in the movie, but he thought meeting a producer would make him sound more important. And Timothy really needed a bit of a boost to his morale.

"We get a lot of them movie peoples here," the clerk said, then asked if Timothy had had a comfortable stay. When he said he couldn't get Internet service, she nodded understandingly. "It's iffy 'round these parts," she said. "Try 'bout five miles south. They got all them cells and bars you could ever want." When Timothy explained that he needed to call for an Uber, the woman looked at him blankly. "A what, dear? If that's like a taxi, I can call Myrtle Smith's husband. He runs the only driving service 'round here." Timothy was just grateful he could get a ride and said he had to get to the set within an hour, no matter how he got there. Fortunately, the car arrived within a few minutes. Timothy climbed into the back with his rucksack, and they headed off.

"Guess you're one of them movie peoples," the driver said, leaving Timothy to think that was the local greeting to anyone who seemed to be from out of town. "I wanted to see that Mercedes actress that everybody talks about, but I hear she's got herself a private house to rent over in Whitehole. She must be rich to afford to stay in that neck of the woods. Yessiree!" the driver whistled.

Most of the journey was spent with Timothy listening to Harv (he introduced himself early on) yammering with gossip he'd heard about the goings-on among all "them movie peoples" staying in the area. Timothy learned that the crew had loud parties. That the stars (except for Mercedes, who apparently spent her free time visiting orphanages and senior care facilities) were "uppity" and "aloof," and that Hollywood had been "going to hell in a handbasket ever since John Wayne stopped making movies." Timothy simply agreed with everything Harv had to say by nodding and uttering the odd "you don't say." However, he feebly suggested that John Wayne had a pretty good excuse for no longer making films. Harv ignored him and continued his incessant jabbering.

Forty-five minutes later, they arrived in a wooded area that had been taken over by large trailers, lights, cameras, and all the sorts of equipment that it takes to make motion pictures. The place was crowded with men and women running around like ants in a colony performing whatever their specific jobs were. Timothy should have known that Harv didn't have the means to accept his debit card to pay the fare and had to root through his rucksack and jeans pockets to find enough money. He couldn't leave a tip, but Harv didn't seem to mind. He was just as excited as Timothy about seeing the film location village.

A split second after getting out of the taxi, a twenty-something guy with a clipboard and a walkie-talkie on his belt rushed up to Timothy as if he were a trespasser. He was all business, not unfriendly, but with an attitude that suggested he was the guardian of the castle. "Right," the guy said after Timothy explained who he was and his purpose for being there and pointed to his name on the visitor's list. "I'm Rylan. I'll take you to his Highness. I'd tell you he's probably in a terrible mood, as usual, but it's none of my business. I'm not paid to rat out the rats, so I won't."

Timothy's empty tummy was rumbling with hunger and trepidation as they approached the trailers. Again, he wondered why Jared couldn't have come here instead of him. Oh, right, the No-Fly List. And what sort of lunatic had Mercedes married? Fabiola called him "sleaze." And now Rylan, the production assistant, said Sage was a rat. Maybe one man's rodent is another's pussycat, Timothy thought, trying to be positive. After all, stories about yelling and screaming on film sets were as much a part of the enigma of Hollywood as the question of why stars usually only dated and married other stars. A total mystery. They finally stopped at the largest trailer on the site, an extra-long, doublewide aluminum palace of a place with a uniformed security guard stationed outside the door. "For Mr. Slater," Rylan said before climbing the two short metal steps and knocking on the door.

"What?" a booming male voice commanded from inside.

Rylan, whom Timothy could tell didn't let little things like stars' pugnacious husbands intimidate him one iota, opened the door. "Your visitor. Timothy Trousdale. You're expecting him," he said, stepping aside for Timothy to enter the caravan.

What Timothy encountered was as he expected from the tabloid pictures he'd seen. Sage Slater was younger than Mercedes Ford by about thirty years, and he was undoubtedly many people's physical idea of a god. Sage had been a stuntman on one of Mercedes's films when they met, and Timothy could definitely see the attraction for his favorite star. Sage's wide smile, straight white teeth, blonde hair, blue eyes, and skin the color of freshly squeezed grapefruit juice made him sexy enough to have been a star in his own right. Now, he was dressed in jeans and one of those muscle T-shirts that are ripped down the sides, revealing everything from thick forearms and biceps to tufts of wispy cornsilk hair in his pits and a long, blue vein that traveled from his right bicep up to his pumped chest. Timothy wondered why he bothered to wear the shirt at all, as there was practically nothing left to the imagination in this outfit.

*His veins are a phlebotomist's wet dream*, Timothy thought as Sage leaned in for a confident hug and said, "Welcome to Hollywood East!" Under other circumstances, Timothy might have found the musky scent from his perspiration seductive, but right now, he just wanted to drop off the pouch and not risk being in Sage's line of fire. Sage wasn't showing any signs of being trouble, but Fabiola's and Rylan's warnings put Timothy on the defensive. And when Sage stepped back from the hug, he seemed to be appraising Timothy like an in-between meal snack that might satisfy a craving.

"Ya like what you see?" Sage said with an arrogant smile and raised eyebrows as he made a fist and flexed his bicep. "Yeah, this is what I get for curling four sets of seventy-five daily," he said. "Try to put your two hands around it. You can't but go ahead and try."

Timothy blushed, completely aware of how inappropriate the situation was but afraid of offending Sage and having him say something unflattering or untrue to Jared and Muriel. Like so many people in show business who have even a small amount of power, Sage was a man who could use his position as leverage to intimidate others, so Timothy accepted the offer and wrapped his hands three-quarters of the way around the mound of Sage's upper arm.

Then, pounding his fists against his chest like Tarzan, Sage added, "And this is from pressing more than two hundred. Diet's extremely important, too." He pulled his shirt over his head. "You can touch if you want."

At any other time in his life, the offer would have been irresistible to Timothy, but at this moment, he felt completely ill at ease and just wanted to escape Sage's presence. Just do your job and scram, he thought, holding out the leather valise he'd been charged with hand-delivering. Again, Sage smiled warmly. "Excellent, dude!" He touched a small key that he wore around his neck. "Excuse me for a sec?" he said, disappearing down the trailer hallway.

Timothy looked around at the fantastic appointments to this mansion away from the mansion. Everything one could want in a posh house, including an indoor Jacuzzi and a huge, flat, wide-screen television, was right here. There was a living room with a bar. And a gym with a lot of workout equipment. Again, Timothy's dad would have definitely said this was "how the other half lives."

A few minutes later, Sage returned and handed the pouch to Timothy, which he could tell was now empty. "Hungry? Thirsty?" Sage said with his winning smile and lips that looked like he'd been sucking on a cherry-flavored lollipop. "Time for my protein shake."

Timothy just wanted to extricate himself from the weird encounter and explained that he had to make haste to return to the Columbia airport.

Sage whistled. "Long way to go, man," he said, putting a heavy arm around Timothy's shoulders. "Okay, well, thanks for coming all this way. Tell Jared he's the man. Tell the miserable little you-know-what that I hate him. A private joke between us. He'll get it."

Just then, the door to the trailer opened, and a voice like the angel in the elevator at The Colton called out, "Did I hear someone say they hate that darling boy, Jared?"

And then the floor fell out from under Timothy. He felt all the blood rush from his face. He was suddenly dizzy and a bit unsteady on his feet because... there she was, the most beautiful sight (other than Brad) that Timothy had ever seen. It was the great and wondrous living legend herself—

Mercedes Patricia Elizabeth Ford. And she was smiling at Timothy. At Timothy! The nobody, wannabe writer from Claberville, Alabama.

"Oh, hello. I didn't know that we had such handsome company," Mercedes said with a beatific smile and a silky sincerity in her voice that made Timothy believe every amazing and good thing he'd ever heard about the star. Mercedes held out her hand. "I'm Mercedes Ford. That's such a lovely ring you're wearing," she smiled.

Even though she was obviously lying about Timothy's cheap-*o*, cubic zirconia rhinestone alloy ring ($22.99 online at Tickytacky.com), she made him feel as if she were honestly admiring the piece.

Timothy was completely tongue-tied, and Sage piped in and introduced him. "This is Timothy. He brought my stuff and your papers from Muriel's office."

Curiously, Mercedes seemed to ignore her husband and concentrated on Timothy as if he were the only thing in the universe that was important at the moment. "It was nice of you to come all this way, Timothy," she cooed. "They certainly take good care of us, those two. But seriously, they could just mail these things rather than spend a fortune for hand delivery. I know what the price of an airline ticket is these days. And coach seating is so uncomfy. I hope you had a decent journey."

"Fantastic," Timothy lied. As a matter of fact, he couldn't think of anything wrong with the world at the moment. Here he was talking to one of the most famous people on the planet, and they were having an honest-to-goodness conversation! Nothing from his past prepared him for the near out-of-body experience he was currently experiencing.

"May we offer you something to drink, Timothy?" Mercedes said as she opened the refrigerator and withdrew a bottle of Perrier. "I'm afraid there isn't much. Sage and I are always on diets."

Timothy couldn't find his tongue. After what he thought was an interminable period, but probably only lasted a half second, he said, "Not a thing, thank you. I'm totally fine." He noticed that Sage had disappeared, and he told Mercedes that he had to leave shortly because the airport was quite a long way, and the flight back was in four hours. Mercedes seemed genuinely sorry that Timothy wasn't staying longer. Then she touched his cheek with her soft hand, and any color left on Timothy's face after Mercedes first came into the trailer completely vanished. It was a miracle that he didn't faint. He was sure he was going to. "Since you're working for the agency, I'm sure we'll be seeing a lot of each other," Mercedes said. "I so very much look forward to getting to know you."

Timothy was quite literally light-headed and wobbly. He thanked the star and then said what probably every idiot who meets the legend says, "I'm such a big fan!" But in his case, it was absolutely true.

"Well, that makes two of us," Mercedes said. "I mean, I'm a fan of anyone who does their job well. I can tell that you're a natural at yours. I admire what I sense is your elevated work ethic. Bravo, Timothy. I hope you won't let working in show business change you too much. Always try to be pleasant to everyone. It won't cost you anything, and they will always remember how you made them feel. I hope we'll see you again soon." Then she gave Timothy a motherly hug goodbye. "Tell the pilot to fly you safely back to Manhattan."

"I will," he promised, then brainlessly added, "You and Sage make such a great-looking couple. No wonder the paparazzi always want photos of you."

Mercedes chuckled. "Yes. For now, he's God's gift to the

universe. Or thinks he is. Check-in with Sage in about 20 years. We all age in the same direction."

Number 9 Cloud Street was Timothy's new and permanent home address. As he left the trailer, he was waltzing on air. Although he knew he had to pretty much race to get to the airport on time, he just had to wander around a bit to see where the mythical Mercedes did her work. After a brief tour of the camp, he found Rylan and asked if he could call an Uber to take him to the airport.

Rylan gave a sweet laugh. "Uber? Not out here, buddy," he said. "I'll get one of the PAs to take you."

Timothy probably didn't need a car to get to the airport anyway because he could have caught a jet stream and simply drifted home to New York. Timothy was so overwhelmed by the star's late middle-aged beauty, thoughtfulness, and ethereal personality that he forgot to tell her he was living in her condo with her housekeeper. But maybe it was best that he hadn't said anything. That might have made things a little too familiar. Just the fact that she was everything Timothy ever wanted her to be and had hoped she would be… and so very much more… made his day/week/year/life complete.

As he waited for the PA, Timothy said to Rylan, "She, Ms. Ford, I mean, is just as great as I've always heard."

"You don't know the half of it," Rylan said with a small knowing laugh. "She flew my girlfriend in from L.A for my birthday last week. It was a surprise. She said she had nothing to do with it, but Gayle told me the truth. And on Fridays, she gets like five hundred dollars' worth of lottery tickets and has me hand 'em out to all the crew. Mercedes pretends she doesn't have a clue where those tickets come from. She does tons of other great things, too, but always denies that she had anything to do with whatever it is. Grant, over in costume, lost his house in the California fires. Someone bought him a new one. Cindy, the script girl, couldn't take this job even though she was desperate 'cause her mother has Alzheimer's, and she couldn't get away. Now, there's a full-time nurse and a special trailer for Cindy's mom. But of course, Mercedes Ford had nothing to do with that either."

* * *

The flight back to JFK was a blur. At least Timothy had a window seat. And by the time his Uber crawled through Manhattan traffic and reached The Colton, he was exhausted.

Timothy went through the biometric routine and rode the elevator to the penthouse. In a highly unusual move, Fabiola was actually waiting to greet him with a semi-cheerful "Welcome home" and offered him a glass of chilled white wine, which he happily accepted.

They sat down together in the living room, clinked glasses in a toast, and just as Timothy was about to gush and tell her all about meeting Mercedes Ford in person, Fabiola said, "What do you want first, the bad news… or the other bad news?"

"Oh shoot," Timothy whined. "I haven't even been home for five seconds, and already drama is stalking me." He took a sip of wine for fortification and rolled his eyes. "Fine. I'll take the category, 'Bad News' for $500, Alex."

Fabiola should have been in showbiz because she was a pro when it came to sucking in an audience and keeping Timothy in suspense. Timothy waited for her pregnant pause to end. And when it finally did, Fabiola announced, "Jared came over after you left yesterday to check on a few things."

Of course, Mr. Sunshine had to be part of the bad—and the other bad—news.

"Yeah, and he said you have to be his Plus One at the

*Obsession Magazine* party tomorrow night. Said that Muriel has other commitments and can't go."

Now, most people on the planet would have been thrilled to be invited to a party hosted by one of the world's premier fashion magazines, even if they had to be evil Jared's date. Timothy would have been happy, too, if he weren't so busy and going nuts with preparation for their own big soiree at the penthouse. He shook his head. "No! No way!"

Of course, that's when he heard Jared's voice. "Yes, way," Jared said as he wandered into the living room from the hallway. "And it's formal," he added.

So that was the other bad news. Jared offered Timothy an evil smile, apparently knowing that there was no way he had a suit, let alone a tuxedo. And, on his salary, he couldn't afford to buy one before the event. "Not to worry," Jared said, reading Timothy's mind, "Muriel has a contact at a rental place."

Oh, great. Timothy didn't know what was worse, not having his own tux for a high-fashion cocktail party and thus being laughed at by the devotees of haute couture or wearing a rented tux and being laughed at by those same elitists if the cut wasn't precise. Honestly, living in Manhattan was expensive enough for him without the added pressure to look successful when he was actually nearly penniless and not far from being homeless, too. "But I have a ton of work to do for Saturday's party," Timothy pleaded, begging to get out of going to the damn event.

"You'll just have to get your tush in gear now, won't you?" Jared said, his ferret face begging to be punched.

It's not a stretch to believe that no one else in the office wanted to go with you, Timothy thought, getting rather tired of being afraid of this poor excuse for a boss.

"When you're all cleaned up, you'll be tolerable," Jared

said, then asked him for the leather pouch he'd given him the day before.

Timothy realized that was the real purpose—or ruse—of why he'd come by the penthouse.

"By the by, how'd it go?" Jared asked, hinting at gossip.

Now, that had to be the real reason for his presence! Jared wanted dish. As Timothy handed him the pouch, he remembered the thrill of meeting Mercedes Ford in person and how swell the legend had been to him. He could still smell the hint of lavender that seemed to emanate from her silky, magnolia-color skin, and he could visualize the little crinkles of laugh lines around her smiling mouth. However, Timothy was not about to give Jared the satisfaction of knowing that he'd actually made one of his all-time big dreams come true. No way. Instead, he told him how disastrous the flight had been.

"Nothing else?" Jared pushed. "What'd you think of Mr. Ford?"

"You mean Mr. Slater?" Timothy corrected. He hesitated for a moment, imitating Fabiola's lordly pause. "He told me to tell you—and these are his words, not mine, so don't shoot the messenger—he said, quote, 'Tell the miserable little you-know-what that I hate him.' He said you'd understand. But then he laughed, so I'm sure he was joking."

Fabiola burst into hearty guffaws, which made Timothy start laughing too.

Jared chuckled uncomfortably. Then he scuttled away.

## Chapter Seven

Prepping for Saturday night's big-budget, star-studded, mega-donor soiree was a thousand times busier for Timothy than any post-theater meal rush he'd experienced working at The Chili Exchange. The entire day had been a constant nightmare, and the anxiety was nearly overwhelming. He was too busy to get a fitting for his date-night-with-Jared-suit and ended up accepting something from the tailor's rack of used rental tuxedos.

    Among Timothy's six million trillion things to do in prep for the next night, he had met with Colton's security team to discuss the guest list. He changed the catering order three times because Jared and Muriel couldn't decide on the hors d'oeuvres to serve: tuna Niçoise crostini, grilled scallops wrapped in prosciutto, or the Asian mini crab cakes. He confirmed that limos would pick up the two most important guests at their hotels, and he personally filled 125 swag bags with herbal teas, mints, skin creams, and a footcare product that guaranteed to keep rich people's heels from getting dry and cracking. He also brought in a plumber to snake all the toilets just to make sure there weren't any disgusting accidents. In addition, he arranged for all of the windows to be washed—which, on a building as tall as The Colton, was generally done on a specific, rotating schedule. But when he contacted building maintenance and said it was for Mercedes Ford, the guy said he'd do anything for his favorite tenant, who tipped lavishly at Christmastime and remembered birthdays and anniversaries. One last thing: he hired an interior cleaning crew because, obviously, Fabiola never even dusted.

Timothy was pleased with himself for intuitively knowing that this was how the wealthy prepared for a party. Everything had to be absolutely perfect for the special evening. All of the guests were philanthropic and expected only the best in return for their support of research to cure icky ailments.

Although Timothy would never really be finished with the prep work, he stopped at 6:30 to put himself together for the *Obsession Magazine* party. He sniffed his underarms. Yep, he had man stink and needed to shower. After a quick splash and dry and dressing for the first time ever in a tuxedo, Timothy arrived in the lobby of The Colton just in time to greet Jared as he entered the building. Surprisingly, in formal dress, the boss was almost decent-looking. If Timothy didn't know there was a reptilian alien living in Jared's body waiting to break out through his chest at any moment, he even might have considered him dateable. But no, Jared's penguin suit might fool Satan, but Timothy had come to know that he was vile both inside and out.

They Ubered to the Argyle Hotel in silence (Jared spent his time scrolling through his phone), and almost from the moment they arrived in the Grand Ballroom, Jared was absorbed into the ritzy crowd and disappeared. Timothy wondered why Jared bothered inviting him in the first place. Perhaps it was not a done thing to arrive alone at such a party. Apparently, the rich and famous have different values and accept, or at least tolerate, unctuous little toadies like Jared. Timothy was actually glad he disappeared. He would have been mortified if anyone thought they might be a couple. He suspected that Jared felt that way about him, too.

Curiously, although generally introverted when it came to making small talk in large crowds, Timothy felt a bit more emboldened than usual. The fact that he was wearing a tux helped, and he subconsciously assumed a different posture and a more confident demeanor. The champagne he was drinking didn't hurt either, and he found himself wandering into little knots of people, smiling, and nodding in appreciation of a gown or jewels on the stylish ladies in the room. And the superficial conversations he heard were great for future characters he might write about:

"Paris, in August? Not if you drove needles straight into my eyes!" declared one blonde woman to another who looked just like her, their identical hairstyles boasting braided buns accented with clips of diamond flower petals.

"I'd rather breathe greenhouse gas emissions from a landfill in India than be caught dining at La Plume!" he overheard an anorexic-looking older woman with chopsticks for arms tell the group she was with.

"Oh, I have oodles of insurance, so I don't worry about little things like climate change and nuclear winter," said a dude who couldn't have been more than twenty-five years old and yet sounded as though he'd lived several lifetimes—and had been bored to death with them all. A spoiled, rich scion from a real estate development empire family, Timothy surmised.

The noise from people talking and laughing, as well as a dance band playing in the background, not to mention all the champagne flutes clinking, was almost as annoying as the drone of a lawnmower. The vast ballroom seemed claustrophobic, too. Then Timothy overheard someone close by speak Jared Evan's name, followed by the word "pity." It was a woman's voice coming from the small clique behind him. Timothy wanted to hear more, so he surreptitiously inched closer. Although he was late to the conversation, it was obvious that they were discussing something related to Mercedes Ford and her husband. Timothy pretended to be drifting aimlessly among many different groups with his lips resting on the rim of his champagne flute. But when one of the men clearly said, "Jared and Sage deserve each other," followed by another agreeing and adding, "They'll pay the piper eventually," and a woman stating, "Mercedes is nobody's fool," he knew something important or at least gossipy was coming.

But who was the piper that Jared and Sage had to pay? And how did Mercedes fit in, other than the fact that Sage was her husband and Jared helped Muriel handle her career? Timothy was mystified and totally curious. If something terrible was happening to Mercedes and he had an opportunity to help, he'd do whatever he could. But just as he hoped to get more information, he suddenly heard his name being called. Then, his ex-boyfriend, Ted, was at his side. Ted was a sort of cute-*ish* poet who had actually been published and whose only real crime in their short-lived relationship was that he bored the whiskers off Timothy.

They were both surprised to see one another. Well, Ted looked delighted at the meeting, but Timothy had wanted to glean more information about Jared and Sage from what the fashionable blabbermouths were saying. However, it was not to be. Ted gave him a sweet peck on the cheek and started talking, and Timothy couldn't think of a way of extracting himself so that he could continue eavesdropping.

It actually made sense that Ted would be at a party like this one. When his book of poetry had come out several months ago, it had been well received by most of the New York literary critics. "Simon Armitage meets Oscar Wilde…"

and "Elegiac but ethereal..." were a couple of quotes from the *New York Times* and *Publishers Weekly*. He was suddenly being invited to swanky parties and galas. But that was after Timothy and Ted had broken up. Timothy only knew the Ted who collected and used coupons (he annoyingly pronounced them "Q-pons") at the grocery store and was excited that he'd get a free breakfast on his birthday at any of Denny's chain restaurants nationwide. As sweet as Ted was, Timothy knew from the start that he could never have a long-term and meaningful relationship with a man who was so untidy that he left his used dental floss to pile up on his bathroom sink. Otherwise, he was a swell guy. Timothy thought of himself as probably an idiot for not planning a future with him.

It was actually good to see Ted again. He looked great in his tuxedo, although Timothy suspected it was also a rental. Frankly, he was surprised when Ted told him that he'd come to the event alone. For all of Ted's idiosyncrasies, he was probably considered a catch. He was smart and apparently talented. And he had rather seductive green eyes and a full head of brown hair. Plus, he was being paid by a publisher to write another collection of poems. Those are attributes that a lot of other guys in the city would have considered bankable assets.

Ted hung out with Timothy for the rest of the otherwise dull evening, and to be honest, Timothy didn't mind despite his interrupted snooping for Jared-related gossip. As they spoke about the several fun months they'd spent together, it occurred to Timothy that maybe it all ended because he was envious of Ted's talent. Timothy's self-confidence about his own work was so low that he thought that anyone who actually had a book contract with a New York publishing house was probably a genius.

Finally, near midnight, Jared wended his way over to

Timothy and Ted. He announced that he was leaving, and that Timothy could expense an Uber back to The Colton. *Yippee, I don't have to share a car with this jerk,* he thought. Jared was totally dismissive of Ted and never even looked him in the eye when Timothy introduced them. He wondered how this man's lack of manners could be tolerated at Muriel's agency and in fashionable settings such as this one. He summed up Jared's lack of manners to poor potty training when he was a kid.

Timothy was bleary-eyed. He'd only had three glasses of champagne the entire night, but after such a long day of working on multiple projects, he was yawning and eager to snuggle into bed and hug his pillow. Ted, bless his heart, ordered an Uber for Timothy from his own phone, and didn't leave his side until the car arrived. He kissed Timothy on the cheek again, and they agreed to see each other "around."

Timothy rode home thinking that in just a few hours, Mr. Piano Man would be in his condo again. Well, obviously not his condo, but the place where his bed was. And Timothy pictured Brad in that very bed.

## Chapter Eight

Oh, the horrors of the hours leading up to the guests arriving for Muriel's big night. The streets outside The Colton were blocked off for a time because a fire hydrant had exploded, and it was touch-and-go whether or not the party would have to be canceled. Then, the building's air-conditioning system had blown out from overuse. And a window washer had to be rescued outside the penthouse when his harness melted, leaving him dangling 45 floors above the street and broiling in the heat and humidity. By the time all the problems had been resolved, Timothy had dressed in his tux (yes, the same one he wore the night before) and rubbed a scent-strip of *Hermés Eau de parfume* on his neck (a sample he found in a *Vogue* magazine advertising page), he was so tired that he was entirely at ease when security announced they were beginning to sign the guests in.

Okay, call Timothy presumptuous for feeling no pressure at that moment. In retrospect, he should have known that this was the calm before the storm. He just didn't see the tsunami coming! Yes, everything was under control. But, as they say, "never judge by appearances." When Timothy came down from his bedroom to the living room, he saw Fabiola looking absolutely divine in a red Armani tailored suit with a white collar and gold buttons down the front of the jacket. She was already settling in on one of the sofas with a flute of champagne. Timothy's first thought was *the kid cleans up well!* His second thought was, *why isn't she pitching in to help the catering staff?* His third thought, as he looked out through the terrace windows and saw Muriel and Jared was, *oh rats, the window washer's harness equipment is still there.* Timothy put on his best working-boy face, which was mostly just a goofy expression, and sidled up to his two bosses. "We're in for a memorable night," he said, suggesting nothing more than they were about to have a lot of fun.

Jared scanned Timothy up and down and sniped, "Did you sleep in that?" referring to his tux, which, admittedly, he hadn't had time to have pressed.

Muriel simply said, "Make sure it goes back first thing Monday."

Changing the subject and attempting to impress Jared, Timothy rattled off a list of everything he'd done in preparation for the evening. The last-minute details included calling the piano tuner to be on standby just in case a string broke or a pedal stuck. Of course, the fib was merely to plant a suggestion as to why Brad would be attending later. It didn't matter, as neither Muriel nor Jared seemed to think it was any sort of brilliant idea on his part. In fact, Jared sniffed and said, "Your time would have been better spent supervising the cleaning staff." Then he pointed to a teensy-weensy smudge on one of the glass accordion sliders that was suddenly evident with the inside lights meeting the outside dusk. "Got it," Timothy said while silently cursing Jared's eagle eye and quickly stepping back into the penthouse to find a rag and bottle of Windex.

The kitchen was a beehive of activity as the caterers buzzed about, placing trays filled with yummy-looking canapés into the ovens and finalizing the decorating of the buffet table with miniature plastic lungs, hearts, kidneys, and hypodermic syringes (sans needles). They all seemed to know exactly what was expected of them and didn't require any guidance from Timothy. So, he moved on to the utility closet for the Windex.

And, just as Timothy retrieved the cleaning supplies, he heard the elevator wind chimes and the first guests stepped into the foyer. He couldn't very well greet them while holding a dirty rag and a bottle of cleaning fluid, so he made a beeline for Fabiola. He took away her champagne flute, gave her the rag and bottle, and said, "All hands on deck! Jared found a smudge on the sliding glass door."

Fabiola's jaw dropped, and she looked as though Timothy'd just directed her to take a holiday at the public garbage dump.

"Get busy, babe!" Timothy added, in a manner that even surprised him in its authority. He was equally stunned when Fabiola replied, "Yes, sir! I guess I done been told!" She got up and did the cleaning deed. At that moment, Timothy realized he should have been bossing the help around from the start. Duh! If only he'd had it in him. He was already blushing at the thought of how rude he had just been.

Timothy quickly made his way to the foyer and began playing host. Well, actually, he was nothing more than a Walmart greeter as he pointed the visitors toward the hardware, lingerie, and home decor departments, in other words—the bar and bathrooms. And each time the elevator chimed, it seemed that all of hoity-toity New York was entering the condo. He thought this might be a fun evening after all. Timothy and his dumb ideas!

Jared, who was nursing a martini, decided that Timothy's charms could be put to better use if he simply stayed out of the way. "Keep an eye out for anyone looking for mementos," he said, gesturing toward a tuxedoed guest examining a small stone carving he'd picked up off the console table under the painting of Diana Ross/Billie Holiday. That was fine with Timothy. He was a people-watcher by nature. And, since he didn't know a single soul at this posh party, he was happy to step aside. If only it were that easy.

The moment that Jared wandered away to creep up next to "a woman of a certain age," as they say, a man of a similar "certain age" moved to Timothy's side. "I think you need a drink, sexy," he said, noticing Timothy wasn't holding a glass.

Timothy wasn't in the mood for a pick-up line, and "sexy" was so pre-#MeToo harassment objectification. He just smiled and lied that he was a recovering alcoholic. That should have been enough to make the guy go away. On the contrary, the man raised his Waterford crystal glass filled halfway with a clear fizzy liquid and a slice of lemon. "How can you stand being here without medication?" he said, taking a large swallow from his glass. "I'm Bud," he added. "How'd you get trapped into attending this dopey do?"

Boy, those certainly weren't the manners that Timothy had been raised with. Any time he had been fortunate enough to be invited to someone's home, he was taught to at least pretend that he was grateful for getting a freebie meal. And this menu included trays of Wasabi shrimp with avocado rice crackers being passed around by hot-looking catering staff.

"Don't get me wrong," the man continued, "Muriel means well. But don't you think it's a bit untoward that she takes advantage of a client by holding what she considers a 'smart evening' in Mercedes' private home? I wouldn't want the likes of some of these people defiling my bathroom, let alone my personal living space."

Timothy gave a small shrug. "Mercedes and Muriel probably have an understanding," he said without knowing a thing about their professional or personal agreements. "Plus, Mercedes doesn't seem like the type who would care."

Bud harrumphed and said, "You're right. She's too busy creating great acting art. But that slug she picked up and married is another story."

Now Timothy wished that he could grab a glass of vino for himself. He didn't want to hear anything negative about his celebrity idol. Still, he was also desperate to hear more gossip about Sage. He figured that since Mercedes married him, surely, she must be head over heels in love. At least that's what Timothy wanted for her. "And how do you know Muriel?" Timothy interjected, trying to steer the conversation to another topic.

"She's my manager," Bud said. "Got me my first Broadway show. I'm a loyal guy, but if she retires or kicks the bucket—heck, she's been around since the Paleolithic period—I wouldn't let that little scuzzball Jared handle my dog's poop, let alone my career."

That's when Timothy suddenly realized that the guy he was talking to had to be Bud Sellers! *The* Bud Sellers. The Bud Sellers who made his Broadway debut in *Come Hither* and won that year's Tony Award for Best Actor in a Play. Timothy may not have been able to afford theater tickets, but he knew all the plays and musicals and their casts. Bud Sellers was iconic. Like Helen Hayes—but alive. He'd never seen him in a show, but his picture was in Muriel's office, and everybody knew his name. Bud must have seen the color drain from Timothy's face, and his eyes widen from embarrassment because he reached out to shake Timothy's hand and said, "And you are?"

Timothy actually forgot his own name for a moment because he was suddenly feeling enormous gratitude to Muriel for hiring him to do a job that brought him into contact with living legends. First Mercedes Ford. Now Bud Sellers. Whom might he meet next, Meryl Streep or Glenn Close? He realized that it was definitely possible. He finally managed to squeak out an introduction. "Timothy. Timothy Trousdale," he said. "I work for Muriel."

Bud nodded in approval and then leaned close to whisper in his ear. "Don't let Jared know I called him a sleazeball."

"Actually, you called him a scuzzball," Timothy corrected with a smile. "And not to worry, he only talks to me when he's in the mood to yell and tell me that I'm a moron and obliterate any little remnants of self-esteem I still have."

Bud Sellers' next question was one that Timothy had started asking himself. "Why, if you're being disrespected, do you continue to face being tortured by Jared?"

"I'm a masochist. He's a sadist. We make a lovely couple." Timothy thought that was a clever reply. It was neither a lie nor a cover-up but could be taken as a joke. "Plus, I get to meet nice people like you."

Well, that did it. Bud Sellers gave him a huge smile and told Timothy to hang in there and not let happen to him what transpired in the lives of the previous assistants. He said he had the feeling that Jared might have met his match with him. But now Timothy was really curious. He'd thought about the long line of PAs who had the job before him and wondered why they'd all left. He played coy and asked what they'd been fired for. Bud raised an eyebrow and shrugged. "They just come and go so quickly," he said. "I'm fairly astute at reading people, and although I never asked about the details, I did overhear Jared explaining to someone that the bodies were piling up because 'Sally was slow, Betty cried too much, Gretta stopped showing up, and Alexa blinked her eyes too rapidly.'" Bud looked around to make sure that Jared wasn't within earshot. "One bit of advice, dear Timothy," he whispered. "You might survive longer if you and Sage Slater don't…"

Oh, drats! Rotten timing. At that very moment, when Bud was just about to tell him the secret of success in the job, a skinny, older woman with short, spiked hair, clownishly rouged cheeks, wide shoulders, and wearing a sequined outfit more suitable for the cabaret stage than a chic soiree came up and, without even looking at Timothy, gushed to Bud. "Sweetums, you heavenly thing! You must come and meet Travis Danton! You know, the brilliant author of *Dandelions on My Grave*? His new play sounds divine, and from what others are saying, there will be Tonys, Tonys, Tonys to go 'round for everyone lucky enough to be associated with the production." And with that, as Bud was yanked away, Timothy's life and future were left in limbo. But only for a quick moment because Jared suddenly appeared by his side with another task to perform.

"When you're through boring Broadway legends with whatever it is that you do to bore them, find out why Virginia La Paloma hasn't arrived," he spat. "We're paying her a bloody fortune to entertain. Oh, and where did you find that terrible piano player? Don't you know better than to let him play movie music in the midst of all these Broadway people?"

How was Timothy supposed to know what the pianist was going to play? And who decided it was a social affront to have tunes that Frank Sinatra had sung in old film musicals? Most of those movies were actually based on Broadway shows in the first place. But he quickly ran down the hall to the office and grabbed his cell phone to call the driver of Ms. La Paloma's car.

He dialed the number, and when the chauffeur answered, Timothy suddenly froze. La Diva not only never showed up in the lobby of The Pierre Hotel, but she wasn't even registered there. "What about an alias?" the driver asked. "Could she be using another name? That's what famous people do."

Holy smokes! Hadn't Timothy sent the message that the driver was supposed to ask for… oh shoot, what was La Paloma's name when she wanted to be incognito? The more Timothy tried to recall the name that Jared had given him, the farther it receded into his memory. He told the driver to stand by and that he'd get right back to him. He opened the security app on his phone and unlocked the bookcase wall. Then he raced into the small room and entered the code for the safe. He grabbed the laptop and searched for the email Jared had sent with Ms. Diva's fake name. Got it! He speed-dialed the driver. "She's under the name "Rolfstead. Emily Rolfstead. You've gotta get her here A-SAP. These snooty, self-important prigs are getting cranky, and my boss is about to strangle me." He returned the laptop to the safe and closed the secret room.

"Oh, for heaven's sake! How could I have screwed up like this!" he demanded.

Then Timothy was suddenly startled by a tsk-tsk sound, followed by a male, British voice that repeated, "Snooty? Self-important? Prigs? My, my, such an elitist observation of these fine rich people."

Timothy looked around the semi-dark office and found the light switch on the wall beside the slightly ajar door. To his horror, he discovered one of the tuxedoed guests holding an empty champagne flute… and his cell phone.

"Interesting setup in there," the man said with a devious smile and cocked his head toward the secret room.

Timothy was completely unnerved. He'd neglected to lock the office door behind him. This guy must have come in while he was checking for the opera singer's fake name or while he was on the phone with the driver. Not only had he seen the open bookcase, but Timothy suspected he'd taken photos of the secret room, too! This was catastrophic, and he figured he might as well resign right then and there. Or better yet, jump over the terrace wall.

He instantly went into damage control and begged the man to please forget what he'd seen, and please, please don't tell Jared. "I'll do anything if you keep this a secret," he begged. "I'll lose my job."

"Anything?" the man asked, giving Timothy a lascivious, raised-eyebrow appraisal.

Phooey! Now Timothy was being blackmailed. And the guy's sagging jowls and turtle-like eye-sacks weren't on the list of Top-100 physical traits that usually turned Timothy on. Timothy looked at him and decided that nothing good would come from playing this game, so he looked him straight in the eye and said, "Honestly, just forget it. I'll simply tell Jared I committed all seven deadly sins at once. He'll kill me, of course. Then he'll fire me. But I'm not sure I can take much more anyway."

The man reached out his hand to introduce himself. "Clive Holgate. From *The Post*. And I'm just teasing you. It's Timothy, isn't it?"

Timothy didn't know how to react to Clive Holgate knowing his name. They hadn't met earlier in the evening. And then Clive explained. "Jared and I are, shall we say, acquaintances. He's an insufferable little rogue, and he said the most dreadful things about the new hire, Timothy. It didn't take much to deduce that you are he."

Of course, Timothy was appalled that Jared was telling people about his apparently already terrible reputation. He wondered how many people knew he was considered an idiot and inept at his job. "What exactly did Jared say about me?"

Timothy asked, insulted that he'd been branded in such a mean way. "I work so hard! He'll never appreciate anything I do!"

"No, he won't," Clive agreed. "But I won't give him any more ammunition to fire you as he's done to the others."

Timothy breathed a sigh of relief. "But now you know about this place," he pointed to the bookcase. "I've let Jared down. Again."

"Jared is one of my least favorite people in all of New York City," Clive said, speaking in a soft and oh-so-charming voice. "He has a propensity for causing trouble. There are too many detestable people in this world, and he's one of them. I'll probably never forgive him for…" Clive caught himself divulging too much information and changed the subject. "I wouldn't give him the satisfaction of sacking you. Of course, he'll do it eventually, and I trust you already know that, but it won't be on my account. No, what I like most about this serendipitous revelation is simply the knowledge of it all. Gives me a tiny bit of power over him."

All Timothy could utter was a heartfelt thank you and "Can I get you another glass of champagne?"

"Just direct me to the bathroom. It's what I came in here for in the first place," Clive said, looking eager to find the potty.

Timothy personally escorted Clive down the hall. The very moment the bathroom door closed; Jared's vicious voice was in his ear. "La Paloma! Where? When? Now!" he growled.

Thankfully, Timothy was all set with an answer. "A small mix-up at the hotel," he said with confidence. "On her way."

He could see the veins in Jared's temples throbbing. "And get rid of the caterer with a black widow spider tattoo on his hand. People are talking!"

***

Finally, the evening actually seemed to be going well. The only guest that Timothy could absolutely tell was dying of tedium was the way-too-young wife of the way-too-old CEO of a way-big bank in Manhattan. The squat old man looked like a cross between Buddha and a garden gnome. She looked like a hamster with post-traumatic stress disorder. Poor thing was entirely unsuccessful in hiding her yawns and seemed nearly comatose from listening to her husband talk to a clique of equally decrepit listeners about the economy and the miserable state of Off-Broadway productions. It seemed pretty obvious that the wife couldn't have cared less.

Timothy looked at his wristwatch a few times, praying for the opera diva to arrive. The bug scientist who obsessed over giant beetle species in the Amazon rainforest had been engaging the guests for the past hour, but now Jared was looking at him and at his watch, too—and scowling at Timothy.

Finally, with an entrance worthy of Cleopatra entering through the gates of Rome, the elevator doors parted, and Virginia La Paloma, the world's most beloved opera star, elegantly dressed in a red velvet off-the-shoulders ballgown, breezed into the penthouse foyer. She stopped by the Lalique table of Casablanca Lilies to humbly receive an ovation that instantly rippled from those closest to the elevator all the way to the farthest edges of the terrace. The piano player started playing arias from random operas. Although, from the dubious looks of a few men standing near the keyboard, Timothy got the feeling that the music wasn't anything for which Ms. Diva was personally renowned.

Now, the evening was definitely in full swing! Even Fabiola had moved through the crowd to see the legend and receive a warm embrace from her. Apparently, the Diva was just as gracious as Mercedes Ford, and Timothy loved her instantly! He also decided that if he ever became a famous novelist, he would emulate these great stars and their big-heartedness.

For once, it seemed that Jared was happy, too. He and Muriel were buzzing so intently around Diva Lady that they didn't have time for anything else. Which gave Timothy the freedom to sneak a glass of wine and check his hair and appearance in anticipation of Brad's arrival. He looked at his watch and prayed that Brad would indeed show up. Timothy needed a friend if he were to get through the evening without killing someone—or himself. Then, as if the gods had just read his text message, the elevator doors opened, and Brad stepped into the penthouse.

However, his clothes were too casual. Too informal. Timothy had failed to tell Brad it was a black-tie event. Lovely Brad was wearing a sports jacket but was otherwise dressed in jeans, a T-shirt, and tennis shoes. It had been ages since Timothy could afford to attend the theater, so he had no idea that a night out no longer required wearing slacks, a tie, or polished leather shoes. Still, Brad looked smashing in Timothy's eyes, and Timothy was over-the-moon-thrilled to see him.

The moment Brad arrived; Timothy dragged him down the hall to the office. Although he claimed to merely want to fill him in on all that had occurred during the evening thus far, he really wanted time alone with this adorable man. He couldn't get enough of his deep dimples and blue eyes! And his kisses! But he had only a moment before he had to get back out to the party. And he was worried that Brad was so inappropriately dressed that someone might make him feel uncomfortable. Or worse, that Jared might have him ejected.

Brad, the smart guy he apparently was, picked up on Timothy's anxiety. "I didn't know it was formal," he said. "Every other guy here is wearing a tux. Do you want me to leave? I don't want you to get in trouble because of me."

No way was Timothy letting his savior go! He needed him to be his moral support. The evening was only half over, and if he was going to survive, he needed backup! He suggested that Brad make himself a little camouflaged by blending in with the kitchen staff. Of course, he felt guilty because it was his fault for not telling Brad that this was a very big do. Lots of deep pockets being coaxed into giving some of their overflow moola away to Muriel's pet charity.

They returned to the party just as Jared approached the piano. A microphone had been placed at the curve of the instrument, and he picked it up and tapped the black ball. "Ladies and gentlemen," he started, and the room began quieting. "I'm Jared Evans, and before the entertainment, I first want to introduce you to our lovely hostess, Muriel Maynard."

After polite applause, he went on for about a minute, telling the crowd what they probably already knew about Muriel, *Infectious chronicosis*, and the importance of fighting this scourge of a disease.

Muriel then took over and offered even more banal information about what *Infectious chronicosis* was and how so many people around the globe were benefiting from the bucks raised from people such as the ones currently in the room. Another polite wave of applause ensued, and when she got to the end of her dreary recitation about sickness and describing in too vivid detail the various nightmarish ways to suffer, she introduced the great opera singer Virginia La Paloma.

The entire penthouse erupted in a loud and enthusiastic

ovation. Ms. Diva bowed and blew kisses. Timothy was so excited to be among the witnesses to the star performing in a private residence. Just for them! The thrill and exhilaration made Timothy want to buckle down and get an agent for his book so he could become a wealthy novelist and philanthropist and have parties with internationally famous singers performing for his own famous guests. He never wanted this evening to end!

But end it almost did the minute the piano accompanist played a medley of famous opera arias. Everyone in the room looked to Ms. Diva, who smiled politely but seemed a bit flustered. She leaned over and whispered something into the pianist's ear. Everyone saw him blush as he nodded and fumbled in his folio for specific music. He sheepishly looked up at Ms. Diva and shook his head.

At that moment, Jared came to Timothy's side and, through gritted teeth, angrily accused him of not sending the singer's music to the pianist ahead of the party. Who knew that he was supposed to do that? Jared had certainly never even given him any sheet music! Oh god, just as he thought he may have gotten through the night without too many hiccups from his lack of anticipating all that needed to be done, the rug had been pulled out from under his feet again.

The gracious Diva kept smiling and tried her best to make suggestions for how else she could entertain the guests. "I know a few 'Knock-Knock' jokes," she said to enormous laughter. "Maybe even a naughty limerick or two?"

Timothy felt especially sad for the piano player, who was humiliated. And then the most wonderful thing happened. Brad, as inappropriately dressed as he was and apparently not giving two hoots about what the others thought of his attire, wended his way through the crowd and reached the piano. He whispered to the pianist, and the musician nodded his head. Then Brad said something to Ms. Diva, whom Timothy could tell was as intrigued by Brad's eyes, dimples, and nose as Timothy himself was. She smiled and shrugged as if to say, "Let's give it a try."

Well, if Timothy weren't in love with Brad Bradbury already (which he definitely was), he would have been totally besotted when he started to play the piano. Brad knew Ms. Diva's repertoire from listening to her albums. Turns out he was a great fan and even knew her favorite key in which to sing each piece. They turned out to be an excellent duo. And during the wild applause following Ms. Diva's first few arias, dreadful Jared returned to Timothy. "Who the hell is that at the piano!" he demanded. "He looks like a Skid Row bum!"

Timothy smiled demurely and sighed, "Skid Row bums rarely play Verdi and Puccini with such virtuosity. Do they?"

It was obvious that Jared was burning up inside. Either he was aghast that the night was almost ruined, or he was upset that Timothy had somehow saved the night from being a disaster. As another round of applause ensued, and it was obvious that Diva Lady was actually having a fun time, Jared once again returned to Timothy. With his voice still sounding calm but vicious, he said, "I can't do this anymore, Timothy. We hired you because we thought you'd be reliable. But we need to talk. Monday morning. In the office. Nine o'clock."

Timothy nodded his head with indifference. He didn't care anymore. He turned around and rolled his eyes. The only thing he wanted to do was to watch and listen as Brad played and Diva sang and try to keep himself tethered to the ground so that falling in love didn't cause him to float away. He'd think about being sacked later.

## Chapter Nine

The next thing Timothy knew, the alarm on his phone went off. It was morning. Drats! How could the next day have come so quickly? Totally not fair, and he wished now that he hadn't had that last (though emboldening) sip of wine. He wasn't hungover, but he certainly didn't want to face the world either. But then… he realized it was Sunday! His day off! If he wanted to stay in bed all day, he could. Yippee! But of course, he wasn't going to waste his free day. No way! So, he hightailed it into the shower.

What was Timothy going to do with the day? Of course, he wanted to spend it with Brad, but Brad always spent Sundays with his mother in Connecticut. (On top of all his other amazing qualities, he was apparently a good son, too.) Timothy would definitely work on his new book, for sure. Well, first, he wanted to take a stroll through Central Park. Then, browse his favorite bookshop. And there was a movie at the AMC 25 that had gotten good reviews, and he really wanted to see it. And after that, he had to do some laundry. But after that…!

He ended up calling his old boyfriend, Ted, to see if he wanted to grab a bite for lunch. Ted was up for it but said he first had to finish editing his latest poem for the new collection. This was the reason Ted was becoming successful. He was totally disciplined when it came to his writing. He was a true artist, while Timothy... well, he didn't want to think about his own lack of motivation.

Lunch was at Larkspur Diner, over on Belmont. They liked the place because the atmosphere was casual, and the food yummy and cheap. Ted had the nutty quinoa and alfalfa cottage cheese mix, and Timothy had a chicken quesadilla. With a side of cheesy fries. And a Coke. But he quickly lost his appetite when Ted asked how the job was going. Timothy didn't want to tell him the truth. He didn't want his Ex to think it wasn't working out and that he was a failure. So, he shrugged and dodged the question. "All jobs have their challenges," he said vacantly.

And that's when Ted started to play Oprah. "What's the hardest part of the job?" he asked.

At least it was a softball question. "It's the evil guy I report to. You sorta met him the other night at the *Obsession* party. He's a total ball-buster! He hates my guts. Everything is my fault. If it rains, I'm to blame. There are times when I literally want to kill him," Timothy said.

"You could always get another job," Ted said matter-of-factly. "You're young... and cute. Are you even looking around for something else? You'd be an asset to any employer."

Timothy didn't believe that for a second. He obviously wasn't an asset to Jared or Muriel Maynard Management. Plus, he wanted more than just an employer. He wanted Mercedes Ford. And no, he couldn't just go out and find another job. It had taken him his entire life to get this far. Plus, he'd been so beaten down by Jared that he now felt like a total failure. Who would want to hire someone who totally sucked at their job? "I'd give anything to be a published author like you," he said.

Ted shook his head. "No, you wouldn't. Not really." He

took a sip from his glass of sparkling water. "If you wanted to be a writer, you'd be a writer. Really, it's that simple. I gave you notes on the chapters from your book you asked me to read. I bet you haven't worked on those pages since we broke up. Am I right? And there's totally nothing wrong with that, Timothy. You'll get to it someday. Maybe. Maybe not. And the world won't stop turning if you don't follow your dream. Not one single person on the planet will care. Not your mother. Not your girlfriend, Mercedes Ford. Absolutely no one. Except you."

Oh, wow! That hurt! Mainly because it was absolutely true. Timothy was crestfallen and could barely swallow his bite of chicken quesadilla. *Got the dream, yeah, but not the guts*; he heard Bernadette Peters in his head singing Sondheim. "In other words, 'If it's to be, it's up to me,'" he quoted something Dan Rather said in a motivational YouTube speech. "But I'm way too busy right now. I'm swamped with work. I'm under tons of pressure. I can't be creative with all this anxiety in my life. And I'm not as talented as you," Timothy moaned his unlimited excuses.

Ted nodded in fake sympathy. "If that's what you believe..." he said cryptically, moving away from the uncomfortable subject. And by the time lunch was over, Timothy felt like a bigger failure than ever.

The summer heat was still oppressive in the city, and rather than walking around as he'd planned, Timothy headed back to The Colton. He was worn out, and a Sunday afternoon nap sounded like a good idea. Timothy loved naps but seldom had time for one. And when he arrived at the penthouse, he was ready to take off his shoes and curl up with Brad—although he'd have to settle for his pillow—which was now named "Brad." He noticed that the office door was slightly ajar. This took him by surprise because he clearly remembered closing and locking it. He tentatively peeked in. There was Jared seated at the desk and typing on his laptop while referencing something on Timothy's computer. Two screens for Jared, of course, and now he's checking up on me in person, not just remotely, Timothy thought as he opened the door farther and saw that the bookshelves were rotated to reveal the secret room. "Don't you ever take a day off?" he asked.

"I work. It's what I do," Jared snapped. "If you were capable of performing the very simple tasks that we pay you to do, I wouldn't have to be here on Sunday. Believe it or not, I have dreams of my own that don't include playing babysitter to you or being second-fiddle to Muriel Maynard. Achieving success in this business, or at anything of value, requires real gut-wrenching sacrifices. I'm willing to do what it takes."

Then he stopped typing as a new caustic thought occurred to him. He turned to face Timothy. His brown eyes were riveted to the assistant's blue ones. Timothy stared back, not knowing how else to react. What could he say? There was nothing. As the uncomfortable moments of dead silence ticked by, Timothy could literally see in Jared's eyes how much Jared despised him. They were in a staring contest, and neither of them blinked.

*Is he a sadist or a psychopath*, Timothy wondered, as he often had over the past week. *Don't most people go out of their way to avoid hurting others? Is he even aware of the anguish he inflicts? Maybe not. And that would place him plainly in the psychopath category*, Timothy reasoned.

At that moment, Timothy didn't really care where Jared fell on the mental health spectrum or whether or not he worked all day and all night and put himself into an early grave. Timothy was tired of all the fear, apprehension, and anxiety that had consumed him since coming to The Colton.

Now, as he was certain that his employment would be over tomorrow anyway, and with nothing left to lose, he finally spoke up in defiance. "I'll probably never really know why you've hated me from the start, Jared," he said timidly. "In your eyes, I've been a catastrophe in the job. I know that. You've said as much. I did the very best that I could, but you've slammed me at every opportunity. Apparently, you did the same to the assistants who came before me. I sort of doubt that we could all be equal-opportunity losers. So maybe you're the problem, Jared. Maybe you need to take a good, hard look in the mirror. You might not like what you see."

Jared continued staring at Timothy without expression for another long moment. Then, he spoke the most profound words Timothy had ever heard from this man. "Don't you think I already know that about myself?"

What? Jared agreed with Timothy's assessment of him as a loser. Had Jared just confessed to having enough self-awareness to realize that he might be the root of his own misery and the misery of everyone in his orbit?

Jared inhaled and released one of his famous deep sighs. "You remind me of someone else I know," he said, speaking in the monotone of a person in a magician's hypnotic trance. His mind's eyes seemed to be viewing the panorama of a sad memory. "I've never liked him. He's desperate to not be ordinary. But he is ordinary. Like you. He isn't especially clever, either. Like you. You and he aren't outstanding in any way at all. The most tragic thing about the whole situation is that he knows he's as common as blue jeans. There isn't a single thing that makes him unique. Oh, he wants to be distinguished. Maybe even famous. Please, dear God, make me successful in some way! If not in my lifetime, then in my mother's lifetime. How pathetic is that? To be so needy for approval and attention that you pray every night that you'll be a star in some way, even if you're not alive to enjoy it. He has no real talents, so he's found ways to be around interesting people… showbusiness people, and people in the arts… as if some of their reflected glory might rub off on him. And it has rubbed off on him. But it's had the opposite effect of what he'd expected. It only makes it clearer that he will always be lackluster at best. He could never in a million years be their peer. It's soul-crushing. But what can you do?"

Jared seemed to return to the moment, and he looked at Timothy. "That's you, Timothy," he said. "That's why I don't like you; I don't like people who have potential and waste it. Plain and simple. Prove me wrong. I dare you."

Timothy's eyes were now brimming with tears, and his lower lip quivered because his mirror metaphor had flipped over and made him realize that maybe other people saw him differently than he saw himself. Perhaps he really was an untalented loser. All of his insecurities bubbled to the surface, and he was as paralyzed as if he'd been zapped with a sci-fi ray gun. If Jared was right, then Timothy was a worthless human being. "You'll make a great evil character in the book I'll write one day," he said with a catch in his voice.

"The book you'll write one day. One day?" Jared scoffed with a sadistic laugh. "You'll never write a novel, Timothy. At least not a very good one. You talk about it. And you say you're about to be published. But that's not true, is it? I know your type intimately. You don't have the courage or the discipline. Writing is something you have to work at. Mercedes works at her acting. Virginia La Paloma works at her singing. Even your ex-boyfriend Ted puts his writing above everything else in his life, and he's making well-deserved headway in a very tough business. They've gone to school to study and hone their skills. Success isn't simple. It's not magic. It's not luck. Oh, sure, becoming a celebrity is easy-peasy. Anyone can be famous—or infamous, at least for Warhol's promised 15 minutes. But true success takes more than you're capable of doing. That's a fact."

This was the second time in one day—in one hour—that Timothy had been slapped in the face with his lack of creative discipline. Somehow, the cut was deeper coming from Jared. He'd hit a nerve made raw by Ted's previous comment. Timothy could feel tears running down his cheeks because he knew Jared was probably telling him a truth that he'd always suspected but hoped others couldn't see.

"And no, I wouldn't make a good character in your book or any other book," Jared said. "Because I'm as unremarkable as you are."

Timothy was shattered. There were a lot of mean words that he could throw back at Jared, but at that moment, he couldn't think of a single one that would hurt badly enough. He had the voice of a mute and the energy of a rag doll. And so, he closed the office door. But not before Jared reminded him of the next morning's meeting with Muriel. With that comment reverberating in his ears and knowing that his unhappy time of employment here was almost over, Timothy wiped his tears and decided to go upstairs and start packing. On the way, he noticed Fabiola on the terrace, clearly asleep in a chaise longue, her book dropped to her side. The heat must have gotten to her. When he reached his room, Timothy decided that the packing could wait. He took off his shoes, removed his sweaty shirt, stretched out on the bed, buried his face in the pillow… and cried himself to sleep.

When Timothy woke up, the bedroom was bathed in early evening light. He looked at the time on his phone. He'd slept for three hours! He couldn't believe it. But it was totally understandable after all the work and anxiety of the past few days and his afternoon altercation with Jared. Still, he was annoyed that his day off had come to a wasted end. He got up with plans to see what the caterers had left in the fridge and have a glass of wine, then maybe do a bit of writing on the new book—that would show Jared—before going to bed again. The new week would start, and his job here would end after meeting with Jared and Muriel. He was resigned to his fate.

Timothy splashed water on his face in the bathroom, dropped Visine into his swollen red eyes, and checked to see if Jared was still in the penthouse. Thankfully, the office door was closed, and he sighed in relief. Then he headed to the kitchen, where he found an open bottle of wine. He poured a glass for himself, then stepped out onto the terrace where Fabiola was seated with her own glass and reading another book. "Gosh, how many books do you read a week?" he asked, genuinely interested, as he'd seen her with at least five different titles. Timothy used to be a voracious reader, but he'd become too busy recently to read more than one novel a month.

"There's nothing else to do around here," Fabiola said. "I have to live in Fantasyland."

*Nothing to do?* Timothy said to himself. *How 'bout washing the floors and making the beds?* Although he had to confess, the place always looked pretty good, so maybe Fabiola was a night owl and did the chores while Timothy was asleep.

Timothy took his first satisfying sip of wine. He surely needed this and tried his best not to think about his earlier humiliating run-in with Jared—which proved impossible. After a long moment, he finally said, "I found out today why Jared dislikes me so much. He came right out with it. He reeled off a whole list. Apparently, I'm the most common and unremarkable thing on the planet... the spitting image of someone he hates because they're ordinary and not even mediocre. Apparently, he's hypersensitive about anything run-of-the-mill. He said I'd never achieve any success because I'm garden-variety."

Fabiola grunted and shook her head. "He's failing as a human being himself," she said. "He's an insecure little runt with below-average size hands, if you get my drift. He's a venomous bully. Like that Voldemort guy who used to be President."

"He said something really odd," Timothy continued. "When I found the nerve to tell him that he should take a look in the mirror because maybe he was the problem, he said, 'Don't you think I know that about myself?'"

Fabiola took another sip from her glass and nodded in understanding. "That speaks volumes about the little pisher. He doesn't like you because he doesn't like himself. You remind Jared too much of Jared."

"I'm nothing like Jared!" Timothy squealed. "For one thing, I'm a nice person. I think. Everybody likes me... well, with a couple of exceptions. I'd jump off a cliff if I thought everybody hated my guts."

"You're so naïve," Fabiola said. "I think Jared resents that you're a decade younger than him and way cuter, and you've got potential. Heck, you've written a book. What has he done with his life? Not a lot. He's a suck-up to people who have done something."

In that moment, Timothy realized that maybe Jared had been talking about himself when he revealed that there was someone else he hated. Perhaps Jared was seeing his own inadequacies in Timothy. *Projection* he remembered something from his Psych 101 class in junior college. *Unconsciously taking behavioral traits you don't like about yourself and seeing them in someone else.* In fact, Jared had said, "Please, dear God, make me successful in some way! If not in my lifetime, then in my mother's lifetime." Jared had said that was pathetic. Timothy agreed. But wasn't that exactly what Timothy wanted for himself too? He wanted his mother—and a slew of others—to see him as successful. Even if success came posthumously. He fantasized about returning to his hometown when he became famous and graciously accepting all sorts of accolades and tributes while benevolently forgiving the sorry little butts of anyone who had ever mistreated him because, well, he was obviously too busy being rich and famous to even think about them anymore. "You might be right," Timothy said, recalling all the terrible things that Jared had told him. "He said, 'I'm as unremarkable as you are.'"

"I rest my case," Fabiola said, pouring herself and Timothy another glass of vino. "But you've definitely gotta find some self-esteem somewhere, buddy," she added. "I know you don't rock the boat because you dislike making waves. But seriously, you might think about walking into Muriel's office tomorrow and demanding two full days off. While you're at it, call Brad and tell him that you're hopelessly in love with him and want to buy a house together in the Hamptons and live happily ever after."

Timothy laughed uncomfortably. "Dream on. I could never do that!" he said.

"You could. But you probably won't."

"Yeah, yeah. It all sounds good in theory, but when it comes to any real strength, I don't have the guts," Timothy said. And yet, he intuitively knew that until he stopped allowing himself to be manipulated by others and intimidated by all of the "what ifs" of potential failure in life, he'd never have any sort of success. He looked at Fabiola and raised his glass. "You're a wise woman, my friend. I should hire you to be my life coach."

"Here's your first lesson: Brie and crackers go good with this Merlot. I'm starving."

Timothy got the message and realized he and Fabiola were having their first good evening together. They certainly weren't besties yet—they weren't swapping recipes or gossip—but they were at least getting on. The wine helped. And when it was time to go to bed, Timothy was sort of sorry to see the day end. Especially since he had to face Muriel and Jared in the morning. That called for one last glass of wine.

* * *

The blasted alarm on Timothy's phone went off at 7:00 a.m. Although it was physically painful to wake up (maybe this time, he did have a wee bit too much wine the night before), he was raised to always be on time for appointments. So, he hopped in the shower, brushed his teeth, slipped into his jeans and an Oxford cloth button-down shirt, grabbed his phone, and waited in the foyer for the elevator.

What's wrong with this picture? he asked himself, sensing that something was slightly not right. "Ah! The Casablanca Liles! They're gone," he said, looking at the empty Lalique table. He hadn't noticed before that the floral delivery guys hadn't replaced the bouquet yesterday. Didn't Jared pay the darn bill for crying out loud? But did Timothy really care? Let Jared deal with it after Muriel fired him. The elevator arrived, and off he went.

The Uber to Midtown was slow, but Timothy really didn't mind. Would it be normal for one to rush to their execution? He wasn't eager to be cast out on the street. And that's precisely where he was headed. Unless he got some sort of severance pay, he didn't even have enough dough to cover the first month—let alone a deposit—to rent a place. Finding an apartment in New York was its own form of medieval torture.

Timothy was suddenly and miraculously calm when the car finally pulled up curbside in front of Muriel's office building. He didn't feel a single butterfly in his stomach. He was resolved. The crowded elevator ride to the 15th floor was swift, and when he walked into the office of Muriel Maynard Management, he was greeted by a clone of Sandy, the rat receptionist who had occupied the front desk until Jared fired him. Again, this new sentry wasn't exactly rude, but he was definitely preoccupied. Timothy was just another task for him to deal with. But at least he was expecting Timothy, and without any fanfare, Timothy was ushered into the same conference room where he'd had his original interview a mere week ago. This time, he asked for a cup of coffee.

As was their way of showing how busy they were, Muriel and Jared made him wait twenty minutes. Actually, it was Muriel alone who made him wait. For once, Gopher wasn't with her. Muriel was never very warm to Timothy, and this morning, she seemed colder than Uncle Walt's brain in a freezer at Disneyland.

"Where's Weasel Boy?" Muriel snapped (she already had a new name for him), taking a seat and acting as if Timothy would know Jared's schedule.

"Running late, is he?" Timothy said. "I thought he'd be here early just to get a ringside seat to my execution. Perhaps he's sticking pins in a voodoo doll with my name on it."

"I don't have the time…" Muriel dismissed his joke. "Darling," Muriel began, "it's come to my attention… Well, here, you read this." She opened a manila file folder and withdrew a sheet of what appeared to be personal stationery. Timothy saw a florid monogram embossed in metallic blue stamped at the top. Muriel took a moment to reread the handwritten message and then handed it to him.

Timothy took the paper, and his facial expression gave away his bewilderment. It certainly wasn't what he had been expecting. Far, far from it.

> Dearest Muriel,
> Just a quick note to let you know that we very much like your new assistant, Timothy. He and I had a lovely conversation the other day here on the location of *Blind Trust*. I think I intimidated him at first, but he was totally professional, and you know how much we value that attribute. I surely hope that Timothy doesn't run away, as all your previous assistants have. He's a keeper. In fact, if (or when) he decides to seek employment elsewhere, please send him our way.
> On another note, Sage says he is sending back the contracts via overnight express.
>
> With enduring love and appreciation,
> Mercedes.

What? Timothy couldn't believe that the great Mercedes Ford even remembered who he was! Again, the living legend had totally surprised him, and he was floating on air. He looked at Muriel with a huge, stupid smile. Stupid lasted. The smile did not.

"This complicates things a bit, dear," Muriel said. "Jared has quite the opposite opinion of your work. In fact, he has a list of infractions that I simply can't ignore. But I also can't ignore Mercedes' commendation, either. Jared thinks it best for you to write a lovely note to Mercedes and Sage telling them that we shared their correspondence with you and that while you appreciate the acknowledgment of your work ethic, a terrific new career opportunity has opened up, and you're taking the job. She'll understand."

Timothy was, of course, taken aback—again! He had been right that Jared and Muriel had planned to fire him. But Mercedes Ford had gummed up the gears with that wrench of a letter. A part of him was giddy with delight, but another part was furious that after making such a good impression on their star client, they still wanted to nail his butt to the wall.

Timothy recalled his conversation with Fabiola the night before and decided to stand up for himself. "This is bullspit!" he challenged, flashing anger at Muriel. "I've done pretty much everything Jared has thrown at me. I've somehow withstood his harassment and vile, vicious, despicable, and cruel insults. I've accepted that he hates me and thinks that I'm a worthless piece of loser trash and wants me to feel like a brainless knobhead. I'm willing to take responsibility for the time I forgot to pick up your dry cleaning before they closed, but the other so-called offenses he berated me for were out of my control."

"Do I need to call security?" Muriel asked.

Timothy suspected Muriel felt a need for personal protection, and that was just the way he wanted her to feel. Timothy quickly stuffed Mercedes' note into his back pocket, to Muriel's surprise and frustration. "A letter of recommendation!" he declared, folding his arms across his chest as Muriel gasped with fury. "And by the way, Saturday night at the party, I met a lovely man from the Arts section of *The Post*. He'll keep your secret about the hidden room in the penthouse unless I tell him to do otherwise."

Now Timothy was in very unfamiliar territory. He'd never blackmailed anyone before, but it felt rather good! He started to leave the room and got as far as opening the door when Muriel demanded that he return the letter. Then she waved a dismissive hand and said, "Never mind. It's addressed to me. Anyone who wants to confirm your employment will have to go through me, and I'll simply tell the truth—that you're a thief and stole that letter."

Drats! But Timothy didn't let on that Muriel was right. He said, "I'm the subject of the letter. I'll say that you gave it to me. Which, in truth, you did." Touché! Plus, he still had Clive from the party as a trump card.

"As for Clive," Muriel said as if reading his thoughts, "he has a very rich and elderly wife who may find it less than amusing to learn that her attractive British husband keeps another apartment in SoHo, which he regularly visits. And that apartment is occupied by, let me see," she pretended to search her memory for a name, "Oh yes, Santiago. Santiago Gonzales. And neither of them is a naturalized citizen of the U.S. and, therefore, easily deported. Get my drift, dear?"

Timothy was sunk. He should have known that anyone as powerful as Muriel Maynard would have the scoop on everybody who was anybody in town. Darn it all! And then he said something that just popped out of his mouth. It wasn't planned. He was making stuff up as he went along, but it had been rolling around his head since his conversation with Bud Sellers at the party. "Mercedes might like to know about her own husband, too," he said calmly.

Muriel swallowed hard.

"Let's just say... No, it's none of my business. As a wise man said to me very recently, "I simply like the knowledge of it all." Timothy had absolutely no idea what he was talking about. He was bluffing. The words just poured out after being stored along with the thoughts and memories of Sage from the day they'd met in the trailer on the film location. He couldn't think of any other explanation for why he blurted out such nonsense.

Muriel looked at him for a long moment. Finally, she said, "One better be very careful about what one says and does in this town, dear." And with that, she stood up and passed Timothy in the doorway.

Timothy guessed that he was free to leave. And he still had a job. At least for the time being. He left the building and took a bus home.

## Chapter Ten

Back at The Colton, as Timothy rode the elevator to the penthouse, he kept thinking about the can of worms he may have opened concerning Mercedes' husband. He rationalized that he was just making stuff up to protect his job—and his tiny wedge of self-respect. He couldn't let Jared's maliciousness get him unjustly fired. It simply wasn't fair. And he felt an unusual strength knowing that he'd stood up for himself. For once, Timothy was proud of Timothy!

And when he walked into the penthouse, he had one more thing to be pleased about. Although the office door was closed, Timothy discovered it wasn't locked. One demerit for Jared, he thought with glee. And Timothy found that the computer hadn't been put away either. Two demerits! Finally, something to lord over the jerk. Equally good was that there were no new phone messages from the loathsome donkey. He was able to get a ton of work done. He replied to dozens of emails and forwarded a request for pictures to Mercedes' publicist; he even sent a quick message to Brad, letting him know that he was available for dinner the next night if he was up for it.

And then it was time for what had become Timothy's end-of-day routine, pouring a glass of vino, and sitting out on the terrace with Fabiola, enjoying the serenity of being above the fray of the city. And, in defiance, he closed the laptop computer and left it just where Jared had. He wouldn't lock it away in the safe, either. That'll show him, he thought!

Relaxing on the terrace and sipping his glass of Shiraz, Timothy started to think that something didn't seem right. For one thing, his phone's whooshing sound whenever an incoming email arrived was practically silent. It had been that way all day. Part of him didn't want to jinx the peace and quiet by acknowledging it. Still, another part of him thought it was strange that Jared hadn't at least been in touch to ream him for the way he'd faced off against the all-powerful Muriel Maynard that morning. Even Fabiola seemed to be in a different and pleasant mood. She wasn't as antagonistic as she usually was.

And then something strange happened. Muriel, who never called Timothy, called, and asked to speak to Jared. Muriel seemed confused as she grilled Timothy about Jared's whereabouts. But Timothy had nothing to offer. He hadn't seen nor talked to him all day. Neither had Muriel, which made the whole situation a bit creepier. Jared was a workaholic. He never stopped. He was tethered to his phone. Timothy even pictured him sleeping with the darn thing at night—although he definitely didn't want to imagine Jared in bed—especially if he slept in the nude. He suspected Jared's pasty complexion was probably due to the screen shine from his phone. Of course, Timothy said he'd tell Jared to call Muriel right away the next time they spoke.

Fabiola looked up. "Lapdog is MIA?"

"Seems so. He wasn't at the meeting this morning, either. Muriel hasn't seen him. He's not answering his phone. Probably out drowning puppies in front of hysterical kiddies."

"Nah, if he's the psychopath I think he is he got tired of animal abuse when he was a child and has moved on to torturing adult animals—such as office assistants," Fabiola smirked.

The image of Jared as a kid holding some poor, defenseless little critter underwater in Central Park Lake was an easy one for Timothy to see in his mind's eye. Timothy was instantly ashamed of himself when he blurted out, "Yeah, and I suspect that all the assistants before me weren't fired. Jared murdered them and keeps a couple of arms and legs in his freezer as souvenirs."

Fabiola looked at him with a wry grin. "What goes around, comes around," she said.

\* \* \*

Timothy tried calling Jared several times throughout the evening, but he didn't answer. He stopped leaving messages because he figured it was overkill. Plus, Jared would never call him back. He'd only check in with Muriel because Timothy was the lowest form of a single-cell organism. To be honest, Timothy didn't really care anymore. He eventually went to bed and slept like a log. It was so good to have had a day without too much pressure. And that's all that Jared was to him—pressure. He felt sick whenever he saw Jared's name on his caller ID.

Sometime in the night, Timothy received a call of another kind—from nature. While in the bathroom, going through the routine with his sleepy eyes closed and with the silence of the penthouse all around him, he was suddenly vaguely aware of the faint sound of a cell phone ringing downstairs in the distance. It wasn't his ringtone, which played Queen's *We Are the Champions*. And it wasn't Fabiola's, which he remembered was the Stones' *Get Off of My Cloud*. However, the ringtone was familiar. It sounded like *Mack the Knife*. Of course! It was

Jared's phone! That's why he hadn't heard from him. Jared must have left his phone in the office. Duh!

But heck, it was the middle of the night. No way was Timothy going to retrieve the darn thing until morning. So, he skedaddled back to his comfy bed to finish a dream about Brad. Heaven!

When the morning sunshine crept into Timothy's room, he felt well-rested and great. He had no problem getting himself out of bed. After his shower and getting dressed, he wandered into the kitchen, where he found that Fabiola had actually set a mug for him next to the Keurig coffee machine. This day was starting out well. He placed a coffee pod into the machine and waited for his java to drip. Then, he dropped a slice of bread into the toaster. With a bit of butter and orange marmalade, he was all set, and he went out to the terrace to sit for a few minutes with Fabiola.

It seemed that the city was finally cooling down. The air wasn't as muggy as it had been for the past week and a half, and Timothy could sense that autumn wasn't too far off. Fall was his favorite time of year, no matter where he was during the season. Being in New York when the leaves start to carpet the ground in the park is an altogether fabulous time of year. There's a scent of freshness, although it's actually the scent of death—decaying leaves. And he loved walking around with the sound of crunching under his shoes.

"How'd you sleep?" Timothy asked Fabiola, who actually looked up from her book, to wish him a good morning. Fabiola said she'd had a few interesting dreams—albino kangaroos and alien abductions—but otherwise, she'd slept straight through until she got up at 6:00.

It was Tuesday, and Timothy remembered that The Suits would be coming to exchange folders again. He still wondered what the heck was so secretive. Why did it seem so clandestine, and why did the material have to be locked up in the safe? But his was not to reason why. And then he remembered that he had to retrieve Jared's phone from the office, too. However, he wanted just a few more precious minutes of peace before being bothered with work and contacting that jerk. So, he grabbed his coffee mug, made another cup, and sat down to scan Fabiola's copy of *The Times*.

Eventually, when he couldn't put off work any longer, Timothy heaved a heavy sigh and toddled back to the office. He started looking for Jared's phone. It wasn't on the desk. It wasn't on the sofa. He checked under and between the cushions, but it wasn't in the room. For a moment, he thought that he might have heard Fabiola's phone during the night after all. Or maybe it was a lucid dream. Whatever, Jared's phone wasn't his responsibility. If he found it, fine. If not, Jared could easily get another; he had boasted about being well-known at the Apple Store. And then Timothy's own phone rang. Although the caller ID said it was Muriel, he suspected Jared was probably using her phone because his was missing. Reluctantly, he answered the call.

But it was Muriel, and she still hadn't heard from Gopher. She said she was really worried and asked if Timothy knew of any emergency contacts. But why would Jared ever have provided a name or number to Timothy? "What about his personnel file?" he asked. "There's gotta be something in there. A friend? A family member?"

Muriel said she'd already checked, and the only name and contact number were for Jared's mother. However, she died six months ago, and the file hadn't been updated. Muriel wanted Timothy to run over to Jared's apartment. "Maybe he has Covid."

*Or he's wedged in an elevator shaft, or struck by falling construction debris, or suffocated in the coffin he sleeps in.* Timothy thought of all the fun things that could have happened to his nefarious boss.

Muriel gave him Jared's address, and Timothy promised to tell Jared to call her right away. When he hung up, he thought, I'll go over to his place when I darn well feel like it. He looked at the time displayed on his phone and realized that The Suits would be arriving at any moment, and he'd better get a file out of the safe.

However, just as he was about to punch the security code into his phone to access the secret room, he heard the elevator chime in the foyer. He couldn't count on Fabiola to greet the guys, so he left the office and hustled down the corridor. As expected, the men entered the penthouse while Fabiola continued reading on the terrace.

Timothy offered bottled water to Messrs. Suits, but they declined. They just wanted to return last week's file and obtain a new one. That was fine with Timothy. The sooner he could get rid of them, the sooner he could run over to Jared's and settle down to do some real work. He took their yellow folder and went back to the office. He punched the code on his phone, and the bookcase began to open. And then he heard that cell phone ring tone again. The same one he'd heard last night. It was louder. And getting even louder. It was coming from inside the secret room.

And there it was…

…On the floor…

…Next to…

Jared Evans.

Dead.

Crumpled up like a bag of trash.

Eyes open and staring at… nothing.

…Jared's phone kept ringing.

## Chapter Eleven

If there were ever a time to burgle one of the other gazillion-dollar condos in The Colton, it was now because pretty much the building's entire security team was in Mercedes Ford's penthouse. And all of their attention was riveted to a sight they never wanted to view in that supposedly super-duper-safe residential tower: a dead body.

Despite what the building's security chief Griffin insisted (after all, his reputation was on the line), it sure didn't look like natural causes to Timothy. For one thing, he'd noticed a bruise on Jared's right cheek and dried blood on his right temple. And he saw what appeared to be a little bit of dried blood on the top left edge of the safe, too. But what did he know about dead bodies and how they got that way? Okay, so it could have been an accident, as Griffin next insisted (he vacillated like a politician). He'd pointed out that the desk chair was tipped over, suggesting that Jared had probably been standing on it and lost his balance while reaching for one of the shoeboxes on the upper shelves. "Yeah, that's definitely what happened," Griffin declared, sounding just like a child blaming a cookie theft on his invisible friend. This was obviously for the police to determine. And they arrived within minutes of being summoned.

Naturally, Muriel nearly had a heart attack when she heard the news. Even Fabiola, who detested Jared almost as much as Timothy did, had to take a Valium chased with a shot of whisky to calm down—after capturing a few photos with her phone of Jared lying on the floor with his eyes wide open and his tongue lolling out of his mouth like a possum squashed by a truck. It was the stuff of which nightmares were made.

And, of course, Timothy and Fabiola, being the only ones in residence at the time of Jared's death, were subjected to a lot of questioning about discovering the body. Did they know the victim? Who was he to them? When was the last time they saw him alive? Blah, blah, blah. But everything they'd ever seen on TV police procedural shows still didn't prepare them for the harsh grilling, which left Timothy feeling that he might even be arrested as a suspect.

It made sense since he revealed to the police detectives that he was probably the last to see Jared alive. And he knew the code for opening and closing the secret room. He also let it slip that Jared had been a real pain in the neck to him. Detective Sloane had given his partner a dubious look when Timothy recalled hearing Jared's telephone ringing in the middle of the night but didn't investigate. Timothy could almost hear Detective Sloan saying, "You might've saved him."

Even though Timothy couldn't have known that Jared was dead or, at the very least, that he needed help since he'd assumed that Jared had left the penthouse sometime during Timothy's Sunday afternoon nap, he couldn't help but think about all the 'what ifs.'

By the time the police were finally gone, it was nearly 4:00 p.m., and Timothy wandered aimlessly into the kitchen, looking for something to do, anything that might take his mind away from Jared's death. Fabiola was there too and actually offered him half of her Stouffer's cheese enchilada frozen dinner. However, even though Timothy hadn't eaten since that bit of toast in the morning, he wasn't at all hungry.

A glass of wine was what he needed. He poured one for himself and one for Fabiola, and they sat on the terrace—and stared into space.

"The thing is, and it's terrible to admit," Timothy mused aloud, "but I sort of understand someone wanting Jared dead. Murdered, even."

"It was an accident," Fabiola said. "Griffin said so. It looks like the police think so, too."

As if he hadn't heard Fabiola's pronouncement or didn't buy what appeared to be obvious to others, Timothy continued to ponder Jared's demise at possibly another's hand. "He was mean, and other than Muriel and Mercedes, not many people will miss him. I know I won't. But how could he have been so loathed that it caused someone to kill him?"

Fabiola frowned and poured more wine, letting Timothy continue his monologue. Jared's death came out of the blue, but perhaps it was natural causes. Maybe he fainted. Or maybe it was an accident. Maybe he fell off the chair. Either could have resulted in a broken neck and a head injury. After all, it was hard to conceive that a killer had entered the penthouse while they were both there. Security in the building was White House tight, and they hadn't seen or heard anything strange or out of the ordinary.

"We were both napping," Timothy agreed, "but when someone is getting themselves killed, shouldn't they make a lot of noise? Wouldn't we have woken up?"

"We probably would have heard it if he was being attacked. But maybe not if it just happened spontaneously, like Griffin and the police think," Fabiola said. "When you slip on an icy sidewalk and go down, you don't have time to yell. It just happens. And if Jared fell and broke his neck, he would die instantly."

It was all way too upsetting, and neither of them wanted to go to bed. As much as they wished the day to end, they both knew that they'd either lie awake with insomnia or fall asleep and have nightmares in which they saw Jared's life being ripped away and abruptly ending. But eventually, they called it quits. It had been an unbelievably harrowing day, and they absolutely needed to sleep. They went their separate ways.

As Timothy tried to sleep in the quiet of the penthouse, he imagined hearing Jared's cell phone ringtone. Of course, that wasn't possible because the phone had been confiscated by the police as evidence, along with his computer. So, he was just hearing phantom sounds. Fortunately, Timothy was so exhausted that he didn't remember anything else until his own phone woke him in the morning.

The caller ID said, Brad. Timothy thought he must have heard the news and was calling to cheer him up. But no, Brad hadn't heard a thing and was shocked when Timothy told him the horror that had happened right under his nose and where he lived. Beautiful Brad argued that it was his duty to dash over and console Timothy. But as wonderful as Timothy knew it would be to snuggle into Brad's strong arms and to feel protected by the man he was falling in love with, he had to insist otherwise. The police were expected to interview Muriel in her office at 10:00, and they wanted to see Timothy there, too, and to get his official statement. But Mr. Sweetie-pie insisted that Timothy allow him to play host for dinner that evening. "Our place," he said, meaning La Strega, the Italian restaurant where they had dined before. Finally, there was something fun to look forward to.

It was a gray, drizzling, and depressing day, and by the time Timothy had showered and made his bed, Fabiola had prepared a light breakfast for them. They took seats opposite each other at the dining room table. The fact that Fabiola had actually prepared scrambled eggs and bacon for them was not lost on Timothy's appreciation meter. Apparently, Fabiola was genuinely getting to like him. This, of course, made Timothy like her more as well. He so needed a friend right now who completely understood what he was feeling about the whole Jared death situation. Even Brad couldn't really fully empathize. Fabiola was the only person on the planet who knew exactly what Timothy was going through. And he was the only one in a position to console her, too.

When it was finally time for Timothy to Uber down to Muriel's office, he grabbed an umbrella, and Fabiola wished him good luck. "Stand up for yourself," she growled affectionately as Timothy stepped into the elevator and the doors closed.

This time, when Timothy walked into Muriel's office suite, the new receptionist introduced himself as Lyle and treated him like a celebrity. "Mr. Trousdale, may I get you a coffee or tea?"

"Tea, please."

"Mr. Trousdale, would you like sugar or lemon?"

"Lemon, please."

"Mr. Trousdale, is it true that you were the last to see Jared Evans alive, and did you count how many times he was stabbed?"

"Stabbed?" Timothy gasped, nearly freaking out. "Where the hell did you get the idea that Jared Evans was stabbed, for crying out loud?"

"Oh, it's all over the office," Lyle said gleefully as if he were the keeper of juicy gossip. "Susan heard that someone stuck it to him with a fork a total of 17 times! Amy is starting an office pool, betting on who the killer is, with extra bonus points for the correct number of stabs. You can help me win!"

Timothy was feeling really sad that the employees had turned Jared's death into a game. Yes, Jared was a jerk, but his life was cut short at a young age. Timothy said as much to Lyle. Lyle blushed and apologized and said that he'd heard someone else say that Jared got what he deserved. Timothy begged Lyle to stop passing around totally untrue information. "Let the man's soul rest in peace, for God's sake!"

Timothy didn't wait for his tea or to be escorted to Muriel's office. He was angry with the world and anxious about the upcoming interview. He walked on his own through the reception area and down to where the police were waiting. "Just a few more minutes," a female officer said to him when he arrived. Timothy tarried outside Muriel's door, looking at framed photos of her clients that adorned the wall. Wow. I'd forgotten that Muriel represented Marsha Willis, the jazz singer; he nodded approvingly. His stomach churned with worry. Would the police think he was capable of killing Jared? Of course, they would. Could they blame him for not finding his body earlier? Sure thing. Would they think it suspicious that he and Fabiola had fallen asleep during the day? No doubt. He started pacing to distract himself from the uneasiness and nausea that were threatening to overwhelm him.

Timothy found himself wandering in front of a desk with an engraved plastic nameplate that said, Jared Evans. It was directly outside Muriel's door, which now made clear Jared's actual position in the company. He was just an assistant but aspired to far greater heights. Fake it until you make it. Jared certainly faked being a boss to perfection. Timothy noticed that most other employees, men and women, wore business-casual attire. Jared had always been dressed in a suit. Other desks exhibited framed photos of loved ones, but there was nothing personal on Jared's desk. His life was his work. The only thing that hinted at outside activities was a pair of tickets to a Broadway show that was paper-clipped together. Timothy looked at the performance date. The tickets were for last Saturday. It made him a little sad that Jared had these expensive tickets and probably looked forward to seeing the show, only to find that he had to work at that blasted *Infectious chronicosis* party. Talk about dedication to one's job. Timothy bet no one heard him complain about being unable to go to the show.

"I could've used those," a woman said as she passed by and noticed Timothy looking at the tickets. "He wouldn't even let me buy them from him," she said, obviously still pissed off that the seats went unused. "He was selfish. He didn't want anyone else to be able to boast about seeing that hit."

Just then, Muriel's office door opened, and Timothy was summoned by the female police officer. Muriel was blotting tears from her eyes with Kleenex and stepped out of the room. The officers introduced themselves. Timothy was now alone with Detective Alan Sloane and Officer Anna Corda. Both were pleasant but professional. They said they just wanted to go over his story again.

*Story?* Timothy thought to himself. "The facts I told you yesterday weren't fiction," he said. "Not a story."

"Oh, right," Sloane said. "You're a wannabe writer, aren't you? Words, especially truthful ones, are just as important to you as they are to us."

Timothy once again recalled the details of Sunday, Monday, and Tuesday. He gave the police a full timeline of his activities during those days and everything he knew about what occurred in the penthouse. Muriel had given her version of those days as well, and they pretty much matched.

Neither mentioned the incident with the letter from Mercedes, as clearly, it was best to keep the big star's name out of this investigation as much as possible. After all, she could not have had anything to do with Jared's death. Not only had she belonged to the very small group of people who liked Jared, but she was also hundreds of miles away. That suited Timothy to a T.

And apparently, it was common knowledge that no love was lost between Jared and Timothy. "Is it true that Mr. Evans called you an idiot in front of Ms. Maynard?"

"Um..."

"When Mr. Evans publicly berated you, did you feel so humiliated that you wanted to kill him?"

"Sure, but..."

"Is it true that you received another public dressing down by Mr. Evans at a party this past Saturday and that you were overheard telling another guest that you were thinking of the best method for his murder?"

"Yes and no," Timothy said, flummoxed. "Yes, Jared was upset with me. But no, I never said I wanted to murder him—even if I did want to."

"So, you did want to kill Mr. Evans?" Detective Sloane said forcefully.

"I'll bet if you asked anyone who knew Jared Evans if there were a time, or two or three, when they wanted to push him off the roof of a tall building, they would all say they did. But no one really means that," Timothy insisted.

Sloane seemed to relax and actually smiled. "Sounds just like my boss," he sniggered. He looked over to Officer Corda. "Doesn't that remind you of Captain Hays? Bosses are all the same, aren't they? They bust your butt, and you never get a word of appreciation. Don't quote me, but sometimes I'd like an accident (he used air quotes) to happen to the captain like it did to Mr. Evans. Clean and quick. God, I can't wait to finish my 20 years on the force."

Accident? Really? Do the police actually believe that? Timothy thought and decided maybe they were right. But Timothy's gut told him otherwise, so he couldn't help himself and asked, "Are you sure it was just a sad twist of fate? Just a tragic mishap?"

"Looks like it to me," Officer Sloane said. "I see these things all the time. One minute we're here, and the next… pfft." He made a sound of finality. "Poor chap had the indignity of falling off that swivel chair and breaking his neck. Not how I want to go for sure. But maybe way better than…"

The detective's voice trailed off. Timothy suspected the man probably just wanted to wrap things up, file an easy-breezy report, and go home to a pizza and a six-pack of beer. At least Timothy's fears of being arrested for murder were on hold. For the moment. He wasn't convinced that Sloane actually knew what he was talking about, but he didn't want to push his own theory about Jared's death. *Just leave it*, he silently instructed himself. *Now go… before Sloane has a change of heart and suggests that you had motive and opportunity. Which you did.* "We're done here?" he said slightly nervously.

"Sure, Sloane nodded. "Get lost. Send me an autographed copy of your book when it's published."

As Timothy left Muriel's private office and headed toward the exit, Lyle cornered him. He wanted Timothy to know how horrible he felt about being insensitive to Jared's death. "He was just such a toxic guy, and I won't be losing any sleep over his death," he said. Timothy nodded in understanding but reminded him that Jared had once been someone's little boy and therefore loved, if only for a short while. It made him sad again to think about what Jared had become and how nobody cared that he died.

But Timothy couldn't leave without asking Lyle to explain what he meant about Jared being "toxic." Of course, he pretty much knew the answer: Jared was impossible to work for. He was bombastic and vile. Probably even a sociopath. But Timothy was stunned when Lyle added, "Because of Jared, I lost a role in a Broadway show."

Well, that was a biggie! Timothy wanted to say, *Does every receptionist/assistant who works here want to be a Broadway star?* Instead, he asked a limp, "What happened?"

Lyle was apparently someone who couldn't let go of a perceived personal slight or injustice. Timothy could totally understand. Heck, he harbored his own personal resentments toward others: a cheap-*o* friend who never offered to pay for drinks at a bar and a neighbor who, for whatever reason, wouldn't speak to him. It turned out Lyle was fixated on the fact that Jared kept him from an open-call audition for a walk-on part in a road company production of *Les Misérables*. Jared apparently wouldn't let him take an entire afternoon off from work without docking his pay for the time away. He totally blamed Jared for losing out on the part. It didn't seem to register in his brain that the chances of ever getting the job in the first place were pretty slim. But Lyle wouldn't let it go. To him, Jared had personally sabotaged his rightful stardom.

Lyle added that Jared had rubbed salt in his wound when he said that he wasn't smart enough to be a Broadway success. "It takes more than talent," he quoted Jared. "You've gotta have a brain, too. Like Streisand, Lansbury, or LuPone. And, if you haven't made it by now—hell, you've never even been in a show—it ain't happenin', kid. Not ever!"

Yikes! Where had Timothy heard those words before? At that moment, he actually could sort of understand someone killing Jared for being so mean. Who was he to trash others' dreams and career fantasies? Although Jared was probably right that Lyle's fantasy was doomed from the start. Timothy could only say, "I suspect you have all the talent you need to be a big shining star. Don't let Jared's mean words hold you back from going for it." He also wanted to strongly suggest that he keep his day job, but that would have meant that Timothy didn't fully believe in him. So, instead, he told Lyle to save him a ticket for his big opening night debut.

When Timothy was finally out of the building, rather than Ubering home right away, he decided to wander the city. As hard as it was to survive in Manhattan, the place still held a great fascination for him. One could always find something interesting to do here, even if it was just a stroll through Central Park. And that's what he decided to do.

Timothy stopped after an hour or so, and it was while he was sitting on a bench overlooking the lake and watching the ducks paddle around and squawk for breadcrumbs from park visitors that he began to seriously consider Detective Sloane's supposition about Jared's death being an accident. Timothy was the farthest thing from a professional dead body investigator, but in this case, death by desk chair just didn't sit well with him. He made a mental list of all the people he knew who disliked Jared. The list wasn't all that extensive because he hadn't known Jared very long. But it included the obvious suspects: Fabiola, Sage Slater, drunk Sandy from the bar, indignant Lyle from reception, and the party guest who was a newspaper columnist for *The Post*. Even Bud Sellers could be considered, though the idea of a famous Broadway star killing Jared did seem a little far-fetched. For a split second, he even included his old BF, Ted. Although Ted wouldn't harm a fly, he was still someone who had not been well received by Jared at the *Obsession* party.

List. List. Timothy kept thinking about people who might have wanted to harm Jared. Then…! He realized that he had pretty much Jared's entire circle of acquaintances, or at least the agency's contacts, on his phone! He remembered that Jared had merged all the names, numbers, and email addresses to his new smartphone on his first day on the job.

They say that most murder victims know their killers. So, Timothy thought that maybe, if he went over all those names, something might trigger a good reason to suspect a specific someone of being Jared's killer. With newfound purpose, he stopped watching the ducks and hailed an Uber from his phone.

## Chapter Twelve

Arriving back at The Colton, Timothy headed for the elevator and was just about to do the biometric thing when the no-neck-hulk head of security, Griffin, stopped him. Although never cuddly while on the job (if ever), he was particularly crusty that afternoon. When he ordered, "In my office," Timothy took a deep breath and prepared himself for another grilling.

Griffin's questions were lame. "How did you know the deceased?"

"Um, he was my boss."

"What was your relationship to the deceased?"

Timothy merely gave him a look that said, *Didn't you hear my last answer?* He wanted to say they were lovers, but he knew the security boss wouldn't appreciate that brand of levity. Plus, just thinking of kissing Jared made his whole body feel icky.

"When was the last time you saw the deceased?"

The third time he asked about the "deceased," Timothy bristled and brought forth his newfound pluck. "The 'deceased' has a name. It's Mr. Jared Evans!" he said, proud of himself for being assertive. "And the last time I saw Mr. Evans, he was dead. Departed. Expired. Passed away. Out of my hair—I mean out of *his* misery." Weary of answering questions and knowing that this pseudo-tough guy Griffin was just playing pseudo-cop and had no real authority,

Timothy turned the tables and started asking him questions.

"When was the last time anyone unfamiliar to you entered Mercedes Ford's penthouse?" he challenged. "Have you reviewed all of the surveillance footage for the entire day and night of the tragedy in question? You must be personally embarrassed by having a suspicious death in your ultra-secure building!"

Ouch! That last one shredded Griffin like a ripsaw, and he angrily cocked his head toward the door. "It was an accident!" Griffin shouted as Timothy left.

But as hard as he tried, Timothy just couldn't let go of the idea that Jared's death wasn't what it appeared to be. His gut churned and wouldn't let him leave Jared's death in peace. Maybe it was the guilt for wishing Jared dead on so many occasions, or maybe he was just naturally curious; he was, after all, a creative writer, and this was as thick a story plot as any.

Riding the elevator to the penthouse, Timothy realized that the only people who could have gotten into the penthouse were residents or friends and, thus, had their biometric patterns extracted, or they were persons who were admitted by someone expecting them. It made sense that Jared's killer—if there was one—had to be someone with whom he was familiar or on the security staff's list of regular visitors. It wasn't rocket science, and he was suddenly rattled by the idea that he, too, might know the killer. And just maybe, if he'd followed the sound of the ringtone on Jared's phone that night, perhaps he would have interrupted the killing and ended up joining Jared in the afterlife. But he snapped out of this awful feeling when the elevator doors parted and saw Fabiola… and Brad!

That darling man couldn't stay away; he had to come over to make sure that Timothy was okay. And Timothy could certainly use Brad's brand of comfort right now. As thrilled as he was to see this marvelous man, he was also a bit jealous of Fabiola for being there alone when he arrived. Of course, he'd never have been permitted entrance to the penthouse if she hadn't vouched for him with her own biometrics, but nevertheless, Timothy wasn't wild about sharing him for even a brief period.

Fabiola picked up on Timothy's vibe of quasi-resentment. She excused herself and headed back into the condo, but not before giving Brad her best Polydent denture clean smile. Thankfully, Timothy's smile was a younger, Pearl Drops gleam, and Brad quickly turned his attention to him. *Sorry, Fabiola, but this is where I play the gay youth card!* Timothy thought.

Brad was everything Timothy had hoped he would be: totally concerned about his safety and well-being. He also believed Timothy that something nefarious had happened. He even suggested Timothy move out of the penthouse and stay with him until Jared's killer was caught. And boy-oh-boy, did that sound great. However, as far as Timothy was concerned, he still had a job, and that job required that he stay right where he was. But it was definitely great to have a strong and talented man to make him feel safe and wanted.

And when Brad kissed him goodbye at the elevator, it was a real kiss. Not one of those friendly pecks between friends or playmates, but a real knee-buckling, heart-racing, mind-bending incinerator! When Timothy finally came up for air, it occurred to him that if it weren't for this job, he would never have met Brad. And, if it weren't for Jared being dead, Brad wouldn't have a reason to be here right now. And if... Well, he stopped the barrage of questions and decided to just be grateful for the best kiss of his entire life.

* * *

Fabiola's sixth sense knew when the coast was clear, and after Brad left, she joined Timothy on the terrace for a glass of lemonade. Timothy told her about his gut feeling that Jared was murdered and that they might both know the killer. Fabiola confessed that she somewhat agreed, despite what the police and The Colton's security team thought. Timothy pulled up the contact list on his phone, and they began going through all the names, weighing each possibility for potential killers.

The early afternoon bled into early evening, and by the time they were down to the Z section of the list (which only contained one name: Zöe Zalinski), they were both still mystified—and in need of food and a glass of vino. Surprise, surprise! Fabiola actually prepared a cheese platter and opened a Pinot Noir. Yes, Timothy was totally impressed. More than that, he felt that they'd definitely turned a corner with each other. He guessed that sharing in the discovery of Jared's dead body in their home was their bonding moment. They were now friends.

Of all the people on the contact list, they only added two new names to their list of suspects. Fabiola said she'd heard that one of them, Walter Staples, a minor star in musical comedy, had written a letter to Muriel promising to "rip Jared's heart out of his puny good-for-nothing, skinny-ass body and feed it to subway rats," all because Jared had convinced Muriel to drop him as a client. It seems that Walter had become more famous for his backstage bad-boy behavior than his singing and acting on stage, and producers weren't taking a chance with him anymore. He wasn't even being considered for auditions. But, as Fabiola pointed out, that was months ago, and it was now common knowledge that

Walter had found Jesus, opened his own church, and left the theater altogether. Not exactly a good suspect for murder.

And then there was Marsha Bressler, the one-time critic's darling after her stunning debut in the musical *Cat Caller's Code of Conduct*. She, too, had made it public knowledge that the planet would be a better place without Jared Evans. She had openly commented that either Muriel Maynard was sleeping with him (rather far-fetched, Timothy thought) or that he knew where the agency's bodies were buried. (That sounded closer to reality.) Otherwise, she couldn't imagine why Muriel kept him on. However, Marsha had since gotten married and moved to California. So that was it for the new suspects. Perhaps they should have another look at their original list. Or perhaps it was all a figment of their imagination, and Jared had simply died in an unfortunate (for him) accident?

But those were the only people on Jared's list of acquaintances who might be interested in seeing him dead. "What about people we don't know?" Timothy said.

"Or maybe someone that Jared didn't know," Fabiola agreed.

"No, it had to be someone familiar to him; otherwise, they'd never get as far as the lobby, let alone the penthouse," Timothy said.

Fabiola was quiet for a long moment, considering that what Timothy had said was more than likely correct.

And then Timothy had a sudden and intriguing idea and snapped his fingers. "I know this sounds totally stupid," he said as Fabiola perked up and leaned forward to hear him out. "What if the killer was someone he knew but didn't know?"

"Riddle me this?" Fabiola said, sounding a bit annoyed.

"Jared worked in a business where six degrees of separation was practically invented," Timothy said. "It was even the name of a Broadway play. With social media and all that, we're probably known by tons of people we've never even heard of. They may even be friends, like Facebook friends."

Fabiola gave him a look that suggested she wasn't getting it but was willing to listen. She said, "I used to belong to that Face thing, but I kept getting faces from my past. I finally stopped. If I'd wanted to keep in touch with those losers from school, I would have contacted them sometime during the 20th century."

In that moment, Timothy picked up his phone and called Detective Sloane. He asked how much longer they'd have Jared's personal laptop computer. He lied that he needed it for work. To his surprise, Detective Sloane said they'd transferred all the required information onto another hard drive, and he could have it back any time. Timothy gave Fabiola a high five, and off he went to the police station.

\* \* \*

Timothy practically got the Uber driver arrested for speeding as he insisted he race back to The Colton. As Fabiola followed Timothy into the office, they were practically salivating, anticipating what they might find among Jared's emails and other files. Although Timothy wondered how anyone as busy as Jared was could find the time to post stuff on social media.

Still, he hoped that something might offer insight into his killer.

Of course, his email account was password-protected. Duh! They should have known. But apparently, Timothy was a good liar because when he called Detective Sloane again, the policeman totally believed that Timothy had permission to use the computer. Sloane looked up the password: **UrAnIdiOt**. Oh really? Even from the grave, Jared seemed to be harassing Timothy. But at least he was able to log in to the email account. And he wasn't surprised by how many new messages he hadn't been able to read. But he also didn't know what he was looking for regarding something that might bring light to the mystery of Jared's death.

Fabiola looked at the screen and shook her head. "It'll take you ages to get through all of this." However, as she looked over Timothy's shoulder, she suddenly gasped when she saw a subject titled Beverly's New Home.

"What the…?" Fabiola said, reaching for the keyboard and brushing Timothy's hands aside. She clicked on that message. As they both silently read the text, Fabiola filled the air with one curse word after another. Timothy didn't have a clue about why she was so upset. According to the message, Jared was following orders from Muriel to arrange for someone to be a resident at Glenwood Farms Retirement Village in rural Pennsylvania. Along with Fabiola's salty speech, Timothy noticed she was also blinking tears away.

Fabiola finally said, "Never have children!"

Confused, Timothy opted for the best response to this baffling statement and said, "It's wine time."

## Chapter Thirteen

Timothy brought the computer to the terrace and met Fabiola, who had already uncorked a bottle and filled two glasses with a Pinot Grigio.

"Drink up, Mister, 'cause I've got some crazy stuff to tell you," Fabiola said. From her tone, Timothy could tell that something momentous was about to be revealed. And after a few sips, Fabiola quietly said, "I'd like to reintroduce myself. My name is… Beverly. Maynard."

"I beg your pardon?" Timothy said, confusion coating his words.

Fabiola/Beverly rolled her eyes. "What do you think I just said, 'Beverly Hills? Mayonnaise'? I said, my name is Beverly. Beverly Maynard," she repeated. "Here's another kicker for you. I'm Muriel's mother."

Timothy nearly spat out his wine. Questions tumbled past his lips in a muddle. "Beverly? Muriel? Daughter? You're your daughter's housekeeper?" he said incredulously.

Fabiola looked at Timothy as if he were a complete chowderhead. "Seriously, Timothy, do I look like a Fabiola? Do I look like a housekeeper? Have you ever seen me so much as rinse out a wine glass? You're a smart guy. Where is your deductive reasoning?"

Although it took Timothy a moment to answer, all this woman was saying seemed plausible and now oh-so-obvious. How often had Timothy asked himself if the maid had ever learned to use a dust rag? She wandered around the penthouse as though she owned the place. "Then, who is Fabiola?" Timothy asked.

"The hell if I know," Fabiola/Beverly cracked. "Maybe someone in Guatemala." This person, now named Beverly, added, "I made her up. And I never said that I was the housekeeper. You made that assumption."

Indeed, Timothy had. When Jared told him, "The old bird isn't long for this world," he simply thought they were trying to find a way to fire the maid without it looking like ageism. "But you supported my impression when you said your name was Fabiola."

"It was the first name that popped into my head. You kept using the word 'fabulous.' Fabulous this. Fabulous that. You repeat yourself a lot."

"When you didn't pick up the shattered glass from the picture frame that first day, I thought there was something fishy," Timothy said.

"The truth is, Muriel's been trying to relocate me for a while," Fabiola, or rather Beverly, said. "Now it looks as though she's found a place. I'm resigned to it. No worries. No more shattered bottles against the bedroom wall. We never did get along that well, Muriel and me. And when I was forced to move in with her last year, it all quickly went very wrong."

For a split second, Timothy thought about what it would be like living with his own mother again. He couldn't do it. That's not to say that they didn't totally love each other despite his mother's lack of warmth and affection. They did. And in a pinch, they'd do anything to help the other. But they were entirely different people. Their politics alone would drive one to kill the other, not to mention their completely contrasting views on so many social issues. Timothy's mom didn't have a single opinion that wasn't parroted from what her friends thought. Timothy thought he might be the same way, but he rationalized that at least his friends had broader points of view. So, he could understand why Muriel and Beverly might not get on if they lived together.

"Muriel decided that since Mercedes is never here, this would be a great holding pen for me," Beverly said.

"Holding pen?"

"Those were her exact words. But it's certainly a beautiful, gilded pen," Beverly said. "No complaints here. Although it wasn't in your job description, and you were never told, the reason you're required to live here is to keep an eye on me. To make sure I didn't fall—or die and stink up the place. That's what I meant when I said you were a spy.

"Until you came along, it was lonely here," Beverly continued. "I knew that the assistants before you wouldn't last long, so I never made any attempt to make friends with them. I tried to do the same with you, but you won me over. I suppose finding dead people lying around the house will do that."

They both chuckled in agreement. It's true that calamities bring people together. Still, Timothy liked to think that he and Fabiola—er, Beverly—were growing on each other without a corpse to cement the deal. He said as much, and Beverly actually put a hand on his.

"I may be an old gal," Beverly sighed, "but I still have my dignity. And I certainly don't want to be a burden to anyone or be anywhere I'm not wanted. I'm not interested in charity. But my lovely daughter could have at least given me a few options. I wish I had input on where I'd be deposited for my final years. Is that too much to ask?"

"Of course not!" Timothy said. "And Jared should have kept you in the loop, too."

"He was just following orders, I guess," Beverly said.

"Still, knowing him as I did, even if only for a short while, I suspect he took pleasure in planning to make your life miserable," Timothy said.

Beverly was suddenly rueful. She whispered, "I've had a pretty good life. At least it lasted longer than Jared's. You know, he actually had a soft side to him. You won't believe this, but when it rained especially hard, he would buy a bunch of umbrellas at the 99 Cents Store and hand them out to the homeless people he passed on the street. It's a pity that hardly anyone will miss him. Not that I will either."

Timothy reached out his hands and cupped Fabiola's in his. He squeezed gently and told her that he would certainly miss her. He added that he hoped she'd be around for a very long time, even though they both knew that was highly unlikely. Timothy also suggested that Beverly follow her own advice about standing up for oneself and let Muriel understand how strongly she felt about being in on any decision about her future living accommodations.

But Beverly wasn't very optimistic about that. "No," she reasoned, "Muriel is incredibly headstrong, which is how she became so successful. Once she makes up her mind about anything, there's no changing it. She's a smart cookie but has very little empathy. Rather sad, I think. What she should have had a long time ago is a boyfriend. I wonder if she's ever even had sex. Some men like a dominatrix."

"The thing that's especially sad," Timothy said, "is that she doesn't value her mother." Of course, Timothy knew that there were always multiple sides to a story, and he'd experienced firsthand that Beverly wasn't always a picnic in Central Park either. But this wasn't the time or place for judgment. All he cared about was that Beverly was obviously in emotional pain. The poor woman was afraid of her future.

Her life was not her own, and she had no idea where she'd soon be living.

"Let's go online and look at that Glenwood Farms retirement place," Timothy suggested. "Maybe it's not so bad."

In a moment, they were at the retirement home's website. Timothy's first response was that, for an assisted living facility, it actually looked like a decent place to live. Of course, the photos of smiling, smartly-dressed seniors in newly coiffed gray hairstyles, wandering the bucolic setting, playing golf, dining in a lovely on-site restaurant, and lounging in professionally decorated apartment units were just PR. They certainly wouldn't show the actual residents, who were probably wearing moth-eaten bathrobes, shuffling in slippers down drab-colored corridors, or parked in wheelchairs and connected to oxygen tanks. And a website can't produce the stinky smells of medicines, leaking body fluids, and decaying human flesh. But it didn't look like a terrible location to spend until one's passport to Earth expired. Beverly agreed, although she said she would miss the sounds and excitement of the city.

They were still contemplating a diminished life on a seniors-only campus when they heard the sound of an incoming email message. "Bry@seemail.com," Timothy read the sender's name and looked to Beverly for an agreement that it was okay to open Jared's mail. He clicked on the message, and they were instantly distracted from Beverly's problems by the subject line: DEADLY SECRETS?

"What the...?" Timothy said and read the text aloud:

"Joe, if you had anything to do with Jared's death, I'll sadly but understandably watch as you fry in hell."
—Bryony."

Timothy and Beverly glanced at each other. "Who's Joe?" Beverly asked.

"Who's Bryony?" Timothy countered. "And why is Jared getting their emails?"

"And why would someone message a dead man and tell him they suspected who killed him?"

Timothy noticed something else that was weird. "It wasn't necessarily meant to go to Jared. It's addressed to Bwaybound@mmmail.org. Jared's email is JVE@mmmail.org. And look… next to his name… it says BCC: blind carbon copy. It was sent to him confidentially."

"Or inadvertently. You, of all people, know about stupid mistakes that can happen with sending emails to the wrong person," Beverly sniggered.

"Maybe it wasn't a mistake Timothy said. "Maybe this Bryony didn't want Bwaybound to know that Jared was included on the recipient list. But you're right. She suggests that this Joe character had something to do with it. It wouldn't make sense to send it to Jared."

Timothy and Beverly sat for a long moment, their brains churning with theories. "Unless… It could be a clue," Beverly suggested. "Bryony might be cryptically sending a message to whoever might be reading Jared's email, hinting that someone named Joe is responsible for his death."

Timothy nodded in agreement that that was a very definite possibility; perhaps Bryony was providing a tip-off to Jared's killer. But his thoughts were taking a different path. "Is it too far-fetched to imagine that the message maybe wasn't meant for either Jared or the police?" he asked. "Maybe there wasn't a covert agenda, and the email that's addressed to Bwaybound is, for whatever reason, automatically forwarded to Jared?"

Beverly made a face that suggested she wasn't necessarily

buying that idea, but anything was possible. "How do you figure?"

Timothy shook his head in uncertainty and wondered if there was any value to an idea that had popped into his head. "Jared used to monitor my emails, right? What if Bwaybound—who apparently works in Muriel's office because they used Muriel Management's mmmail domain name—was someone Jared didn't trust, so he got access to their emails? Or maybe Bwaybound is someone who no longer works at the company, and Jared just wanted to collect any stray messages that might still be coming to that address. I mean, Jared wouldn't risk missing something important that might otherwise be floating around."

Timothy started considering the Bwaybound email address. He concentrated on the word Bwaybound. "Bway," he said, "maybe a contraction for Broadway? Broadway-bound?"

Beverly was beginning to show a little excitement as if they were close to answering the mystery title in a game of Charades.

"Someone working in the theater," Timothy suggested.

"That would be virtually everyone in Muriel's circle," Beverly reminded.

"Maybe a handle for someone who loves Broadway. A fan. Someone with Broadway aspirations. Someone like…" Timothy snapped his fingers and said, "Remember the afternoon I had to stop at La Maison Eleganté to pick up something from that Max guy when I was going to the *Blind Trust* set? There was someone at the bar. Sandy. He'd been fired by Jared that morning. He talked a lot of nonsense about being destined to be a Broadway legend but had done something seriously wrong, and Jared fired him. Bway bound!"

"But this is Jared's laptop. How could…? Beverly couldn't admit that she totally failed to understand anything beyond the basics of 21st-century technology.

"It's easy-breezy to go into a computer's settings and forward emails to another device and email account," Timothy said. "Let me try something." He picked up his cell phone and typed a test message to Bwaybound@mmmail.org. The very moment after he pressed Send, the email popped up in Jared's Inbox.

Then, Timothy had what he thought was another great idea. "Whoever used Bwaybound as a username at Muriel's office may have also used the same address at a private account. Perhaps Gmail or, Yahoo or AOL. He typed another message to Bwaybound@gmail.com. "Hope you're feeling better and have found another job. Wishing you the best. Keep in touch as you become a star," he wrote. Timothy looked at Beverly. "Just a hunch, he said. Then he pushed Send. And waited. And waited. And…

Heck, he didn't even know if this was a working email address, although his message wasn't bounced back as undeliverable. Rather than wait around indefinitely, he decided the best thing for him to do was to just get on with life and work assignments. If only it were that easy! Timothy was the farthest thing from lazy, but he sometimes put off doing the necessary chores in favor of more fun things—in this case, it was going through Jared's email messages. So that's what he did.

Then, another idea popped into his head, and he entered the name Joe into the email search field. Bingo! There was a long thread of messages to and from Joe@seemail.com and Bry@seemail.com, with Bwaybound BCC'd on all of them. It seemed they had all been forwarded to Jared. They'd hit the jackpot, and Timothy and Beverly started eagerly devouring the entire thread of written conversation, which went back several months.

They thought it was curious that the first email from Bryony to Mercedes was generically addressed in care of Muriel Maynard Management. The correspondence between Bry@seemail and Joe@seemail started out innocently enough. In the first message, Bryony introduced herself as a fan of Mercedes. She wrote about her love and admiration for the star and her animal rights activism. She wanted to be an actress too and added that she thought Mercedes had made an excellent choice of a husband. Bryony wrote:

> "I saw a picture of you and Sage in *FanFoto*. He's a hottie. If (or when) he decides to leave you, please point him in my direction."

The message was followed by a line of laughing emojis.

That last sentence sounded awfully familiar to Timothy. He felt vaguely sure that he'd read it somewhere else recently. But never mind; this Bryony person had also attached a picture of herself, and when Timothy clicked on the image, he nodded with approval. She had the right looks to be in movies, that's for sure. But again, Timothy had to ask himself, who are these nut jobs who write such inappropriate things to this wonderful star? Or, for that matter, to anyone they didn't personally know?

But it was Joe's response to Bryony that especially bothered Timothy. Joe claimed to work directly for Mercedes, although his texts were sent from a seemail domain email account rather than Muriel's mmmail domain. To make things even weirder, Joe had written that the picture Bryony had attached was incredibly sexy and asked for more. He said he'd pass them on to Mercedes' husband Sage, who "was always doing his best to help young talent break into modeling or acting."

"So inappropriate!" Timothy huffed.

The volley of subsequent emails ended in a downright steamy crescendo of Joe suggesting that since he and Bryony had so much in common, they should meet at a hotel to become better acquainted.

The excitement in each message from Bryony was palpable. She was apparently falling in love with her pen pal, Joe. And yes, she would keep it all a secret because she totally understood the nature of Mercedes' celebrity and how anyone who worked for such a big star—as Joe claimed he did—had to maintain rigorous moral ethics. At least in public.

"OMG! If Jared had read these messages, this Joe guy would be sacked instantly," Timothy said. "Jared would never have tolerated this behavior from anyone at Muriel Maynard Management. Remember how he reacted to my dumb but innocent-by-comparison email boo-boos?" And then Timothy discovered that Jared had indeed obviously found out about the messages because the last one was addressed directly to Joe@seemail.com. It said:

> "Joe. I know who you are. You're really the big, stupid, idiot blockhead that everyone thinks you are. You've been hitting Replay All on your emails to your "pen pal" Bry@seemail, so they've all gone to my former assistant, who forwarded that original message to you in the first place, and now I have the entire thread in my files. Someone very near to you will be very interested when I show them to her. That dandy little document called a "prenup" will cause you more pain than anything I personally could do to you. Many of us can't wait to see you suffer."

By now, Beverly was weary of all the drama and decided to return to reading one of her novels. But Timothy was too invested in playing Peeping Tom. Not only did it provide hours of intrigue and speculation about the relationship between Joe and Bryony, but an equal amount of amusement (loonies asking for tickets to the Academy Awards, another asking if he could stay in Mercedes' guest room, one even asking if Mercedes would donate one of her Oscars to a local theatre for a raffle contest).

Also in the mix was a startling message from Jared to that British fan, Fiona Carter. Timothy instantly recalled who that was. How could he forget after that terrible incident in which he accidentally sent that mean-spirited email? Fiona Carter was the one who believed that she was Mercedes' long-lost daughter.

## Chapter Fourteen

The message to Fiona Carter was from Jared's personal email address and sent to FCarter@mymail.co.uk. It read:

> Dear Ms. Carter. There appears to be a serious miscommunication between the email account Bwaybound@mmmail.org and your email address. Please ignore all previous correspondence that you have received from that address. We hope this hasn't caused you any inconvenience.
>
> Sincerely,
> Jared Evans

Well, apparently, there was a whole lot of inconvenience because Fiona Carter's response was a doozy! She wrote:

> Dear Mr. Evans. My relationship with Mercedes Ford is hardly anything you need to concern yourself with. She's my mum, and she's sending me money any day now to fly me to America for our reunion. Any further attempt by you to invade my privacy will make you quite sorry.

In Timothy's opinion, Jared should have just left well enough alone and not continued to poke at a hornet's nest. But Jared was good at poking. He replied:

Dear Ms. Carter. I'm sorry to have to contact you again, but please know that the person you have been corresponding with is not Mercedes Ford. Therefore, please cease and desist from future communications. Thank you.

And that's when the hornets swarmed. Fiona's subsequent stinging emails became more and more hostile. She decried that Jared was attempting to cut her off from Mercedes Ford—her "Mum." She insisted that she and Mercedes had legitimate email conversations in which they had determined they were related.

Nothing would dissuade Fiona Carter from what she understood to be both her destiny and the truth. She vowed to reconnect with her loving mother, no matter what. The final email, which was received two days before Jared died, flatly stated:

Mr. Evans. I know who you are. I know where you work. I will not allow you or anybody to stand in the way of me and my mum. You will soon be very sorry that you ever wrote so unkindly to me!

"Jared's killer!" Timothy stated matter-of-factly and excitedly called out to Beverly and summoned her back to the office. He asked her to read the messages between Fiona Carter and Jared.

"Threatening messages backed up with action," Timothy exclaimed. "She's the one!"

Beverly wasn't convinced. "We were both here that day," she pointed out what Timothy knew but didn't want to hear. "There weren't any unusual visitors. Plus," she added, "there's no way on earth this sick-o from England—even if she somehow knew Mercedes' New York address—would have any idea that Jared would be here and available for easy execution."

Timothy couldn't stand it when people were logical—or at least more logical than he was. Although he was 99% sure that Beverly was right, he couldn't be entirely certain. He thought it was too much of a coincidence that this Fiona Carter character had threatened Jared only two days before his death. Perhaps she only pretended to live in England. What if she actually lived right here in the city? Some rabid fans know everything about their celebrity of choice, including where they live, what they eat for breakfast, and who does their weekly mani-pedis.

But it sure looked like Timothy was back to square one. Or square two, depending on whether or not he was correct about Sandy's Gmail address. Beverly shook her head and suggested they call it a day. "We both need our beauty sleep," she said. Timothy blew her a kiss and went up the stairs to his room.

But Timothy couldn't sleep. Just knowing that a person with whom he'd personally corresponded could be a murderer made his skin crawl. As he lay in bed, he kept trying to remember what totally inappropriate words he'd written to Fiona Carter in that first email message he'd sent. He'd only get rest if he reviewed the text. He quietly returned to the office.

When Timothy retrieved the old email message, he once again felt terrible about how he'd inadvertently treated Fiona Carter. He hadn't intended to press the Send key that day. Now, he thought that perhaps his behavior was what sent the Brit over the edge and that he might be peripherally responsible for Jared's death. He'd made it appear that his message had come directly from Mercedes, the woman Fiona believed to be her flesh and blood. That was totally inexcusable on Timothy's part, and it had come back to bite him. But if someone was corresponding with Fiona Carter and pretending to be Mercedes or someone working for her, that was downright despicable, too.

Timothy left the office and wandered into the living room. He opened the tall glass doors and stepped into the cool night air. He sat down on a patio chair and stared into the night sky. The impact of what he'd done by merely trying to be funny had possibly sent a maniac over the edge of sanity and resulted in someone's death. He vowed to himself that he would never again be flippant. Why, he asked himself, did it amuse him to make light of a serious situation that affected others' lives? At that moment, Timothy considered himself a total loser, just as Jared had said he was. He shook his head, and for a split second, Timothy thought, I could climb over the terrace wall, and no one would really miss me. Well, he hoped that Brad would, but they actually hardly knew each other, and Brad would quickly forget him. In fact, he probably wouldn't even admit to knowing someone so unstable as to take such a drastic and final action.

"I can't sleep either." Beverly's voice came from behind. "What's on your mind?"

"That my stupidity may have been the cause of Jared's death."

"Nah, that fan was crazy to begin with. And we don't know for sure that Jared was killed. He might have had an accident like everyone thinks." Beverly tried to assure him that even though Timothy's original message to Fiona Carter had been totally irresponsible, she was certain it had not been a factor in Jared's murder. But she agreed that Timothy should be more careful with his words. "You know what they say about the pen being mightier than the sword."

***

Although it had only been about eight hours since Timothy had sent that message to Bwaybound the night before, and to a Gmail address that may not have even been valid, his impatience was obvious. Maybe Bwaybound wasn't Sandy. Or that Sandy wasn't tethered to his phone and hadn't seen the text. Timothy was eager to get on with his investigation, so it was time for a call to the former agency employee. The best thing that Jared ever did for Timothy was to merge all of his contacts to his phone, and Sandy Blair's number was instantly available.

When 8:00 arrived, Timothy sat on his bedside and touched the Contacts icon on the phone. He scrolled down to Sandy's name and made the call. Of course, Timothy didn't expect him to answer at this relatively early hour. Plus, since Timothy wasn't in Sandy's own Contacts when his number came up on his caller ID, there'd be no accompanying name, so he might think it was from a telemarketer or bill collector. Timothy was actually happy that Sandy didn't answer because it gave him an opportunity to leave a voice message explaining, without too much pressure, why he was calling in the first place. He hoped Sandy wouldn't recognize his voice as he casually fibbed and said he was the office's new hire and hadn't had any training. And, since Sandy had the job before, he was hoping he could answer a few questions about how to deal with certain personalities in the office, such as Muriel. Timothy even managed to sound as if he were weeping from all the anxiety and pressure that he was under at work. Which wasn't really much of an acting stretch.

After Timothy ended the call, satisfied that he sounded

like an overworked and underpaid staffer at Muriel Maynard Management who just needed a wee bit of counseling, he hopped into the shower. However, he kept the phone close by on the vanity just in case Sandy called back. And naturally, darn it all, while his hair was plastered with shampoo chemical suds and his body dripping with lather from his favorite jellybean-scented bath wash, that's when the phone rang. Timothy didn't have time to rinse off, so he opened the glass shower door and stepped onto the bathmat, water was flying everywhere. But he managed to pick up the call by the fourth ring. It was indeed Sandy. He'd fallen for Timothy's little boy lost ruse and wanted to reach out to dish the dirt about all the stuff that he knew went on at the office.

Timothy grabbed the towel he'd hung on the hook beside the shower and gingerly walked into the bedroom, careful not to let his wet feet slip on the travertine floor. He sat his wet butt on the edge of the bed and continued acting like he needed guidance from someone who knew all of the ins and outs of the job. After an opening statement about how much more work there was than initially agreed upon, how he didn't understand why he had to live in Mercedes' penthouse, and how he'd been bullied by Jared before he died, he asked, "Mind if I ask why you left?"

Sandy gave a good impression of someone who had no idea Jared was dead. He may have been a better actor than Timothy gave him credit for. And Timothy didn't blame Sandy for lying that he was offered a better position elsewhere, instead of the humiliating truth that he was fired. That probably would have been Timothy's own response too. Timothy pressed on and said that although he'd only known Jared for about a week, he was happy he wasn't his boss anymore. "Sometimes the best boss is a dead boss," he said. "I could never do anything right."

By now, Sandy seemed totally at ease with Timothy. He agreed with Timothy's assessment of Jared and added, "I'm not sorry he's dead, either. He had it out for me from the first day I started working there. And Muriel just let him do whatever he wanted. If she only knew what that little troll was up to, spying on me and my work…" Then it seemed that Sandy had suddenly become aware of his gossip and reigned himself in.

Timothy pretended to know exactly what he was talking about and told him about Jared monitoring his emails. He found himself suggesting that he, too, had already amassed a list of infractions that would have gotten Jared in trouble with Muriel. "The dude is dead, but he left a lot of unfinished business," Timothy added.

They continued chatting like old chums, and Sandy slipped back into a gossiping mood about all the important celebrities he'd interacted with when he was sent out to do errands for clients, especially the trips to wherever Mercedes was working. Timothy was surprised to find that Sandy had managed three trips to film locations during the 6 months he was employed by Muriel Maynard Management.

Timothy lied that he was supposed to visit the set of *Blind Trust* next week and asked what advice he could give for dealing with Mercedes. And Sandy walked right into his trap.

"Not to worry about Mercedes," Sandy said. "She's swell. But keep your distance from her husband, Sage. Don't let him fool you. Yeah, Sage is super sexy and all that, and he'll act like your bestie. But it's all a way for him to gain power over you. And when you give in to temptation, he has total control. Just ask Mercedes."

"Control over Mercedes Ford?" Timothy said. "She's a strong independent woman. How could anyone control her?"

"You know how it is," Sandy continued. "When you look

as amazing as he does, and you're as old as she is, well, you'll sorta do anything to keep your man around. Or at least ignore a lot of stuff. Sex stuff, even. He's definitely scorching hot. You'll see."

Timothy was eager for as much information as possible but was afraid that he might go too far. Still, he hedged his bet. "Are you suggesting that Mercedes ignores that Sage sees other women?" he asked.

Sandy made a slight laugh that sounded like a cough and said, "… and men too. Mercedes is nobody's fool. And Sage is a lizard of the lowest order. I know someone in the office who actually had a thing with him. A huge mistake, for sure. But the guy said he couldn't control himself. He was hypnotized. Sage does actually have it all if you know what I mean. Plus, the guy said it was fun to be with someone who had kissed a movie star. But I can't say anything more."

Although Timothy was appalled that Sage apparently cheated on Mercedes, he had to confess to himself that he actually understood why anyone could be seduced by him. Timothy conceded that if he hadn't been distracted by his burgeoning love for Brad, he, too, might have gone down the wrong path the day they met. Sometimes, it's impossible to keep it zipped up, he told himself, quoting an old friend.

Then Sandy returned to the subject of work. "But the email stuff can get kinda dull," he said. "So many losers who don't have interesting lives of their own. You have to get creative."

"Any suggestions?" Timothy asked, genuinely interested in what Sandy meant by getting "creative."

"You'll figure it out," Sandy said. "Just don't get caught the way I did. It's not a good idea to start corresponding long-term with these loonies. They just want more and more of your time, and you can get in so deep that it's almost impossible to stop without causing an international incident. Whatever you do, never send a message that implies it's actually coming from Mercedes. You won't last a day."

Timothy was silent for a long moment, and Sandy must have intuited his thoughts because he suddenly interjected, "Never mind. Just don't let stupidity get in the way of the emails you write on behalf of the overrated Mercedes Ford."

*Overrated Mercedes Ford?* That was the wrong thing to say to Timothy about the movie star he loved best. Timothy wasn't about to let this nobody trash-talk the most wonderful celebrity on the planet! Thankfully, Timothy was able to control his voice so that he didn't offer a clue that he suddenly detested Sandy. Instead, Timothy brought the conversation back around to the subject of answering emails from fans. Then, he tried ever-so-subtly to work in his curiosity about Joe, Bryony, and Fiona Carter in England. "My gosh," he said, "there are so many emails from crazy fans. What's up with the one who thinks she's Mercedes' daughter?"

Suddenly, other than heavy breathing, there was total silence on the other end of the line. After a long moment, Timothy asked, "Still with me?"

"Right. Yeah," Sandy said. "I got distracted. Sorry, what were you saying?"

"I was trying to figure out what to do about the fan who thinks she's related to Mercedes and is coming all the way from England to meet her. Did Jared know about this? Does Mercedes know? What do I do?"

In a manner that made Timothy realize he'd definitely stepped over the line, Sandy hurriedly said, "Yeah, she's okay. Mercedes, I mean. No worries. I'm sure that Jared took care of things with the Brit. Listen, I gotta go. Good luck with the job." And then he hung up.

"Well, that was a bust," Timothy said aloud. But then it dawned on him that he'd actually inched forward into Jared's mysterious death. First, he now knew that Sage was unfaithful to Mercedes, and he'd had a thing with someone in the office—probably that Joe guy—and maybe other assistants. Maybe that's why so many didn't last all that long on the job. Of course, he was so good-looking that Timothy wasn't surprised he was a schmuck. But Sandy said something interesting: Jared had "taken care of things."

Timothy quickly wrapped the towel around his waist and grabbed Jared's laptop, which he'd stopped keeping in the safe. With his hair still a wet, sudsy mess, he raced to the terrace where he knew Beverly would be reading. "I think we have another breakthrough!" he announced and sat down beside her.

## Chapter Fifteen

With the summer air drying his bare chest and arms, Timothy was almost hyperventilating as he told Beverly what he'd learned from Sandy about the Brit, Fiona Carter—with her insane ideas about Mercedes Ford being her "Mum." However, he withheld the big news bulletin about Sage's infidelity.

Beverly divided her attention between Timothy's milky-white skin, the feather dusting of dark hair on his chest, and his enthusiastic announcement.

"She had a major motive, to meet Mercedes in person, but Jared got in the way and rejected her and the idea of her family ties," Timothy panted. "But I'm also wondering if maybe Sandy did the deed. He totally hated Jared for firing him. If security wasn't aware that he'd been booted out, he maybe could have gained access to the penthouse because they wouldn't have deactivated his biometrics ID."

However, Timothy's excitement about possibly linking Sandy to Jared's death was short-lived. The telephone rang, and it was Muriel. She wanted Timothy down at the office immediately. "Now what?" he said to Beverly as he hung up the phone.

"Maybe she remembered that she forgot to fire you," Beverly said. "By the way... totally inappropriate... but you're cute naked."

\* \* \*

In the offices of Muriel Maynard Management, Lyle, the receptionist, who had expressed so much remorse about the shameful way he'd addressed Jared's death, escorted Timothy down to Boss Lady's office. On the way, he tried to be nice by warning that Muriel was not in a playful mood. "She's already made one of the other junior managers cry," he said and nodded toward a guy wiping his eyes on his shirtsleeve. "He'll be gone soon," he said with authority.

"Wish me luck," Timothy said when they arrived at Muriel's door. Timothy knocked.

"What?" Muriel snapped.

Timothy opened the door and stepped inside her office. The meeting was over in only a few minutes. Timothy was told in no uncertain terms that he'd be out on the street if he made one more misstep. "I've lost my right-hand assistant. I'm left with a bunch of incompetents!" Muriel screamed at him. "If you don't have enough work to keep you busy, I can always find plenty more!"

Timothy wasn't entirely sure what he had done wrong this time and was upset by Muriel's vitriol. He hated it when people yelled at him. It made him feel stupid and degraded. When Jared was alive, Muriel was, if not exactly a pussycat, at least almost oblivious to Timothy. It occurred to him that one of Jared's indispensable jobs was to play bad cop to Muriel's good cop. Muriel could appear to be a friend while instructing Jared to drag a razor across someone's jugular. Timothy knew the routine. He saw it happen all the time at The Chili Exchange. Another reason he wanted to become a rich and famous author was so he could just stay home and not have a boss making his life miserable. He'd only have to report to an editor. Of course, in his imagination, Brad would be by his side to ease any and all unpleasantries.

Being the little toady that he can be, Timothy crossed his heart and hoped to die and would stick a needle in his eye rather than ever do anything to cause Muriel to be upset with him again.

Muriel harrumphed, then told him to get lost.

Well, how was that for being just a tad immature? When someone told Timothy to get lost, he generally did as they suggested. However, he had something more than just his job to worry about now. He had information about what he strongly felt was a murder, and he was determined to keep investigating until he could go to the police with definitive proof of who the killer was. He may have intensely disliked Jared, just like almost everyone else, but nobody deserves to be a dead murdered body and not have the wrong-doer brought to justice. And now that Timothy realized what Muriel was really like, he had some (though still very little, to be honest) sympathy for Jared. Had he known this before, he may have been less unkind in his thoughts and feelings towards the guy. To assuage his guilt, Timothy resolved to pursue his suspicions and find the killer.

Timothy returned home, and when he told Beverly what Muriel had said, Beverly just shook her head. "She was never a sweet little girl, but when she got to high school, the nightmare really began. Perhaps she turned out this way because her miserable, no-good, but oh-so-sexy daddy left us early on. I know she hated that we were so broke that I had to work three jobs just to keep food on the table and lights on in the apartment. She resented not having any money and was embarrassed at school by her lack of fashionable clothes. She always said that one day she'd be rich. She's done a pretty good job of that. At least I know that she can afford to keep me in a decent place when she sticks me at Glenwood Farms."

Timothy felt sorry for Beverly, who, he suspected, considered herself a failure as a mother. And now her daughter was exercising her authority by sending her to a senior living community and essentially throwing away the key. It was heartbreaking. Timothy hoped that nothing like that would ever happen to him.

Exhausted from his run-in with Muriel, Timothy decided to take his mind off the experience by engrossing himself in a good book. He asked Beverly if he could borrow one of hers.

"Have you read *Murder Is Murder*?" Beverly asked. "It's on my nightstand."

As Timothy walked into Beverly's room, he saw that the bed was neatly made, and the vanity was tidy. The walls were still stained from the shattered perfume atomizers—and maybe if he squinted just right, he could see the *Madonna and Child* in the splatter—but otherwise, the place was in shipshape. Even the books on the nightstand were neatly stacked. He looked at the titles, searching for the one recommended, but it wasn't there. He looked around the room and saw several other paperbacks on a chair next to the floor-to-ceiling windows. There it was. *Murder Is Murder*, by Ben Tyler. As he picked it up, he noticed it had been on top of a sheaf of papers that looked like printouts of emails. He looked closer; indeed, they were correspondence between Beverly and Mercedes Ford. Of course, they would be acquainted since Beverly's daughter represented Mercedes, but Beverly never hinted at a close relationship. He guessed that Beverly had no reason to brag about being a friend of the greatest star on the planet.

Timothy can be really nosey at times. Even though he understood that personal correspondence is private, he was intrigued by the subject line SAGE/JARED. He had to read further. There was no salutation and only one line of text:

> You take care of Jared, and I'll take care of Sage. – MF

Take care of Jared? Take care of Sage? Take care of them, how and why? Timothy thought as he looked around to make sure that Beverly hadn't come looking for him. He was baffled. What could that cryptic message mean? "Take care" could be anything from selecting Christmas presents to offering back massages and, let's face it, up to and including—murder. Could Mercedes have meant that Beverly should kill Jared and that Mercedes would do the same to her husband? No! Impossible! That was the stupidest thing Timothy could ever have imagined. He would not allow himself to even consider such a ridiculous thought. It was absurd! Beverly was not a murderer. And definitely, neither was the most renowned actress in the universe! Never! Ever!

Timothy had to read more. The subject line on the next message said, THE END? The short text of that was:

> It's not his deceit that hurts me as much as he thinks I'm blind and stupid. Someone's about to have a very short existence. – MF

Timothy couldn't risk being gone any longer, so he grabbed the book and wandered back to the terrace. "Thanks," he said to Beverly and sat down to read. Or pretend to read. He opened the book and turned to page one of Chapter One. But he couldn't concentrate on a make-believe murder mystery when he had a real one to think about. Now, there was no doubt in Timothy's mind that Jared had been murdered. There he was, sitting on Mercedes Ford's

New York penthouse terrace with a woman who had lied about her name and who she really was. Heck, Timothy never even saw her interact with Muriel Maynard, the woman she claimed was her daughter. Even on the night of the big party, the two had no apparent connection. And, although she hadn't exactly fibbed about being a friend of Mercedes, she was guilty by omission. And yet, Beverly knew Mercedes well enough to have an ongoing email correspondence with her.

Timothy turned page after page of the book without reading a word. Was he flipping too quickly? If so, could Beverly tell? If she thought Timothy wasn't really reading, might she become suspicious? Timothy said to himself that he shouldn't even entertain such a really silly idea that Beverly could be involved in Jared's death. Beverly was an old lady. She didn't have the strength to push a floor mop, let alone shove Jared's body against the safe with as much force as it would have taken to kill him. Well, she did know about the secret room. And…

Suddenly, Timothy jumped to another thought, a more logical one. Beverly might not have been the killer, but she may have aided and abetted! What if she had allowed the killer into the penthouse? She had claimed to be napping during the time of Jared's death, but she could have been lying about that too; she may have woken up and let the killer in. Now Timothy was back to the totally terrible thought that Beverly might be somehow involved. And that's when he started to freak out.

Timothy absolutely could not let on that he was having any such crazy ideas. Again, he thought, no way Beverly is involved! But he was desperate to go back to Beverly's room and read the other emails to confirm or reject his suspicion. He was kicking himself for not taking photos of the emails on his phone—James Bond would have never missed such an obvious opportunity! However, as long as Beverly was conscious, he couldn't take that chance. And Beverly never left the penthouse. Still, Timothy had to figure out a way to distract her long enough to get back to her room. But what could he do? Perhaps if he plied her with enough wine, Beverly would get sleepy and take a nap. But he knew Beverly never liked to imbibe before 6:00.

Timothy thought maybe he could say that his bathroom toilet wasn't working and ask to use Beverly's. He could lock himself in her room with a bit of privacy. But there were five other bathrooms in the place. He could use any of those. At that point, Timothy wished he were a better liar. Or at least better at coming up with plausible stories. No wonder his book manuscript wasn't attracting an agent. He was a terrible teller of tales! All the agents and editors were right! With that tragic thought in mind, Timothy put down the book he wasn't reading and blurted out, "I know it's wrong, but I read your emails!"

Beverly looked up from her book and gave him a quizzical stare.

"I'm so sorry," Timothy begged. "I was looking for this book and saw a couple of messages between you and Mercedes. I know it was wrong, but I couldn't help myself. Do you know who killed Jared? Did you have a hand in his death?"

"That's a really rotten thing to say to me!" Beverly sneered. "Kill Jared? Kill anyone? How could you even think that?"

Of course, in that very instant, Timothy knew Beverly was right. "I know. I know!" he tried to apologize. "But the two messages suggested…"

"Go get them," Beverly barked. "Bring back the entire stack! There should be half a dozen. Go on, you little sneak!"

Oh, shoot. Timothy had made Beverly angry. And now that he'd blurted out the accusation, Timothy knew he was completely wrong. A part of Timothy wanted to just apologize and say that no, he didn't need to read the other messages, but the other side of him thought, "Darn right, I want to read those emails." The reading/snooping side won. He got up and headed straight for Beverly's room.

When he returned, Beverly had uncorked a bottle of wine and filled two glasses. "It's way too early, but I need fortitude," she said. "Read the damn emails!"

Timothy finished and looked up at Beverly with a sheepish grin. "You're on the good side."

Beverly put down her wine glass and let out a deep sigh. "It's not fun spying on your own daughter's employees," she said. "But since Muriel was incapable of keeping her eyes on Jared, I had to play double agent."

"What did Mercedes mean by 'Take care of Jared?'"

"For some bizarre reason, she liked Jared," Beverly said. "She saw a lot of potential in him. Of course, Jared was always on his best behavior around her. She knew that and wanted me to watch him for her."

"And Sage?" Timothy said. "How was she going to 'take care' of him?"

"Let's just say she's now seeing Sage in a different light."

# Chapter Sixteen

Timothy thought his job had been overwhelming when Jared was alive, but now he had the additional enormous weight on his shoulders of figuring out who killed his boss and proving it to the disbelieving police. Nobody seemed to care that Jared was dead, perhaps except for Mercedes, and certainly, nobody believed his demise was anything but an accident. But Timothy's guilt about his less-than-charitable thoughts about Jared when he was alive, meant he had to find out the truth. And now he had several suspects with motives. Did they also have the opportunity to kill Jared? It was time to check alibis. But he couldn't do this alone.

In addition to Beverly, whom Timothy now considered beyond suspicion, there were only two people on the planet he trusted and who wouldn't think he was a total idiot for pursuing an investigation: Ted, the ex-paramour (whom Timothy briefly suspected but quickly dismissed as he had neither the disposition nor motive) and Brad (the hopefully) new paramour. With his penchant for solving crosswords and composing intricate poems like sonnets and villanelles, Ted certainly had the analytical brains to help. But Brad was the one who could probably more clearly understand Timothy's personal commitment to the project. Both men, Timothy was sure, would have been happy to help. But Timothy didn't want to be beholden to Ted and risk having him think their relationship could be revived. However, he did want to draw

Brad closer into his life. So, of course, the cry for help went where? To sexy Brad, of course.

They chatted on the phone for a few minutes about a handwritten note Brad received from Virginia La Paloma, thanking him for being her savior and accompanist when she sang at the *Infectious chronicosis* evening. Brad read the text to Timothy, and when he got to the part where she suggested "thank you drinks" at the Carlisle Hotel the next time she was in Manhattan, Timothy made a mental note to make sure he kept an eye on the diva's website and monitored her tour dates—to make certain Brad was unavailable when New York was on her schedule. Finally, Timothy got around to suggesting dinner for that night. He said he had something important to discuss.

Oh, pooh! Of course, Brad had another commitment. A guy who looked like Brad probably had dinner commitments well into star date 47457.1! But Brad quickly amended his answer. "Let me cancel my other thing. I'd much rather have dinner with you." Timothy couldn't feel too bad for Mr. or Ms. Other Thing being disappointed. And his heart nearly burst when Brad suggested they meet at "Our Italian place."

For the remainder of the afternoon, at least when his thoughts didn't drift to Brad's eyes, eyelashes, lips, smile, and every other inch of his body, Timothy did a bit of work. He answered fan mail. Muriel's new temp office assistant had forwarded the latest photos of Mercedes to add to the official Facebook page and her Instagram account. There were pictures of Mercedes on the set of *Blind Trust*. Others included her visit to an orphanage in South Carolina. Additional images showed her wearing a floppy-brim hat, mugging for the camera with movie crew members. She looked absolutely happy and radiant in all of the pictures. Although she'd been a star for over 40 years, it didn't matter how old she was. Time did not seem to touch her. And even if she had obviously changed slightly over the years, it didn't matter to movie audiences or critics. In fact, age allowed her to portray more diverse characters.

It was now nearly 4:00 in the afternoon. Although Timothy wanted to shower and make himself especially alluring for dinner with Brad, he conscientiously opted to check emails one last time before signing off. He should have just closed the darn computer and put it away in the safe. But no, he had to open a message from an address he didn't know: Doxdox@seemail.com, with the intriguing subject line that said: BEWARE!

The text was succinct:

"Watch your step! I know where you live."

Timothy was totally creeped out. He looked at the sender's email address. It wasn't one that he recognized. In fact, as he searched in the Incoming Mail folder, there wasn't a match. Of course, he was aware that anyone could have multiple email addresses, so it was indeed possible that he knew the individual who sent the missive. But who was it? And was Timothy too close to finding incriminating information about the person responsible for Jared's murder? And the threatened price he'd pay for not watching his step was what? OMG! The price might be his own life. This was too freaky. Shaken to the core with fright, Timothy logged out of the email account, turned off the computer, and put it away correctly.

After he closed the safe, Timothy stood in the quiet, hidden secret room for a long moment. In his mind's eye, he could see Jared's lifeless body on the very spot where he was now standing. He'd only seen one other dead body in his life, his dear Aunt Louise's, after the sudden heart attack that took her away. Timothy had been sixteen years old and so bereft at the wake that after all the other family members had filed past the coffin and were out of the mortuary room, he had leaned into the casket and kissed Louise's forehead. He instantly realized that he wasn't kissing the real Aunt Louise. His lips touched what felt like room-temperature plastic. It was a horrible experience. Only the sight of Jared's body with its vacant, dead eyes and bloody temple was worse.

Timothy tried to understand again why Griffin and the police thought Jared's death was an accident. Griffin had insisted that Jared was probably standing on the desk chair and reaching for something on the top shelf next to the safe. The chair had probably swiveled and slipped out from under him, and he landed on the floor in such a way that his head snapped off from his brain stem. "Quick and easy," Griffin had said. But that didn't make sense to Timothy. Pragmatic Jared would have used the steady step stool resting against the wall. Timothy shook his head and left the room, pivoting the bookshelves back into place.

As unsettled as he was about the threatening email message and still wondering who may have sent it to him, along with visions of Jared's broken neck and twisted body, he decided to take his mind off the subject with a shower and prepare for his dinner with Brad.

\* \* \*

Before leaving the penthouse, Timothy told Beverly he was dining with Brad. He didn't tell her about the ominous message, but considering that his life may be in danger, he thought it best to let someone know where he'd be… just in case. Beverly didn't seem surprised that Timothy was rendezvousing with Mr. Sexy and gave him an approving nod and smile. As Timothy entered the elevator, Beverly called out from the terrace, "If he has a widowed grandfather with a temperature of 98.6° and blood pressure under 180/120, I'm interested and available!"

The debilitating heat and humidity of the previous week had been supplanted by a lovely cooling trend, and the evening air was so pleasant that Timothy decided to walk to the restaurant. He'd save the cost of an Uber for afterward. Although the car horns and sirens from emergency vehicles were as noisy as ever, he hardly heard them. Timothy's thoughts were fixed first on seeing Brad and then on how to enlist his help in identifying Jared's killer. Even if security guy Griffin and the police didn't believe that Jared's death was suspicious, Timothy did. And now, with what appeared to be a direct threat to his life, he intuitively knew that he was on the right track and, terrifying as the thought was, that a killer was somewhere in relatively close proximity.

Timothy must have been preoccupied with those thoughts and his date with Brad because when he arrived at the restaurant and the hostess asked for the name under which a table had been reserved, he merely sighed and said, "God's gift to the world."

The hostess nodded knowingly and said, "Gotcha. Follow me, Sweetie."

When they arrived at the table, Brad stood up to greet Timothy and was beaming his captivating, dimpled smile. Timothy could tell that the hostess was mesmerized too, and he caught her not-so-innocently taking stock of Brad's full lips, medium-length black hair, broad shoulders, and Roman nose. Timothy wanted to say, "He's all mine, Sweetie." But, of course, he was too shy for such a comment. But he couldn't blame the hostess for being jealous.

If Timothy had had any worries about asking Brad for help, they were dispelled in one evening. Timothy really couldn't believe how truly easy Brad was to be with. Their conversation was nonstop, and they always had something mutually interesting to talk about. So, when it came to Timothy speaking about the most important reason for this dinner meeting (other than wanting to be in Brad's company), he knew Brad would try to be of service if he could be. And Timothy was not disappointed. Especially when he revealed the cryptic threat he'd received. In fact, Brad was eager to play amateur sleuth, if only to serve Timothy and act as his protector.

Throughout the evening, Timothy provided Brad with character descriptions of all the people whom he knew had a hostile or antagonistic relationship with Jared: Sandy, Lyle, Beverly, Sage, Clive, and even Bud (though a major and aging Broadway star seemed a little far-fetched as a suspect) and the fans Fiona, Bryony, and someone named Joe, who may or may not have been employed by the Muriel Maynard Management, were the most obvious. As hard as it was to include Beverly, he felt it necessary to at least suggest that her relationship with Jared hadn't been cozy. But, then again, no one he knew had a warm connection to the guy. Brad gently asked why Timothy was so keen to delve into this mystery, considering how unpleasant Jared had been to him. For the first time, Timothy had to put his motives into words. When it came down to it, it was the combination of sadness at the thought that nobody cared about Jared's death, a little guilt about how he had thought about him, and downright curiosity.

After they'd finished their lasagnas and shared a bottle of Pinot Noir, and as Brad signed his credit card receipt for the bill (Timothy suggested splitting the check, but sweet and generous Brad refused), he made a troubling statement. "Why isn't Mercedes Ford on your list?"

For a moment, Timothy was floored. He would never put the amazing and oh-so-talented star on any list except Santa's Nice List. It was inconceivable to him that Brad might consider Mercedes as someone to investigate. "No! Never!" Timothy insisted.

But Brad reminded him that Mercedes had apparently stated in an email to Beverly that "Someone was about to have a very short existence." Timothy could see why Brad might get the (wrong) impression that Mercedes could be implicated in Jared's murder, even though she was all the way down in South Carolina filming a movie when it happened. "And Jared died in Mercedes' home," Brad nudged his memory.

So, just for the sake of covering all the bases (and not wanting to fall out with beautiful Brad), Timothy reluctantly agreed to at least place Mercedes on the list of possible suspects. Still, he felt guilty deciding to even consider such an impossible idea. Not his Mercedes! No way. Not ever!

As Brad and Timothy left the crowded restaurant, he noticed people looking admiringly at his date. Of course, it made Timothy feel special to know that such an attractive man wanted to be with him, but red flags were being raised in his mind. A guy like Brad, who was charming, intelligent, talented, and sexy, would forever be the object of many men's (and women's, too) appreciation. Timothy would have to be on his toes to keep Brad interested only in him. But that was a challenge he'd happily accept, even while he was preoccupied with writing best-selling novels. Me and my imagination! he sighed to himself.

When their romantic night was finally over, and as they waited outside for Timothy's Uber, Brad leaned in and kissed him. It was just as passionate as the first time, and Timothy never wanted to come up for air. He'd heard the saying "lost in his kisses." That's precisely how he felt. Completely transported to a fictional fairytale land. When the car arrived and dragged them out of Paradise, Brad said, "Send me Sandy's contact information in the morning. I'll pay him a visit."

As Timothy waved goodbye, he was disappointed he couldn't bring this man home to The Colton for the night. Well, at least not for the type of night he wanted, which would include serving Brad breakfast in bed. *Breakfast at Timothy's*, he smiled at the pun he'd just made up. But it was against the rules. Or was it? Now that Jared was dead, who would know? Oh, right. Beverly would know. But would she mind? Might she even encourage it? It was the same problem he had with all his previous roomies: No privacy! But at least he had Brad's commitment to help find Jared's killer. And with his extra-sexy looks, he knew that Sandy would be putty in Brad's large hands. Oh, he wished he could be a fly on the wall when Brad and Sandy met and not just to hear the conversation.

# Chapter Seventeen

When Timothy returned to the penthouse, Beverly had already gone to bed. The place was dark, and looking through the terrace doors, Timothy could see a carpet of city lights stretching out like a sequined cape to the edge of the island. He kicked off his shoes, turned on a light in the kitchen, dropped a K-cup pod into the coffeemaker, and placed a mug under the spigot. He merely wanted to enjoy the peace and quiet of Mercedes' amazing condo and unwind after a fulfilling, if exhausting (and somewhat unsettling), day. For Timothy, there was nothing like alone time. It was really a necessity in his life.

When the coffee was ready, Timothy brought the mug into the living room and sat on one of the fireside sofas facing the piano. Other than the soft sound of faraway traffic filtering up from the city, there was only silence in the vast room. This place still amazed him. But he was saddened, too. He suspected that his time here wouldn't last much longer—either because Muriel would eventually fire him, or he'd end up dead at the hands of whoever was warning him to "Beware."

Neither thought was fun to consider. Where will I go? he wondered. It was stupid to think that he'd live with Brad. Heck, they hardly knew each other. A couple of kisses do not a romance—let alone a relationship (budding or otherwise)—make. Yep, it was probably back to his mother's home in

'Bama, at least until he could get back on his feet for a return to his beloved NYC.

So, Timothy quietly sipped his coffee and fell into thoughts about Jared, who had left this planet in a room just down the hallway. Timothy wondered if Jared knew who killed him. He wondered if he himself knew the killer. Was Jared aware of being on someone's To-Kill list, or did it just happen spontaneously, perhaps after an argument? A thousand previously considered questions flooded back into his thoughts.

For instance, what would Jared have done with the rest of his life if he'd lived? Was he romantically involved with anyone? Probably not. But then why were there two tickets on his desk for that Broadway show? Maybe they had been given to him as a present. Or were they freebies since he was in the business? But, given by whom? And who liked him well enough to provide such an expensive gift? Was Jared gay? Timothy's gaydar often malfunctioned, but in showbiz, everyone was considered gay until proven otherwise. What had been his relationship with his deceased mother? Did he have any siblings? The last Timothy had heard, the police were still looking for next of kin. How sad, he thought, that not only had Jared died abruptly and brutally, but it also appeared there was no one to collect his body. Of course, Muriel wouldn't let him go to a pauper's grave. Timothy was almost certain of that, and if not Muriel, then Mercedes definitely wouldn't. Still, Timothy had never known anyone so seemingly alone and friendless.

As Timothy continued to think about life and death and how each of our fortunes seems to be at the mercy of some invisible force or puppeteer, he suddenly thought about the night of the *Obsession* cocktail party and the man who said that Jared and Sage would have to "pay the piper." That sounded ominous at the time, but it seemed even more sinister in light of all that had happened over the past few days. It had been lovely seeing Ted that night, but Timothy wished that he hadn't come along at the very moment he did. Now, he'd never know who spoke those words and what they may have meant.

Timothy suddenly remembered what Clive had said about New York being "a small town." That got him thinking. Clive had claimed to dislike Jared intensely. But why? Timothy opened his phone to see if Jared had included his name in the contacts list. He couldn't recall his last name, but when he searched for Clive, it instantly popped up among the last names, starting with H. Bingo! Clive Holgate! He made a mental note to call him first thing in the morning and invite him to lunch. There was so much about Jared that he needed to know, and he hoped that Clive would be a good source of information.

\* \* \*

For once, morning couldn't come quickly enough. And when Timothy woke up at 7:00, he promptly checked messages on his phone. He squealed with glee when he saw one from Brad. It simply said: 🖤

Now, Timothy was super excited to start the day. Forget fifty-carat diamond rings and bouquets of red roses with shiny mylar balloons; Brad had sent him an emoji heart! Nothing could be better! Suddenly, it was Christmas Day, Cinderella's foot filling the glass slipper, and a royal coronation in one extravagant 4th of July fireworks explosion. Yes, the gods were giving Timothy a big, fat, sloppy, wet kiss.

Beverly was halfway finished with her crossword when

Timothy finally bounded onto the terrace with a very bright disposition. "More coffee?" Timothy offered as he set his full mug on the glass-top table.

"TV role for Clooney or Wyle," Beverly said, ignoring Timothy's greeting. "Eight letters. Starts with E. Ends in R."

"ERDOCTOR?" Timothy suggested almost instantaneously. "In this case, the answer's in the question."

"Smarty pants," Beverly said sweetly and filled in the squares. "And by the way, Noah Wyle is just as sexy as George Clooney, if you ask me!"

"That ER casting director certainly had a sweet tooth for good-looking actors!" Timothy agreed, then switched the subject as quickly as possible; otherwise, he knew he'd get stuck solving all of Beverly's crossword clues for her. "Do you remember a guest named Clive Holgate at the party? British guy. He works for *The Post*," he asked.

Beverly looked up from the paper. "He has a reputation. I've heard he's not exactly faithful to his Miss Havisham," she said.

Timothy asked, "Do you have any idea why he despised Jared? He told me there was something he'd never forgive him for."

Beverly thought for a moment. She picked up Timothy's coffee mug and took a long sip before saying, "He writes celebrity gossip, which means he's a tattle-tale. Maybe Jared had a problem with something he'd written about one of Muriel's clients."

That made sense to Timothy. It was indeed something to ask him about when they met. If they met. He looked at his watch and realized it was probably a reasonable hour to make his calls. He took his mug out of Beverly's hands just as she was about to take another sip and said he had to work. He made a beeline for the office.

Timothy's first call was to darling Brad. He thanked him again for a terrific dinner and conversation the night before. He wasn't lying when he said it was one of the best evenings he'd had in years—maybe ever. There was something so fulfilling about being in Brad's company. He hoped that they would do that more often... maybe for eternity.

But, of course, the second main reason for his call was to provide contact numbers for the man he wanted Brad to personally interview. However, he warned that Sandy would undoubtedly be beguiled by his charms and sexiness. "He might try to ensnare you in his web of love," Timothy joked (in humor, there is truth!).

"What's a 'web of love'?" Brad laughed and poo-poohed Timothy's idea that Sandy would find him even remotely interesting. (Is this beautiful man an idiot about his charms, or just charmingly gallant?)

Timothy's next call was, of course, to Clive Holgate. That Clive actually remembered him was a good sign. That he was available for lunch that very afternoon was an even better sign. "The Galaxy Grill," Clive suggested. "West 46th. Noon."

Timothy was definitely ready to set out. But first, he felt compelled to do some emailing on Mercedes's behalf. And there was plenty. One, from Muriel, stated that she had tasked her new temp office assistant with some of the chores that had been Jared's, such as being the intermediary to whom Timothy had to report before getting through to Muriel on the phone. Timothy rolled his eyes. "Good lord, I have seniority over this assistant—if only a week's worth— and I have to go through a gatekeeper again." He decided to just do his job and not worry about the new gopher.

He scrolled through the email subject lines, looking fc something especially interesting. The usual theme ran throu most of them: "I'm A Fan." "Loved *The Final Curtain*!" "Please Adopt My Cat." By now, Timothy had spent enough time on this job to be able to practically answer those messages without even reading the full text. And by now, he should have learned not to go looking for trouble. But no, he was a masochist to his core. And when his eyes fell on a message heading: "BLOOD ON YOUR HANDS," he was suddenly simultaneously terrified and curious. He looked at the sender's email address. Just as he feared, it was Doxdox@seemail.com. With trepidation, Timothy clicked on the message:

> As Mercedes' assistant, you know more than is healthy for you.
> Be careful. Be wise.

* * *

The Galaxy Grill was notoriously noisy, and at lunchtime, it was always crazy busy. When Timothy arrived, Clive was already seated and looking at the extensive short-order menu. Although he tried to rise to greet Timothy, the crowded seating situation was such that his chair was basically wedged between the wall and the table. No matter, Timothy reached out his hand for a shake and sat down. He wasn't happy about having to speak loudly in this place for Clive to hear him. After all, he was about to ask some potentially sensitive questions. But it also occurred to him that Clive selected The Galaxy Grill over a fancier and less crowded restaurant specifically because of the noise and the relative anonymity provided by being in a cacophony of other human voices.

Timothy didn't bother to look at the menu. When the server came to collect their orders, he simply requested a tuna fish sandwich on toasted whole-wheat bread with a side of chips and a pickle. And a Coke. Clive ordered a burger on a toasted bun, no onion, and water. And then he asked Timothy straight out about the urgency of his needing to see him.

Wow. No time to ease into a conversation and somehow find the right moment to start investigating. So, Timothy came directly out with it. "It's about Jared Evans. The security guys in Mercedes' building and the police say his death was accidental. He supposedly fell off a chair, hit his head, and broke his neck. It's possible, but I doubt it. I just wondered if you knew anyone who hated him enough to kill him?"

Clive smiled, which Timothy thought was totally inappropriate. Clive must have read the expression on his face because he said, "Sorry. I sometimes smile at the least appropriate times. It's a response to sad news that I know I should feel bad about but don't."

"Then you're not sorry that Jared is dead," Timothy continued.

Clive shrugged. "I'm always sorry when I hear of someone's death. Especially someone relatively young. But I knew him well enough not to be all that sorry. You know what he was like: Disagreeable. Ill-tempered. Took advantage of everyone he could. Thought he could do the same with me, but I pushed back."

In the short period that Timothy had known Jared, he had displayed all of the attributes Clive had listed. Plus, he was arrogant, confrontational, and a know-it-all. But Timothy had to find out what it was that had caused a division between the two men. "Was there a particular incident that made you dislike him?" he asked.

As Clive was about to respond, the waitress delivered their

lunch orders. "Fast service," Timothy said, genuinely impressed.

"Lots-a hungry folks waitin' for this table, honey," the waitress sassed, suggesting that they should chow down quickly and leave.

Clive poured ketchup on his burger, took a bite, and after he was satisfied with the first taste, said, "Muriel had set up an interview for me with her client Kritzi Lawrence before Kritzi opened in her last show. She was in one of her legendary moods when we met backstage in her dressing room at The Music Box. And, apparently, she didn't like the questions I asked. She said I was too arch. She hadn't given me much to work with, that's for sure. And I think Muriel and Jared were afraid of what I'd write.

"Jared called me up and insisted on reviewing and approving the article before it went to press. I don't do that. Not for LuPone. Not for Midler. And certainly not for the overrated Kritzi Lawrence. Jared didn't understand journalism and went straight to my editor. I'm one of the most widely read columnists in town. Of course, my editor totally backed me up. I have a stellar reputation. As expected, Jared hated the piece when it appeared in the Sunday edition of the paper. Apparently, Kritzi disliked it, too, because she tweeted a bunch of nonsense about me. You may remember all the drama."

Timothy was passionate about gossip from Broadway—even though he couldn't afford tickets to those super-expensive shows—and remembered what Clive was referring to. He nodded in understanding. "The shoplifting thing. Did Jared try to…"

"He tried. Or at least threatened," Clive said. "But I didn't take his bait. He didn't understand that no one in this town gives two figs about what consenting adults do in their private lives. Sure, maybe twenty years ago, there might have been a ripple of gossip that could hinder one's career, but now, short of murder, people are too busy raising their families, trying to make ends meet, and getting ahead in their professional lives. So, when Jared went to various important people in town with the so-called news of my *une liaisons*, they just laughed at his naiveté. They instantly recognized that he was a troublemaker, and if it were not for Muriel's good standing in the biz, they would have drummed the little scandalmonger out of town. End of story." He finished talking and took another bite of his burger.

But was it the end of the story? On the one hand, Timothy was proud that his beloved New York City was a live-and-let-live town, but on the other hand, he wondered if ultra-rich spouses of not-rich cheating husbands were equally mature and accepting of their partners' extramarital indiscretions. What if, in failing to exact the revenge against Clive that he wanted from the city's movers and shakers, Jared then threatened to go a step further and have a candid conversation with Mrs. Gossip Columnist? Timothy asked, "Why, if Jared didn't succeed in getting even with you through your peers, did you still have it out for him?"

"I never had it out for the little bugger," Clive countered. "But that doesn't mean I ever wanted to see his evil ferret face again, either. He was like a terrier mutt in that he wouldn't let go once he got his sharp teeth into something. Ever. But I'm a bigger man than he was—intellectually, professionally, and creatively."

Clive stopped for a moment to take a sip of his water. Then he said, "But why are you asking me these questions? Are you thinking that I may have sent Jared to his just reward?"

What Timothy wanted to say was, "You're a pretty good

candidate for the role of the hangman." But instead, he laughed, "No! No! Of course not! Never even thought of that. But I hoped you might have a clue as to who could have done the deed."

Clive was still wary of Timothy's questioning him. "But you don't even know if there was a deed," he said. "You admitted that the police and the security staff at The Colton believe it was an accident. What makes you think that something nefarious occurred? Jared apparently simply fell and hit his head. I once had a friend whose hands were in his pants pockets as he skipped down a flight of stairs in his own home. He tripped. Couldn't grab the railing. Broke his neck. Dead. Done. It could happen to anyone. Perhaps you should leave well enough alone, eh?"

Of course, Timothy knew that accidents happen all the time. One minute we're alive, and the next minute… boo-hoo. And he wouldn't have had a problem with letting Jared go to his final resting place—but for the way-too-strange fact that he had found him in the secret room with the bookcase entrance closed. He obviously wouldn't have locked himself inside. And only a few people knew that room existed. Clive was one of them. But, of course, Timothy didn't remind him of that. Instead, he said, "Knowing that Jared would be at the party last week, why did you accept an invitation? You said you never wanted to see his 'evil ferret face' again. Surely, you knew he'd be at the event. If I had a problem with someone, I'd go out of my way to avoid being within a ten-mile radius of them."

Clive shrugged again and pursed his lips. "In my business, it's hard to avoid people who, for one reason or another, don't like me or what I write about them," he said. "If I wanted to avoid them all, I'd have to never leave my apartment. Plus, I was covering the event for the paper. And

I happen to like Virginia La Paloma. I have all of her CDs. Yes, I know, CDs date me."

Okay, Timothy thought, so he's a fan of opera and had a job to do. That made sense. What still wasn't entirely clear to him was that during the evening, when Timothy was in the office searching for Ms. Diva's fake name for the limo driver, Clive came in and watched while he was frantically opening the safe in the secret room. He'd later said he was looking for the bathroom. But why did he not go on his merry way when he wandered in and saw that there obviously wasn't a bathroom there? And for once, Timothy got the courage to ask a pointed question straight out. "If you had to go tinkle so badly at the party that night, why did you hang around watching me in the office and the secret room?"

Clive smiled again, apparently uncomfortable with Timothy's question. "I'm simply fascinated by bookcases that lead to hidden rooms. Aren't you? Plus, it's my nature—and apparently yours, too—to be inquisitive. And... I thought you were cute. I'd had my eye on you all evening."

Timothy blushed but couldn't say that he was totally buying Clive's story. And he didn't want to waste his day—or his tuna fish sandwich—by going around and around with Clive on this issue. The way the columnist answered or, more precisely, didn't answer his questions actually put him smack dab at the top of the suspect list. Yes, Clive seemed to know something but wasn't going to budge and reveal any secret he may have.

The waitress came along and slapped the bill down on their table long before they were finished. She wanted to hurry them along and make space for the next growling tummy. Timothy was pretty much done with Clive anyway. And the tuna sandwich wasn't all that good; it had too much mayo. So, he thanked Clive and removed his debit card from his wallet. Fortunately, Clive waved away any thought that Timothy would pay for lunch. "This is why we have expense accounts," he said, placing his Platinum American Express company credit card on top of the bill.

As Timothy pushed his chair away from the table and stood up, he thanked Clive again and asked if he had any thoughts about who else he should talk to, to please let him know.

"Have you chatted with Lisa Lambert?"

"Lisa…?"

"Jared's former boss."

Surprise must have registered across Timothy's face. For some reason, he never considered that Jared existed before Muriel employed him. Of course, he had to come from somewhere. The chicken or the egg.

"A not-so-successful casting director," Clive said of Lisa Lambert. "She might have an idea about anyone else who despised the old boy. I'm sure I have her number somewhere." Clive opened his phone and scrolled through his contacts. "Ah, yes!" he said, and Timothy wrote down the number as dictated.

# Chapter Eighteen

By the time Timothy returned to The Colton, it was early afternoon. He was eager to contact Lisa Lambert, but first, he wanted to research her. Google listed only a few entries. He clicked on the first one and found a brief article about The Lisa Lambert Casting Agency. According to the report, Lambert had cast a few amateur stage shows in her hometown of Lansing, Michigan. After moving to Manhattan to forge a career in the big city, things didn't work out well. Although the article listed the Off-Broadway shows *China Shop Bull*, *Glad to Leave You*, and *Across This Land*, as her casting credits, after two years of trying to make it, the agency closed. Timothy could feel a bit of empathy for Ms. Lambert. Like Timothy's writing dreams, her New York dreams so far had not materialized. Armed with very little information, Timothy placed a call to her.

Lisa Lambert sounded stressed out and explained that she was inordinately busy. And on hearing that Jared was dead, she seemed genuinely shocked. She was now working for Preston/Middleton, one of the biggest PR firms in the city. Understandably, she wasn't interested in rehashing the painful period during which she had to give up her own business. Of course, it must have been hard for her, but Timothy pushed for a meeting and told Lisa that it was really urgent. He lied that he was a grieving friend of Jared Evans and just wanted more information about his life before Jared joined Muriel

Maynard Management. Lisa gave in, and they arranged to meet for drinks at 7:00.

Drinks at seven sounded good to Timothy. What didn't sound good was the location for their meeting: The Palm Court in The Plaza Hotel. Talk about a pricy place! Timothy still needed to receive his first paycheck, and he dared not look at the available balance on his debit card. One drink at The Palm Court, and he'd probably be getting a convenience charge for being overdrawn. But heck, this was important enough to take a chance on personal bankruptcy.

Timothy had several hours before he had to skedaddle, so he decided to call Brad to ask if he'd had any success contacting Sandy.

Of course, it was great to hear Brad's rich and seductive voice, and as they talked, Timothy pictured him smiling and staring into his eyes. They were so into discussing their personal feelings that it wasn't until the end of the conversation that Brad remembered to tell him that he was meeting Sandy for coffee at the same time that Timothy was meeting Lisa. They could meet after their respective appointments and compare notes. Timothy would text Brad when he was finished, and they'd determine where to rendezvous. And, he hoped, plan their next real date.

\* \* \*

After ending his call with Brad, Timothy was happy to see Beverly sipping iced tea on the terrace. He stepped outside for a visit and to ask about what she'd been doing all day. Beverly wasn't in the best of moods.

"Muriel called me a few hours ago," Beverly said. "She wants me to travel with her to Pennsylvania. Says it's a business trip and needs the company. She never ever calls me.

She hates my company. And I loathe hers. Obviously, she's making plans to deposit me in that Glenwood Farms place. This is the beginning of the end, my dear."

Darn! Timothy had hoped that with Jared's death, Muriel might have forgotten all about Glenwood Farms. "Maybe she only wants you to tour the place. If you really hate it, tell her so," Timothy suggested.

"A lot of good it'll do me," Beverly said, shaking her head. "Once Muriel makes up her mind about something, she's intractable. Still, it's bound to beat living with her. But I'll miss this place. I love the privacy. And I sorta like you."

Suddenly, Timothy felt a wave of sadness wash over him. For one thing, Beverly was saying that she actually "liked" him. For another, he could feel her sense of doom. He thought, please, dear God, don't ever let me be dependent on anyone! Timothy didn't know how he would be able to handle going through what Beverly was facing. The end of our days on Earth can be challenging enough with decreasing health or mobility and maybe financial concerns. To add uncertainty about housing is a rotten cherry topping to the melted sundae of life. He felt really bad for Beverly. If he had any money of his own, he'd adopt the woman.

"Never mind," Beverly eventually stated. "Let's talk about something fun—like birth control."

Timothy refilled Beverly's glass with iced tea. He really didn't know what else he could say about her situation that wouldn't sound pathetically naïve. After all, Timothy was young, and Beverly was old. Beverly had far more experience and wisdom about life and death. What did Timothy know other than the superficial? So, he decided to fill her in on what he'd gleaned from visiting with Clive Holgate. "I don't know enough about his relationship with Jared to come to any conclusions," Timothy said, "but I left feeling that he's not to be completely trusted. Although, he suggested that I talk to Jared's former employer."

"Someone else hired that little twit?" Beverly declared. "I thought that Muriel was alone in being so foolish."

"A Broadway casting person. Lisa Lambert. Having drinks at The Plaza with her tonight. If nothing else, it's a way to get more background information on Jared. Maybe someone from his past killed him. Someone we haven't met. That would actually make me feel a heck of a lot better. I can't stand thinking that I may know someone who has the capacity to murder."

Beverly growled. "Heck, look at me. I'm ready to kill Muriel, and I actually sort of mean it."

Timothy knew it was just a figure of speech. He could more easily see Muriel Maynard taking someone's life than Beverly. Oh, early on when they'd first met, Fabiola/Beverly was someone to be wary of. But now that Timothy knew her better, he could see that the old woman was just a frightened human being on her way out the door—no more than used furniture going to a charity shop.

\* \* \*

The Plaza. That oh-so-elegant and historic hotel on Fifth Avenue and Central Park South was a place Timothy had only seen from the outside. The 1% Hoi Polloi could afford to stay or dine there, but not him. As he arrived via bus, he was more intimidated by the doormen than by meeting with Lisa and talking about Jared.

Trying his best to act as though he'd been there a gazillion times, Timothy walked up the carpeted steps and nodded at the uniformed attendant, who welcomed him with a smile and opened the door. Timothy didn't want to look like a tourist, so he didn't stand around gazing at the elegant lobby, although he definitely wanted to gawk. Instead, he walked with purpose up to the lighted lectern at the entrance to The Palm Court. The host, a middle-aged, balding guy in a tuxedo, looked over the rims of his eyeglasses at Timothy.

Acting confident, Timothy offered a weak smile before the man could make a judgmental comment and said, "I'm joining Lisa Lambert. Has she arrived yet?"

Tuxedo Guy's expression instantly changed. He went from a disapproving grandfather figure to a helpful manservant in the blink of an eye. "Indeed, sir. Please follow me," he said and guided Timothy to a table in the corner of the posh bar/restaurant. Whatever Timothy may have expected Lisa Lambert to look like, she didn't.

"Hi. I'm Timothy Trousdale," he said, reaching out to Lisa. The woman looked at Timothy and nodded as the maître d' ushered him into a wingback chair. So here he was, opposite a woman who looked maybe 35 years old, her brunette hair mixed equally with gray. Her puffy eyes reminded Timothy of someone crying and/or sleep-deprived for a decade. She held a martini, and because of her lack of warmth, Timothy suspected their time together would be short, so he didn't waste any of it with introductory chitchat. To ask about Jared's character would have been stupid since he was pretending to be Jared's grieving friend in search of material for his memorial speech. And he didn't care about things like Jared's work habits or personal life. So, Timothy opted for the direct approach and blurted out, "I don't believe Jared's death was an accident. Any idea who disliked him enough to commit murder?"

A waiter arrived, and Timothy confidently ordered, "Perrier in a wine glass with a wedge of lime, easy on the ice, please." He'd seen an elegant woman at The Colton party last week place that order and thought it sounded good—and cheap. He looked back at Lisa with questioning eyes. "I know some people considered him a pain in the neck, but…"

"I found Jared to be an outstanding worker," Lisa said as if dismissing Timothy's assessment of his former boss. "I'm extremely sorry that he's dead."

She seemed totally unphased by the idea that Jared might have been murdered, which Timothy found interesting. However, he wasn't given much time to ponder this as Lisa continued talking.

Without prompting, Lisa Lambert went into an analysis of her and Jared's work relationship. Lisa recalled that Jared had come to her unannounced. She hadn't even posted an ad for an assistant, nor did she think that she needed one. "It was rather curious," Lisa said. "He'd obviously done his homework and knew not only where I lived—my office was in my loft apartment—but that I like onion bagels. So, this guy somehow gets into my building, rides the service elevator to my floor, and hands me a warm bag from Murray's Bagels when I answer the door. I can still recall the aroma. He didn't look dangerous. Strange, maybe—it was unbearably cold outside, and he was wearing a suit but not an overcoat—so I let him in. Smooth talker that Jared was, I agreed to let him work with me—for free. I was a casting director, and he said he just wanted the experience and knowledge of being in the biz."

Timothy could tell that Lisa's memory was taking her back in time as she sipped her martini. Just then, Timothy's Perrier arrived. "Cheers to Jared," Timothy said, raising his glass to Lisa's.

Lisa continued. "Before I knew it, I started giving Jared money for the bus, lunches, and even help with his rent. Finally, after a couple of months, though I really couldn't afford it, I hired him full-time. I'd never seen such a self-starter. He came in and, without any direction, started organizing my office. I admit it was a mess, and he straightened it out. I started inviting him to casting sessions, too.

"But Jared definitely had a dark side. One evening, after I'd come back from seeing a play, he told me the reason my business was in the toilet was that I listened to what other people had to say about particular roles and the actors who might fill them and that I didn't have the guts to follow my own convictions and instincts and to fight for what I knew was right. I thought he was joking, talking to me like that. But he was serious. I cried. I'd never been insulted like that, certainly not by someone I was employing. I hate to cry in front of other people. But actually, he was telling me the truth. I guess that's what hurt the most."

*I hear ya, Babe,* Timothy thought, remembering Jared's similar castigation of his character traits. This was the Jared that Timothy knew and hated. The sting of his tongue was numbing. But the sad thing was Timothy realized that if Jared had phrased his words differently, Lisa would not only have listened to him but also remained friends. That was Jared's life in a nutshell; he alienated people, perhaps without meaning to.

"I was struck dumb by how he spoke to me," Lisa continued. "Seriously. I couldn't speak. When he left, I sat down at the computer and wrote him a letter. Regardless of how terrific he may have been as an assistant, and one who, until then, I liked very much, I was not going to be mistreated and insulted by him. Heck, I had to put up with everyone else in this sick business making my life hell. But when he arrived at the office the next morning, he told me he was going to work for Muriel Maynard Management. He deprived me of the opportunity to hand him that letter and to show some strength. Quite honestly, I didn't have much strength. He was right; I wasn't very good at standing up for myself. I was weak in a very tough business. Not long afterward, I knew I'd never make it in casting, so I quit. Now I'm working for a beast and hating every waking moment of my miserable and worthless life." She lifted her glass and took another swallow.

Wow! Timothy never expected such a personal disclosure. Lisa assured him that Jared wasn't the reason she closed her business but that he was responsible for opening her eyes to the fact that she was a failure. Although her confession helped Timothy see how Jared got his start, he still had nothing substantial that would bring him any closer to finding Jared's killer. They both took another sip of their drinks. Then Timothy asked why Jared had left her casting agency for Muriel's talent management firm.

"Money, for sure," Lisa said. "I don't know what Muriel offered him, but it had to be more than I could afford to pay. But it may also have had something to do with Sonia Chartsworth."

"Sonia Chartsworth? The singer?" Timothy asked. "She's dead."

"Yep. Walked off stage during intermission and killed herself," Lisa recalled.

"But what did she have to do with Jared leaving you? They weren't…"

Lisa offered a soft, scoffing laugh. "Involved? No. As a matter of fact, Sonia disliked Jared intensely. That was another problem for me.

"On the one hand, Jared was a tireless worker and very bright. But I had complaints from a lot of actors about how uncomfortable he made them feel. Not uncomfortable in any sort of physical way; I mean, he wasn't hitting on anyone that

I know of, but they sensed something dark about him. There were times I had to defend him. 'That's just Jared being Jared. Don't take it personally.' That sort of thing. But it made me uncomfortable to have to do that at all. It was only that final night that I saw what others had warned me about."

"But what did Jared do to Sonia or vice versa?" Timothy pushed.

Lisa was silent for a long moment. She took another sip of her martini and looked at the piano player serenading the room with something from *The Phantom of the Opera*. Then she turned back to face Timothy and said, "He called her a 'never was.'"

Timothy looked perplexed. Lisa leaned forward and said, "A 'has-been' is better than a 'never was.' Do you follow me? It's one of the cruelest things you could say to an artist, especially one as vulnerable as Sonia. She was a star, for crying out loud, a minor one for sure, but still. He preyed on her self-doubt. Frankly, I think that's why she killed herself. She knew she'd never be an Audra McDonald or Bernadette Peters. She hated being second fiddle."

Now Timothy was really intrigued. What on earth would possess Jared to have said such a terrible thing to anyone, and what were the circumstances? "Why?" he asked. "What did she ever do to him to deserve such a harsh comment?"

Lisa seemed to wonder just how much more she should reveal to Timothy. After another sip from her glass, she said, "Sonia was a pill, okay. The insecure ones always are. Jared was young and naïve, and I think he thought shoving her face in the truth would make her work harder. You know, reverse psychology or something. She had come to the office to read for the role of Martina in *Flags on the Moon*. In my opinion, she nailed it. I told her so. I was ready to call the director and send her over for an interview. I remember Jared said he would walk Sonia out of the loft to get a cab. They left, and the next day, Sonia called to say she was no longer interested in the role. At the funeral, Sonia's fiancée told me what Jared had said to her. Kent, Sonia's fiancée, basically accused Jared of killing her. Or at least killing her spirit. In a manner of speaking, I suppose Jared was complicit in her death."

As Timothy sat listening to Lisa, he was stunned by this revelation and excited to realize that for the first time, he now had someone in sight who had a significant motive for killing Jared: Sonia Chartsworth's fiancée! Perhaps he wanted revenge for what Jared had done to Sonia and, by extension, himself. This night had turned out much better than Timothy had anticipated. And when he asked Lisa for the name and phone number of Sonia's boyfriend Kent, Lisa happily opened her phone, went into her Contacts, and provided all the details.

"Kent Isaacson," she said. "He's in the chorus of the latest revival of *Pests*. God knows why they keep bringing that dead horse back," Lisa said. "Avoid it like the plague. Unless you like musicals about The Plague." She gave a small laugh.

"I'll take your recommendation," Timothy said. Heck, Lisa didn't have to know that he couldn't even afford a movie ticket, let alone a seat for a Broadway show. Even the cheap prices at the TKS booth in Times Square would have taken all his savings. If he'd had any savings, to begin with. Timothy looked at his watch, which was his nonverbal way of saying it was time to go. And when he reached into his wallet to withdraw his whimpering Visa debit card, Lisa waved it away.

"I've got it," Lisa said. "You only had a Perrier. I'm going to stay and have another martini. Gotta numb what's left of my rotting soul after a day like I've had and the one I'll have tomorrow. And the next day after that, and…"

Well, that was certainly big of her! If Timothy had known

she'd be so generous, he'd have had a martini too. Timothy hadn't had to spend any money that day except for a couple of Ubers and the bus. He thanked Lisa profusely and suggested drinks were on him the next time they got together. Of course, he never expected to see Lisa again as long as he lived, but the gesture is what counted in his book. He left The Palm Court and, now armed with new information about Jared, sat on a red plush velvet settee in the lobby and checked his messages. As he'd hoped, there was a text from Brad: "Meet me at our place." It ended with another ♥. Oh, goody, Timothy thought, *Our place*. A late-night Italian dinner with the sexiest man in Manhattan. He immediately ordered an Uber and was off.

\* \* \*

When Timothy arrived at La Strega, Brad was already seated and sipping a glass of red wine. Sweet, sexy man that he was, Brad had poured a glass for Timothy, too. "Hope you haven't been waiting long," Timothy said as he boldly gave Brad a kiss on his cheek. If only he had the guts to publicly move his lips just a few more centimeters to the right! But Timothy was as insecure about love as Sonia Chartsworth had been about her talent. They lifted their glasses and toasted, "To interesting times."

"Interesting, indeed," Timothy added excitedly. "I think I've found another suspect, and with a good motive." Then, he launched into reciting his meeting with Lisa and all she had revealed. Brad nodded a lot, allowing Timothy to keep yammering about his evening. "And that's that!" Timothy said when he finally came up for air. "There'll be a call to Kent Isaacson first thing tomorrow!"

Brad was excited for Timothy. They ordered their meals,

and then Brad made an announcement of his own. "Sandy had some decent info, too," he said triumphantly. "If I believe him, someone else had an excellent reason for keeping Jared quiet."

Timothy was totally intrigued. Wow, two suspects in one night, he thought. Then Brad began to reveal what he'd learned. Timothy pictured him being all suave and charming and easily making Sandy feel comfortable enough to let down any defenses. Sandy probably got all giggly and stared at Brad's deep dimples, then lost himself in his root beer-color eyes while unintentionally offering top-secret and personal information.

Brad would have used his seductive charisma and maybe even rolled up his shirtsleeves to reveal the treble clef tattoo on his left inside forearm and unbuttoned an additional shirt button to reveal a hint of flesh and tufts of chest hair to lure Sandy into his confidence. Surely, he would have paid attention to Sandy's every word and looked intently into his eyes, making him feel that he was the most important person on the planet. Brad would have effortlessly steered the conversation so that even if Sandy knew what he was telling Brad, he would trust him to keep his secrets. Timothy only surmised this because he, too, was a fool for Brad. Almost anyone would be.

"And then Sandy said..." Brad stopped mid-sentence and took a fortifying sip of wine, creating a cliffhanger. "He said that Jared seemed to be in some sort of trouble. He was upset about a letter he received. It's a physical letter, not an email. He said that first of all, receiving personal mail in the office was a no-no. So, when Jared was delivered an envelope, it was noticed by some of the other staff. They figured that Jared getting personal mail was just him lording his self-importance over the others. As if rules didn't apply to him. But Sandy said that when Jared opened the envelope and read the correspondence, his face turned bright red, his hands shook, and he angrily crushed the paper into a ball and threw it into the trash can under his desk. But get this…"

Again, Brad paused to sip his wine, and Timothy did the same, anticipating some great revelation. "Apparently, Jared stormed out of the office and went to the restroom. When he returned, he went to retrieve the letter… but it was no longer in his trash!"

Timothy gave Brad a quizzical look. He was wondering why anyone would be interested in Jared's trash. Then it occurred to him. Jared was so disliked that someone was happy he had received bad news and wanted to know what that news was.

"Tell me! Tell me!" Timothy squealed, probably sounding like a little girl demanding to know the secret to a magic trick. He couldn't help himself. He'd naturally become so invested in this mystery that he was starting to become nagging, which he knew was unattractive behavior.

Suddenly, Brad looked sheepish. He looked Timothy in the eye and said, "All that Sandy could tell me—and I don't think he would have lied—was that Jared was afraid of something or someone…"

What? After all the suspense build-up, Brad left the story's ending unanswered. No! Brad saw the disappointment on Timothy's face and said, "So, Sandy said that Jared came back to his desk, couldn't find the letter, and just stood there looking around the common room and giving everyone the stink eye. No one would give him the satisfaction of saying who took the paper from his trashcan."

"Who did take the letter?" Timothy asked.

Again, Brad paused to take a sip of wine. He looked at Timothy and said, "Muriel Maynard."

## Chapter Nineteen

One of the things Timothy liked best about living in Manhattan was the gazillions of people who visit from all over the planet. There was such a variety of humanity, and he felt that most were terrific people who try to do the right thing and follow The Golden Rule or whatever their version of that is. Before he arrived in the city, he believed the stories of muggers and random individuals meeting their deaths by being shoved in front of subway trains. And sure, that happened, but during his time in New York, he also experienced being lost and having ordinary New Yorkers stop to ask if he needed help. In fact, twice he'd lost his wallet, and twice it had been returned to him with nothing missing. Perhaps he just had good karma. Or maybe the news media sensationalized his great city's negative aspects.

New York had also given him opportunities. He firmly believed that if he just went with the flow, so to speak, everything would work out well. Maybe not how he'd initially planned things to sort out, but perhaps even better than he could have imagined. For example, his working for Mercedes Ford and living in her fabulous penthouse condo. Timothy could never in a squillion years have conceived that such an opportunity would come to him or that he'd make a friend like Beverly. He also couldn't have known he'd fall so deeply in love. And Brad was turning out to be so much more than just a talented piano tuner/player and a fun person to be around. But Timothy knew he was getting ahead of himself. "Just let things work out the way they're supposed to. Can't force love," he admonished himself a dozen times daily. Even though he was definitely past the point of no return.

During this reverie of gratitude, Timothy realized that by letting go and seeing every moment as an adventure, he was living a larger life than anyone he knew. For instance, none of his friends or relatives could claim they'd found a dead body in their home. He could guarantee that he, Timothy Trousdale, was indeed the only one in his circle with such an exciting life. It was far more interesting even than his cousin Jackson, down in Alabama, whom everyone in the family admired because he was brave enough to work in pest control. Sure, he got to have adventures crawling under old houses in the stultifying humidity of summers in the deep South and had great stories about horrifying giant mutant spiders and millipedes and snakes and scorpions and other critters he encountered. But Timothy was working in showbiz. Or at least, showbiz-adjacent. He was thrilled to be where he was in life. Thrilled—until he finally got hold of Sonia Chartsworth's fiancée Kent Isaacson—and Kent told him to take a hike.

Timothy could be such an idiot. He made the mistake of calling Kent and using the same tactic he had used on Lisa Lambert, lying that he was a friend of dead Jared Evans and wanting to learn more about him to build a fuller picture of Jared's life for the memorial service. If Kent was shocked to find out Jared was dead, he hid it well. Timothy should have appealed to the ham in every actor and said he was writing a story for *Playbill* and wanted a chorus boy's perspective about breaking out of the background and into the spotlight. Darn, he thought, why do I usually think of these things after it's too late?

So, Timothy decided to do the most totally wrong, unethical, and utterly sackable offense imaginable. He found Kent on Instagram and sent him a message identifying himself as one of Muriel Maynard's junior talent managers. He figured that even if Kent decided to check on him, he'd call the office, and the new rat-girl assistant would truthfully say that Timothy was indeed employed by Muriel. His skills at lying were getting really good. This time, Timothy sent Kent a message saying that he had seen him in *Pests* and that Muriel Maynard Management was always looking for unknowns with a lot of potential and who were ready to move on to the next level of their careers. He said that he thought Kent was a standout in the show and that they should meet up with an eye toward "a mutually beneficial professional relationship."

Sometimes, Timothy had to pat himself on the back for how his written words could manipulate others. Kent fell for the ruse, clearly not recalling that Muriel Maynard Management was where Jared had worked. Kent eagerly agreed to meet for lunch and suggested they rendezvous at Quinoa Bites, over on 43rd. One o'clock.

When Timothy finally arrived at the restaurant ten minutes later than planned, Kent was already seated at a table and examining his face in a pocket mirror. Timothy knew it had to be Kent because aren't all Broadway chorus boys exceptionally good-looking? Timothy picked out the most attractive guy in the small restaurant, and—bingo! Kent smiled warmly, showing off his perfect white teeth. His head of blonde hair and reddish-blonde facial stubble would have made Timothy's knees go weak if he weren't already enamored of someone even sexier. It's a good thing that Brad was in his life—well, in his life enough to have kissed him— or he wouldn't have been able to concentrate on his mission with Kent.

Timothy suggested that they order their food right away and then talk about Kent's career. The chickpea quiche looked good to Timothy. Kent ordered the cauliflower-potato-kale-lentil soup. If you've ever seen sexy chorus boys, you understand why Kent selected such a healthy meal. He knew he looked great and wanted to keep it that way for as long as possible.

Sweet-faced Kent couldn't contain his enthusiasm for why he thought they were meeting, and the moment their server left to place their lunch orders with the kitchen, he gushed. "So you obviously liked me in the show, I've had bigger parts, but I think this one really shows off my dancing and singing skills, and even though I only have one line, it's important because it sets up the next scene for the audience, I'm sort of the glue that holds the entire show together, don't you think so, too, of course, what I really want is the lead in a Sondheim revival, *Sunday in the Park* would be ideal, I know that Muriel Maynard is the right agency to get me there, you obviously agree, otherwise, you wouldn't have picked me out of the cast, right, and…?"

Yipes! Timothy's first thought was that this guy definitely doubled his morning dose of Adderall. Talk about a positive self-assessment. But then he realized that if any actor didn't have a sense of enthusiasm and confidence in himself, he probably would not make it in a business where rejection was part of everyday life. Thespians have to have an elevated level of self-assurance to survive emotionally. Timothy wished that he had that attitude about his own work. He could obviously learn something from this guy.

"Absolutely right." Timothy agreed with Kent's suggestion that Muriel had spotted him in the cast and believed he had star quality. "So, let's chat about your career thus far," Timothy said while simultaneously taking a pen and notebook from his rucksack and pretending that he needed some background information. But Kent, as if always prepared to be discovered, reached into a shoulder bag that he'd placed on another chair and withdrew an 8" x 10" color photo of himself leaning into the frame with a wide white smile, wearing a muscle shirt, and showing off his pumped arms. "All my credits are on the back," he said. "Notice that besides acting and singing, I can also tap dance, skateboard, am excellent with dialects, and do impressions. Oh, and I can bench press up to 280 lbs."

*Two-eighty with the weights, eh?* Timothy thought, wondering why on earth that was an attribute that casting directors might be interested in. Timothy then looked at Kent's picture and reviewed his credits. Feigning intense interest, he made sounds that implied that he was impressed with the titles. "*Hairspray,*" he said. "*Legally Blonde. Urinetown. Mama Mia! Oklahoma!* You note they were Off-Broadway productions. How far off-Broadway?" he asked.

Without seeming to be the least bit self-conscious, he enthusiastically admitted that they were local productions in his hometown of Peabody, Massachusetts. "Rave reviews," he said. "Go online and check out what Ben Pitman wrote about me in *The Daily Item*. He says that I'm destined to go far."

*It's not that far from Massachusetts to New York*, Timothy wanted to say. Instead, playing to Kent's distended ego, he said, "Totally agree." He tried to start questioning him about his deceased fiancée, but Kent was steering the conversation. Timothy really couldn't blame him. Kent thought they were lunching together to discuss his future. And when their meals were delivered, Timothy settled into listening to Kent prattle on about his acting classes and how far he thought he'd come in a relatively short period. Of course, he believed that the trajectory of his ascent to stardom was on a fast track. And from the way he was dropping celebrity names and how they had all expressed interest in his work, he apparently wasn't opposed to doing whatever he had to do to achieve his ultimate career goal.

As Kent monopolized the conversation, Timothy was getting a little antsy because he didn't want their time together to end without discovering more about Kent's link to Jared. Finally, it seemed that Kent had exhausted his autobiography because he said, "I've told you enough about myself."

Phew! Timothy thought, finally, a chance to ask a few questions.

"What was your favorite part of my performance in *Pests*?" Kent quickly absconded with the fraction of a moment between his self-aggrandizing promotions.

This was one totally vain dude, and since Timothy hadn't really seen him on stage, he didn't know exactly what to say. He covered himself by offering that Kent owned all the scenes he was in. Of course, the young actor agreed completely. And then the darn check arrived. Not only had Timothy not gotten a word in edgewise, but he could also tell that Kent expected him to pick up the bill, which it was entirely his place to do since he invited Kent, and this had ostensibly been a business lunch. And after having gotten away twice the day before with others paying his way, he decided that fair is fair. But no way was he going to let Kent go without him coughing up some sort of information about Jared as return payment. And that's when he pounced.

When their waitress picked up Timothy's debit card, he looked at Kent and said, "By the way, I'm really sorry about your tragedy."

For a moment, Kent looked perplexed, as if he were searching his memory for anything that resembled misfortune. Then, a light dawned, and as if on cue, he hung his head in grief. "Thanks," he said. "A minute doesn't go by when Sonia's not in my thoughts. It's so hard to move on."

Timothy knew that he was treading on a potentially high-risk minefield. Still, he wasn't paying for Kent's cauliflower-potato-kale-lentil soup without getting some solid info in return. "Sonia obviously meant the world to you," he said. "You were engaged to be married, weren't you?"

Kent nodded. "New Year's Eve. Hawaii."

At this point, Timothy wanted to sound like a grief counselor, hoping that Kent would feel comfortable talking about his loss. But it was tricky. He decided that if he made his questions relevant to the suicide and how it affected Kent, the guy might keep talking. Timothy reached out his hand and touched Kent's arm. This was his way of letting him know he was there to offer comfort. Not that it really seemed necessary. He asked Kent a bunch of you questions. "When and where did *you* and Sonia meet? When were *you* first aware that you loved her? Did *you* know that she was unhappy? I heard *you* accused Jared Evans of contributing to Sonia's death…"

… Oh boy, that was a stupid thing to say, especially to a potential killer! Kent looked at Timothy with searing, inquisitive eyes as if he were seeing him for the first time. He said, "Jared Evans? How do you know about that evil little sniveling piece of human trash?"

Timothy stuttered as he tried to dig himself out of the sinkhole he'd just opened up for himself. He apologized for hitting a nerve and said that he totally agreed with him that Jared Evans was nothing more than dreck and that he, too, was aware of how horribly he treated people. But then Timothy stepped even further into the pooh when he foolishly said, "I don't believe that Jared's death was an accident. He was murdered. Someone who detested him. Someone like…"

"Like me?" Kent exploded. "That no-good, sorry excuse for a human being killed my Sonia! I hold him totally responsible for her death. If it hadn't been for him being so despicable to her, she'd be starring on Broadway in *Flags on the Moon* right now. It's a huge hit, and she would have been a bigger star than she already was. Jared Evans deprived her of that success. And he deprived me of the woman I loved!"

Kent became quiet, but he'd gotten the attention of almost everyone else in the restaurant. New Yorkers are famous for being blasé when it comes to seeing people behave oddly. Still, Kent's outburst definitely unsettled the other patrons around them. Timothy tried to ignore the stares and concentrate on defending his inquiry. But the young actor was having none of it.

"You work for Muriel Maynard. Jared Evans worked for Muriel, too," Kent said, connecting the dots for the first time. "You said that you believe Jared's death was murder. We're not really having lunch to discuss my career, are we? So why are we here?"

Timothy hated doing anything in public that might attract attention to himself. And no doubt his face had turned bright red. That always happened when he was embarrassed. Whenever a teacher called on him to answer a question in school, he looked like a guy with a severe case of rosacea. It also proved how weak he really was. Surely, Kent could smell blood and was ready to tear him apart.

"I'm really sorry, Kent," Timothy tried to act less mortified than he actually was. "I know what Jared said to Sonia about being a 'never was' and how upset that made her. And then she killed himself. That's a terrible tragedy, and I agree that Jared had blood on his hands, but…"

"But you think I killed Jared."

Although Timothy adamantly denied Kent's suggestion, he hoped it was true. Kent obviously had a motive. And he sounded off about Jared's contemptible nature and lack of conscience. So yes, he thought it was possible that Jared had been murdered by Kent. "So, sue me," Timothy said without thinking.

And that's precisely what Kent said he was going to do. Sue him and Muriel Maynard Management for a lot of money and things like libel, slander, character assassination, and malicious gossip. Although Timothy suddenly wished he'd never met the guy, he rather doubted that he'd slandered him. So, what if he asked a few nosey questions? Kent would have a tough time getting a lawyer to take a case with zero merits. But then, these are litigious times… That aside, Timothy decided that he had nothing to lose by continuing to prod Kent.

"I saw the letter you sent to Jared after Sonia's death," he lied, not having any evidence that Kent was responsible for Jared's mail at work that upset him.

"What are you talking about?" Kent growled, again becoming obviously agitated.

"The one you sent to him at the office. The one in which you threatened him for killing Sonia."

Kent gave Timothy one of the nastiest, most withering looks he'd ever received. Then he did what Timothy had only seen people do in movies to drive home a point: He picked up his glass of water and tossed the contents into Timothy's face. Talk about being dramatic. Was this taught in his method-acting class? Timothy was stunned, and time actually stood still as everyone in the restaurant turned to look at the altercation. A few customers made audible gasps. A few even chuckled. And as Kent stormed out of the restaurant, their waitress came rushing to Timothy's side.

"Your card was declined," she snarled, crossing her arms indignantly.

## Chapter Twenty

Timothy was more embarrassed about his worthless debit card than by the water running down his face. Counting out cents from the bottom of his pocket and rucksack to pay for lunch was the real humiliation. And, as he took the bus back to The Colton, he phoned Brad to report what had just happened. Sweet man that he was, Brad insisted that Timothy come over to his apartment straightaway. Timothy had been accosted, and Brad wanted to see for himself that he was all in one piece. *Where do such great guys come from?* Timothy thought, smiling to himself. In a short while, he was ringing the bell at Brad's place on East 52nd.

When Timothy heard the buzzer unlocking Brad's door, he walked into the small entrance hallway of the narrow, three-story, pre-war building. There was no elevator, so he had to walk up a flight of stairs to the second floor. For a minute, he wondered why Brad had chosen to live in what was probably a less-than-primo building in this otherwise decent part of town. But then he checked himself. Heck, he's probably paying a fortune for it. Rent in New York is over-the-top expensive. And no doubt Brad's personal space would be as terrific as he was. Timothy was right. When Brad opened the door and welcomed him in with a big hug, he saw that Brad had sophisticated decorating tastes. The furnishings were not cheap. No IKEA build-it-yourself, flatpack pieces here. They looked like genuine heirlooms.

The rooms were spacious, and the ceilings were high. There were two bedrooms, a large kitchen, a designated dining room, and a large living room with a fireplace and two floor-to-ceiling multi-paned windows that looked out over a small, fenced-in park. The white walls displayed original art. Side tables boasted framed photos of concert musicians and conductors at Carnegie Hall and Lincoln Center (as well as one of legendary comedienne Carol Burnett tugging at her earlobe), each personally autographed to Brad. And the hardwood floor was accented with a large Persian rug. The chairs and sofa were beautifully upholstered in what Timothy could tell were expensive fabrics. The room's highlight was a shiny black grand piano next to an exposed brick wall. The wall was adorned with a dozen Hirschfeld caricatures in identical black frames. Timothy's eyes grew wide as he identified the drawings of such Broadway legends as Ethel Merman, Liza Minnelli, Carol Channing, and the original cast of Cabaret.

Brad brought them iced tea, and they sat down to discuss the events of Timothy's very weird day. After hearing his review of the Kent episode, Brad said, "Yeah, he's an actor, all right. Such drama! But he should save the histrionics for the stage. What made him so livid?"

"Oh, just a tiny, silly, little ol' thing. I suggested that he killed Jared Evans."

"Oops," Brad said, grimacing. "Bold move on your part. Do you think he really could be guilty? His motive is solid, but how did he know where Jared was, and how did he get past the security system at The Colton?"

Timothy shrugged, heaved a deep sigh, and said that he thought it was odd that Kent hadn't seemed to be in too much grief over Sonia's suicide. "I know we all handle death differently, but when I told him I was sorry for his loss, he had to think about it for a long moment."

Brad was right to play devil's advocate and to suggest that since Sonia's death had happened months ago, Kent might have been successfully moving through the tragedy. "Do we even know how long they were a couple?" he asked.

"Regardless of their history, this dude can't stop talking about himself and his career long enough to shed tears for anyone," Timothy said. "And there's the questions of the incendiary letter which Kent denied sending."

That elusive letter. For crying out loud, Timothy didn't even know what was in the letter—which may or may not even really exist. It was Sandy's account of an incident he claimed to have observed in the office.

Timothy's mouth went dry as he considered what he had to say next. He took a sip of iced tea and stalled for a long moment. Then he said, "I think you need another meeting with Sandy. He needs to give you more—more information, that is." *Am I a fool or what?* Timothy asked himself. Why on earth would he actually suggest throwing this handsome man into Sandy's den of potential iniquity? He instantly regretted his words. He took another sip of iced tea and looked at Brad, who seemed to be weighing his suggestion. Then, dear man that he was, Brad said, with reluctance, "If you think it's for the best. But I'd much rather meet with you instead."

Timothy wanted to lean over and kiss the heck out of Brad. So, he did. And it was fantastic. And Brad tasted of the apple, cinnamon, and honey tea he'd been drinking.

Then it happened. No, not THAT! Timothy's phone rang. He looked at the caller ID, and his happy feeling turned to dread. He rolled his eyes and then tentatively answered the call. "Hi, Muriel."

\* \* \*

Within an hour, Timothy was back in Muriel's office being reprimanded for allowing fan email to go unanswered for several days and forgetting to meet The Suits, whom Timothy was interested to hear, worked at Nautilus Books. Oh, darn, he neglected to exchange those stupid folders. So, he did something he had recently become rather good at. He lied. Since he couldn't tell Muriel that he was investigating Jared's death despite the police classifying it as an accident, he said he'd had to take a few sick days. Of course, Muriel wasn't buying that baloney. And Timothy hadn't worked there long enough to accrue any sick days. At least not paid ones. He watched as Muriel wrote a note, and he intuitively knew that his lie would get his paycheck docked. Phooey!

"Oh, you young people are all coughing and sneezing around me," Muriel sneered. "Even my temp, What's Her Face, is out with something icky. It's all the processed foods that you kids eat. And rap music. Listen, dear," Muriel finally said, getting to the real reason Timothy was called into her office. "I'm going out of town for several days and taking your roommate with me."

Timothy pretended to be stupid. "Vacation?" he asked, but he shouldn't have because it was still supposed to be a secret that Muriel and Beverly were mother and daughter. Muriel answered with a change to Timothy's regular assignment. "You'll have to work from here. I need someone to cover the desk. It's only for three days or until What's Her Face comes back."

Little did Muriel know that this was something of a miracle. Was she reading his and Brad's thoughts? They had agreed that they needed the letter sent to Jared, and now Muriel was practically welcoming him into her office with open arms—unsupervised. It was a perfect setup for Timothy to look in every nook and cranny without being busted by the boss for breaking and entering.

Muriel must have noticed a look of glee on Timothy's face because she added, "You're still behind with answering emails. And you haven't posted to Facebook lately. Or Instagram. Or X." She shook her head. "What am I paying you for, and why do you people need so many ways to communicate anyway? In my day, we only had a landline and a residential mailbox."

Timothy wanted to say, "In your day, they communicated with hieroglyphics." But of course, he didn't. Instead, he said, "I'm happy to do whatever you need me to do."

\* \* \*

When Timothy returned to the penthouse, Beverly was in her bedroom, packing a suitcase. She looked tired and older than she had even the day before. She puttered back and forth from her closet to the bed and neatly laid sweaters and slacks into the luggage. "If I don't come back, it's been nice knowing you."

Timothy thought he might actually cry. Not because they were all that close, although they had become fond of each other, but because he saw how pointless Beverly thought her life had become. She was no longer in charge of her own affairs. Not that she'd had any real autonomy for years, but this was the final march to her permanent incarceration. She'd be caged in a home for old people and never really be free again. It was like she was a different species and was being sent to live with "her own kind," all of them waiting for angels or unicorns to usher them to the pearly gates.

Timothy knew better than to reach out and hug Beverly in

any sort of loving fashion, so he merely said, "I'll meet you on the terrace at wine time."

Again, Beverly didn't respond, but Timothy suspected it was because she was lost in her own thoughts about how quickly her life had gone from childhood to motherhood to a burdensome old lady. Timothy thought about his own family, and even though his mother could be a shrew, Timothy didn't think he could ever remove her from her home and put her somewhere "convenient" to wither and die.

As Timothy walked away from Beverly's door, he figured that since he was in the area, he might as well go into the office and grab a folder for The Suits so he wouldn't forget it in the morning. He opened the secret room and looked at the side of the safe where Jared's blood had turned the color of rust. Timothy promised himself to look for cleaning materials and remove the last evidence of Jared's life. It didn't seem right to leave a blood stain in Mercedes Ford's apartment. Then he looked up at the shelf from which Jared had supposedly tried to reach for—something. He pulled over the swivel desk chair and the stepstool.

And why hadn't Jared used the stepstool instead of the chair? This question had bothered Timothy since he discovered Jared's body. Why was Jared reaching for something on that upper shelf? Nothing much was stored there, just a few shoeboxes. And none of them seemed to have been moved. He decided to perform an experiment.

Timothy placed the swivel chair in a position that he thought was as Jared might have done. The room was small, so there were few variations on how he could arrange the chair next to the safe. Then he set foot on the seat, followed by the other foot. It wasn't hard to keep his balance, and the carpeted floor kept the chair from rolling. He reached the shelf, touched one of the boxes, and brought it down. Easy breezy. It seemed odd that Jared would have lost his balance in the way Mr. Griffin and the police insisted. Although it wasn't impossible, it still didn't seem right to him.

While Timothy was at it, he thought he should see what the boxes contained. What could have been so important that Jared lost his life over it? He opened the one he'd just retrieved. Lo and behold, it contained—shoes! Black-leather high-heels. From Michael Kors. Big deal, he thought. A shoebox containing shoes should have been no surprise. But why would Jared have been reaching for something so mundane? It seemed lame to think that Mercedes, who was on a film shoot, would have called asking for her pumps. If she'd needed dress shoes for something, the film's costume department could have arranged for that. And why were there shoes in a secure room? It seemed a strange place to keep them. Timothy placed the box back on the shelf and set the chair aside.

Timothy had come to get a file from the safe, so he did that. But this time, since Jared wasn't around to discover that he'd disobeyed the rules, he decided—as he suspected the assistants before him had also done—to see why there was so much secrecy about the contents. As he took a folder out to the desk in the office, he was feeling brazen and unconsciously looked around to make sure that he really was alone. With a bit of trepidation and an equal amount of curiosity, he opened the folder.

The pages were handwritten and appeared to be a chapter from a diary. From the first page, he realized this was Mercedes Ford's autobiography! No wonder it was handled with as much secrecy as an FBI investigation. It made complete sense. The two Suits who arrived each Tuesday to return and exchange folders were from Nautilus Books. Duh! Nautilus Books is one of New York's premier publishers!

Now Timothy realized why he was told not to review the material—because portions of the book might get out before publication. And then he wondered if Mercedes' book could have had something to do with Jared's death. Was there something in the pages that someone else didn't want to be revealed to the world? That seemed incredibly farfetched, considering that his favorite star had led an exemplary life as far as he knew. There were never any scandals. She worked steadily in movies and on Broadway while raising three great kids and still grieving the death of her beloved first husband. In fact, Timothy suspected that, other than being a movie star and marrying an incredibly sexy younger man, Mercedes Ford probably led a relatively dull life of all work and little play. Just totally mundane stuff like being photographed walking the red carpet at her film premiers, collecting acting trophies and humanitarian prizes, and traveling first class or on private jets.

However, as Timothy spent the next several hours reading the pages in all the folders, he discovered that Mercedes' life had been far from ideal. In fact, she revealed great unhappiness in her personal life: Her mother had left the family when Mercedes was only twelve years old. The auto accident she'd had in high school resulted in the death of her best friend. Her cancer diagnosis and treatment stopped her from graduating college. Timothy was just getting to the part where she married Sage when the text ended. "This is going to be a huge bestseller, and I, Timothy Truman Trousdale, am among the very first on the planet to read portions of the book," he said, thrilled to know more about one of the world's most celebrated stars.

If it were possible, Timothy loved Mercedes even more because she was brave enough to reveal her innermost feelings and social concerns, even at the possibility of disappointing or offending some of her worldwide admirers. Timothy returned all but one of the folders to the safe. The Suits would be coming around in the morning, and since he'd be in Muriel's office, he'd take it with him and have the guys meet him there. He supposed if Muriel knew he was removing the pages from the penthouse, she'd have a conniption, but what was he to do? He couldn't be in the office and penthouse at the same time.

The thing to do now was to find Beverly and share a much-needed bottle of wine.

Beverly beat Timothy to the punch. When Timothy arrived on the terrace, she had a glass filled and waiting for him and was reading the evening edition of *The New York Times*. She seemed to be in much better spirits. "Stocks are up," she said. "That Disney World incident is still in the news. Mickey is no longer allowed to touch kiddies during photo ops in Naughtyland," she added gleefully. "I love it when the mirror shatters, and we discover everything's an illusion. Especially in The Magic Kingdom."

"When do you leave for the tour of Glenwood Farms?" Timothy asked, knowing full well that it was tomorrow morning.

"As soon as Her Highness picks me up in the a.m.," Beverly said. "And who knows, I might love the place."

"You'll be back in a few days," Timothy assured her. "This is just to check it out, I suspect."

"Maybe. Maybe not," Beverly said. "Part of me just wants a decision to be made quickly. No sense in drawing out the inevitable. The sooner I know what's what, the better."

Timothy took a small sip of wine and didn't know what to say to Beverly. They were much alike in that they didn't want lingering situations that could easily be solved by someone just making a decision. But Timothy didn't want to sound ignorant or simplistic. He decided to offer a bit of philosophy. "I once asked a friend who was really old if he could live his life over again, what would he change."

"Having kids?" Beverly cracked.

"He said that he wouldn't have worried as much."

"Good advice," Beverly sighed. "Why worry about things we can't change? But if I got to live my life over, I'd marry your boyfriend, Brad."

"Brad's not my boyfriend," Timothy laughed and blushed. "Of course, I wish that he were, but I suspect he's too good-looking for me."

"You're nuts," Beverly said. "I saw your skinny little bod the other morning. Some men go for substance over brawn. Just hit the gym for a couple of months, and you'll be smokin'!"

Timothy giggled with embarrassment. He was shy about his body and a bit mortified that Beverly had taken such a close appraisal.

"You wear a bath towel really well, if you don't mind me saying so," Beverly continued. "I can definitely see you and Brad naked together. Also, we seldom know exactly what others see in us. How many times have you seen a giant marshmallow stuffed into a bikini pushing a baby stroller with an impossibly good-looking spouse or playmate by their side? You already know that Brad likes you, for crying out loud. Take it from me, an old lady. If you don't catch this guy, you'll end up wishing you'd at least tried."

Of course, Beverly was right. Timothy was the opposite of one of those marshmallow people. And Brad seemed to enjoy kissing him as much as he loved kissing Brad. At that very moment, Timothy decided to make his feelings for Brad much clearer. No ambiguities.

However, almost as important was solving Jared's murder

mystery. To be honest, he was hooked; despite Jared's horrid behavior and lack of interest in his death from everyone else around, Timothy just had to know what had really happened. He was excited about getting to Muriel's office in the morning and finding that letter. He was sure it would prove that Kent Isaacson had threatened to kill Jared.

Timothy felt a bit guilty being so excited about his own life and adventures while Beverly was facing her worst nightmare. But the wine had made Beverly mellow, and now she didn't seem too upset about her prospects. They sat quietly listening to the traffic far below until, out of the blue, and without thinking, Timothy stupidly said, "I'll give you five to one that Mercedes' memoire will be a huge hit."

Beverly looked at Timothy oddly, and Timothy instantly knew he'd let his mouth race ahead of his brain again. He tried to wriggle his way out by adding, "I mean someday. I'm sure she'll unload lots of gossip when she feels like writing her autobiography. Don't you think so, too?" He attempted to laugh, but it sounded more like he was clearing his throat.

And then Beverly said, "You obviously know better than I do." She was plainly aware that Timothy had ignored one of the cardinal employment rules, not to read the material stashed in the safe. But Beverly also didn't seem at all concerned. Timothy suspected that she didn't care much about anything anymore. "Mercedes deserves everything she's worked for. Well, except for Sage," Beverly added. "As you've probably discovered, all the closets—and graves—will be opened." And then she cackled like an old witch.

## Chapter Twenty-One

Timothy didn't sleep well that night. Perhaps he was still in a bit of shock over having Kent Isaacson publicly toss a glass of water in his face. He could still feel the liquid cascading over him. Or, perhaps, it was the anticipation of working as Muriel's office assistant the next day that gave him a restless night. Or, more than likely, it was the excitement he felt about rooting through Muriel's office in search of the mythical letter that was sent to Jared. It didn't help that he was also anxious about making Brad aware of his true feelings. Regardless of which of those scenarios was most prominent, they collectively made him edgy all night. And he was already totally awake when his alarm went off.

When Timothy arrived in the kitchen, Beverly had a mug of coffee waiting for him. She was dressed in black slacks, and a brown-marled, open cardigan accessorized with a small heart-shaped black stone necklace surrounded with diamond chips. Beverly looked like a million bucks. She was certainly dressed to impress any of the other seniors she'd encountered at Glenwood Farms. And if she hated the place, she'd surely have made an excellent case for being too good for unacceptable living accommodations. "Brava!" Timothy said, admiring Beverly's outfit. "Be sure to wear those awesome butterfly sunglasses you wore a few days ago. They say, "Don't screw with me!"

"Got 'em in my purse," Beverly assured him and took a

sip from her coffee mug. "I've decided to make this an adventure. I'm even going to be nice to Muriel. If possible. She thinks I'm too stupid to know what she's up to, so I have the upper hand. I'm prepared to play naïve."

When the elevator arrived, Beverly and Timothy were seated at the dining room table. The chimes gave them a few moments' heads up, and they were prepared to greet Muriel. Timothy shouldn't have been shocked by Muriel's lack of warmth toward her mother, but he was. There was no cheery greeting. No hello, kiss on the cheek. Not even a "Are you ready?" Instead, Muriel barked, "Hop to it." And her only acknowledgment of Timothy was a nonverbal "Hmm." Not that Timothy cared. He was well aware of how little Muriel thought of him.

When Timothy leaned in to hug Beverly goodbye, he whispered in her ear, "Fabiola."

Beverly grinned and nodded in understanding. Timothy meant that her alter ego, the woman he'd originally met, was strong and uncompromising. A tough cookie, as they say. "Invite me to your wedding to Brad," she whispered back.

After the elevator doors closed, the penthouse was inordinately quiet. The pulsating beat from his own heart was the only sound Timothy could hear, and it was racing. Timothy realized how much adrenaline he'd pumped just being in the uncomfortable presence of Muriel Maynard. Authority figures make me jittery, he said to himself as he moved to the kitchen and emptied his coffee mug into the sink. He did the same with Beverly's and lovingly held the mug for a moment longer. He really hoped that she would return to the penthouse.

Timothy had to get to Muriel's office. He wanted to be there before anyone else arrived so that he could search for the letter unobserved. He ordered an Uber, and off he went.

Unfortunately, he didn't manage to arrive at an empty office; a couple of other people were already at their desks. However, Timothy wasn't going to be defeated. He decided on another tactic. He would wait for an opportune moment and stroll into Muriel's office as if he belonged there.

He parked himself at Jared's old desk and powered up the computer. He was dreading the first call of the day. Muriel had left only minimal instructions, and Timothy was afraid of making a mistake, possibly insulting a Broadway legend, or doing something to make Muriel fire him sooner. For his new plan to work, he now needed people in the office to see him and realize that he was covering for the sick temp before he ventured into Muriel's office willy-nilly. He was terrified of being seen going through Muriel's things and thus suspected of ransacking the office.

And then the phones started ringing, and Timothy was swamped! "Muriel Maynard's office. How may I assist you?" he said every few seconds. It was insulting to his ego. He should be writing novels, not lying to people, and telling them to have a nice day when he really didn't care if they did or not. Most of the morning passed in a blur. And his own day turned out to be less magical when he finally got a moment to go into Muriel's office. The door was locked!

What? No! This can't be happening, he screamed to himself. It had all seemed so perfect the day before: Muriel would be away. Timothy would be working at her temp's desk. He would have a couple of days to find that blasted letter. Muriel would never know that Timothy had been in her space. Darn! Timothy was mere inches away from his goal. Separated by a locked door. "The Lord giveth, and the Lord taketh away!" he muttered.

Timothy returned to his desk, and in between calls, he mulled over his options. He certainly couldn't pick the lock and break in. There might even be an alarm on the door for all he knew. And maybe there were hidden cameras, although the way the office was decorated, he doubted that Muriel had done anything high-tech since electric typewriters were the height of modern office equipment. And then Timothy had an inspired idea that cheered him up in an instant, he thought about the building superintendent's department. Surely, they would have keys to all the doors.

When a guy named Larry in maintenance answered the phone, Timothy explained his predicament. He put on his best panic-stricken voice and half lied, "I'm Muriel's assistant for a few days, and I've locked myself out of her office. She'll kill me for sure. You know how she is! Please help me!"

"Hey, I understand how you feel, buddy, but that's the one office I don't have no keys for. Sorry," Larry said. He was sorry? Timothy's luck had run out. He was devastated. All his plans for solving a murder mystery had hit another barrier. But, just as Timothy descended into despair again, Larry said, "Call Mark in janitorial. Maybe he's got a key."

Timothy wondered why he always went to a negative place instead of trusting the Universe to bring him everything he needed. Well, probably because the Universe hadn't brought him a book contract yet. Nor had the Universe listened to his plea for winning the Mega Millions lottery. But here was a case where the Universe, indeed, had come to his rescue. Oh heck, he knew that we're all interconnected, so he should just sit back and let the world turn and trust that he'd always be all right. Like his old friend who'd said he wouldn't have wasted his life worrying. Timothy had to start putting that philosophy into action.

Within ten minutes, Mark from janitorial was unlocking Muriel's office door. Timothy looked around, but nobody seemed to think there was anything unusual about an assistant having their boss's locked door opened by janitorial.

When he finally decided that the time was right to search for the letter, Timothy casually walked back into the office and opened a filing cabinet. He had no real idea where he'd find the blasted note. If he could find it at all. Would it be in a folder? Under a stack of other papers? Would it be hidden among the pages of a magazine? The office was relatively small, but it still seemed that he was searching for a needle in a haystack. There were way too many places where the letter could have been stashed. Timothy was suddenly incredibly demoralized. All the "what ifs" came rushing into his thoughts. But he soldiered on.

After going through all the folders in the filing cabinet, Timothy moved on to the drawers in the credenza behind Muriel's desk. On either side were built-in cabinets crammed with old *Playbills*, restaurant receipts, and miscellaneous office supplies, like envelopes, pens, and yellow highlighters. Just stuff. It was all so unorganized and daunting. Timothy was just about to give up and head to lunch when he discovered a locked drawer in Muriel's desk. He pulled the drawer handle several times but to no avail. Yep, it was definitely secured. And a locked drawer meant only one thing. There were important contents inside. Timothy called janitorial again, and Mark returned to help out.

Timothy looked around to make sure he wasn't being watched. When he eventually opened the drawer and discovered the familiar leather pouch he'd carried to the set of *Blind Trust*, he picked it up. The little padlock was fastened, but he figured it probably wouldn't take much to pick it open. And he was right. A paper clip was all he needed, and when he looked inside, he was thrilled by the contents. Among a sheaf of other papers, he found one that had obviously been crumpled, then smoothed out. And, buoyed by his success, that's when he decided to go to lunch.

Timothy left the office with his treasure and headed back to The Colton. It was the only place he could think of where he'd have complete privacy. But when he arrived in the lobby, The Suits were waiting for him. Darn! He'd totally forgotten to call them and arrange to exchange the folders at the office or to take the folder with him to Muriel's. Had they been waiting all morning? He brought them up to the penthouse, and when they entered, their eagle eyes immediately rested on the folder on the Lalique table where Timothy had left it this morning to help him remember to bring it with him to the office.

Drats! Busted! Timothy thought and expected a verbal dressing down for leaving the folder in the open. But as he'd previously discovered, for guys who work in publishing, they were certainly men of few words. Yes, there were cryptic looks and body language that spoke volumes about the transgression. Still, they simply glared at him and then turned to re-enter the elevator. And Timothy made a big show of promising to immediately deposit the returned folder in the safe. "Swear to god, hope to die," he joked, wishing them a good day. He'd file it away when he darn well felt like it.

By now, Timothy was desperate to check the contents of the pouch. He eagerly brought the zippered folio to the twin sofas opposite the fireplace and withdrew the pages. The only item he was interested in was the letter. And that's the first thing he read. And reread. And read for a third time. And then he called Brad.

Timothy had to return to Muriel's office pronto, so he asked him to come to the penthouse that evening. "Oh, yeah, this is major," he said. "Can't tell you over the phone, but trust me, it's absolutely amazing."

For once, Timothy personally needed the safe in the secret

room. Along with the zippered folio, he grabbed the folder left by The Suits, stashed it inside the safe, and checked twice to ensure it was completely locked.

It was tough going back to the office. Timothy totally disliked the atmosphere, which had a negative vibrational feel. The other employees weren't necessarily unfriendly, but they didn't seem to want to engage with Timothy, either. He felt that by sitting at Jared's desk, he had become Jared in their eyes. And he didn't have answers to all the questions callers asked him. All he could do was take notes and promise to have Muriel call them right away. Of course, every time he tried to reach Boss Lady with someone's urgent message (they were all urgent), the call went straight to her voicemail. As Timothy wasn't getting any feedback, he had no idea if Muriel was even receiving his messages. But heck, Timothy couldn't worry about that. What he really had to worry about was far greater than some Broadway actor complaining about a co-star with halitosis or a director who was a wimp about directing his megalomaniacal leading lady. Timothy already had three calls from Mandalay Constanzo, the stand-up comic, griping about the small size of her name on the billboard for her show in Vegas. Timothy didn't care. He had a strong lead to a murder to contend with.

When the workday was finally over, Timothy was exhausted but eager to get home and see Brad and discuss his amazing find. Brad arrived at The Colton and Timothy decided to play it cool. First, he posed as the Lord of the Manor and gave him a tour of the penthouse. Then he offered Brad a glass of wine. Then he invited him into the inner sanctum of the secret room. He was thrilled to be able to impress this man with not only where he lived but also with the hidden amenities. And when he opened the safe, he acted like a game show spokesmodel, revealing what was hidden behind Door #3. "Voila!" he said as he withdrew the zippered folio and handed it to Brad. "I'll leave you to it. Be prepared to tell me how amazing I am," he said. Then he left the room to refill his wine glass and turn on music.

Ten minutes later, Brad wandered into the living room carrying the documents. Timothy gazed at him and registered how great he looked in his tight, faded red T-shirt, Jeans, and cowboy boots. And Timothy loved the smile that showed Brad's perfect white teeth and made his dimples pop to life. He handed him a refilled wine glass and said, "I would never have believed it. Would you?"

Although Timothy referred to the documents, his sentiments would have worked just as well to describe how he felt about being in Brad's company. He could never have imagined that he'd have not only an exciting job (although he was aware of how tenuous it was) but that he'd also be reeling toward love. He reminded himself of how life can change so quickly. He was thrilled. But just as he was thinking so highly of the Universe for giving him such an amazing life, Brad brought him back to reality.

"Okay, so just as you suspected, Kent Isaacson sure didn't like Jared. And he knew where he worked after leaving Lisa Lambert," Brad said. "But writing to someone and telling them…" Brad looked at the paper and read a paragraph aloud, "…There's a special place in hell for pathetic little good-for-nothing weasel losers like you. Let's see how many people attend your funeral. I'll be there, but just to make sure you're dead. You're going down, freak boy."

"I know!" Timothy gushed. "Isn't it exciting? We have something worth taking to the police."

Brad shook his head, which instantly deflated Timothy's spirit. "Honey (he called Timothy honey!), there's nothing substantial here. Sure, it's obviously written by an angry dude, but telling someone that…" again, he referred to another paragraph of the letter, "'…The wrong person is in their grave… Watch out. Life can be as dangerous as black ice,'" is not real evidence.

Timothy had planned to specifically point to that last line to make his case. But he now knew that Brad was right. There were no real death threats in the letter. Warnings, for sure. And a bit of philosophy, too. But it was far from a warning that Jared would soon be a dead man—and at Kent's own hands. And there was the not-so-small matter of explaining how he got into The Colton. Timothy was certain that Beverly wasn't involved, and blockhead Griffin was not a man to bribe or easily fool.

Of course, Timothy was not pleased with Brad's analytical brain. It would have been so much more fun if he had agreed that Kent was the guy who probably murdered Jared. Timothy would have been so much happier, and Brad would have been so much sexier (nah, it was impossible for Brad to be any sexier) had Timothy's own hypothesis been determined to be logical. He took another sip of wine and pouted for a moment. And then his darling man reached over, tapped the bridge of Timothy's nose, and brought his lips close to Timothy's. He looked intently into Timothy's eyes and, with his seductive voice, said, "You obviously didn't read the other documents, did you?"

Timothy blinked a few times in stupidity. He had expected a kiss.

"But be prepared," Brad warned. "You'll be rather upset because there's a reference to your girlfriend—Mercedes Ford."

## Chapter Twenty-Two

All the other correspondences in the folio were copies of email communications between that dubious fan Bryony, who had set her sights on that other someone named Joe. Brad looked at Timothy and said, "These are duplicates from Jared's computer. Why would Muriel have them?"

"He monitored all that was written and received, and Jared must have given the copies to Muriel," Timothy said, remembering Jared's attention to his own email activities. "And what about this Post-It?" Timothy took a page from the folio and read a hand-printed note: "Stop! This game has turned lethal!"

As they'd previously read, the most recent message from Bryony to Joe was that she no longer wanted anything to do with him. "Jared Evans is dead. I don't want to believe you had a hand in this, but I'm no fool. I'm completely mortified that I ever started this game. I'm done," said the last one.

Brad listened intently to Timothy, and he could tell that all sorts of things were running through his brain. "Read the next one from Joe," Brad said.

"Actually, you are a fool," Timothy read. "But don't blame yourself too much because people like you are easily manipulated. I have quite a few starry-eye peeps in my back pocket. And trust me, they don't abandon me. Well, at least not without paying a very high and painful price. When we meet—and I'm already making arrangements—you'll really wish you hadn't ever become a fan of Mercedes Ford."

Timothy looked up and stared at Brad. "Don't try to tell me this message isn't a threat," he said. "If I were Bryony, I'd be terrified of this Joe guy. But we still don't know who he is. There isn't anyone named Joe in the office. Must be a former employee who still has access to Mercedes' email account?"

After ruminating and sipping more wine, Brad moved over to the sofa and sat closer to Timothy. Timothy wasn't sure which was the more powerful thought, the possibility that Brad would take him in his arms right then and there or trying to figure out who Joe was and how to stop him from continuing to harass Mercedes' fan, Bryony.

Brad solved the problem. He kissed Timothy. Passionately. After that, he said, "Taking into account all that we've just read, I think this Joe is our strongest suspect. I think we should contact him and draw him out."

Timothy was lightheaded by the smoldering kiss, so at first, he didn't fully take in Brad's suggestion about contacting Joe. "How? Who? Where? He's a phantom," he reminded.

Brad shrugged and said, "We have his email address. Let's pretend that we do know who he is. Call his bluff. Lure him into the open with some sort of bait. It's worth a try."

Timothy kept thinking about how amazing this man was, and Brad kept proving him absolutely right. And Brad's new idea was, he thought, brilliant. "Oooh! This sounds like fun!" he said enthusiastically. He should have known better.

For the next hour, Timothy and Brad went a bit crazy trying to think of what to say in an email to this Joe character. No matter what they tried, the messages all sounded like indictments or blackmail. They had no real idea who Joe was and, therefore, no idea how to lure him out of anonymity. They finally took a break and opened another bottle of wine. Timothy accessed Pandora on the condo's music source and selected a program titled *All Frank. All Sinatra. All the Way.*

Brad and Timothy stepped onto the terrace and gazed at the sparkling lights below. It was chilly. A light breeze whispered against their bare arms. Timothy remembered that he had been melting in the city's heat just a couple of weeks ago. Now, he almost needed a sweater. Then Brad enfolded him in his arms, and he had all the warmth he needed. And Brad smelled sexy, too. The heat from his body radiated a clean Ivory soap aroma. They started swaying together to the sound of Sinatra singing, *Strangers in the Night*. Heaven was where they were at that very moment. It was really like an old Hollywood movie musical. But a set decorator couldn't have created a more romantic atmosphere. A screenwriter couldn't have written better dialogue. And a choreographer couldn't have given them better dance moves. They were their own director and audience. And then Brad whispered the most shattering words Timothy had ever heard: "Pretend you're Bryony."

What? Is he insane? Timothy stopped mid-sway and looked at Brad. Why is he even thinking of this Bryony person while holding me?

Timothy's thoughts instantly transmitted directly into Brad's brain, and Brad realized that the romantic mood was broken. "What I mean is we don't need to create a fake person to reach out to Joe," Brad explained. "All we have to do is hijack Bryony's name and send a message that will coax him to come forward and identify himself."

Timothy looked up at Brad, ashamed of himself for his initial gut reaction. He was grateful that they had a mutual interest. And really, what could be more romantic than—murder? "So now I'm Bryony. What should I say to Joe?" Timothy asked.

Brad thought for a long moment. "You're the brilliant

writer," he said. "But, as Shakespeare said, 'Brevity is the soul of wit,' so make it concise and to the point, just to test the waters. How about starting with some sort of apology for even thinking he was capable of Jared's murder? Make Joe think that Bryony realizes she's made a mistake and wants him to come back into her life."

The romantic mood was still broken, so Timothy reluctantly returned to the condo. He picked up his glass of wine and led Brad toward the office. After a deep breath, he sat before the computer and began typing.

> Dearest Joe. Please accept my sincere apologies. I overreacted. I haven't been able to sleep or think of anything but you and the plans we made. Please forgive me and take me back. I am good for you. And you are good for me.
> —Bryony.

Brad nodded his head in approval, and Timothy clicked Send. "Now we wait," Brad added, slowly running his hand through Timothy's hair. "I think I know what we should do in the meantime." Then he gently pulled Timothy up from the chair. "It's time I had a tour of the upstairs," he purred. Jared's ban on visitors was well and truly forgotten.

\* \* \*

When morning arrived, and there still was no word from Joe, Brad suggested that Timothy take the laptop to work with him. Who would know? Jared was in the Afterlife, and Muriel was out of town. "It'll drive you totally nuts to have to wait until you get home tonight to find out if Joe responded to you, er, Bryony," Brad said.

*No. What will drive me nuts all day is thinking about you and remembering last night… and the middle of the night… and waking up with you this morning… and…* Timothy wanted to say.

***

It was another busy day at Muriel Maynard Management. Bobby Bunch, the musical comedy star, called a dozen times to complain about the billboard he'd seen advertising his concert series in Kansas City. He raged that his picture wasn't large enough, and the type-font used for the performance dates didn't stand out clearly enough. Maggie Lamour called several times, too, demanding to be allowed to meet with the director of the revival of the musical *Blast Off!* And Muriel was still not answering Timothy's calls.

People were shouting over the phone, and the office was again in bedlam. It appeared to Timothy that even the rat girls and boys in the office seemed to take pleasure in watching him suffer. With every passing second, he vowed to buckle down, start writing his next book, and pester agents to represent him. He didn't want to live like this forever and decided he couldn't count on anyone (probably not even Brad) to save him from a life of menial office labor. If he wanted to succeed, it was entirely up to him.

By the time Timothy was ready to leave the office at six, he still hadn't heard back from Joe. He checked for messages every twenty minutes, but the In Box only contained spam. The one bright spot in Timothy's life was that he was meeting Brad at La Strega for another dinner. "My treat," Brad had said before kissing goodbye at the condo that morning. But then, Brad had never let Timothy pay for anything in the past. He was as generous as he was gorgeous, and Timothy suddenly knew the meaning of the phrase, "If I can't have him, nobody will!" Of course, he'd never really hurt anyone, especially sexy Brad, with whom he was definitely falling hard, and wasn't about to let him go.

When Timothy arrived at the restaurant, Brad was already seated and checking messages on his phone. Timothy waltzed right past the hostess, ignoring her "Do you have a reservation?" command, and kissed Brad on the cheek. *Yeah, I have a reservation, all right,* he thought to himself. He sat down and stared at Brad's eyes and dimples. He couldn't decide which of the two was more seductive.

"Any news?" Brad asked.

"A lot of nil and nada," Timothy said, withdrawing the computer from his rucksack and placing it on another chair. "I'll show you in a minute."

"Well, I have something interesting to report," Brad added. "Sandy was eager to meet with me and said he wanted to clear his conscience about something. He invited me to his place for coffee in the morning."

Timothy must have looked jealous because Brad offered a small laugh and insisted, "It's nothing like that. Really. Nothing for you to worry about."

Oh sure, Timothy thought. A sexy guy invites an even sexier guy over for coffee, and it's 'nothing like that?' He remembered the ginger-haired FedEx driver in his hometown and how many women invited him in for "a cup" after he delivered a package. "It's nothing like that," his mother answered when Timothy commented that the birthrate in Claberville quadrupled, and there were a lot of redheaded kids being born into families with otherwise brown-haired people.

"As a matter of fact, I told him to meet me at The Caffeine Canteen over by Carnegie Hall," Brad said, easing Timothy's fears. "You can join us if you want to."

Of course, Brad knew Timothy had to work. There was no

way Timothy could get out of the office to join him and Sandy, even to spy on them. And spying was not something Timothy wanted to start doing anyway. He had to face the fact that they weren't a couple—at least not yet. So, he pretended to be excited about Brad's meeting with Sandy and convinced himself that it could only be about Jared's death. "What do you think he wants to discuss that he didn't tell you before?" Timothy asked.

"He said it was about Mercedes' husband, Sage."

\* \* \*

Another delightful dinner with Brad had ended, but then he surprised Timothy. "It's nice outside, and if you feel like walking back rather than getting an Uber, I'm up for it."

Timothy tried not to appear too giddy about Brad's invitation. Still, he was obviously transparent because, without a word from him, Brad said, "I hoped you'd feel that way. Let's go. And maybe afterward…"

They left La Strega, and Brad took Timothy's hand in his. They strolled in the cool night air, heading toward The Colton, and Timothy was as happy as he could ever remember being. With Brad, he realized that although the planet may be a mess, and a lot of bosses and politicians made life hell for everyone else, and gazillions of people were lonely and unhappy, there was still an excellent reason for living and for being optimistic about the future. Namely, love.

During their stroll, Brad revealed personal information about his past and why his last boyfriend had left him. The guy had fallen for a trumpet player Brad had introduced him to. He talked about all his years of studying piano and how his family had expected him to become a great concert pianist. They'd given him every opportunity and hadn't spared any expense for lessons and training. But the sudden death of his beloved father had so grieved him that he couldn't continue his studies. It had taken a couple of years for him to feel creative again, but by then, the musical fast-track to stardom that he'd been running on had ended, and he had lost all interest in performing.

Timothy, too, felt comfortable telling his life story. He described his lonely childhood in a small Southern town where he felt completely out of place because he didn't fit in even at home. His family was dysfunctional. His parents didn't like each other. And his worship of celebrities like Karen Carpenter and Doris Day, instead of Beyoncé and Jay Z, was asking for trouble among his peers. Zero dating in high school. His only friends were books. And, of course, his big dream of being a *New York Times* bestselling author. Brad was completely supportive, and when they arrived outside at The Colton, they embraced and became totally lost in another deep kiss.

"I like you a lot," Brad said with earnest sincerity.

"I really like you a lot, too," Timothy grinned flirtatiously. "Tonight was really special. Last night was especially special! Hell, every moment I'm with you is amazing," he gushed. "Let's go upstairs."

Brad smiled as he looked deeply into Timothy's eyes. "You're amazing," he said. "I really want to make our time last as long as possible. Like maybe forever. I'll call Sandy and move our meeting back a couple of hours, so I don't have to rush away in the morning."

Timothy was already fantasizing about spending another night with Brad and agreed that he should call Sandy. "And I'm not even going to check if there's a message from Joe." He shook his head. "Nope. No thoughts of Joe or a message… no Joe… no… JOE!"

Timothy was suddenly apoplectic with horror. "Joe! The laptop!" he shouted. "I left the laptop at the restaurant! I was so carried away by the fun time we were having. Oh my gosh! We've got to get it back!"

Brad looked as if he'd just had a stroke. Any bonus points Timothy might have accrued for being charming and bright had just blown up. Timothy was an idiot. He knew it! A simple-minded bonehead. He wanted to die.

Brad immediately hailed a cab, and they hopped in. "La Strega, over on 8th," Brad cried to the driver. "It's an emergency!" Then he turned to Timothy. He took his hand and said, "Remember, twice you've lost your wallet, and twice it's been returned, you said. You have good karma. Everything will be all right."

Together, they burst into the restaurant and dashed to the table where they'd been seated. The table was unoccupied, and the computer wasn't there. Brad sprinted back to the hostess' lectern. Although she was about to sit another couple, Brad pulled her aside. "I'm really sorry," he said, "but we left a laptop computer at our table." He pointed to where they had been sitting all evening. "Did someone turn it in?"

Although this was the same hostess who had previously given Brad a covetous eye, she was not amused by him interrupting her as she was taking care of new diners. "I'll see," she said coldly and proceeded to bring her charges to their table. Apparently, Brad's sexiness didn't always work. Not everyone drops whatever they're doing to be of service to him. Other than Timothy.

They watched as the hostess seated the couple, then disappeared into the kitchen. It seemed ages until they heard her voice asking, "Is this what you're looking for?" Brad and Timothy turned around, and there she was, holding the laptop. She saw their expressions of relief and gratitude. Brad reached out for the machine. "Not so fast, cutie," she said, pulling the computer to her chest. "You'll have to prove that this is yours. Is your name on it?"

"It's actually mine," Timothy said. "And no, my name isn't on it. It should be. And I'll make sure that doesn't happen again."

"I need proof," the hostess said, looking down her nose at Timothy.

"Oh, come on," Timothy urged. "You've seen us in your restaurant several times. I'm sure that Brad even leaves good tips. Can't you take my word that the computer belongs to me?"

The hostess didn't respond verbally, but Timothy could tell she wasn't impressed with how often they'd patronized La Strega.

Brad interrupted. "Timothy knows the password. Only the owner would know the password." He took the machine from the hostess' hands and set it down on her lectern.

Timothy opened the cover and typed in the code. A bright red banner flashed across the screen and screamed: PASSWORD INCORRECT!

"What? No!" Timothy said. Although he'd committed all the passwords to his own devices to memory, he hadn't bothered to learn Jared's code. "I'm just nervous," he said. "Let me try again." He knew he only had three tries, and if he were locked out, only Muriel could override the system. But then Muriel would also know that he'd taken Jared's laptop. The moment was dire. This time, instead of placing his fingers on the home keys and risk having his less-than-nimble fingers miss a stroke, he held the shift key while he depressed another for the first character. Then, he slowly pressed a series of other keys with his index finger. He lingered over the Return key and looked up at Brad, who nodded in support.

He went for it, and the computer instantly came to life. Timothy and Brad simultaneously smiled and exhaled "thank gods" as the hostess made a sound that suggested she was resigned to handing it over. "Take better care of your things," she said snidely.

"So much for our favorite restaurant," Timothy said when they stepped outside.

"We'll just have to find a new favorite."

Apparently, even if Brad had thought Timothy was a numbskull, he still wanted to see him again. Although Timothy was still embarrassed by his stupidity, he was grateful that Brad seemed not to have let that potentially disastrous situation affect his feelings for him. At least, that's what he was hoping. "This time, I'll Uber it home," Timothy said, tapping his cell phone app. The car arrived in minutes, and Brad kissed him goodnight. Not the sort of kiss he gave Timothy after their romantic walk, but considering the drama they'd just shared, he thought it was more than adequate.

Timothy held on tightly to the computer during the drive back as if holding a winning lottery ticket. Nothing would cause him to let go. Nothing except a call from Beverly that came in. He placed the computer on his lap to answer the phone.

Beverly was calling from Pennsylvania. Just as she'd expected, Muriel had taken her to visit Glenwood Farms. They'd argued during the tour, and both had said terrible things to one another. Beverly was in tears.

They were still talking when the car arrived at The Colton, and they continued their conversation as Timothy took the elevator to the penthouse. Once inside, he put Beverly on speaker, and they chatted while Timothy poured himself a glass of red wine. "Wish you were here, my friend," he said. "You've only been gone one day, but there's so much to tell you."

"Brad or the investigation?" Beverly asked.

"Both! But I don't think we should talk about the latter until I see you in person," Timothy said, always concerned that someone may be eavesdropping. "When are you back?"

"Muriel's back the day after tomorrow."

"Can't wait to see you," Timothy said, ignoring that Beverly hadn't answered his specific question.

Timothy really wanted her home. Now, he was the one who was beginning to cry. And the penthouse seemed lonelier than ever. If he had any guts, he would have called Brad and asked him to return and spend the night. But he decided to save his Knight in Shining Armor Loyalty Rewards Coupons for when he really needed them.

# Chapter Twenty-Three

Timothy was seated at the desk outside Muriel's office the next morning when... Muriel unexpectedly returned. "Messages!" she snapped in place of a greeting. "And get me Karl Bevel, Robert Kant, Eva Swallow, and Rupert Gallows on the phone. In that order. Now!"

Yep, the shrew was back. Sometimes, although he hated to sound sexist, in his personal experience (and with ol' Jared being the exception), men were more comfortable to work for than women. Although he would bet his life that Mercedes Ford would be a perfect boss. If only Timothy really worked for her instead of Muriel *Mean*ard.

It was two o'clock before Timothy could take his lunch break and call Brad. Practically starving to death, he left the office and headed to a hot dog cart parked at the curb. Two boiled dogs with mustard and relish and a Coke later, he called Brad. He was desperate for an update on his meeting with Sandy.

Brad had just left The Caffeine Canteen and was headed home, where he could write up a few notes about his meeting. "Just give me the gist," Timothy prodded. "Anything especially creepy?"

As a matter of fact, Brad did have some information that was a bit disturbing. However, all he would say over the phone was that Sandy had completely understood why Jared fired him and no longer held any serious animosity toward him. He knew he'd deserved to be sacked. There was, however, a bigger fish that Brad deemed worthy of catching and filleting. He suggested Timothy rendezvous with him at the Bethesda Fountain in Central Park at 6:30 to hear more.

In the meantime, Timothy was illicitly carrying the stolen satchel from Muriel's desk in his rucksack. He had to replace it ASAP, so he returned to the office to wait for an opportunity to smuggle it back before Muriel noticed it missing. But Muriel was too busy even to use the bathroom. Timothy kept bringing her cups of coffee, hoping to induce the need to pee, but she just kept yammering on the phone and yelling to Timothy to call this director and that actor and to make other calls here and there.

While pouring more java for Muriel, Timothy noticed a half-eaten birthday cake in the break room and a card signed by everyone in the office. "Kammy" was written on the envelope. Before returning to his desk, Timothy popped his head into Muriel's office and suggested she go over and wish Kammy a happy birthday. "You do it for me," Muriel said curtly. "These contracts are due tomorrow."

Timothy rolled his eyes and tried to find another ruse to get her out of the office. "There's cake," he teased.

"No thanks," Muriel said without even looking at him.

"Gluten-free," Timothy added, not really knowing if that was true.

Finally, Muriel looked up. She was obviously irritated by the constant interruptions.

"It's just that you'd make Kammy's day by personally wishing her a happy birthday," Timothy said, hoping Muriel would feel guilty enough to make an effort. "It's what bosses do."

With a heavy sigh and a pen that bounced off the wall when she flipped it, Muriel finally got up from her desk and left the office. "Which one is Kammy?" she asked. Heck, Timothy didn't know for sure, so he pointed to an anonymous desk that was farthest away. Without wasting a second, he grabbed the pouch from his rucksack and raced to Muriel's desk. He pulled on the drawer handle. No! The darn thing was locked again! Timothy should have noticed it was one of those self-shutting locks—it did make that clicking sound when he pushed it closed, he now remembered. Naturally! This was exactly what his world was like. How could this be happening? he screamed to himself. Timothy saw his boss returning. He was trapped. He had the clutch in his hands but couldn't get back to his desk quickly enough. He remembered the cluttered cabinets in the credenza, so he opened the one on the left and shoved the satchel among the office supplies. But, of course, Muriel caught him.

"Need something?" Muriel asked suspiciously.

"Got it," Timothy said, holding up a highlighter that he had been smart enough to retrieve. "I'm out of yellow."

Muriel gave Timothy a dubious look but went back to working on the contracts and ignored him.

Darn! If Muriel opened the cabinet, she'd find the bag and know for sure that Timothy had placed it there. And, if she looked in her desk drawer, she'd rightfully accused Timothy of taking the blasted zippered thing. Timothy couldn't risk waiting for the day to end before doing something. What if she stays late after I leave? Timothy thought. He was definitely in the middle of another self-inflicted mess. If only he hadn't been such a procrastinator and had placed that sack back where he found it when he first came in, everything would be fine. So, Timothy answered phones for the rest of the day and couldn't even chance checking the computer for a response from Joe. It was truly a rotten afternoon.

Eventually, people in the office started going home, or out

to the theater, or whatever these people did when their workday was over. Timothy looked at his watch and was happy to see that it was finally six o'clock. But Muriel was still slogging away at her work. Timothy gathered up his rucksack, then leaned into her office to ask if Muriel needed him for anything else.

Muriel looked up and, for the first time, gave a slight hint of a smile. "Have a good one," she said as she put down her pen and stretched. "I'll be in late tomorrow. Meeting with the guys at Powers and Powers to go over this ridiculous contract. Only a fetus without a fully formed brain would sign the draft they sent. They'll be sorry."

Timothy felt a slight, yet cautious, sense of relief. If he got into the office early enough, it was still possible that he could get maintenance to unlock the desk drawer and replace the folio. Though what reason he would give them now that Muriel was back, he didn't know. He decided not to worry about it until he had to worry. He'd come up with something. Maybe he could still get away with his crime. He was prepared for the worst but hoped for the best. As there wasn't much of anything he could do about it right then, he summoned an Uber to Central Park.

Of course, Brad was already waiting for him at the fountain when he arrived. He really had a thing for being on time. In another man, Timothy might have found his punctuality adorably irritating, but in Brad, well, in his book, the guy couldn't do anything wrong.

After their greeting kiss and tight hug, Brad suggested grabbing a hot dog from a street vendor instead of going to a restaurant. Of course, Timothy lied and said it was a perfect idea, not telling him that his tummy was still barking from the dogs he'd swallowed at lunchtime. He was just happy to be with Brad and the anticipation of hearing what had been revealed during his coffee meeting with Sandy. They grabbed their food and sat down on a park bench.

Between bites and wiping mustard off his chin, Brad said that Sandy told him he had been feeling guilty about a few things that had happened while he'd worked for Muriel. He cut to the chase. "He had an affair with Mercedes' husband, Sage."

Timothy choked on his soggy hot dog bun. He was never as close to requiring the Heimlich maneuver as at that moment. After a couple of swallows of Coke, he was still alive but in total shock. "He told me that someone in the office had had a 'thing' with Sage. He neglected to mention it was his *thing*!" Timothy wheezed, still trying to catch his breath.

Brad cocked his head. "According to Sandy, they saw each other whenever he delivered so-called 'contracts' to Mercedes. He said that 'contracts' was a euphemism. He was delivering something far more private and personal to Sage that Mercedes didn't know about—a government-banned food supplement that was supposed to be the equivalent of the fountain of youth—and himself. Their relationship went on for a few months. He also claimed that Sage initiated the affair. He said that's why the so-called 'contracts' were hand delivered instead of sent via overnight mail. He'd met Sandy once in the office and liked what he saw. From then on, Sage would insist on hand delivery of the material."

Wow! What a shocker! Not what Timothy was expecting at all! "So why is he coming forward now and telling you instead of Muriel or an attorney?" Timothy asked. "Is it a feeling of empowerment now that there's been a universal shift in workplace hanky-panky?"

"Maybe," Brad said, "To a degree. But he's also being threatened. Jared found out about the affair, which is why he was fired. But someone else knows and is now threatening him. Someone named..."

Timothy had no idea where his response came from, but he hesitantly said, "Joe?"

Brad simply nodded. And Timothy dropped his mustard-stained napkin and the empty can of Coke.

Brad looked at him and said, "You're not going to like what I have to say next, so keep an open mind. Sandy thinks that Mercedes Ford is behind the threats. He thinks this guy Joe may be like a private eye that Mercedes hired."

In yet another shock moment (Timothy had so many of them lately), he decided, "Good for her! Take down the man who's trying to steal your man!"

But Brad brought him up short. "First of all, the affair is apparently long over. If Mercedes was ever aware of it, surely, she would have said or done something long before now. Don't you think?"

Timothy certainly didn't know. He'd never had an affair with a movie star's husband. Heck, he wouldn't think of taking anyone's temperature, let alone their husband or boyfriend. But he was curious. "What sort of threats is Sandy receiving?"

"The 'I know what you did last summer' sort of threats," Brad said. "With a few specific references to the liaison that nobody else would know unless one of the lovers talked about it to someone else. And Sandy insists he's been a clam." Brad asked, "Would a woman hold a grudge long after her husband's lover was out of the picture?"

"I would," Timothy said. "Maybe even more if I were rich and famous and concerned about my image and how foolish I might look to my friends who had warned me about Said Husband in the first place." When viewed from that point of view, Timothy realized that it actually might be possible that

Mercedes could try to manipulate someone into keeping such a sensitive secret. "What did Sandy say were the actual threats?" he asked.

Brad took a moment; then, he withdrew a small notepad from his back pocket. He looked at it and read aloud, "It happened to Jared Evans. It could just as easily happen to you."

Timothy was taken aback. "It's Jared's killer. Or someone alluding to the fact that Jared is dead, and that Sandy could join him in eternal rest if he's not careful."

"Want to know the most interesting part of all this?" Brad asked. "Sandy showed me printouts of the emails. They came from…" Brad looked again at his notebook and said, "Doxdox@seemail.com."

Timothy's eyes widened, and his jaw went slack.

"That's the address from a threat that I received a few days ago," he said, as his face drained of color, and he almost passed out.

\* \* \*

Timothy tried to explain to Brad that he hadn't said anything about that email threat to him before because after Brad had disregarded the note from Kent Isaacson and said it wasn't really a threat, he realized the menacing tone in the message he'd received wouldn't stand up to the test either. "And, quite honestly, I'd almost forgotten about it," he said. "I've been swamped working for Muriel and following leads to connect someone to Jared's murder."

Brad was amazing. He apologized profusely for being responsible for making Timothy think that his own threatening note was not to be paid attention to. He said he'd only been thinking about a lack of concrete sinister language in the other messages and that the police probably would have required specific threats to take them seriously. He drew Timothy to his side and cradled him in his arms. They sat on the bench, and he slowly rocked him like the protector that he was. "I'm so sorry, Sweetie," he cooed. Timothy liked that so much that he pretended to be more upset than he really was. Heck, if Brad wanted to hold him like this until the street sweepers came by in the morning, that was totally fine with him. But finally, he said, "Someone's going to get hurt again if we aren't careful."

Timothy thought that made Brad feel even more guilty because Brad said, "Not on my watch! Now, let's get a real dinner."

## Chapter Twenty-Four

Brad and Timothy switched their restaurant allegiance to Ragacci's over on 47th and spent the evening dining on the restaurant's signature lasagna and sipping Chianti. But mostly, they talked about their cast of characters and potential suspects whose common denominator was that they totally disliked, and maybe even hated, Jared Evans. While the list was not extensive, there were several who they both thought more likely than the others to do away with their nemesis: Kent Isaacson, Fiona Carter, Sandy Blair, and Bryony and Joe—and whoever was hiding behind those anonymous emails.

Kent had blamed Jared for the death of his fiancé. Fiona had accused Jared of trying to stop her from meeting with her supposedly long-lost mother, Mercedes. And Joe and Bryony were, well, that was a mystery unto itself. Timothy didn't know who the heck they were. Still, they sounded devious and manipulative. But Timothy and Brad still didn't have evidence that might make nailing the right person to the crime easier to figure out. One can't be a suspect based purely on a dislike of the victim.

Brad and Timothy eventually called it a night and ordered separate Uber cars—even though they both agreed that their next planned Friday night rendezvous was too far away.

The moment Timothy stepped out of the elevator and into the penthouse foyer, he set down his rucksack and the laptop, reclined on the sofa, and redialed Beverly's number. No response. This time, he left a message telling her how concerned he was, especially as Muriel had returned to the city and she had not. "If you're in that senior living place, I want to know," Timothy said in his message. Then he opened the computer.

Finally! A message from Joe!

> Bryony. You're a little late with the crocodile tears. The Forgiveness Train has left the station, and I'm not on board. Anyway, I don't know why I ever bothered with a freak like you. Go back to the rock you crawled out from under. I'll be in the city tomorrow. If I see you… you'll wish I hadn't.
> —Joe

Although Timothy had made a promise to call Brad the moment a message from Joe arrived, the wine he had drunk at dinner and the memory of Brad's strong arms made him reckless, and he was so livid with the way Joe was treating him, er, Bryony, he couldn't help lashing out at him immediately.

> Joe. Your message is insulting. I've done my research, and I now know who you are.
> —Bryony.

Of course, that was a complete lie, but who cared? Joe was being a total jerk. He didn't deserve the truth from Timothy. And then he noticed yet another new message.

> Please tell Mercedes I don't need her to send money for my plane ticket. All has been sorted out. We will soon be

together.

—Fiona Carter

"Can life get any more complicated?" Timothy said, suddenly overwhelmed by the prospect of murder suspects raining down on him—or at least coming to town. And then he literally jumped. His phone rang, and it startled him.

It was Beverly! She described the few days she'd spent with Muriel, and they didn't sound like anybody's idea of awesome family fun. "After touring Glenwood Farms, Muriel insisted that I'd be more comfortable there than in New York, so I took off," Beverly said. "I'm acting the way she did when she was a teenager when I told her she couldn't have a pony. She ran away for a few days. I had been so worried, and now… Too bad she came back." There was a sadness in Beverly's voice hiding behind the bluster.

Beverly let Timothy know that she was in town and staying with an old friend in Brooklyn, but she planned to sneak back into the city and, with Timothy's help, hide out in the penthouse until she could find other accommodations. They agreed that although they couldn't foresee the future, they would figure it all out together. Beverly said she'd be back on Friday. Only a few hours away.

Timothy was taken further aback when, after his conversation with Beverly, he returned to the computer and found that Joe had already responded to his note from Bryony. That was fast. For a moment, he considered calling Brad and asking him to join him for the reading of the message. However, it was late, and he didn't want to drag Brad out at this hour. But he also would not have been able to sleep had he not opened the email. He clicked on the message and read:

Bryony. Or should I say, Timothy? Yeah, I've done my homework, too. I've had a change of heart. Let's rendezvous tomorrow. Lots to discuss. I'll meet you in the penthouse. Time TBD.

–Joe

Now Timothy was really stunned and wished that Brad was there. Joe knew who he was and where he lived! Timothy considered marking the message as unread and pretending that he was opening it for the first time in Brad's presence the next day. But he was also antsy to respond to Joe. He didn't know what to do. Should he make him wait and agonize the way he'd made Timothy wait? Or should he suggest another place to meet?

And then, another call came in. This time from Muriel. "Sorry. My fault," Muriel said without salutation. "I should have fired you when Jared asked me to. Don't try to deny that you broke into my desk and removed—stole—the bag. No doubt you've read the contents. Never mind. I'll come 'round tomorrow afternoon with your final check. Be packed and ready to leave by the end of the workday." She disconnected the conversation without giving Timothy a chance to say one word.

"Oh, damn! Damn! Damn!" Timothy exploded as he let the phone drop onto the floor. And then he burst into tears. Life had become too overwhelming. He was a failure in everything he tried. From living on his own in New York to working a crummy job to writing a novel to solving a murder mystery. Timothy felt like a total failure. Why would a gorgeous man like Brad even want to continue dating a failure like Timothy? But at least there was no ambiguity in his world. He now knew who he really was—a miserable loser—just as Jared had said.

## Chapter Twenty-Five

Timothy woke up Friday morning feeling unexpectedly well. A night of crying and panic about his future had somehow washed away his fears. The fact that Muriel had decided that Timothy was no longer of value to her was actually reasonably okay. At least he knew where he stood. Of course, no one likes to be told they're useless dolts. And being fired from a job can sure screw up one's self-esteem for a while. But he was determined to see this not as any big setback but merely as the end of a chapter in his book of life. "Turn the page," Timothy told himself firmly. At any rate, there'd been way too much drama in his world since working for Muriel and Jared. It was time for some peace and working a less stressful job.

Of course, Timothy would miss living at The Colton. And he hoped that Beverly would continue to be a friend, even if only as pen pals. But his major disappointment was that he'd look like a failure in Brad's eyes. Brad deserved someone strong, smart, and successful. Timothy was obviously the opposite. Would there be other Brads in his life? None like the original; he knew that for sure.

Being let go from this job also meant he would no longer have to worry about who killed Jared Evans. Sure, Timothy was still extremely curious, and he had very deep suspicions about who the murderer was, but it was time to calm down and reclaim his sanity. He felt he had done all he could to find out the truth, and any guilt he'd had about wishing Jared dead evaporated when Muriel told him that Jared had wanted him fired. And Timothy was on a roll here with the positivity; being expelled from the Colton had the benefit of disappearing from Joe's radar.

So, after taking his clothes out of the closet and bureau drawers and placing them back in the boxes in which they were delivered, he decided to take a long walk and start planning for his future.

The weather outside was absolutely glorious. Autumn was just around the corner, and people seemed to be in good spirits. Even the usual cacophony of car horns and emergency vehicle sirens seemed muted that morning. Since he would probably have to move back to his mother's home in Alabama, he should do something in the city he'd put off for too long. Something fun that tourists do but that New Yorkers seem to ignore. He decided to check out the famous Guggenheim Museum. Then he'd return to The Colton, call his mother to say he was coming home, and wait for Muriel.

Timothy couldn't have known then that being away from The Colton and spending a few hours at the museum was one of the best decisions he could have made. He later learned that an Uber had pulled up to the curb in front of The Colton shortly after he left the building, and when the passenger got out of a black Prius, he'd entered the foyer of the building and went directly to the bank of elevators without stopping at reception. He pushed the call button, but as he waited, he was distracted by what appeared to be an argument between the concierge, Mr. Fulton, and the head of security, Griffin, and a plump older woman with a British accent.

Griffin noticed the man at the elevator and called out to him. "Mr. Ford, er, Mr. Slater," he said. "Perfect timing."

Sage Slater walked over to the group. He looked at the woman, who appeared to be in her 60's, her gray hair in an unruly mop, and said, "S'up?"

It was quickly revealed that the visitor's name was Fiona Carter. She was Mercedes' biggest fan and claimed Mercedes Ford was her mother. She said that Mercedes had been writing to her for many months until someone named Jared Evans abruptly interrupted the dialogue. She had proof and presented copies of the emails. Fiona had come from England to America that very morning, expressly to be reunited with her "Mum."

Although Fulton and Griffin could hardly contain their amusement that this woman, who looked many years older than Mercedes Ford, could even for a moment think that she was the star's daughter, Sage was suddenly struck with an idea. To the security chief's surprise, Sage said, "She's cool," and escorted Fiona to the elevator.

When the doors opened to the penthouse, Fiona Carter had arrived not only in Mercedes Ford's home but also in her deluded idea of Heaven. She was stunned, senseless, to realize that she was standing in the very spot where Mercedes had stood. She was breathing the air that she thought Mercedes had inhaled. She touched the Lalique crystal pedestal foyer table, knowing that Mercedes had also touched the art glass. And now she recognized Sage as Mercedes' husband. It was almost too much for her to take in. This was far more momentous than anything she'd ever imagined. It was the most important day of her entire life.

Sage looked around the room and called out Timothy's name. He'd just concocted a scheme and was ready to put it into action—with Fiona's help. He offered her a drink.

"I can't be impolite," Fiona said. "I'll have a wee something if you do."

Sage poured gin and tonics for both of them. A charmer of the first order, that attribute, along with his classically handsome face, gym-built body, and knack for exploiting any personally advantageous opportunity, had taken him much further in life than would have ever been predicted for a guy from a small town in Ohio with only a high school education and no discernable creative gifts. As with many pretty faces, people instantly trusted him or gave him the benefit of the doubt, even when evidence suggested that perhaps one should not judge by appearances. This was just such a moment for Fiona. But she was oblivious to any inner voice of reason.

As Fiona sipped her drink, Sage gave her a tour of the penthouse. He captivated her with anecdotes about what Mercedes was like as a real-life person and how she was such a great mother—despite Fiona's claim of being abandoned in favor of Mercedes' acting career. He told her how excited Mercedes would be when they finally met again, but that Fiona better prepare to discover another very big secret in Mercedes' life.

When they'd completed the tour, Sage guided Fiona onto the terrace. He suggested that she be seated at the table to receive some news that she might find distressing. "Did you know that there's another big fan who believes that he, too, is Mercedes's child?"

Fiona was dumbstruck. Totally uncomprehending. "But… I'm…"

Sage comforted Fiona. "No worries. I'm on your side," he said. "I'm not like Jared Evans. But FYI, your rival is named Timothy. Timothy Trousdale. He's even living here in the penthouse."

As Fiona became agitated, Sage explained that he was merely giving her a heads-up to the challenge ahead. "You'll have to do something to get rid of him today," he said. "Are you willing to do whatever it takes to earn your rightful place in your mother's life?"

Fiona was, at first, stunned into silence. But soon, her face twisted into rage. She squared her shoulders and clenched her fists. "My mum loves me. And I've waited all my life to be with her. Nothing can get in our way!"

Sage reached out and gave Fiona's shoulder a reassuring squeeze. "Timothy will probably be home soon," he said. "I think you'd better figure out how you'll handle this."

Fiona looked into Sage's sparkling and hypnotic eyes. She seemed to draw strength from them. "I'll do whatever you want me to," she said.

Sage shrugged and shook his head. "I can't tell you what to do," he said. "It has to be entirely up to you. But I'll say this: Timothy is a gold digger. He's taking advantage of your mum's good nature—and her money. You have to be stronger than he is because he'll do anything to make sure that nobody gets in the way of his scheme. Of course, when Mercedes finds out the truth, she's going to be devastated. You won't let your mum be lied to, deceived, and cheated anymore, will you? Of course not. You have to make some really tough life-or-death decisions today. Yes, life and death. I have faith in you, Fiona. Faith that you'll handle this in the best possible way—for you and your mum."

Fiona finished her drink, and Sage refreshed the glass with another G&T. "Liquid courage to confront Timothy," Sage smiled. "You're a loving and dutiful daughter," he said as he guided her to the terrace. Then he walked over to the glass balustrade and looked over the side. "It's certainly a long way down to the street, isn't it? Forty-five floors is a long distance." He whistled a loud and gradually descending note that trailed off into silence as if a pebble had been dropped into a bottomless well.

Sage continued, "I should step out for a while and let you wait for Timothy and to think about how you'll handle things when he gets here. I know you'll do fine all by yourself. It's all for you and your mum." Again, he whistled a descending note.

He had planned to wait outside the building until he knew Timothy had returned. But just as Sage was about to leave the terrace and the penthouse, the elevator chimed, the doors opened, and Timothy stepped into the foyer—then out and onto the terrace.

Timothy was shocked. The last thing he expected was a visit from Sage Slater! For a moment, Timothy wondered whether Sage had heard he was fired and wanted to ensure he wasn't running off with any souvenirs.

"We've been talking about you," Sage said when Timothy made eye contact with him.

Timothy smiled too quickly because, in his next breath, Sage said, "I'd like you to meet a significant person in Mercedes' life. This is Fiona Carter—Mercedes' daughter."

Of course, Timothy instantly recognized the name. He looked at Fiona and saw pure hatred in her eyes. She was seething with rage. Was it because of that first message Timothy had accidentally sent to her? This woman looked like an escaped rabid animal that had been caged for too long and was now about to lunge for the jugular of its captor.

And then Sage said, "You two need some time together. I'll be back when it's all over. Er, I'll be back soon." And then he left the terrace.

Timothy certainly did not want to be left alone with Fiona, who looked like a mad woman. But he was now face-to-face with the person he knew so much about from reading her messages to Mercedes. "How's the weather in England?" he lamely asked, trying to tap dance around the obvious tension. "You've come an awfully long way. Are you totally exhausted from your long flight?" Timothy was trying to gauge the level of her hostility.

Yeah, those were idiotic things to say, but Timothy honestly didn't know what else to do at that moment. He truly felt that, at any second, this woman would eat him alive. Timothy glanced around for something with which to protect himself in case Fiona became physically hostile. The only thing he could see was a small gardening spade that Beverly used for potting plants, and it was several feet away from his reach. Then, for some reason, Timothy said, "Mercedes will be thrilled to finally meet her little girl."

Fiona blanched as if Timothy had slapped her out of a dream.

"She talks about you endlessly," Timothy lied, stalling for time, and hoping Fiona could be lulled into passivity.

"Yes, that's right," Fiona said. "She told me that in her emails." Then, returning to her state of anxiety, she added, "Mercedes Ford is my mum, not yours!"

Well, that was a surprise because Timothy never said he was Mercedes' son. A huge fan, of course, but nothing more. Where did this woman get the silly idea that Timothy claimed to be kin to a movie star? And he said as much.

"Sage told me everything," Fiona said through gritted teeth. "You're crazy. Demented. You're out to ruin Mum's life. I won't let that happen. She deserves better than you."

*Crazy? Demented?* Timothy wanted to say, I know you are, but what am I? Instead, he told the truth. "I'm only working for Mercedes. I love her as a superstar living legend, but that's all. She's your mum, not mine."

Fiona seemed suddenly unable to know what to believe. She stuttered, "But Sage said… That you… Living here…

Mercedes' condo…"

"Because I'm an assistant who answers her fan mail and takes care of the penthouse when she's not here," Timothy said, trying to sound as though he had no ulterior motive. "I swear, I've only ever met Mercedes once. And I have my own real-life mum who lives in Alabama."

As Fiona contemplated what Timothy had said, Sage returned to the terrace doorway. "What? You're still here?" he said, looking at Timothy, then at Fiona. "Um, we don't have much time. Let's get this over with." He seemed to be reminding Fiona of something she had to do.

Fiona looked at Sage. "I'm Mercedes' only child," she said proudly.

"Of course, you are," Sage said. "But Timothy says that he's her son. Perhaps you're twins separated at birth, eh?"

"What?" Timothy spat to Sage. "You know that I only work here. You're leading this poor woman on."

Timothy could tell that Sage had had enough and just wanted to move on to whatever nefarious business he had in mind.

"But why else would Timothy be here in Mercedes' penthouse if he wasn't related?" Sage suggested to Fiona. "You don't think Mercedes would give a key to just anyone, do you?"

"Maybe. If they worked for her."

Sage smiled. "Fiona, who are you going to believe? I'm married to Mercedes, so I think I know better than anyone else on the planet what she would do." Then he pointed to Timothy. "He's trying to confuse you. He wants you to do something that would make Mercedes reject you."

For a long moment, they were all at a standoff. The three of them were still determining what the others might do. Any sudden move could prove fatal. Timothy looked at Fiona, then Sage. Both were wondering about Timothy, too and what he might do at any second. What he wanted to do was retreat into the condo and flee the building.

But Sage was standing guard. In a steely voice, he looked at Timothy and said, "Why are you making things so difficult for us—Bryony."

Timothy shouldn't have been stunned, but just for an instant, he was. And at that very moment, he knew to whom he was talking and who Jared's killer was. "Joe," he said.

Sage's smile answered any doubt in Timothy's mind. "Can't believe I figured it out before you did," Sage said. "I'm not as thick as a few of Mercedes' friends think I am. And by the way, thanks for all the emails, but you look nothing like the picture you sent."

"Who's Joe?" Fiona asked.

"The same man who has been lying to you," Timothy said. "The man who sees your mum merely as a piggy bank. The man who… murdered Jared Evans."

Sage heaved a heavy sigh and said, "Everyone thinks it was an accident and I intend to keep it that way."

Fiona looked on, confused. She turned from Jared to Timothy like a spectator at a tennis match.

"People around here seem to think I'm fairly stupid, too," Timothy said. "But at this moment, I think I'm rather smart. I'll just call 911 and tell them the truth about Jared's accident." Timothy took out his phone.

Sage chuckled and shook his head. "You really are an idiot, just as Jared said." Then he grabbed Timothy's arm and snatched the phone out of his hand. He held it like a softball, then smiled as he pitched it underhand and over the side of the terrace. "Oops! You're a klutz, too," he said.

"No worries. It's not even my own phone," Timothy said.

"But you are responsible for company property," Sage

added. "And I think Fiona will be a witness to the fact that you tried to catch the phone and lost your balance. Whoops!"

Timothy was suddenly terrified. He realized that, indeed, if he were pushed over the railing, it might appear that he'd reached too far for his phone and fallen over. Such accidents actually happened from time to time.

"When I'm through with you, the only witness will be Fiona—a crazy woman who will be found all alone in the penthouse. She doesn't have the biometric credentials to leave the building, but I do, and the closed-circuit video monitors will show that I left the condo before your fall. I'll be all shocked and saddened! That poor kid, Timothy! I'll modestly claim that it was my fault for leaving you alone with a mad woman. My bad." Sage sniggered. "I'll be questioned, of course, but, ultimately, Fiona will be arrested and spend the rest of her pathetic little life in prison or hooked up to a bunch of tubes dripping with chemicals for her execution."

Timothy looked at Fiona to see her reaction, but she seemed to have lost the plot and looked like she was in another world. He considered what Sage said and realized it might be a good plan. Sage might actually get away with another murder. The whole high-tech security system may indeed be his cover and alibi. But would the police really ignore Fiona if she told a different story about how Timothy ended up like Humpty Dumpty? Who could tell? And surely, another death occurring in this same condo would raise suspicions. But it would be scant consolation to Timothy, who would be a dead, splattered mess on the pavement.

Sage, taller and much stronger than Timothy, was now far from the good-looking man Timothy had met a week ago. In fact, his ugly soul was on full display as he moved menacingly toward Timothy. Timothy started backing away from him and suddenly found himself trapped between Sage's muscled body and the mid-chest-high railing of the terrace barrier.

"Mum would not approve…" Fiona began but was cut off by Sage, who turned to face her.

"Mum!" he snarled. "Mercedes Ford is not your mum, you stupid, demented, old woman! Trust me; if Mercedes ever met you, she'd laugh in your ugly old face. You're a crazy freak! Why don't you know this? All you fans are freaking mutant idiots!"

This verbal slap seemed to snap Fiona out of some sort of mental hallucination. "Mummy's been writing to me for ages."

"Yeah, yeah, so you've said! Reality check—she wasn't writing you, you psycho," Sage spat back. "Those emails were written by an assistant. Someone named Sandy who got a really big kick out of screwing with your empty head. He was mocking you. It was a charade. He was bored with his job and just having a bit of fun. Don't you get it? You're a pathetic nobody. Why would you think, even for an instant, that someone as famous as Mercedes Ford would take the time to play pen pal with a nobody loser? She's a world-famous celebrity. Unlike you, she has a real life. You could join Timothy by jumping off this building right now, and she wouldn't ever know that you even existed, except as a story on the 11 O'clock News. As a matter of fact, why don't you do just that? Take a leap. It's probably the most exciting thing you'll ever do. You're less than a worthless piece of trash, and you'd be far better off exiting this world. You know it's true!"

Fiona was trembling, and her lips were quivering. She was trying to hold back tears of frustration and rage. She was thinking about all that Sage had just said and how he was probably right.

Timothy's life, on the other hand, seemed to be moving at a rapid clip as Sage turned back to focus on him. In nanoseconds, Timothy's memory flashed on that day he visited the set of *Blind Trust*, and Sage boasted about how much weight he could curl and bench press. Sage would have no problem picking him up and tossing him over the railing. He was King Kong to Timothy's Fay Wray.

Fiona suddenly started to wail, "Mummy! Mummy!" And at that moment, when Sage was distracted for only an instant, Timothy again saw the hand spade resting next to a newly potted plant. He reached out for it, intent on slashing Sage's pretty face.

But Sage was too quick for Timothy. He slapped him hard across the cheek, and with the sudden impact, he lost hold of the spade. It fell to the terrace floor with the sound of metal scraping stone. Timothy was stunned into immobility. But as Fiona witnessed the assault, she was drawn away from her own emotional pain. She seemed to know Sage's plan for Timothy and began to rage at him to let Timothy go.

No one in the nearby buildings could hear Fiona's screams. That was a disadvantage to secluded living. The only other penthouse on the 45th floor of The Colton was separated by walls so thick that noise from either unit could never be heard—even with an opera diva blasting out high C's. Timothy knew he was doomed!

Then, in the distance, Timothy vaguely heard the sound of the elevator chimes. Muriel! Thank God! However, he was too preoccupied with fighting to save his skin as Sage easily tackled him around the waist and dragged him to the terrace railing. Sage had full control Despite Timothy's kicking, twisting, and squirming. "No! Don't!" Timothy begged. "I'm too young to die. I have to become a famous writer first!"

And then they all heard a familiar voice. It was stern but stable. And though it held no discernable panic and was almost soft in tone, it exuded strength and authority. "You've deeply disappointed me, Sage." It was Mercedes Freaking Ford!

Ordinarily, Timothy would have been out of his mind with excitement, but at the moment, he had a rather big problem. And did he hear Mercedes say that Sage had disappointed her? That had to be the world's biggest understatement. Timothy was the one about to be tossed over the wall like a stray frisbee that had ended up on the wrong side of a fence. And Mercedes seemed way too even-tempered for this specific predicament. She wasn't playing the docile nun Sister Esperea in her Oscar-winning movie role about convent corruption, for crying out loud.

But, at the sound of Mercedes' voice and words, Sage turned around and involuntarily released Timothy, who immediately scrambled to the other side of the terrace.

"Being vicious and cruel to others doesn't become you," Mercedes continued, speaking to Sage in an even tone. The color in her voice was more like what one would hear from a mother dissatisfied with her child's school report card than one pleading to save another's life.

Sage looked at his wife with an expression of anxiety and denial. He was trying to find the words to explain the unexplainable.

With her inimitable poise, Mercedes continued expressing her grief over what she'd exposed about her husband. With only her steady voice, she managed to subdue Sage into inaction. Timothy wondered how in the world Mercedes learned to have the effect of a stun gun. He was witnessing a master class in acting, the star playing a delicate scene in which life and death stakes could not be higher. And Timothy believed her every word. He suspected that Sage did too. "I don't judge you," Mercedes continued, "because I'll never know what it's like to be you or behave as you are now."

Sage finally found his voice and tried to hold anyone else but himself accountable. "Intruders!" he said to Mercedes. "I found these two in our condo."

"Liar!" Those words came from Beverly—who suddenly appeared in the doorway to the terrace. Timothy would later find out that Mercedes had collected her while visiting her sister in Brooklyn, and they returned to The Colton together.

"You're a crazy old lady," Sage spat at Beverly.

Mercedes said, "I'm the crazy old lady, Sage. I'm crazy for trusting you. For loving you. You're everything that my friends said you were… Joe."

Sage looked dumbstruck. "Joe?" he said, as if not comprehending the sum of two plus two.

"Allow me to introduce myself," Mercedes said. "I'm Bryony. Joe, you and I are very well acquainted."

Timothy thought, Holy moly! A lot of people around here lie about their names. First, there was Fabiola/Beverly. Then La Paloma/Rolfstead. Now there's Sage/Joe and Mercedes/Bryony! Heck, he was guilty, too, when he also pretended to be Bryony.

Mercedes went on to explain that several months earlier, when checking how her fan mail was being handled, she'd sent a fake message to Muriel's office pretending to be an admirer named Bryony—a fan of Mercedes. She had written in her message that she thought Mercedes' husband Sage was sexy. Jared saw that and instructed Sandy to forward it to Sage to feed his always-famished ego.

Mercedes continued, "You liked the idea that this purported fan, Bryony, thought you were hot, so you started to correspond with her. I even sent you a stock picture of a young actress to heighten your interest. The funny thing is that for the longest time, I thought you actually knew it was me that you were corresponding with and just fooling around.

I mean, how many times have I used the name Bryony when we travel under false identities? And you always go by Joe. But you were too dull-witted to pick up on that trifle, weren't you? In my deluded mind, we were having a fun game between lovers. Like in *The Piña Colada Song*. Never mind. That was long before your time. But I was always excited to receive your messages. They were so steamy. And since you'd long ago stopped giving me more than a quick kiss goodnight…"

Sage tried to laugh it off. "Of course, I knew it was you, sweetheart," he said. "I don't do fan mail. That's his job," he said, pointing to Timothy.

"Not just any fan," Mercedes countered. "A fan whose words made you think of having an affair with her. The way you did with the others… and even Sandy. I knew all about that, too. And what's his name, the one from the Hallmark Channel, head of publicity, I think, whom we met at that cast party? I didn't need Jared to tell me. And… Well, it doesn't matter anymore." She waved away her thoughts. "What you failed to understand is that if Bryony had been real, I wouldn't have stood in your way. From the beginning, I knew I'd never have you all to myself. But as long as you kept your *affaire de coeur* private and came home to me, I was inclined to turn a blind eye. But then—you murdered Jared."

"Jared?" Sage repeated. "Murder? I didn't… I'd never…"

Timothy had moved away from the terrace wall railing to a safer place near Beverly at the glass doors into the penthouse. Then, feeling out of immediate harm's way, he found his voice. He looked at Sage and nodded his head in understanding. "It took me the longest time to figure out how someone got past security and into the penthouse the day that Jared was killed," he said. "Then I remembered that it had happened on Sunday, the day after the party and the day the floral delivery guys brought the weekly arrangement."

Suddenly, it all fell into place; Timothy saw the whole scenario in his mind's eye. "Sage arranged to meet Jared in The Colton to try to talk Jared out of being a tattletale about the affair with Sandy. Maybe to bribe him. Or threaten to have him fired. Whatever. Sage arrived in the lobby coincidentally at the same time that the delivery guy was taking last week's floral arrangement away. Sage must have had murder on his mind, or perhaps it only occurred to him on seeing the delivery people that he could enter the Colton unobserved and get rid of Jared once and for all. Whatever his motives were, Sage offered to take the new flowers to the penthouse. He was camouflaged behind the vase of Lilies. Later, when security looked at the camera video footage, Sage was unidentifiable as he went up to the penthouse. People see what they expect to see, and Mr. Griffin chose to see the delivery guy. Although, upon closer examination, it'll be obvious that it was Sage in the elevator. All one has to do is compare the arms of the person holding the vase with the many photos of Sage."

Timothy continued with his assessment of how everything had played out. "When Sage stepped into the penthouse, he saw Beverly asleep on the terrace. Perhaps it was only then that he thought of murder. Jared must have arranged to meet Sage at the Colton, hoping that the presence of Beverly and Timothy would offer him protection.

"Sage walked in and begged Jared to keep quiet. And Jared, loyal to Mercedes, wouldn't go along with Sage's plea to keep his secret. They had an argument. Sage is a strong guy. And in no time, he was backing Jared into the secret room. There, he put his arms around Jared's neck in a full nelson, and in one quick snap, he separated Jared's neck from his spinal column. Instant death!

"Then, Sage tried to make it look like an accident. He laid the desk chair on its side, hoping that it would seem that Jared had been standing on it, reaching for something on a shelf, and it slipped out from under him. Then he picked Jared up and smashed the side of his head against the top corner of the safe to make it look like a fall. When it was all over, he closed the bookshelves. Jared was sealed up in the wall, just like in an Edgar Allan Poe story."

Then Beverly spoke up and asked, "But then how did Sage leave the penthouse undetected? All the cameras."

"I was wondering that, too," Timothy said. "I thought about the emergency stairwell exit in the kitchen. But cameras are on every floor, and he'd have been spotted."

"A disguise?" Beverly offered.

"No. And according to Griffin, everyone who came and left the penthouse was accounted for. And then I thought of the craziest thing. It seemed totally insane. But there was really no other way for the killer to escape."

By now, Timothy had a mesmerized audience. It seemed that even Sage wanted to know how he'd escaped. Timothy walked over to where the building's window washer had left his harnesses and equipment from the day of the party. "I can't imagine what bravery—or insanity—it takes for someone to do this type of job," Timothy said about high-rise window washers. "Hanging by a thread forty-five stories above the street would give me the willies and a lifetime of vertigo. I could never ever do it in a million years. But Sage had been a stuntman. He's strong. He's adventurous. He doesn't have a fear of heights. He put on this safety harness and lowered himself to the condo terrace on the floor below. Being so high up, I suppose the tenants wouldn't have bothered to lock their terrace doors. And away he went. Am I right, or am I right?" Timothy said with satisfaction in his voice.

Sage started laughing. He looked at Timothy as if he were performing a stand-up comedy routine. His laughter was genuine. For the first time in Timothy's life, it seemed he'd actually succeeded in telling a funny story. Then Sage said, "You've made the point a bunch of times that cameras are everywhere. In the corridors. In the elevators. Even if I did as you said and made it to the floor below, I still couldn't get out of the building without being spotted on CCTV. Unless I jumped over the terrace and flew away like a little birdie. And then, maybe I brought the window-washing rig back up here so it wouldn't be missed. Nice and neat."

"He's right," Beverly said. "The Colton has the best security this side of that bunker in the White House. I feel paranoid whenever I enter this place because I know that probably a dozen cameras are watching me. Also, remember, I was asleep on the terrace. I would have woken up and seen something like that."

Drats! Beverly had two solid points. And for a long moment, Timothy started to doubt himself and Sage's guilt. But no! Sage had to be the killer. Timothy just needed to prove that he found a way out of the building that Sunday afternoon without being seen.

Then something totally weird occurred to him. His memory clicked back to the day of the murder, and he started to see specific images, like slides in a PowerPoint presentation. He remembered that the Lalique crystal table in the foyer was empty! Timothy had realized that on Monday morning when he was leaving for his meeting with Jared and Muriel. He had noticed that the Casablanca Lilly bouquet wasn't there. At the time, he thought Jared hadn't paid the florist bill, so they may have stopped bringing new arrangements. This brought Timothy back to his original theory that Sage had entered the elevator behind a vase of flowers. It made sense that he exited the same way. It was Timothy's Ah-ha Moment!

"Sage left the penthouse hiding behind the same vase of lilies that he'd brought up in the first place!" Timothy nearly shouted. "Mr. Griffin and the security team hadn't noticed, or perhaps it hadn't registered that the delivery guy had already left with the previous week's arrangement!"

At that moment, Sage's face dropped, and he stopped sniggering. He knew Timothy was right.

For a split second, Timothy patted himself on the back. And accomplishing this in the presence of his favorite movie star idol was especially rewarding. But then he realized he was responsible for proving to Mercedes that she'd married a killer. However, Timothy didn't have time to feel sorry for Mercedes because, with the speed of a panther, Sage lunged and took him hostage. "I killed Jared because he was a sniveling little toad who was about to ruin my life," Sage cried. "He wasn't playing fair! He deserved what he got!"

Sage's body strength was killing Timothy, too. He could feel the crook of Sage's left arm tight around his neck, making it hard for him to breathe. But, for some inexplicable reason, Timothy felt a certainty that Mercedes Ford would somehow save his life.

Mercedes slowly walked toward her husband. When she was standing just inches before him and Timothy, Mercedes looked into Sage's eyes and almost whispered, "So much of this is my fault. I wanted, or at least hoped for, unconditional love from someone other than my fans. I had that once with my dearest Gerard, bless his beautiful soul. I know you don't like it when I talk of him, but that was true love. What passed as love between you and me—was an illusion. My whole life is an illusion. It's what I do. It's why I'm famous."

Mercedes folded her arms over her chest and looked at the others on the terrace. "We all have fantasies," she said, still speaking as calmly as a mourner reading a eulogy. "Beverly tells me that she wants a loving daughter. Fiona, it appears, wants a mother. Timothy desires to be a famous writer. Sage wanted to parlay his physical beauty into a life of leisure and 24/7 playground time. There's absolutely nothing wrong with any of those dreams and with wanting our lives to be special and fulfilling. But I'll go to my grave wondering why we, who actually have so much compared to billions of others on this planet, can't find contentment with what we already have."

"Easy for you to say," Sage snarled. "You've always had everything that anyone could ever want! You were always popular and well-liked as a kid. Then you went to Hollywood, and audiences and critics instantly fell in love and handed you fame, fortune, and Oscars! Your career came easily! Don't stand there all self-important and pass judgment on me!"

"Judgment?" Mercedes said. "I said I'm not here to judge you, Sage. But you had it all, too," she said casually. "In addition to your physical beauty—oh, your kisses used to be so wonderful—all that belonged to me was also yours. I gave you the freedom to do as you wish. Why did you have to kill poor Jared?"

"Your poor Jared Evans—who no one but you could stand—was about to ruin my life!" Sage shouted and began to drag Timothy into the penthouse. He stumbled over the slightly raised track of the terrace's accordion door, and they fell backward together onto the floor. "Jared didn't understand," Sage yelled as he got back on his feet. "That little weasel got exactly what he deserved. And no one misses him."

"What didn't Jared understand, Sage?" Mercedes asked. "That you're a narcissist? An egoist? A showboat? A very mean human being. Oh, I think he understood that, as does everyone else in our circle. I did, too. But I guess I wanted you regardless. And by the way, you're wrong that I have everything. I don't have… you."

"I'm calling security," Beverly said as she raced to the house phone in the kitchen. However, Sage tightened his grip around Timothy's neck and demanded that everyone stay planted where they were and not move a muscle. Timothy knew better than to struggle. Sage had effortlessly broken Jared's neck, and he could easily do the same to him in an instant.

"Let Timothy go," Mercedes demanded, although it sounded more like a suggestion.

Sage pulled Timothy farther into the penthouse toward the elevator, and Timothy began questioning his faith in Mercedes as a savior.

Then Mercedes said, "This is one of those rare times when my fame could actually be of use to someone," the world's biggest star said in an almost untroubled and reassuring voice. "You can literally get away with murder if you release Timothy and take me as a hostage. The police would never shoot at Mercedes Ford. We can go to our farm in Connecticut. We have friends in the Maldives where there's no extradition treaty."

Sage was clearly frightened and confused. He looked around, and his eyes focused first on Beverly, then on Fiona, and finally on Mercedes again. He was trapped, which made him angrier, frightened, and frightening. He backed up to the elevator door and blindly punched the call button with his fist a half dozen times.

Presently, the elevator chimes rang. Sage exhaled a long

breath and seemed to calm down slightly. He said in a very tired voice, "If it explains anything, Mercedes, I know I've been a failure all my life. I'm not smart. Or talented. I'm not witty like you and your famous friends. I had only one thing that I could use to take me to a better life. I couldn't risk losing everything. Being sexy isn't easy."

Under ordinary circumstances, Timothy would have rolled his eyes and scoffed, "Boo-hoo. Poor baby. Being sexy is such a tragedy." But this wasn't the time or place because he was being kidnapped and probably about to die. Then, he heard the elevator doors open behind them, and he freaked out as Sage began to haul him into the elevator car. He struggled to be free and then—

—The next thing Timothy knew; he was soaking wet and covered with flowers. Sage was in an unconscious heap. Muriel stood over him, and Brad cradled him in his arms! What, in the name of...

Brad had come to The Colton to surprise Timothy with a vase of posies and to apologize for being so unintentionally insensitive the day before. He'd arrived at the same time as Muriel, who was there to give Timothy his last paycheck and to make sure he vacated The Colton. She'd allowed Brad to ride the elevator to help collect Timothy's personal things.

Muriel later said that when she saw the hostage situation, her natural instinct was to do to Sage what she'd always wanted to do to Hollywood studio executive bullies during contract negotiations. She'd grabbed Brad's vase and clobbered Sage into unconsciousness with the full weight of her temper.

## *Epilogue*

Timothy had to love Muriel for that. Well, perhaps love is the wrong word for "The Beast of Broadway." But she and his beautiful Brad had saved the day. And possibly his life, too! Timothy was out of a job, but he was still alive! As challenging as the past few weeks had been, Timothy decided it was all worth the effort and horror because he got to meet and become friends with his favorite star. Mercedes was everything Timothy ever hoped she would be.

Sure, Timothy was no longer employed by Muriel Maynard Management, but Mercedes had convinced Muriel to add a few more zeros to the sum of his severance check. (Timothy suspected the money came directly from Mercedes' own pocket.) It was enough for Timothy to afford a deposit and a full month's rent on another shared apartment. Brad had suggested they could share his space, but Timothy is still terrified that once Brad truly got to know him, he'd stop being in love with him. It's an Aries thing.

The Chili Exchange in Times Square also needed more staff. But Timothy just couldn't bring himself to go back to that awful place. So, he reapplied at SwellHire Top Temps. And, although their motto, *Out with the Old, in with the New!* was being investigated by the New York Department of Fair Labor Practices for ageism, Timothy suspected that they'd find an appropriate position for him.

Also, Timothy's name appeared in all the news articles

about Mercedes Ford's husband, who was arrested for murder, attempted murder, and even kidnapping. *The National Intruder* and gossip magazines had pictures of Timothy, and in one caption, he was identified as *Timidly* Trousdale, a novelist. Sure, they misspelled his name. And "Timid Timothy" was an appropriate nickname. But the really important thing was that an agent called and asked to read his book. The agent ultimately decided not to represent it, but instead of a form rejection email, he had sent a personal message that said, "If you have anything shorter, and less depressing, and with better sentence structure and fewer typos, I would be willing to read a few chapters." That was the closest Timothy had come to publication since arriving in New York! And it gave him the confidence and encouragement to buckle down and seriously pursue his writing career. That'll show Jared—if Jared keeps an eye on him from wherever his soul ended up—and Timothy suspected he might be watching.

Dear Beverly decided that Glenwood Farms Retirement Village wasn't such a bad place to live after all. Initially, she'd only put up a fight because she wanted a direct say in where she would spend the rest of her days. Of course, Timothy promised to visit her. And they were only a phone call away.

Timothy couldn't feel too sorry for Fiona Carter. Although she eventually understood that Mercedes could not be her biological mother and that she needed a lot of psych meds, she was happy to have met her film idol. However, now she was insisting that Audra McDonald is her sister.

As for Mercedes herself, she was darn strong. Although Timothy was certain that Sage had broken her heart to bits, she almost instantly went on to her next film assignment. And naturally, she got another Oscar nomination for *Blind Trust*. She probably wouldn't win because the Academy voters were said to be bored with giving the statute to her year after year, but they couldn't overlook the fact that she was the biggest and most talented star on the planet.

The next time Timothy saw Sandy was when he was invited to The Comedy Cure, a club in the Village, to see Sandy and Lyle doing a stand-up act as a team. They were dreadful: "Did you hear about the Italian chef who died? He pasta-way." You get the picture. But Timothy faked hearty—if insincere—laughs anyway.

Sage? Well, you guessed it. He's behind bars. *The National Intruder* did a follow-up story about him recently, and the photo they used showed that he was missing a front tooth. It seems that Bumpy or Spider or Tank or Knuckles, or some other cuddly cellmate felony guy had knocked him around. And he was sporting tattoos of Chinese characters on the side of his neck, too. When he gets out of the pokey, there'll surely be a place for him in a Los Angeles street gang.

And now Timothy is really writing up a storm. He's definitely carving out creative time every single day. Jared and Ted, the poet, had been darn right about one thing: he'd never achieve his dream of publication if he didn't do the hard work. There was no getting away from that fact. He didn't want to become one of those middle-aged people who looked back on their lives and regretted not following their hearts. It was now or never, and he wouldn't let anyone—especially himself—stand in his way.

With Brad's loving encouragement, he's working on a new book. He decided not to waste any more time on that first opus. *Suffer Fools*, indeed! He'd given Beverly a physical copy of the manuscript to take with her to Pennsylvania. She wrote back and said—and this is a direct quote: "Oh man! Worse than the unventilated air in the dining room here at Glenwood Farms after we've all had a meal of beans and cabbage!" Why couldn't someone have been that straight with

Timothy sooner instead of tap-dancing around the truth and trying to spare his feelings? He could have saved a lot of agents' eyestrain.

Muriel sold her business and moved to Florida. She says she'll let Beverly visit for a few days at Christmastime. But Beverly insists that there isn't enough vino and Valium on the planet to get her through such an ordeal.

As challenging as the past couple of weeks had been, Timothy decided to just be grateful for almost every moment. Definitely, not the moment when Sage had his arm around Timothy's neck, and his life flashed before his eyes on the terrace of The Colton, but pretty much everything else. After all, he got to meet his favorite star, Mercedes Ford, and even lived in her penthouse apartment for a while. He was certain they would be firm friends forever.

But, topping even that, he'd fallen really and truly in love for the first time in his life. Brad Bradford was smart, confident, talented—and to Timothy's way of thinking—the epitome of a quality human being. He made Timothy feel loved, appreciated, and protected. In fact, right after the police arrested Sage and everybody left the penthouse, Brad took Timothy hostage again, but this time to the safety of his mother's house in Connecticut.

House? Calling the 500-acre Lynnwood Manor estate merely a house would be like calling St. James Palace a bungalow. Brad's mother was super-duper rich. Queen Elizabeth rich. Thurston Howell III rich! Definitely in the 1%! No wonder Brad enjoyed spending Sundays with her! Although Peggy (Brad didn't call her "Mum or Mother") said that her fortune had been an albatross around her neck and didn't want her son to suffer the same way, so she wouldn't give him a penny until she was dead. Timothy can tell that Brad loves his mother and isn't planning a way to get his inheritance sooner than from natural causes.

Timothy and Brad are now officially a couple. It says so on their respective Facebook pages: In a relationship. And Timothy couldn't be happier. His life is perfect. Well, almost. He still needs to find another temp job.

New York is home for Timothy, and he wouldn't want to live anywhere else on the planet. Definitely not back with his mother in Alabama. And not at Glenwood Farms in Pennsylvania, either. But maybe he could be coaxed to move to a secluded beach house on Pago Pago. With Brad, of course!

The End

# About Richard

RICHARD TYLER JORDAN is a novelist and nonfiction writer. His most recent books are *Breakfast at Timothy's* and *Girl's Night Out*. His cozy mysteries include The Polly Pepper Mysteries series: *Remains to the Scene, Final Curtain, A Talent for Murder,* and *Set Sail for Murder*. He has also contributed novellas to the Kensington anthologies *Summer Share,* and *All I Want for Christmas* (both of which earned nominations for the Lambda Literary Award) and *Man of My Dreams*. Jordan is also the author of *But Darling, I'm Your Auntie Mame*, a history of the fictional icon created by Patrick Dennis. Writing as Mike Melbourne, Kensington Publishing Corp. published *Tricks of the Trade, Hunk House, Gay Blades* (each of which reached #1 on the InsightOut Book Club Bestsellers List), and *One Night Stand*. As a senior publicist and staff writer with The Walt Disney Studios for thirty years, he worked on the marketing campaigns of over 500 live-action and animated feature films. An American expatriate, Richard Tyler Jordan lives in England in a 16th-century cottage (complete with a playful ghost).

Take a detour to Richard's digital domain and read his blogs.
richardtylerjordan.com
He loves to hear from his readers.

Printed in Great Britain
by Amazon